P9-DOD-600

FIC
WOL

Wolfe, Swain.

The parrot trainer.

31442306

$24.95

DATE			

SNYDER COUNTY LIBRARY
1 N HIGH ST
SELINSGROVE PA 17870-1599

BAKER & TAYLOR

SNYDER COUNTY LIBRARY
1 N HIGH ST
SELINSGROVE PA 17870-1599

THE

PARROT
TRAINER

Also by Swain Wolfe

The Woman Who Lives in the Earth
The Lake Dreams the Sky

THE
PARROT
TRAINER

Swain Wolfe

St. Martin's Press   New York

Note on Illustrations

The images on each chapter heading were drawn from Mimbres Indian bowls by Harriet Cosgrove in the 1920s during the time she studied Mimbres ruins in Southwestern New Mexico.

The Mimbres parrot trainer bowl image on the title page was reproduced from a photograph by Frank J. Thomas.

THE PARROT TRAINER. Copyright © 2003 by Swain Wolfe. All rights reserved. Printed in the United States of America. No part of this book may be used or reproduced in any manner whatsoever without written permission except in the case of brief quotations embodied in critical articles or reviews. For information, address St. Martin's Press, 175 Fifth Avenue, New York, N.Y. 10010.

www.stmartins.com

Drawings from *Treasured Earth: Hattie Cosgrove's Mimbres Archaeology in the American Southwest,* copyright © 1995 by Carolyn O'Bagy Davis, used by permission of Burt Cosgrove.

Parrot trainer image on the title page used by permission of Anthony Berlant.

ISBN 0-312-31091-9

First Edition: February 2003

10   9   8   7   6   5   4   3   2   1

To Frank and Susanne Bessac,
Burt Pfeiffer, and Uncle Jimmy

THE
PARROT
TRAINER

"Come into my house."
She has no idea where she is.
She has the spirit of the well reared. She says,
"Come into my house," as though
Wherever she is
Must be her house.
"Come into my house," she says.

Not knowing if she is demanding,
requesting,
or inviting,
he goes into her house.

ONE

Jack happened to look up from the bottom of Lacuna Canyon at the moment a red car flew off the east rim. The black stone he was loading into his truck became weightless. A piece of chrome flashed in the thin air as the car defined a perfect arc in the blue sky and fell into the canyon's shadow.

The sickening *wump* of impact caused small creatures to flee and startled birds—red-and-yellow flecked—to fill the sky. Jack held his breath and listened. A handful of feathers billowed up, glowing white in the sun, and fell back into the shadow.

There was no sound, not even the buzz of insects. The birds, tense and fix-winged, glided above the black-thorned mesquite. The silence reminded him of the white room where his father had stopped breathing. Jack wondered if the driver was alive.

It had taken five and a half seconds for the car to fall the five hundred feet from canyon rim to floor. The car, a Ford Taurus, had landed on its wheels at sixty miles an hour. The tires blew. The trunk and doors popped open. Jack was running toward the car before he realized how far away it had landed. He was well out of breath by the time he peered through the shattered windshield at a somewhat startled, intelligent-looking fellow in his sixties. To Jack's surprise, the man's wire-rimmed glasses were in place. His eyes were open, yet he seemed disconnected. Jack searched for a pulse in his neck. There was none. The dead man stared out at the desert—the shock still attached to his face.

Jack's extreme need for oxygen stifled his inherent sympathy. He gasped for air, dizzy and hardly able to exhale. That the man was dead and not dying was a relief—death itself seemed so gentle compared to the terrible process of getting there. Perhaps the man's heart had seized up. Jack imagined the driver dead, falling through thin air.

As the world began to solidify and time regained direction, his eyes came to rest on a blank piece of paper near his foot. He reached down and turned it over, revealing a drawing in the style of an ancient Southwest tribe. The image was of a young woman in profile. She wore a white mask with a small triangular beak, two vertical marks on the cheek, and slits to see through. Black ovals were painted around the slits. She held a hoop in which an excited parrot balanced, wings extended, its beak open. The woman's stance was poised and thoughtful. Her bare breasts were small. Her only clothing was a wide belt, worn low on her hips, that held a sash between her legs. Long woven strings fell from the back of the belt to her calves. Jack studied the set of her shoulders and back and the position of her legs. Her entire body was making a gesture. Something in her stance seemed familiar.

He sat down, his heart still pounding in his ears, and stared at the drawing. There was an indecipherable note in a hurried scrawl along one edge.

He was captivated by the gesture that revealed the woman. The gesture was striking, its meaning just beyond the grasp of words. How had the dead man in the red car come by such an image?

Jack got up and looked inside the car. The man wore khakis and a pink and white seersucker shirt. He had short white hair. Jack raised the man's glasses and with thumb and forefinger closed the lids over the staring eyes.

The practicalities of death demanded specific, methodical attention. He wanted to know who the man was and where he was from. Jack walked around the car to the passenger's side, retrieved a day pack from the floor, and opened it on the hood. In an outside pocket, he found a passport and an ID card from the University of Leipzig.

The man was Hans Becker, a professor of anthropology, born April 7, 1939, Dresden, Germany. Jack wondered if Becker had been in Dresden during the firebombing. Little Hans would have been five.

Jack studied Becker's stoic passport photo, concentrating on the mouth and eyes. Here was a man who had survived a terrible war, who had forty years of socialist cynicism replaced by a Happy Meal, and who died on impact. Jack wondered if the Germans had developed a sense of irony.

There were three kits in the pack. One with medicinals—antiseptics, gauze, a vasopressor for allergic reactions, and the requisite elixirs for pain and sleepless nights. One held small tools—a nice Swedish set. And one included a compass, candles, flashlight, and a suction device for drawing venom from bites. In another pocket he found a brilliant blue and scarlet parrot feather and a silver frame wrapped in chamois with the photograph of a serious, sexy woman probably in her fifties. There was no camera. He repacked everything, mindful that he was tampering with evidence. Evidence of what, he was not sure.

He had picked up the pack and started toward his truck when he noticed several more pieces of paper scattered in the brush around the car. The feathers he had seen fly up after impact were pages from a notebook that had been blasted through the window and carried up by the draft.

He began gathering pages. A few feet away, one had caught on a agave plant. Others were scattered through the mesquite and rock habitat of snakes and Gila monsters. He retrieved what he could and sat on the hood of the broken car to examine his find.

The notes were carefully printed in German with a ballpoint pen. In addition to the trainer of parrots, there were two other drawings and a photocopy of a map. Since his German was rudimentary, he skipped to the newfound drawings—sketches of a zigzagging snake with a lightning bolt along its side and a creature with the head of a coyote, a fish's tail, and the legs of a man. The images appeared to have been copied from the pottery of the Mimbres Indians, a prehistoric tribe who had lived in the area until A.D. 1130. Jack knew the era well. At one time, decorated Mimbres bowls had been the focus of his dealings in Southwestern artifacts. The painted images had been his obsession. Evidently, they still had the power to draw him in.

The Mimbres had painted abstract, playful figures of animals and spirit creatures. Becker's drawings of the coyote-fish-man and the snake could have been exact copies of Mimbres images, but their renderings of humans were usually stylized, often stiff, or abstract. The parrot trainer was different. She had a smooth, rounded shoulder, a graceful back, and exquisite thighs. Even though she was depicted with a mask, the drawing seemed more like a portrait of a particular person. Jack had seen hundreds of bowls from this period and had owned and sold enough of them to make him wealthy. None was quite like Becker's parrot trainer.

If the bowls had been in the car, they would have shattered, but there were no bowls and no shards. It was unlikely Becker would have sketched something he had found and intended to take—perhaps the bowls were not for taking. If he had discovered them in a ruin, why would he leave them behind? Maybe Hans had an ethical dilemma.

The photocopied map suggested Becker had in fact found a ruin. The map depicted trails and geographical details, including a narrow canyon with a creek bed and south-facing cliffs. A small cross marked a point near the canyon's rim. The map must have come with a story so convincing that Becker believed it. The original had been drawn before logging roads were built. That was at least forty years ago and in some places, more than a hundred. The map showed a road added in ballpoint, no doubt by Becker.

Jack tried to match the map with his memory of the immediate area. Nothing came to mind. Perhaps the detail was too small. A series of numbers was written across the bottom with the notation: *Drehen Sie Westen am gelben Metallhaus.* West, maybe yellow, and metal house. *Drehen* probably meant "turn."

He stood up and looked through the splintered windshield at the man who had written the notes and drawn the images Jack held in his hand. The notes, the map, and the parrot trainer now owned Jack as he assumed they had owned Hans Becker. He felt he had inherited another man's obsession.

Jack murmured, "Goodbye, Becker," then he turned and walked the half mile back to his truck.

He spread a Forest Service map across the hood and began scanning for a set of lines that corresponded to Becker's map. None of the numbered Forest Service roads matched the German's numbers. After several minutes, he gave up, hopeful the notes would tie the map to the territory. He had taken only two semesters of German and that was years ago. Now he would have to look up nearly every word. Somewhere, buried in boxes stacked in a storage room of his rambling house, was his German–English dictionary.

He drove the twenty miles north and west to Silverado, a high and hilly mountain town of eighteen thousand, not far from the Arizona border. It was cold in the winter, which saved it from being overrun by the elderly fleeing the ice-encrusted states of Montana, Minnesota, and North Dakota or by boomers fleeing the human compressions of California and New York. In the summer, it was too hot and dry for tourists. Since the underground mines had closed in the sixties, there were no decent-paying jobs.

It was a typical Western mining town, divided by several gullies that collected massive amounts of water during the late summer rains. Cars had been washed through storefront windows, and once a goat drowned in the hotel lobby. Silverado's main claim to fame was the rumor that William Bonney—an Irish man-child known as Billy the Kid—had committed his first murder in a local bar, defending his mother's honor. They say he stabbed the offender three times with a pocketknife and fled into the desert where he wandered for three days and nights. After that, the diminutive Bonney became an outlaw, infamous for killing and terrorizing the good people of the Southwest. He had not lived to write his life story or tell it to *The Denver Post*. This oversight allowed better folks to besmirch his good name, leaving Silverado's only celebrity a nasty little villain.

A thousand years ago, the area had been home to the Mimbres Indians. Their ruins, scattered every three or four miles along the creeks and rivers of the surrounding watersheds, had been worn by rain and wind for nine hundred years, then eroded down to dirt by a century of archaeologists, museum directors, and pot hunters. The town maintained a museum chock-full of lonely Mimbres pots, metates, and mysterious stone objects. The museum's florescence, as they like to say in the archaeology business, had come and gone twenty years before. The museum creaked, but its patina gleamed.

Jack drove into the old part of town from the east side in the after-noon heat. The asphalt was starting to quiver, and the air-conditioning units in the windows of the old stone structures were not performing as advertised. The neighborhood near the business district consisted of small houses made of stone, wood, and a few of brick—with high fences and a sparseness of grass.

He turned up the third gully, known as Arroyo Seco, proceeded past the Silverado Bar, The New Mexico Apartments, and Silly's Bar and Grill, to Carmen's Office Supply and Copy Shop, where he parked and went in. He copied only Becker's notes, keeping the map and drawings for himself. The shy, freckled girl at the register glanced at the copies but could not bring herself to ask about the for-eign writing. She made change and managed a quick smile.

Jack drove up the street to the Silverado County Court House. The sheriff sat in front in his car listening to a deputy spit half-formed sentences from the radio. Sheriff Evans, an obese, wheezing Indian with jumbo jowls and the standard ponytail, stayed in his car for several hours at a stretch. Getting in and out was work and time-consuming. The front seat had been mounted on extra-long rails, allowing him the necessary room. Heavy-duty springs and antisway bars had been installed. What he needed, and claimed to have on order, was an antigravity kit. Evans found the car comforting, like body armor. Car bound, he had decided, was better than desk bound. It got him out of the office and around people, so he could do his job. Evans liked to eat, and if that was a problem for some people, he told them they could always vote for Hurley, the fat *white* bastard.

Jack pulled up next to the sheriff and listened to the patrol car's radio—Edwin, the deputy, was following up on a report that some fool had driven off the Lacuna rimrocks southeast of town. Edwin was having little luck finding the fool's exit from the flatland into the canyon. Jack got out of his truck, walked over to Evans, and handed him Becker's pack. "Hello, George."

"Hiya, Jack." George struggled with the pack, dragging it across his great stomach and onto the passenger seat. "What've we got here?"

"Your fellow came off the rim about two miles south of the Ocate mine. The pack was in his car. Tell Edwin to check near where the Binford Road dead-ends on Foucault Lane."

"Did you see the car go off the road?"

"No. I saw it flyin' through the air after he'd gone off the road."

"Is he dead?"

Jack squinted up at the sun. "He is."

"Anyone you know?"

"Never saw him before." Jack looked down at George. "He's a foreigner. German."

"You didn't tamper with his stuff, did you?"

"Not so as you'd know, George." Jack smiled and handed him a pile of loose notes. "These blew out of his car."

Evans thumbed the pile of notes. "Looks German, all right. What do you suppose these are about?"

"Maybe he was interested in Americana."

"A history buff?"

"They like Indians." Jack smiled and walked back to his pickup. "Tell me what you find out about the German," he called back at George.

"You interested in him?"

"He fell out of the sky, dead at my feet. Of course I'm interested."

George grinned. "Just another dead white man."

"You're a dangerous Indian."

"You're a rich white guy. You got nothin' to worry about."

"You think all white guys are rich."

"The ones who live out here are. Mexicans and Indians are the only folks who're smart enough to survive on nothin'. Poor white guys just curl up and die—maybe drive their car off a cliff. But like I said, you don't have anything to worry about." The sheriff's repressed giggle sounded like the soft neighing of a draft horse.

"Put your name on that. It'd be reassuring if they come for me."

"Call if they come." A stream of tobacco spit bounced on the clay. "I'll send a posse."

Jack backed into the street, shifted into low gear, turned right and right again, and cruised slowly down San Ignacio Street, the second gully, toward the highway. Through a plate glass window he watched a woman with long black hair folding clothes in the Laundra Queen. Two tourists, lost souls anchored in the heat, stared at his truck, hypnotized by its surreal lack of progress. Jack gave them a slow wave. The man began to raise his hand, then stopped, unsure of what it meant to wave to a stranger in such alien country. Jack watched them disappear in the rearview mirror.

Idling along in low gear, he felt as though he were drifting through a child's game of Slowville, a hypothetical town where everything became glacial, ponderous, and deliberate. He had to slow the world down. People were, after all, falling out of the sky, dead at his feet. He took the side roads home.

During a 150-year period archaeologists called the Classic III, the Mimbres had made their most distinctive geometric designs and images of animals, spirits, and people. Shallow bowls, most six to twelve inches in diameter, were the painters' canvases. Some drawings had an Escher-like quality. One famous bowl had spirals made of cubes folding in on themselves or spilling out, distorting the spherical belly of a smiling, round-faced critter with clawed hands. On another pot, a maniacal bat, its wings painted with black and white squares, glared out at the observer. A bowl, perhaps by the same painter, depicted a pear-shaped creature with a long, thick tail that came to a sharp point above its head. No one knew the meaning of these images. They were as much a mystery as the Mimbres themselves, whose cultural memory disappeared with their language. No other tribe even had a story about them.

Jack laid Becker's drawings on his desk. The images in Becker's notebook appeared to have been copied from bowls made at the height of Mimbres culture, also the moment before its collapse.

More likely than not, had the images been copied from a museum collection, Jack would have known the bowls. The images could have come from a private collection. And there was the intriguing possibility that the bowls were newly dug. It was this possibility that had compelled him to keep Becker's drawings and the map from the sheriff. Jack did not want Evans and his deputies getting excited about the prospect of a new find. He did not know what he would do with the site himself, if he could find it, but he wanted time to look things over without the interference of competing state and federal agencies, archaeologists, and the droning do-gooders who would descend on any scrap of the past.

He knew the original set of notes in the sheriff's hands would never be translated. Without evidence of foul play in Becker's death, the notes would be sent back to Germany along with the "deceased and effects."

The idea of finding an undisturbed Classic Mimbres site was extremely unlikely. In the 1970s, when the best bowls started to sell for several thousand dollars, a frenzied race developed between archaeologists and pot hunters—or, as they were defined by the archaeologists, antiquities looters.

Eventually, prices for the most exquisite bowls passed the $100,000 mark. It became illegal to disturb grave sites, and the government began prosecuting looters. Known sites had been churned over two or three times. Archaeologists themselves had gone back and excavated sites that had been studied years before, reexamining shards and bits of charred wood.

Since the passage of ARPA (The Archaeological Resources Protection Act) and NAGPRA (The Native American Grave Protection and Repatriation Act), antiquities collections became a political strain for many archaeologists and museum directors. The new laws gave the tribes the legal muscle to reclaim their ancestors' bones and possessions from the museums.

Then there were the Indians who liked the high moral ground of being here first. They did not want ancient bones examined, because an early skull with distinctly non-Indian, European features might be taken as proof by some, including Aryan racists, that Indians came late and wiped out the white, "peace loving," first Americans.

In 1982, Jack had traded a single Mimbres bowl for his house and one hundred acres. The dwelling extended out in three directions from the original adobe hovel that sat just above the two-hundred-year flood plain of the Joaquin-Jimenez River.

The structural forays that defined the house were the accumulated necessities and ecstacies of seventeen different owners over 150 years. Heavy rains had forced the Joaquin-Jimenez over its banks a few years before. Although the highwater was far short of his house, it inspired Jack's dream that his treasures, washed from their rooms, went swirling through the halls—roots in the shape of cats, devils, goddesses, sex organs, and snakes; Navajo and soap tree yuccas; black alder; giant opium poppy pods; skulls of deer, bear, wildcats, horses, and javelina; faded door panels painted with the ascensions in orange and green, and a yellow bicycle; dried roses, tulips, narcissus, juniper, hop sage, and Russian olive; cones from ponderosa and piñon; a faceless wooden santo, tin *retablos*, and wood panels depicting an epidemic of devils, swarms of saints, an assembly of Christs, a multitude of Madonnas—all awash, surged through the rambling house, out the many doors, pulled through and away, into the storm.

Jack pinned Becker's drawing of the parrot trainer next to a bookcase in his study and stared at it for several minutes. The Mimbres had shown great skill as draftsmen. Their animals could be nuanced and subtle, yet humans were usually drawn in stiff, nearly ritualistic formality—never as realistic individuals. For whatever reason, the Mimbres had not done portraits. Perhaps it was believed dangerous and not allowed. To Jack's thinking, the artist who had painted the parrot trainer had broken a taboo.

When they stopped painting animals and people, the Mimbres themselves seem to have vanished. Every Southwest archaeologist had a theory about where they had gone—north to join with tribes that became the Zuni, south to Paquimé, west to the Hohokam, east to the Rio Grande, or into the mountains above the valleys where they had lived in pit houses generations before. Wherever they had gone, the Mimbres were never the Mimbres again. As a culture they had lost definition.

The accepted theory was that the Mimbres had rapidly increased their population during years of plentiful rain until their numbers began to consume the upper limit of what could be grown and hunted in good times. Then came a series of droughts that brought them down.

The Mimbres had been different from most Southwest tribes, having refrained from slaughtering one another over their diminished resources. Two hundred miles north, the Chacoan-Anasazi, driven by their leaders' savagery, had reduced themselves to paranoid bands living in fortified pueblos and cliff fortresses. Wars of attrition raged for centuries, leaving the Zuni, Acoma, Laguna, and Hopi the victors.

Jack's interest in the Mimbres waned even before he stopped dealing in artifacts fifteen years ago. In the Southwest, anything Mimbres became a merchandizing ploy, a gimmick for the Downtown Associations. Mimbres designs were stamped on plates, bracelets, T-shirts, and paper place mats. Aggressive marketing sponged up the Mimbres mystery.

He quit the antiquities business, because the value of things had come to occupy his mind for too long. Being a dealer had reduced his life to "what can I get for it?" The assessment of everything became a nauseating habit, then an addiction. In the midst of a delight or an ecstatic discovery, the worm of worth would creep into his brain, rendering his joy into appraisal, dead with value. So he quit, with the help of a three-step program. First, sell everything. Second, put half the money in government bonds. And third, study, collect, and make only worthless things—nothing to market. He became a student of the inconsequential.

Jack's wife, on the other hand, long addicted to the assessment of worth, collected her half of the money, twenty-five Navajo rugs, several pots she had purloined on her own, and headed for the grunge-canopied hills of Seattle, where the dark arts of calculation were about to be distilled into a form of greed so pure it would come to acquire the status of theoretical physics.

As Jack studied the parrot trainer's image, he became convinced the German had made a careful replica of the original. It was more likely her distinctive gesture and stance were not Hans's doing but the sophisticated work of the original artist, someone who loved her deeply—perhaps an older sister or her mother. A man might have painted her. Women were thought to be the painters, but no one could say men never painted.

She was an enigma—a moving riddle of hands and feet in the flicker of firelight. Perhaps both the painter and her subject had violated a taboo, revealed a secret, or cast a spell.

He studied Becker's hasty scrawl on the edge of the drawing. It took Jack an hour to come up with, "She dances inside my mind . . . my thoughts turned to clouds."

Maybe she was about to dance—dance for a painter who loved her. In the thousands of Mimbres pots Jack had seen, none matched the intensity of this image, none had the feel of this one. The masked woman's stance revealed something whimsical and mischievous—something particularly human. Her painter had defied convention by capturing her soul.

He stood and stretched and wandered from room to room. In a small room in the south wing, he spent an hour examining Mimbres images from the books and the hundreds of photographs acquired in his dealing days. The more he looked, the more improbable the parrot trainer seemed. He was driven back to the task of translating a language he had not read since college.

Becker's notebook began in New York, waiting for a Delta Air Lines connection to Albuquerque. Jack's struggle with the translation rewarded him with a glimpse of Becker's quixotic view of the world, particularly of America. The words "For my children and my children's children. Notes from my American travels, July 4, 2002" appeared at the top of the first page.

Today is the big day for America—226 years ago she detached herself from an old world and away flew. The angry progeny leaves domineering brutal parents. She should not be smug. She began as a figment of the European imagination. We invented both her need for freedom and her peculiar concept of community as a religious ritual. But where we gave purity of vision, she muddles that vision. She disfigures our romantic fantasy of herdsmen and noble savages, twisting them into ungainly creatures—"cow persons" and "Native American Peoples." She has taken a meat cleaver to her language.

This is my fifth journey to the American Southwest in pursuit of great-grandfather Becker's explorations of the ancient Indians of the new world and their splendid artifacts. This diary begins upon my arrival at America's JFK International Airport.

A man without a country is living in the Air France waiting room. He claims his passport is stolen. The authorities thwart him from America. No other country allows him entrance. For three years he lived on handouts. A man on an island of inbetweenness.

Waiting is a country which represses becoming. The prospect of becoming underlies the reality of being. In waiting one ceases to be. There is nothing else. One only waits.

Translating Becker was hard work. Jack wandered into the kitchen and poured a glass of whiskey. He came back and made some corrections. He was unsure of the paragraph about waiting and becoming. One slip and all that being and becoming could mean its opposite or just fall apart.

He remembered Hans staring out at the desert behind the steering wheel of the rented Ford. Jack guessed he would have liked Hans. He began sampling pages, searching for the German's first contact with the parrot trainer.

There were approximately twenty pages of notes, printed on both sides. Jack began scanning the pages for *Weg*, the German for "road," looking for a way to locate the hand-drawn map of the canyon within the large Forest Service map. He found *Weg* in a passage where Becker complained, "The little roads at home are much better for real driving. Americans are quick and cheap." Several pages later he found another road reference:

> Stopped at Little Grande, a bar off Little Grande Road—hamburger quite good, beer unbearable. Several Cowboy types drinking many beers in small glasses.
>
> One fellow went away, returned with a painted artifact bowl—two men exit the mouth of a large fish. He desires I buy the bowl he says is Mimbres. I ask, "Is it the real McCoy?" With irritation, he reassured me. His woman friend suggests I do not know my Indians, to which I reply I have no Indians.
>
> They think I am funny—for a German. I try to leave. They persist. I escape without injury.
>
> Half a mile east of the bar, I discover Billy the Kid Motel. History makes little jokes. The legendary William Bonney died for a shambles of a motel in the desert. Surely the world is crazy, but nowhere as crazy as America. Anything goes. Thank you, Billy. Goodnight.

The image of the parrot trainer danced into Jack's dreams, emerging from the darkness of an underground room into a shaft of light from an opening in the roof where the frail lines of a ladder disappeared into the bright haze filtering down from the upper world.

Jack opened his eyes. He had fallen asleep on the couch in the study. It was daylight. Out the window he could see The Sisters, as he called them, inspecting the latest mudmen to appear on the creek bank.

Years ago, Came From Under A Stone, a weary half-Zuni who rolled Prince Albert in Blue Danube papers, told his version of the first-people story to Jack. "The first ones were made of mud. Ordinary mud. Like a road in rain. They lived deep in the ground . . . long before time."

The beginning of the story was Jack's inspiration for the mudmen. He made them by building armatures of willow and plastering them with the damp reddish clay. The larger figures, some up to seven feet, took days to construct. The clay had to dry as the figure progressed or the entire structure would collapse. Several figures might be under construction at the same time. There were probably sixty figures in all—not all man-shaped. Many were women and children. Mud snakes curled around poles, trying to reach mud birds perched on top. There were three small horses, five mules, and a cat. Among the figures were several precarious pillars of stones. The Sisters saw Jack's mudmen project as important work that was worthy of their attention—unlike most things that occupied the minds of adults.

The four girls, as young as five, as old as twelve, were new arrivals to Zuma Draw. They came from a trailer house perched on a knoll half a mile upstream. Their mother was a waitress in Silverado. They had taken to wading down the creek to Jack's place to watch him work. The first day they were shy as stray cats. They stayed on the other side of the creek and watched, whispered to one another, and called him "sir" when they answered his questions. All of that had changed rather rapidly.

He could see his own cat crouched in the grass near the girls—the curious scrutinizing the curious. He went into the kitchen with the Forest Service map and spread it out on the counter. While he waited for the water to heat, he found Little Rio Grande Road and searched for similarities in the feeder canyons to Becker's map. Several logging roads emerged from canyons adjacent to the Little Rio Grande, but there was no match between the two maps. He walked down the hall to his study and called information for the number of the Billy the Kid Motel.

He drank his coffee and called the motel for directions. Two scrawny boys, about ten and eleven, who were new to the landscape, joined the girls.

"Billy the Kid speakin'," the clerk answered. Jack asked how he would find the place and the man replied, "We be about eighteen an' a half miles west off the main highway from junction 36."

"Any crossroads nearby?" Out the window, Jack saw the youngest boy furiously whacking a mudman with a stick. How The Sisters would deal with this attack intrigued him.

"Crossroads?" Billy the Kid asked. "No. No crossroads. A few loggin' roads is all."

"Did you have a German tourist staying there recently? A Hans Becker?"

"The professor's a tourist?"

"Why does that surprise you?"

One of The Sisters said something to the boy, but his rage against the mudman only intensified.

"Are you with the sheriff?"

"I understand Professor Becker is interested in Mimbres pottery."

"I can't talk about our guests unless you're with the sheriff."

Sissy, the third youngest, was running toward the house. Jack walked into the kitchen to meet her at the door.

"That's all right," he said to the day clerk. "Are you Billy the Kid?"

There was a long pause before the man answered in a small voice. "Course not. I just say that." He gradually assumed his rightful authority. "It's something I say, that's all." He was getting louder. "No harm to it."

Sissy was pounding on the door by the time Jack got there. "Hang on, ah, Mr. Kid. Someone needs attention." Jack opened the door and put a finger to his lips to quiet Sissy.

"My name isn't Kid, like I was sayin', that's somethin' . . ."

"Right. I understand, there's no harm in it. Well, thanks for your help."

"Don't thank me. I wasn't any help."

"You're right," said Jack. Now both boys were wailing on the mudmen. "You weren't, but that's okay. Goodbye."

"Bye," said the clerk.

Jack set the phone down. "Hi, Sissy."

Sissy was pointing toward the mudmen. "Those boys . . ."

"I know."

"Don't you want to stop them?"

"I don't think so." He took a small camera off the counter and handed it to her. "Take some pictures. Then tell them I said it's okay if they kill the mudmen. Then take some more pictures. It'll be an experiment."

Sissy studied Jack for a moment. He was serious. "Okay, that's a good experiment, Jack." She grabbed the camera.

"Be careful they don't whack you."

"They won't. I'm fast."

Jack watched her run back to the creek. She was a spindly, long-legged girl with short, straw-yellow hair, and she was very fast. The boys were worked up, attacking enemy mudmen with karate kicks.

"What did Jack say?" asked SuAnn, who was standing with Sadie beside a clump of mudmen, far back from the flailing boys. "Is he comin'?"

Sissy showed them the camera and whispered, "It's an experiment." At first the boys did not notice Sissy or the camera. The bigger boy stomped a mudman into the next world, kicking its skeleton of sticks into the creek. He turned toward Sissy, eyed the camera, and looked up at the house. Jack waved.

"It's okay if you kill the mudmen," said Sissy. She kept taking pictures while she talked. "You can probably kill them all if you want. Jack's pretty much done makin' them. And when the rain comes they'll all get washed away anyway."

The boy knew he was being played with. He wanted to call her bluff, but there were too many mudmen. The task of destruction overwhelmed him.

"Who makes this stuff?" he demanded of Sissy.

"Jack." She pointed to the house. "We help some when Mom's at work. Why are you kickin' 'em?"

" 'Cause they're ugly and weird."

"Yeah," said Sissy, still taking pictures. "We thought that at first, but he let us help. You get to like ugly and weird after a while."

"Well, that doesn't make it right. They oughta be beautiful."

"Ought not," said Sadie. "Beauty ain't all it's cracked up for."

"That what he said?"

"Nope. I'm the one sayin' it."

"What's your names?"

"I'm Sissy." She pointed to the one with rounded shoulders, long black hair, and a quick temper. "She's Sadie, and that one is SuAnn. She's oldest." SuAnn was a tall twelve and soon to be a dark-eyed beauty. Although she let Sissy do most of the talking, she ran the crew. "Over there's Snake." Sissy pointed to the dusky little girl with a rock in one hand and a stick in the other standing next to a short, black mudman. "She's youngest. What's your names?"

"I'm Buck an' he's Charlie." Charlie was still at work, furiously kicking at the leg of a mudman, oblivious to the shifting alliances of his older brother. "Our folks is camped down the creek," said Buck. "We've got a mobile."

"What's that?" asked Sissy.

"It's a big old house on wheels," said Charlie, who was wising up. "It's made outta tie-tay-nee-um." He had reluctantly stopped kicking and stood near his brother, waiting for the chance to take action again. In-between stuff bored him.

Snake was guarding Oliver Oil, her favorite mudman. He was exceptionally smooth, with bright, chrome-plated bolts for eyes. She had procured the necessary mud, willows, and bolts for his construction. His smoothness was the result of her own waterproofing technique, which involved a rub-down with a quart or two of used, thirty-weight Valvoline motor oil and a finish coat of axle grease. He smelled like the dirt floor of an old garage. Snake did not subscribe to Jack's infatuation with entropy. She was all for permanence. Nobody was going to mess with Oliver Oil—neither rain, nor Buck, nor Charlie. Snake stood silently with her rock and her stick and stared at the boys.

Buck kept an eye on Snake. Beneath her bangs and thick, shoulder-length hair, all he could see were angry eyes and jaw muscles. She was no older than five, he figured, but she looked like she could do him some damage. "We're on vacation," he explained. "We're not white trash or like that."

"You sayin' we are?" Sadie snapped back.

"No," said Charlie, surprised and defensive.

"Then why'd you bring it up?"

" 'Cause people who live in trailers are called white trash, is all."

"We live in a trailer. Does that make us white trash?"

"If you say you ain't, then I guess you ain't."

"We ain't."

Jack watched the drama on the creek play out, the first episode at least. When he was confident The Sisters could handle the situation, he went back to Becker's map and Billy the Kid. What unrealized expectations caused the clerk's flight of fantasy?

He marked the map at eighteen miles from the highway and began searching the nearby canyons for similarities to Becker's map that showed a road along a ridge marked "south side" and a "deep canyon." The north side of the canyon was "steep" and capped by a mesa. The original map had shown a tiny cross just below the mesa ledge. Jack was surprised by the mark. The Mimbres had not been cliff dwellers. "You be here," Jack whispered. "Treasure be there."

Jack was ten miles past Billy the Kid before he found a faded yellow trailer house a hundred yards off the road among the rocks and sagebrush. According to the Forest Service, the intersecting logging road would take him into an east–west canyon. He assumed the trailer was Becker's metal house. Nearby, a white chicken pecked at the dirt under the rust-red tractor.

He followed the road across a sandy alluvial fan to a dry streambed near the mouth of the canyon. There the road began a zigzag up the hill through the remnants of an early logging operation. A rabble of juniper, fir, blackberry, and scrub brush had taken up residence among the ponderosa stumps. By the time he reached the top, the land south of the road and to his left sloped away into a high open meadow. On his right, the hillside fell off sharply as the canyon narrowed.

The other side of the canyon, to the north, was composed of soft, slate-blue steps. Vertical streaks of crumbled, lichen-black rock divided the cliff face into murals of staggered stone.

According to Becker's map, the canyon was supposed to widen significantly, but that was not happening. It became narrower until it was almost a channel. Then a ridge of black rock jutted up, forcing the road to the left, away from the canyon's rim. He stopped and studied the map—a thin, jagged line that paralleled the canyon represented the rock formation that caused the road to veer from the rim. Midway on the line, Becker had made three tiny, sharp marks directly across the canyon from the cross. Jack drove another mile until he found a distinctive cluster of three sharp stones about eighteen inches high. He got out, slipped a knapsack over his shoulder, and began picking his way over the ridge of black rock until he was looking down on the canyon. Three hundred feet below, the canyon floor had widened from its channel to a meadow about five hundred feet across. A half mile to the west it closed up again. The bottom-land was almost as dry and brown as the hillside grass, but there was enough water beneath the dry streambed to keep several willow trees green. Directly across, in the rising heat, a mesa cantilevered out over the cliff face. If there was a dwelling beneath the overhang, it was obscured by his angle of view.

He began sidestepping his way into the canyon. A dry creek disappeared into the willow trees where the canyon narrowed to the east. After he had descended two hundred feet or so, he felt the air cool slightly. In another hundred feet, the undergrowth began to thicken. He came upon a deer trail and followed it down toward the canyon floor. For a moment, an unexpected scent of water on stone caught his attention. Then it was gone. He continued down the trail. Somewhere in the underbrush the creek resurfaced, slid around warm rocks in the shallow stream, and released that elusive odor that evokes manic joy in young horses and children.

Jack reached the canyon floor and walked the dry bed for a half mile to a place where the stream emerged. He followed the water for a hundred feet, until it disappeared near a clump of willow trees. His curiosity exposed a hidden pool. The water sloped down to a deep groove cut in the rock. During high water, the groove would be submerged, but in dry times it channeled what water there was toward the cliff and into a deep stone basin. The resulting pond hid in the shade of the willow trees. Even a trickle of water would have kept it full. The channel was an odd phenomenon. He could not tell if it was an act of nature or a human intervention.

Jack cracked two rocks together and listened to the sound echo across the canyon. The Zuni diggers who had worked with him in the late 1970s had listened to echoes. They said it helped to see. The sound ricocheted and faded, again and again. As the sound played out, he studied the cliff for signs of habitation. Did the echoes make a difference? Perhaps the Zuni had been having fun with him. After several minutes, he thought he could see steps and holds between some of the ledges and crevices of the cliff—a difficult climb for someone as afraid of heights as he was.

If people had actually lived in a cliff house beneath the mesa, they would have carried their babies, possessions, food, and water up some kind of path. As he worked his way up the first two ledges, he became convinced he had found an ancient pathway. Several holds, invisible from below, had been chipped out for toes and fingers. At first, he watched his feet search for a purchase; then, sure of his footing, he would reach for the next handhold. As he moved higher, looking down became difficult. His heartbeat started to pick up. Twenty feet from the ground, he felt the first wave of vertigo. He drew a deep breath and exhaled. Jack was no longer in awe of the Mimbres or their esoteric pots. But here he was, in desperate pursuit, clinging to a cliff, barely able to breathe, lured by the ancient image of a parrot trainer and her enchanting gesture.

The climb was easy enough. The path had probably been carved out for the women and older children, and even though Jack was strong and agile, his stomach turned, and his body stiffened. He leaned in against the rock and glanced down. One slip, a piece of gravel, a few grains of sand underfoot and he would be supper for pumas. Jack pressed his face against the warm rock and closed his eyes. He wondered if cliff dwellers had to abandon their acrophobes to the marauding tribes. Even Becker, slightly stout in pink seersucker, had apparently made it up and down. Jack thought of the

Zuni boys—always so full of themselves. This would have been nothing for them.

He looked up, refusing to dwell on the journey down, and started climbing again. His mind focused on the image of the dancing parrot trainer while he felt for the next foothold, and the next, and the next. He stretched for another grip and discovered he was reaching over a wall of solid rock that hid a natural terrace. The terrace cut back several feet beneath an overhang to a low, thin doorway. Here was Becker's cliff house and the ancient home of Jack's infatuation.

The doorway appeared to have been no more than a crack that, with great effort, had been widened in the middle and tapered to a point at the top and the bottom. It was large enough for an adult to enter. Jack stepped through the slit into the cavern, then sat with his back to the doorway and waited for his eyes to adjust to the dim light. A long chamber narrowed into the darkness on his left. Except for the doorway, little had been done to alter the natural cave. On the right side of the room, clay fill had been brought in to level the floor. A metate for grinding corn lay in the clay next to a depression that held a plain bowl. There were poles in one corner next to three large baskets. An acrid, pack-rat odor permeated the air.

He got the lantern out of his knapsack and shined it around the room. At its highest point, the ceiling reached seven feet. On the opposite side of the room, five large, plain-ware ollas, a stone ax, several scrapers, chert knives, awls, and bone daggers suggested the cliff dwellers left suddenly—there one day and gone the next.

He ran his fingers over the tight weave of the baskets. The edges of one were so worn and frayed he thought it might have been woven years before the initial retreat into the cliffs. If they had been used for storage, every grain had been devoured centuries ago. The bottom of the frayed basket was covered with a light down of fine grass and feathers. Something had made a nest. A furtive appraisal, the specter of his old addiction, valued the baskets at ten to twenty thousand dollars each.

A small hide bag near the doorway had disintegrated around a handful of pale rose-colored shells. He gathered several and took them into the light. These had come from the Sea of Cortez—several days' journey through dangerous places occupied by dangerous people. Risking death for beauty was an ancient obsession. At one time, stories of daring adventure would have been evoked by the rosy shells—delicate talismans of love and power. The light illuminated the vivid pink ridges and translucent veins of the shells. He imagined Mimbres children standing in the south-facing doorway in a shaft of winter sun, holding the pale rose shells in their small hands, letting the glow warm their faces.

If Hans Becker had left the parrot trainer bowl in the cliff house, it was not in the main chamber. Jack aimed the lantern toward the far end of the narrow room. Winters here would have been perfect misery. Only people escaping death would choose such a place. For whatever reason, this group had been forced to flee their homes and move several miles upriver to the cave for protection. The cold from the floor and the walls must have seeped into their thoughts and frozen their dreams.

Thirteen blue and scarlet parrot feathers protruded from small holes bored in the north wall of the room. A single hole was featherless. He wondered if Hans was superstitious—had Becker felt a pang of guilt when he plucked the feather from the wall?

The height of the room diminished until it was no more than a tunnel, which drifted right, toward the north, away from the canyon wall and deeper into the mesa. The floor was covered with fine sand and dust that showed the marks of Becker's boots. After forty feet, the tunnel opened into a chamber, arcing up from the left to form a domed ceiling of smooth rock about fifteen feet high.

He passed the lantern across the stone floor. It was much too hard for a burial site. On the right side of the chamber was a pile of sand and rock. Against the wall on his left were several more storage baskets and a two-foot-high, unpainted, ceramic olla for storing grain. The olla's belly tapered up to a narrow mouth covered by a flat stone. The neck was wrapped in thin corrugations of flattened clay.

Jack reached for the lid. Even though the pot had not been touched for a thousand years, he hesitated before lifting the stone.

Inside, coiled in a latticework of fine, white bones, was a rattlesnake skeleton—its ever-vigilant skull balancing near the rim of the pot. Something in its eye sockets glittered at him. He set the stone lid in place.

There were mouse droppings in the bottom of only one basket. The last people to live there had left behind some grain. One day they had all gone out, perhaps to work their field, and had never returned. Something had happened—an ambush, even a flood—and the last of their grain became the property of a mouse and her brood.

He crossed the chamber and inspected the pile of sandy clay and rock. The lantern's beam found three bowls nestled in the clay. Two were six inches in diameter. The other was ten. As he approached he could see that their interiors were painted. He held his breath and stepped closer until he could see in. These were the bowls Becker had copied.

As he stared at the parrot trainer in the larger bowl, she blurred and seemed to move, startling him. "She dances inside my mind," flickered through his thoughts. As he turned his head, he assumed he was seeing an illusion and reached down, touching the parrot trainer. She stayed put.

Had Becker found the bowls just lying there in the clay? Jack played the light back and forth along the floor, then across the wall above the bowls. A crevice, starting about waist high, widened toward the ceiling. Evidently the rocks and clay had once sealed the fissure. He was staring into a burial chamber.

He had seen a cliff-house burial once before, though it was Anasazi and in an exterior wall. The Mimbres had buried their dead under the floors of their houses. In a cave, a crevice made sense.

Jack slowly moved the lantern up the crevice, thrilled by the light's revelation. A skeleton sat partially exposed in the clay, the legs drawn up against the chest in a fetal position, with the hands under the chin. The dry mixture of sand and clay had been poured in around the body as the rocks were set in place.

After Becker had removed the rocks, he carefully carved away the sandy clay, revealing the front of the skeleton.

The cluster of finger bones grasped a small, semispherical object.

Jack leaned forward and peered in. He stared at the fingers for a minute, then leaned closer and with his thumb and index finger pulled the finger bones apart, revealing the skull of a bird with a large beak—a parrot or a macaw. This had to have been the parrot trainer.

Becker had removed the two smaller bowls from the burial, leaving their impressions in the clay near the knees of the skeleton. The parrot trainer bowl would have been placed upside down over her skull, the typical Mimbres practice. There was an interesting distinction between this burial and others—it was customary for the skull bowl to have a small hole punched in the bottom, but this bowl was smooth and unbroken. He had never seen a Mimbres burial in which the inverted bowl had no "kill hole," as archaeologists called the mysterious fractures. No one knew why the holes were made. Many believed the Mimbres were directing their ancestors' spirits into the clouds.

The find was unique—a Mimbres burial in a cliff house with a portraitlike image painted on an unkilled bowl. Jack sat down and studied the parrot trainer's bowl nestled in the clay below the burial crevice. Becker had not exaggerated. In fact, the parrot trainer was more fluid and sensual than in the German's sketch. She was exquisite.

She held one leg slightly forward, her foot raised, the toe pointing down. Her hips, pulled by the curvature of the side, seemed to turn as he rotated the bowl. The long, string skirt flowed down behind her like a horse's tail. He analyzed the set of the woman's legs and body line. There was a sense of expectation in her stance, and there was that gesture. What was it? It seemed as though the meaning was held in the bowl itself. He had to take her home. He rationalized his impulse to have—to steal—the bowl, as though rules and statutes did not apply to his parrot trainer. Of course, he would return her to the chamber one day.

He stood up and turned the light on the skeleton in the chamber. She was silent and lifeless, yet beautiful, as bones are beautiful. Once she had danced.

Jack set the two smaller bowls in place next to the skeleton, then began putting the rocks back, sealing the parrot trainer in her chamber. As he rebuilt the wall, stacking rock upon rock, he wondered how she had met her end and who had buried her the first time.

He was determined to take the parrot trainer bowl with him, but the consequences of being caught were serious. He was on Forest Service land, which made taking the bowl a federal offense. Perhaps that was why Becker had left her behind. Besides, he could never have gotten her through German customs. Once Jack got the pot out of the cave and home, there was little chance he would be bothered.

He needed to get off the cliff before dark, but wanted to explore the cave further. Were there other chambers, other rooms with openings to the mesa above, or windows on the valley below? This was where she had lived the last days of her life. He wanted to remember her house. He set the bowl against the wall near the burial chamber and continued to explore.

After thirty feet, the cave floor began a slow slope that became steeper and steeper until it seemed to drop straight into the underworld. The hole swallowed the lantern's beam. The curvature of the floor was gradual and difficult to gauge. Almost too late, he realized he dare not go farther. He was balanced on the slope, about to drop off into total blackness. Both feet were planted on hard rock, but his body was drawn back as though he had seen a snake. As he stood anchored in place, the lantern began to dim. He switched the light off and began moving back an inch at a time.

From the darkness deep in the cave below he heard a murmur. It grew louder, changing pitch—from the flutter of wings to the shriek of excited, hungry bats. The wind of their velvety wings caressed his face as they streamed past, seeking the doorway to dinner. He stood with his eyes closed, euphoric in the dark and blessed by bats.

He liked the strangeness of bats. The Mimbres had painted bats on bowls—happy, demonic-looking creatures. The Zuni told stories about bats. Some said bats were bad. Witchy things. But Came From Under A Stone told him Bat was once a powerful being who led the first people up into the middle world from the first world when they were only mud people. "Bat gave us eyes and skin and teeth and ways to have sex. Always be kind to bats."

Jack wondered what mysteries the Mimbres consigned to the deeper parts of the cave inhabited by hundreds of bats. Had they ever ventured deep into this black hole, believing it led to the mythic world of their beginning? He imagined they had discussed it often and heatedly.

The evening migration of bats from the cave was a warning the sun was setting. He needed to get down the cliff before dark. He moved back through the cave toward the bowl, flicking the feeble light to orient himself with the chamber wall. The last of his batteries was used locating the parrot trainer. For a brief moment, Jack considered the risk of getting her down in one piece. He took a thick wool sweater from his knapsack and gently wrapped it around the bowl. He slid the parrot trainer into the knapsack, stood up, and began feeling his way toward the entrance. In the distance, the dim glow of twilight illuminated the main chamber. He made his way to the doorway and out onto the terrace overlooking the secluded canyon.

Had he been thinking clearly, he would have slept on the terrace and gone down in the morning, but the prize of the parrot trainer had overwhelmed his better judgment. He was on a high of good fortune, a fool in love, with one foot searching for a toehold in the failing light.

In less than ten minutes, the cold sobriety of reason returned, quickly displaced by anxiety, and that by the outright fear of falling. His limbs began to ache. He stopped for a moment to rest and looked out across the canyon. He saw what he thought was a small light moving down the deer trail. At first, it traveled in a straight smooth line, then broke apart, becoming erratic, dancing around for a moment, and resumed its glide toward the bottom of the canyon. At first he thought someone had found the truck and was looking for him, but the light lacked the conviction of a flashlight. There was no beam searching the trail. The light behaved like a luminous moth following a scent. When it disappeared, he waited, hoping to see it again, but it did not reappear.

His muscles began to stiffen in the cool air. After a half hour of struggle, he was nearing the bottom. The cliff became a slant face. If he slipped now he would not die, but the parrot trainer would be shards, or as the archaeologists like to say, "sherds." As he searched for footing, he wondered when shards become sherds. And why? Sherds were nasty, small, and scatological. Nothing you would want to touch with your hands.

He was spent by now and searching for a hold reliable enough to give him a rest. He found a small crevice he could squeeze his fingers into while he studied his next move. Though the light was nearly gone and everything was in shadow, solid footing seemed only a couple of feet away. His toe caught something solid. Maybe it was solid, he could not be sure. He let himself slip down a fraction, carefully testing the surface with little toe taps. How many more times, he wondered, before I get in one of these jams and kill myself?

Something sharp touched his finger, then jumped into his arm. He turned in the air as an electric jolt surged through his body. He fell the last two to three feet, coming down hard on his knees.

His brain cleared enough to think he had been stung by a scorpion. A scorpion's sting could be poisonous, but it wouldn't kill him directly—though he might become disoriented and drive off the road. Becker's flight off the canyon rim came to mind, and Jack remembered why he was there. He reached behind with his good hand and felt the knapsack. The bowl seemed fine. He was probably all right himself—nothing broken. He was alive, but he felt the poison working its way into his body in waves of pain.

He took twenty-five minutes to climb the west side of the canyon, moving one slow step at a time up the deer trail. When he finally reached the truck, his vision was blurred, his right hand and forearm had swollen to nearly twice their normal size, and his head felt cleaved in half. With great care, he set the knapsack on the floor on the passenger side and started home, steering with his left hand. Shifting required twisting his body far to his right—which mashed his throbbing arm—steering with his left forearm pressed against the wheel while shifting with his left hand, then grabbing the steering wheel before he ran off the road. He stayed in first gear coming off the mountain. Once he reached pavement and the hallucinations began, he never got out of second.

At least the sensations in Jack's hand and arm kept him awake. With his good hand, he directed the truck along the line in the headlights between the rocks and cacti. For a long time a thought floated along outside the truck, trying to move in through the open window. The thought had to do with the creation of space, or the idea of space. Then the thought drifted through the window and into his head—the road invented space, and when it disappeared over the horizon it invented space through time. He wondered if this was original or significant. In any case, it wasn't his thought. It had come through the window.

With difficulty, he turned off the main highway onto the dirt road that meandered toward the river and his rambling house a quarter mile away. He could see the tiny, distant house in the moonlight. After a time, it began to show up in the headlights, but something disturbed him. The house stayed the same size. The truck was moving closer, but the house remained static and unchanged, as though he were driving toward a photograph.

Since the house was not getting any bigger, he was afraid he would run it over. He was not sure he could stop. He slowed down, grinding the gears as he shifted into low. Just before his tiny house disappeared beneath the hood of his truck, he stopped. Everything was small but the pain.

Getting out of the truck took a while. He cradled the parrot trainer in his arms and cautiously made his way toward the tiny door. He reached down and with thumb and forefinger turned the little knob. He leaned over and peered inside. It seemed normal. He clasped the bowl to his chest, then crouched down, making himself as small as possible, and slipped through the doorway.

Once he was inside, everything was fine. He stood up and moved around. The perspective shifted—as it was supposed to. It was his real, undistorted house. Before him was the living room, with two sofas, a fat chair, some skinny chairs, and a small bookcase with a globe on top against the wall to his left. The far edge of the large Navajo rug indicated the beginning of the dining room with its massive table, which could easily scat ten people. Beyond the table a sideboard stood against the adobe wall that separated the dining room and the kitchen. To the right of the dining room, a long hall-way connected a honeycomb of rooms that had been added on with varying degrees of craftsmanship by previous owners.

Jack stood with his back to the door. He did not want to look out. His sense of the world had been meddled with—there was a slight disturbance in his thinking. He was afraid if he looked, he might see the giant grille of a '78 Chevy truck leering back, as though the house and its contents, including himself, were normal and the world outside had become big and overstuffed. He decided to let the outside world wait until he had a chance to medicate himself and have a look at the bowl for which he had risked his body and perhaps his mind.

TWO

"Too damn loud," said Lucy. She reached over and pulled the hotel phone toward her ear and yawned a long, drowsy "Hello."

"Are you still in bed?" It was Philip in D.C., sounding mildly irritated.

"Good morning to you, too." She sat up, looking for a clock. "It's six A.M. in Albuquerque." A slit of light from the curtains made a line across the sea-foam carpet, illuminating the pale peach walls. She yawned and sank back into bed. "And I got in late."

"You're already getting another two hours over me."

"I'm going back to sleep."

Philip was excited and persistent. "Can I tell you two things first?"

"Two things."

"Remember Mickey McGregor, a grad student, about four years ago?"

"The skinny screw-up with the birthmark on his earlobe?"

"Good memory. He called last night. He's the chief lab rat at O'Connell Biotechnics in Berkeley now." Philip kicked into high gear, talking faster and faster. "On June thirtieth, someone sent a tech in his lab a human toe for a carbon date. It was an off-record, unaffiliated, nonprofessional request sent by a Jack Miller. The toe dated around fifteen thousand years old. McGregor found out about the date and got intrigued because there was quite a bit of flesh attached and it came packed in dry ice, which means it's been preserved in a glacier. So he ran a DNA with a departmental batch. The DNA showed the toe could not have come from a North Asian–Siberian migration. However, there were European and Southeast Asian markers present that don't show up in early Siberian DNA."

"Philip?"

"What?"

"Why are you telling me this now?"

With a wounded edge, he said, "You used to like it when I called you out of a sound sleep."

She laughed. "That was when you called because you missed me."

He became slightly defensive. "I still miss you."

"And that's why you're calling about a frozen toe at six A.M.?"

"The toe was mailed from Silverado, New Mexico." He paused for a moment of relevance. "That's only a couple of hours south of Albuquerque. Could you find out what you can about Miller? The address is 7736 Zuma Canyon Road, Silverado. If he's smart, he'll tell you where the toe came from and get it off his hands. He's violated several state and federal laws already."

Lucy rubbed her eyes and focused on the slit of light that cut across the room. Philip's rapid-fire stream of words began to sound like complete sentences.

"I think we can assume no one with credentials is involved yet, but we have to move fast. I've talked to Leonard at *GeoGraphic*. We'll have funding in place by the first of next week. Are you awake yet?"

"Yes." She kicked the covers off the bed. "What about the lab tech and McGregor?"

"McGregor can't afford to reveal anything officially. What he did was illegal. The lab tech's in the same bind. He'll lose his job if he talks, plus McGregor never told him about doing the DNA. Jack Miller is our only problem at the moment."

"Does he have the lab results?"

"No. McGregor's sitting on it. Miller hasn't heard a thing."

She pushed herself toward the foot of the bed into the stream of light, letting it slide over her feet and ankles. "Philip, this is incredible. It's huge. Do you have any idea if it came from Alaska or Canada?"

"I don't know. With luck, it'll be Alaska. That's what I want you to find out."

She sat on the edge of the bed, nodding, thinking that none of this was going to be easy. "How can you control the site?"

"A lot depends on where it is. I spent all night researching the applicable laws and tribal agreements where there're glaciers. I hope to God it's not Canada. They're bastards to work with."

"It's their country. What do you expect? They like to make their own discoveries."

". . . Xenophobic screw-ups."

"Let's find it first. You can stew over who you have to deal with later. Besides, you must have students in half their universities, right?"

"I'm weakest in British Columbia, and they're working the western glaciers. They've pulled a lot of stuff out of there lately."

"Whatever happens, it'll cause one hell of a stir." She stood up to stretch, rising up and down on her toes. "This is the one you've been looking for."

"I know it shouldn't matter," he said, "but it does. It really matters."

"Philip, you're a legend, no one can touch you."

"You know what I mean, Lucy."

This latest quest for archaeology's ark of the covenant—the pursuit of the oldest ice mummy in North America, which held the DNA code of the first Americans—seemed obsessive and perverse to her, but it was his quest. Her enthusiasm was for Philip, not the find.

"What was the other thing you wanted to tell me?"

"You remember Ben Wang?"

"Big Writer?"

"Yes. At some point I'd like to pull him in to do a piece on the discovery process and the aftermath. It would be a great coup. Anyway, I mentioned him because he called me for research on an exposé for *Harper's* on private collectors who are buying up artifacts that have been repatriated by the tribes."

Lucy laughed. "Perfect. Is the stuff coming from the tribes or individuals?"

"He didn't say, but I would suspect individuals. He said he'll be in Albuquerque this week and would try to catch the conference, so you can expect to run into him. He'll try to pull you into his little scandal or ask what effect tribal politics has on your work."

"If I can't avoid him, I'll be my sweet, diplomatic self. Thanks for the warning."

"Sure."

"I'll call you as soon as I find anything on Mr. Miller, okay?"

"Okay. Are you ready for your speech?"

"I've looked at the program. I can't believe how many different cliques there are to offend."

"It's the goddamn postmodernists with their thousand theories on the relativity of truth. They should all go back to sociology, where they belong."

"I'll bring you a program. You won't believe it."

"It is the wu-wu-west. Good luck tonight."

"Just a minute." She reached over and got a pad and pencil off the night stand. "Give me Miller's address again." She wrote it down and added a few details. "Call me tomorrow. Love you."

"You too. Bye."

She stood under the shower thinking about Philip—his drive, energy, and curiosity—and how these qualities influenced the arc of his career. Before she had met him, he had become a legend in the field, proving an early Paleo-Indian migration pattern by means of a long and complex analysis of certain flaked tools. What she had seen and loved most in Philip was his great intellectual generosity. Several times a casual comment he'd made on some aspect of human behavior or an anomaly in the archaeological record would be picked up by a student or colleague and turned into a monograph, a doctoral thesis, sometimes an entire book. The ease with which he gave ideas away also made him an inspiring teacher whose classes were packed.

She once spent several weeks researching a paper on the high-glycemic diet of agriculturalists, its effect on personality types, and the resultant warring organizations and behavior of such groups–all because of his casual remark: "Early agriculturalists limited to a diet of cereal with little or no fat would have been an owly bunch of bastards."

He filled her mind. Her heart had no trouble following along, especially after his wife left him. When Lucy asked Philip to be on her thesis committee, he declined. She was stunned. She knew he liked her work. He had always been gracious, encouraging, supportive, and often took her to lunch, testing ideas and listening carefully to her responses.

So, with all the attention he had been investing in her, why did he reject the request to be on her committee? After a day of depression, she confronted him in his office. It was a bad time. He was obsessed by something he was writing. He left her standing at the door while he finished a thought. He looked up, distracted and irritable. She asked why he'd rejected her request.

"Well, I thought it was quite obvious."

"Well, it's not to me."

"I have to say, it would be a conflict of interest."

Subtle courtship is often wasted on the naive. She stared at him, dumbfounded, until the obvious was obvious. Their relationship stayed below the scan of the politically proper, and she got her degree before their affections became public.

As Philip became something of a legend, he was able to loosen the academic grip–teaching at various institutions and running his own show at the same time. He developed his role as grand master into status and money, and attracted a small cadre of graduate students to cowrite papers with him.

He was drawn to Lucy, because he could spend an entire evening with her without his throat constricting–a physical reaction brought on by anxiety and panic, cured by sudden, ungainly flight. He did not want to understand the emotional segues many women required for a relationship to progress smoothly. He fled often.

Lucy was honest, direct, and immersed in ideas and theories, but happiest when she was in the field, sweating and coated with a fine layer of bentonite and quartz dust. Not every man's ideal woman, but Philip wanted a partner, someone with whom he could think. He was getting older and had lost tolerance for coy ninnies, pretenders, sulkers, mood swingers, and the other neurotic behaviors that provoked the male flight response.

The only real hitch was his obsession with archaeological theories about first-biggest-longest. This obsession, which Lucy had come to call BPA—Big Penis Archaeology—had fascinated her since she was an undergraduate. Admittedly, it had drawn her to Philip in the beginning, but after a few years of seeing the obsession up close, the quest became too vague and abstract for her. She did not love Philip less for his grand theories. The gyrations and complexity of his thinking entertained her, but when she was around him for too long, she experienced mind-drift.

There was a defining moment for Lucy that led her away from the domination of Philip's ideas. Early in their relationship she had made a major contribution to his migration theories by suggesting that nineteenth-century photographs of the Ainu tribesmen of Hokido, Japan, showed long cranial features similar to modern Europeans. She joked that they looked like Swedish immigrants. The Ainu were descendants of a maritime culture who had inhabited Japan forty thousand years before it was settled by its current population. Though Lucy's suggestion had a significant influence on Philip's thinking, he had failed to credit her contribution. She assumed it had been an oversight. It should have made a difference to her, but it didn't—and that was her turning point.

Professionally, she gravitated to subtler ways of unraveling the secrets of the past. In conjunction with her field work, she began to sift through the fine grain of the archaeological record—searching archives for the unedited, uncensored notes of trappers, explorers, and early colleagues. As she read, she would caress stone tools, holding their cool weight in her hand for hours at a time. In ancient native stories, she looked for themes that lay hidden in the relationships between humans, animals, and the controlling forces in nature. She studied the motifs and small jokes in the patterns waiting to be found in textiles and pottery. Her questions were always a variant of

"What were they thinking?" How did they know their world? How did they see themselves?

She soaped the washcloth, balanced on one foot, and began scrubbing the other. She had high, strong arches and well-defined toes. She liked the shape of her feet. She had good toe cleavage.

She understood Philip's BPA obsessions. Flashy theories attracted major money and status, the rudimentary forces in archaeology. In the days when she had done field work, the heavy lifting was always finding the money. With Philip's connections and her passion and energy, she had become extremely good at it. Too good. Finding the money gradually became her work, and replaced the joy of playing in the dirt and speculating on ancient thoughts. She had started the Archaeological Preservation Fund to give herself some independence from Philip's work and to protect sites the big boys like Philip leaped over in their quest for validation. The career-enhancing, media-magnet sites the alpha archaeologists were after did not need the APF's protection.

Lucy's attempts to protect sites important to understanding early humans' interactions with their environment called for a more discriminating philanthropist. During the last ten years, she had developed a network of wealthy individuals with the insight to grasp the importance of protecting unglamorous, time-consuming, media-dog projects.

The trip to Albuquerque was a part of Lucy's ongoing effort to widen her net, identify new sites, and educate the public and future donors. She had been traveling for the last three years, speaking at schools, giving interviews, addressing national and regional conventions, and looking at sites the Fund might purchase for future investigation. Before her speech to the convention at two o'clock, she had to deal with correspondence, write a Web chat reply, and do an interview with *The Albuquerque Journal*. In the evening there was a reception at the house of Sylvia Siskin, a famous Southwest collector and culture maven.

Lucy was, even by her own accounting, a success in a contentious, viciously competitive field. Escaping academia for a private foundation allowed her to be less guarded and defensive, freeing her enthusiasm and generosity. The fact that she sought funding for other archaeologists tempered their envy and made for a number of ardent devotees. By focusing on what she believed should be done, she had saved the Fund from the fuddy-duddies and the politicians. She had prevailed, not by means of political adroitness or ambition, but from simple passion.

A downside of her job was that she had begun to view people as stepping stones to achieving her ends. She was always scanning the crowd for the wealthy—"hunting fat birds" was Philip's phrase. At the same time, she left herself wide open to appeals from crackpots, scammers, the impossibly naive, and, when she was lucky, an occasional competent, sincere, straight talker.

Lucy loved Philip, but he had become irritable and morose. The playing field in archaeology had been revamped in the last ten years. Young, quick boys connected to the media were rewriting the archaeological record. Philip's legendary work on twelve-thousand-year-old Paleo-Indian points in the Great Basin was just that, legendary, and his American–Ainu migration theories were being challenged, rather crudely, he felt, particularly by people who were promoting their own theories to the popular press. Most of them, as far as he was concerned, were guilty of sloppy work and manipulating their data.

Philip needed an event, early access to a major new find that supported his migration theory. More than his reputation was at stake. A large endowment from the Benning Center for American Archaeology covered salaries and maintained his offices, but field work had to find its own money. Major press coverage brought in major cash.

Lucy believed a significant find would invigorate Philip's life and open him up again, and she would do what she could to help him. Finding Mr. Miller for Philip was a perfect assignment.

She slipped into a cotton travel robe and dried her hair with a towel on the balcony. An inversion held the smog in the valley, making for a murky morning. To the northeast, the rim of the Sandias was visible, but not the tramway. She ordered a room service breakfast and worked on correspondence until the *Journal* reporter called.

Professor Marion Horowitz pressed his heaviness against the podium and began extolling Lucy's career, her heroic efforts in saving archaeological sites from bulldozers, and her commitment to educating the public on matters archaeological.

"She is, indeed, one of the great heroines of archaeology," said Horowitz in closing.

Lucy winced and made a rueful smile. Too much, she thought. Determined, yes, certainly not heroic. She was ready to stand, but experience told her to wait. Horowitz was not finished. He held the podium with both hands as he would an object of affection, and talked for another three minutes. He was a pink, puffy fellow—a headman who preferred golf, food, and departmental politics above archaeology—another survivor. By the stance and the jut of his chin, she knew he imagined himself powerful and grand—a big sweep of a man who ran an organization that, in his mind, rivaled Harvard's Peabody in complexity and influence.

She had stopped listening, thinking about what she might say that would appeal to the room before her. The crowd was unusually diverse. She recognized the serious types from departments throughout the Rocky Mountains, several state and reservation bureaucrats, a handful of professional renegades, curators from several Southwest museums, and a few collectors. The room was also stocked with the local crystal wavers who had fallen into their own vortexes. They came with vague, mystifying gibberish, putting their spiritual spin on new finds.

Lucy knew the major players and appreciated many of them, particularly when they dropped their hustle and just goofed and told stories, which was what archaeologists did best. However, her passion for her work was slowly being eroded by the people she served. The ever-present envy and petty fights over fiefdoms of status and authority were taking their toll. The treacherous undercurrents of malice that swirled through academia discredited the real work of archaeology. The turmoil caused Lucy to live in that middle state of exasperation—angry, but not angry enough to walk away, passionate, but not passionate enough to ignore her colleagues' clumsy greed. It gnawed away at the nucleus of purpose and meaning that inspired her. She wanted each speech to be her last.

She missed Horowitz's final joke and heard him say, ". . . Dr. Lucy Perelli."

During the applause, she took his place at the podium, smiled at the audience, and returned Horowitz's chin jut with a nod. "Thank you, Marion. It's good to be back in the Southwest again in spite of your cold snap." They laughed—it was ninety-eight degrees outside. "The diversity of interests represented here gives new meaning to the term *multiculturalism*." More laughter, but edgy. "My standard opening joke these days is, What's the difference between a Hopi pot and postmodern relativism?" She paused for a moment before giving the answer. Several people, who had heard the joke, tittered. When the room was quiet again, she said, "The Hopi pot actually holds water." Scattered laughter, a few groans, and some boos followed. From poking the postmodernists, she segued to the need for better tax incentives for conservancy covenants. She gave the short version of her speech, touching on the necessity for better enforcement of the archaeology preservation laws, reducing illegal trade in antiquities, better site protection from vandalism, and funding for field work programs.

"Several years ago I testified at a juvenile hearing for three teenage boys who had vandalized an important mound site near Cincinnati. As part of the boys' parole agreement, the judge had them donate eight hours a week for one summer to work on the survey of the mound with archaeologists from the University of Pittsburgh. That summer, the connection those young men made to the past will stay with them forever. Today, two of them are studying archaeology at the University of Oregon and the University of California, Santa Barbara." She scanned the faces of the audience during the applause. The response was as predictable as her story.

"The universities that glamorize abstract theories at the expense of research and field work are not helping to advance archaeology. There are not *that* many jobs teaching irrelevant relativist theory."

She put on her glasses and picked up a paper from the podium. "As a case in point, let me read to you from one of the more extreme postmodern French relativists:

"'Ultimately, we must ask ourselves—the larger community of philosophers, social scientists, anthropologists, and archaeologists—is this reality we appear to inhabit competent to the task of presenting us with truth? Pythagoras understood man to be the measure of all things, the central observer of a world lacking cardinal essence. Stephen Hawking has stated that clock time is the illusion and dream time the reality. In the Amazon basin and the Australian outback, native peoples believe the waking world is merely illusory, that the world of dreams is the true reality. Who are we to deny these assertions?'"

Lucy removed her glasses, looked up, and smiled at the writer's dreamy notions. "Imagine for a moment the prospect of the new field of Archaeological Dream Theory and its potential curriculum. My favorite would be meteorological altered-states studies, by which we would learn to shuttle inclement weather into a parallel universe."

This brought cackles from the field people. Next to money, weather was the great bane of those who played in the dirt.

"My story about the bad boys who vandalized a precious archaeological site was not meant to be merely a cheery tale about the success of a little education. It is also a story about the social significance of working in the field and recognizing the value of preserving the context of our finds for future generations. Such work does in fact help us consider our relationship to our own culture, to other cultures, and to past cultures. Most importantly, it teaches us respect, and in so doing, we learn that we must save the past for the future. Thank you."

After the applause died out, people quickly clustered around her to say hello, ask questions, or promote a project. An intense female graduate student caught Lucy's attention and asked about applying for a job with the APF. As the student recited her brief résumé, Lucy noticed a small, delicate man in his midforties, wearing all black, with stylish stubble and designer sunglasses, maneuvering untouched through the milling bodies toward the podium. He was followed by an alert, redheaded woman whose tight green skirt and black leotard displayed an aerobicized body—the basic action-lady package—attached to pieces of sound equipment. The woman was talking rapidly to a handsome young man who raised a video camera as the man in black walked into the frame to greet Lucy. The redhead made a sharp little introductory smile and pushed her microphone forward. Lucy maintained calm and smiled back as she surveyed the woman and the man in black. The latter interrupted the graduate student's question about a job and extended his hand.

"Exquisite timing, Dr. Perelli. I am Henri Bashé, and these are my videographer friends, Anita Parker and Billy Myrdal, who are creating a documentary of Bashé in America. We would like you to do a small video segment. I think we might call it, *Whose Past for Whose Future?* Do you like it?"

Lucy stared at him, slightly mystified. She knew the name, but the context eluded her. "I'm sorry, have we met?"

"Only in my dreams, Dr. Perelli." He made a small graceful gesture with the unlit cigarette in his left hand. His accent disguised a tinge of sarcasm beneath the whiff of flirtation.

"Oh, Bashé," Lucy exclaimed, extending her hand. "Of course, Henri Bashé." Standing before her was the French theorist she had just quoted. She tried to deflect her embarrassment with a joke: "I wasn't expecting you." She waited, he smiled, she laughed. "What a coincidence! How nice to meet you. And I cannot resist: touché, Bashé."

"Yes, touché, as you say. Very good to meet." He made a modest bow of his head and a fleeting but playful smile. "Yes. We meet . . . ah, um . . . at last. I do, in fact, consider myself extremely relative, even for a Frenchman."

"Oh, I get it," said Anita. "You're the French relativist she just quoted. Right?" She glanced at Billy. "Is that taped?"

"Yep. Metazoic, babe."

No one in the crowd knew Henri or grasped the awkwardness of the moment, though the camera, the accent, and the spiffy outfit left no doubt Henri was somebody.

The interruption flummoxed the graduate student, whose wide-set eyes were transfixed by the camera lens. Anita's flea-flicker gestures failed to get the girl to move, leaving Billy to his own devices. He tightened the frame on Lucy's self-conscious formality. It was not a shot Anita could use, but Billy made his own little, marketless movies that crackled and popped with obscure cultural references, erratic timing, and disturbing ideas. As to which shots were his and which Anita's, that was sorted out in the editing, leading, often, to an abundance of shrieking and swearing.

Henri backed away. "Please, forgive our invasion, but sublime photo op, yes? We may speak again later?"

"Yes, of course. Again, later." She smiled. "Another day, another humiliation."

"Only one? So fortunate for you." Henri pointed toward the lobby. "We wait for you in the lounge. *D'accord?* Okay?"

"*Oui, certainement.*" She laughed, shaking her head in disbelief, and turned to the grad student. "Always remember whom you quote. Now, were you interested in something administrative or do you like field work?"

Forty minutes later, she had greeted the last of her friends, archaeology buffs, zealots, students, and a lonely old man who claimed that one of his ancestors, a Jewish peasant, fled the Spanish Inquisition disguised as a monk, came to America, made a fortune, and became a territorial governor. In America, he said, anything was possible.

Lucy left the Georgia O'Keeffe Room and walked into the lobby. Massive beams supported the high ceiling and heavy wrought iron chandeliers. Everything was so Western and sturdy. She was standing in the middle of the lobby, staring up, marveling at the great beams, when she perceived they were fakes, merely long boxes painted to look beamlike, attached to the ceiling with bolts. The chandeliers, she guessed, were made of molded aluminum. Someday, archaeology students would mark the precise position of those bits of molded metal, creating enormous databases.

She scanned the room for Henri and the video kids. They were filming him against a window on the far side of the lobby. His face was lit by small halogen lamps bounced against two silver umbrellas and framed in the window against the bright green grass. A low, ominous, steady thumping reverberated through the lobby. Henri used his cigarette for emphasis, took quick drags, and shot short blasts of smoke to the corresponding lurches in his delivery.

". . . Through the window," said Henri to the camera, "you can see a dozen or so Native Americans, ah . . . drumming and singing beneath their canvas awning. They protest against, um . . . what has been going on inside the Posada Duran Hotel today—a meeting of archaeologists from the Western United States. The archaeologists are here to promote their occupation . . . to the media, to politicians, and . . . themselves. Their occupation is not merely territorial—the taking of land and artifacts—it is also the taking of memories. Their unstated, perhaps unconscious, goal is the complete and total absorption of the Indian. The archaeologists pretend to share the belief that digging, ah . . . up the past . . . is of great cultural value and deserving of your money and . . . attention. Some archaeologists even describe what they do as . . . *science*. At a first look that may seem absurd, but given what passes as science today . . . they will have the benefit of our doubts. Shall we go now . . . and meet the Native American people who protest the archaeologists?"

Billy let the camera drop to his side. "Looked good," he said, "a little eerie with the contrast between inside an' out. The smoke's good. He lurches a lot . . . but he's, ah . . . ah . . . *très français*. I liked it."

"Henri, just for the record, you're not suppose to smoke in here," said Anita.

"Sorry. I did not know. There are so many rules in America . . . Ah, here she is," Henri said when he saw Billy raise his camera as Lucy crossed the lobby. "You have caught us . . . having, as you say, our way with you, but all is in fun, yes—no bad feelings?"

"Of course not," Lucy said dismissively. "I started it all by making you the object of my derision in the first place."

"Ah, I see you are angry."

"Not at all, Henri." She smiled sweetly, then turned to Billy and in mellifluous tones asked, "Would you mind terribly, turning that damn thing off?"

Henri laughed. Anita murmured to Billy. He made a slight shrug and put the camera down. He was very good-looking—underwear-ad material—with full, well-defined lips and a square, Nordic jaw. Dark lashes offset his flashy blue eyes.

"Thank you . . ."

Henri laughed. "You are so, ah . . . *stern*, Dr. Perelli. Do you have the history of . . . how you say . . . ah," his lips pursed and his eyebrows shot up in a mischievous angle, "unfortunate relations with the opposing sex?"

"Henri, please call me Lucy. Now that we have insulted each other, we are freed of certain formalities."

"You have a good humor."

Billy corrected him. "You mean, she has a good *sense* of humor."

Henri laughed. " 'Sense of humor' is oxymoronic."

Anita held the door for Henri, Lucy, and Billy as they filed out into the light and heat of the day.

On the green between the Hotel Posada Duran and the street, a group of demonstrators sat around a large drum under a long tarp. Two poles held a banner with the slogan: SAVE OUR SACRED SITES. STOP ARCHAEOLOGY. Propped against a small birch tree was a cardboard sign with the legend: DEATH TO ARCHAEOLOGISTS.

Henri looked at Lucy. "Truth or joke?"

"I don't know. You should ask them."

"Good idea," said Anita.

Henri smiled. "You are suggesting I martyr myself for archaeology?"

"Not for archaeology," said Anita. "For the video."

"You and Lucy should go," said Henri. "Billy and I should video. If they kill you, we will have evidence of their crime."

Anita took his hand. "Come on, Henri. You have to do the talking."

"I suggest you ask permission before you start filming," said Lucy.

An Indian in his early forties, with beautiful, thick lips, obsidian eyes, and long braided hair, wearing a Seattle Mariners baseball cap, sat on an air mattress just under the tarp, out of the sun. The air mattress flapped up on either side, creating a stubby-winged effect. His long braids were pulled forward over his shoulders.

The Indian noticed several people, including a lean white woman with short, spiked red hair, crossing the lawn toward him, towing a slight man dressed in black pants and a turtleneck. The Indian had been inhaling deeply and exhaling slowly, which left him calm and reflective. The people crossing the lawn were not a problem. He could see they were neither angry nor crazed—they had a camera.

"Hi, I'm Anita," said the redhead. "This is Professor Henri Bashé, from France, Dr. Lucy Perelli, and my partner, Billy."

"I am Kills The Deer Burnum."

They said their hellos. Lucy noticed the air was a little dopey. Farther back under the tarp, several young people beat a large traditional drum and wailed an unmistakably sad song.

Kills The Deer pointed at Henri and asked, "Your name is Ornery?"

"Close," said Henri, lighting another cigarette.

"Pretty strange name," said Kills The Deer.

"It's like Henry," said Anita. "But in French it's pronounced On-Ree."

"Close," said Henri. "Could we ask you a few questions for the film?"

"I am here to answer questions. What kind of questions did you have in mind?" asked Kills The Deer.

Billy raised his camera and focused in on Kills The Deer. "Ready, Henri."

"Do you actually kill archaeologists?" Henri asked.

"What are you talking about?" Kills The Deer was used to making absurd accusations, not having them hurled at him.

Henri turned and pointed toward the sign. "Under the tree it says, 'Death to Archaeologists.'"

Kills The Deer craned his head around and squinted at the sign. "Those damn kids must've done that. Are you people archaeologists?"

"Dr. Perelli is the director of the Archaeology Preservation Fund," said Henri. "I am more of a student."

"You are old for a student," said Kills The Deer, not believing.

"We can always be students."

The Indian nodded thoughtfully. "My mother takes classes at the community college."

"What kind of classes?"

Kills The Deer closed his eyes and exhaled. "Did you come to ask about my mother?"

"Would you rather not talk about your mother? Many people feel that way," said Henri. "Myself, I liked my mother. In fact, I wrote a book about her."

"It doesn't matter," said Kills The Deer, resigned to the moment. "My mother is studying to be a midwife. She's already a midwife, but she wants the license so they won't arrest her. They have lots of licenses these days."

"It's much worse in France," said Henri.

"How is that?"

"You need a certificate to pee."

Kills The Deer laughed.

Anita put her hands on Billy's shoulders and expertly rotated him in a half-circle. The camera lens found a policeman in a bright yellow vest walking across the grass toward them. Behind him, the mirrored windows of the buildings reflected the sky in deep blue.

Kills The Deer had a long history with the policeman, whose name was Mendez. The yellow vest against the sky's reflection reminded Kills The Deer of a kachina doll. For many Pueblo people, these dolls were representations of the masked ancestral spirits who mediated between the earth and the sky to make rain. They were sometimes called cloud people or cloud dancers. Kills The Deer was not a great believer in kachinas, but they were good "symbology-wise," which elevated the appeal of his kachina paintings to the New Age market. He liked the idea of a cop-kachina in a yellow vest floating through blue sky, framed in concrete. Add one billowy, Maxfield Parrish cloud and the result would be formal and ironic, yet radiant in mythological meaning. In other words, it whooped with postcard potential.

The cop approached Billy until he was standing directly in front of the camera. "May I see your permit, sir?"

"That will not be possible, Officer."

"Why not?"

Billy turned the camera on himself. "We have no permit. We have not applied for permits."

"Sir," Mendez began lecturing Billy, "you are standing on city property. If you capture images for commercial gain on city property, you must have a permit. I request that you stop filming until I understand the nature and intent of your work."

Anita took charge, delivering her standard reply to standard queries. "We're making a public television documentary with funding from the NEH, NEA, the Lawrence and Lulu Merryman Foundation for Social Research, and support from viewers like yourself. This gentleman is Dr. Henri Bashé, the famous French social theorist and the narrator of the program."

"Well, that doesn't sound very interesting," said Mendez. "I guess you don't need a permit."

"Your support is appreciated," said Billy.

"Billee," Anita hissed.

Mendez shrugged. He looked down at Kills The Deer, who was blowing into a tube connected to the air mattress.

"This pillow has a slow leak," said Kills The Deer. "It needs to be inflated a lot." He blew some more.

"Looks like you could fly that thing, Burnum." Mendez looked up at the tarp. "You come prepared."

"Only mad dogs and white men stand out in the noonday sun," said Kills The Deer. He began giggling, which jiggled him up and down on the mattress.

Mendez peered back under the tarp at the drummers in the dim light. "I smell something I don't like," he said.

"Fe-fi-fo-fum," someone chanted to the slow beat of the drum. "Hi, Officer Mendez."

"You're on probation, Jeremy. Don't screw it up."

"I ain't smokin' nothin'," came the quiet reply.

Officer Mendez turned to Kills The Deer. He looked perplexed and irritated. "You should be keepin' these kids out of trouble."

"Robert, I *am* keepin' them out of trouble. They're poundin' a drum. That's about as out of trouble as you can be."

"I don't like it."

"If you were to go somewhere else, you'd feel a lot better. We'd feel better, too."

"There's some truth in that," he said and walked back toward the street.

"What's this film about?" Kills The Deer asked.

"The death of archaeology," said Henri.

"It's about the ways we define culture," said Anita.

"It's about esoteric French theories no one understands," said Billy.

"An epic work, as you can see," said Lucy.

Henri raised an eyebrow, Anita ignored her, Billy grinned. Three different films were playing in their heads. The final cut guaranteed carnage.

Henri smiled at Billy. "Remind me to tell you about the benefits of respect." Then he stooped down toward Kills The Deer and, marking his phrases with cigarette smoke, said, "I am especially interested in cannibalism."

Kills The Deer stared at the camera lens, filling Billy's field of view with the expression of a man insulted into stupefication. Then, not knowing if he should feel rage or amusement at this haggard, turtle-necked geek, Kills The Deer turned to Henri and said, "You are obviously from some other planet, Mr. Bashé. Only an alien would come here and talk to Indians about cannibalism."

Henri said, rather brightly, "We all have cannibals in our closets. So it is of no great matter to me, who ate whom, nor should it be to anyone." Henri spoke lightly and with slight, poking gestures between puffs, holding his cigarette between his middle finger and thumb, orchestrating his words. "Are you familiar with Christy and Jacqueline Turner's study that documents violent death, dismemberment, and cannibalism in the pre-Columbian Southwest?"

Kills The Deer shook his head in disbelief, a gesture Henri misunderstood to mean that the Indian had no knowledge of the Turners' work. Henri, with childlike enthusiasm, proceeded to explain.

"The authors described a feast that took place in the southwest corner of Colorado about nine hundred and fifty years ago. The feasters filleted the victims from their bones as though they were deer or other large animals. The bones were broken and boiled, causing the sharp ends to rub against the side of the pot—archaeologists call such wear 'pot polish.' Wonderful phrase. And, most dramatic, the feasters used the victims' skulls as kettles in which to cook their brains—a tribute to culinary minimalism."

Kills The Deer looked at the others for signs of collusion. He was relieved to see Anita and Lucy wide-eyed with dismay. Billy was in his camera, considering the possibility Henri had cooked his own brain.

"However," said Henri, finally realizing he had stepped where he should not, "my work is of another nature altogether, having nothing to do with the physicality of ingestion. I am studying the absorption and consumption of cultural cannibalism—the manner in which one culture absorbs another—customs practiced in the act of consumption—the smile, the handshake, the offer of colored sugar water. I mean no rudeness or insult to you or your ancestors in any way whatever."

"I'm not sure I want to understand," said Kills The Deer. "But show a little awe and respect. It's your ticket to hang with the Indians, otherwise . . ." He flicked his finger across his throat.

"*Absolument*," said Henri, with an exhalation of smoke.

"You are fortunate. We find the French peoples . . . hard to digest." Kills The Deer laughed. Everybody relaxed a little. "So you came here to ask me something, or was it my mother you were interested in?"

"No," said Anita before Henri had a chance to screw things up. "We would like you to define what you mean by Indian."

"Indian? You don't want me to talk about my ancestors eating each other?"

"Initially, we would like you to define Indian."

"Indians first, cannibals later. Well, Indians are my people. I'm an Indian. That's all the definition I need."

"About twenty percent of the U.S. population claim to have Indian blood in their veins. Is an Indian anyone who claims to be an Indian?"

"You should ask them."

"The twenty percent?"

"Yes. They'll give you lots of opinions you can use in your *dada* base."

"You mean data," Anita corrected.

"You Indians and we French have much in common," said Henri. "We are both in deep dada."

Kills The Deer laughed. "You too? We should talk sometime."

"How did that look, Billy?" Anita asked.

"Fine." He kept his eye in the camera.

Kills The Deer grinned. "Don't you want to know about my mother?"

Anita squeezed Billy's elbow, her signal to tighten the frame on Kills The Deer.

"Do you want to stop archaeologists from digging on your lands?" she asked.

"I am an artist. I use many images they dig up. A lot of us make a little money off archaeology, one way or the other." Inside he was stirring up a stew of self-righteousness, pride, anger, and superiority with a sprig of guilt, and a dash of remorse, none of which he could articulate. His lips felt thick and flat. His rugged face twisted into a scowl. "The real issue is that Indians are always being screwed by whites. Not all Indians care about sacred sites. What we want is control over our lives. So we're goin' to make an issue out of anything we can. If we have to be a little mean to get respect, we'll be mean." He laughed. "Gentle persuasion hasn't worked so far."

"What makes an Indian an Indian?" Anita asked.

"Today, it's a legal issue. I'm Indian so long as the law says I am. But I don't want to talk any more about bein' Indian. We're goin' to sing now. If you want to video those boys drummin', maybe you could give them a few bucks. Jeremy's '73 LTD guzzles gas like a white girl . . . never mind."

Anita flinched. Lucy snorted, "Now who's the racist?" She touched Anita's hand. "Seventy-three was a very good year, Anita."

Anita rolled her eyes. "Yeah, it was the year I was born. Gas money, huh? Sure. It's the least we can do."

Billy came around behind several boys and young men drumming and dropped down on one knee. He framed the drum and the flailing sticks against Kills The Deer's silhouette. He grabbed shots of young, expressionless faces, then moved in close on the drum head, shooting in slow motion, catching the vibrations of the stretched rawhide as a sheen of undulating light.

"We don't need a whole lot of that, Billy," Anita whispered. She left him to capture beauty and went back to Kills The Deer.

"Fifty bucks for your kids?"

"Thanks. That should buy them burgers and get them back to the rez."

"Are you demonstrating at the reception at Sylvia Siskin's tonight?" she asked.

"Who's goin' to be received?"

"The archaeologists."

"We weren't planning anything. Saturday night on the rez. The kids will be doin' their thing."

"What thing is that?"

"Don't ask, don't tell. At the pueblo they say, Kids rule, elders drool. But I wouldn't mind goin' to your party." He guessed that any reception would be well-stocked with rich, white people who might actually buy art. "Is this party invitation-only?"

She imagined the video ops with Kills The Deer in a room full of archaeologists. "It doesn't matter at these things. It's just archaeologists. It's at six-thirty. You know the house?"

"I've been there," he said in his flat, even way.

"Come as you are."

"As I am is good."

"We'll count on you." She turned and called to Billy, "Anytime, bucko."

The drummers had changed their chant from the forlorn wailing to a muffled phrase Henri was having a hard time understanding. "What are they saying?" he asked Lucy. "Is it English?"

"Frum time n men oreal? I'm not sure. It sounds British."

As they walked back to the Posada Duran the phrase repeated in time to the drum, "Frum time n men oreal, frum time n men oreal, frum time n men oreal."

THREE

Sylvia Siskin's house was a remodeled adobe mansion with a maid, a cook, and a house man who performed butler, driver, and security duties. The house stood near the tramway in the shadow of the Sandias, overlooking the smog of Albuquerque. In the 1920s, an Italian minimalist, craving the beauty and magic of the Southwest, built the original house high above the river road that led north to Santa Fe. The site, an arduous five miles above the meandering river, was chosen in part to avoid the procession of hedonists drawn to the free-thinking cabal of Mabel Dodge and D.H. Lawrence on the high plain of Taos.

Video cameras scrutinized the grounds, the road to the house, and the ravines that funneled skunks, rattlesnakes, coyotes, and other visitors from the Sandias into Sylvia's backyard. Once, wild burros and deer had roamed among the cacti in the moonlight, while pumas waited in the shadows.

An eight-foot-high, wrought-iron fence defined the twenty acres surrounding the house. Sensors in the road alerted the staff to incursions over forty pounds, including big, goofy dogs and wayward children.

Anita and Billy arrived early with Henri, whom they had rescued from a bout of reflective drinking in the hotel bar. A lean, Chicano gentleman in his early thirties was walking toward the gate.

"Good evening. I am Morales. Mrs. Siskin said you would be early. She is waiting for you."

"Hi, I'm Anita Parker." She gestured over her shoulder, "Henri Bashé, Billy Myrdal."

"You can pull your van over by the house for now. May I help unload your equipment?"

"Oh, thank you, but there's not much. Billy can handle it. There's a Native American gentleman with us, Mr. Kills The Deer Burnum. He's coming later, but he isn't on the guest list. Is that a problem?"

"Not at all. I know who he is. A friend of mine has one of his paintings."

"Really? What's it of?" asked Anita, intrigued by the possibility that Kills The Deer had a degree of fame.

"It's a kachina. It's different."

"Oh," said Henri. "In what way different?"

"It's on fire."

"I've never heard of a fire kachina," said Anita.

"It's not really a fire kachina," said Morales. "It's more like a kachina on fire. It's symbolic, I'm told." His bristly mustache turned up at the ends in a sweet, angelic smile. "Enjoy the party." He waved them on. "Señora Sylvia's maid, Inez, will show you where you can put your equipment."

Anita and Billy collected their gear and crunched across the circular drive to the front door, followed by Henri, who was enjoying a warm buzz from the hotel's rough red. The thick walls of the house tapered up for a monumental fifteen feet. The ends of the heavy roof beams, carved by an elite of impoverished Mexican craftsmen, protruded through the wall two feet below the tiled ridge cap.

Inez opened the door before they could knock. "Please come," she said and with an open arm gestured to a room across the foyer to the right of the entryway. Billy turned as he passed by her, drawn, as many were, by the strange beauty of her Spanish-Mayan legacy. Her eyes were large and dark, her hair long and black, and her nose slightly rounded. She stood extremely straight, perhaps to make amends for her lack of height.

"You may leave your equipment in the Scholder Room until it is needed."

Billy unburdened himself of his cases of cameras, lights, and tripod, carefully arranging things on a giant oak table beneath a brightly lit painting of a screaming Indian. He unpacked the digicam and began a pan shot of the room, stopping briefly on the Indian, zooming in and out on the black hole of a mouth edged in white teeth.

"Billy, how do you expect me to use that?"

"I can use it."

"It'll cost us editing time."

"Peaches, babe, we agreed about this."

"That you can waste my time with this nonsense?"

Billy's eyes drifted away to the screaming Indian. "You know, sweetheart, you've gone through a lot of cameramen."

Anita caught sight of Inez, waiting graciously in the doorway, attentive to the gringos' needs and instructions. For a brief instant, Anita caught a flash of her bitch-self reflected in the housekeeper's serene, dark eyes. She glanced away and glared at Billy. "Can we talk about this later?" she whispered.

"If you insist, sure."

She inhaled evenly. "Okay."

Billy was lost in his viewfinder, staring at the ceiling. It appeared that every beam in the house, from every imaginable angle, came together in this room. No two beams repeated an angle, as though a bunch of drunks had been stuffing sticks into a campfire all night, yet the beams fit precisely. You could not slip a cigarette paper between them. There was no architectural necessity for such a display. A remarkable level of skill had forced the timbers into patterns unimagined in nature—a Chicano sorcerer wielding a razor-sharp adz at an ancient conifer.

"Billy," Anita whispered. "Please."

His eyes fell from the ceiling, panning down past the elaborate Caravaca cross above the doorway and into Inez's sweet, waiting face. She smiled, not for the camera, but because Billy had discovered the intersecting timbers. She glanced up at her magnificent timbers, then turned away.

The maid's smile mystified Billy. He looked back at the ceiling, then at Henri, who made a slight hand shrug in French, feigning innocence. Henri had seen the maid's open gaze, her bright, loving eyes, and square shoulders—saw her look at Billy with her entire being. Radical departures were a mysterious business. Henri studied the intersection on the ceiling. Perhaps it was merely an achievement of craft.

Anita glanced at Billy and pointed to the table. "It would be polite if we left the camera until we've been formally introduced to Sylvia Siskin." She strode past the maid to the center of the foyer and waited. Billy and Henri followed, then turned to watch Inez lock the door and pocket the key.

"Now it is time to meet Señora Sylvia," Inez proclaimed. "Follow me, please."

Though Inez and Sylvia occupied the same space, they existed in different spiritual planes. Inez saw her employer in wary detail. She could recall Sylvia's every gesture, and often, she believed, images of her employer's thoughts. Time and service had made Sylvia predictable, yet left Inez deeply puzzled. They only thing they shared was the air they breathed.

Inez saw Sylvia as an aging white beauty, whose purpose and meaning were hidden behind the routine of her life. Inez wished to transmit only a single aspect of her own life to her mistress—she prayed that Señora Sylvia would one day perceive the holiness of the antiquities with which she surrounded herself—objects once used by others in the veneration of God.

Inez led Henri, Anita, and Billy to a large domed chamber off the foyer that opened to the several directions of the house. A high-beamed corridor with sainted alcoves cut in the thick adobe led from the center of the chamber to a tiled veranda. Fragments of light filtered through the wisteria-covered trellis. Inez led them to a random cluster of heavy teak chairs where they could sit and look up at the purple and pinks splashed across the Sandias.

Billy was already shooting a scene in his mind, framing the interview between Henri and Sylvia at the edge of the dancing light, against the purple-pink mountains. When he edited the image, his impulse would be to pump up the colors. To Billy, pretty was suspect. He preferred to tweak nature's colors until they achieved a raw fervor, a form of revenge against sugar coating. He also found if he tweaked all nuance from a scene, screwing up the contrast and color saturation, Anita would like it better. It took a little of that snap, snap, pop, pop action to get past her front desk.

Inez went to fetch drinks for everyone. Billy made a box shape with his hands and pretended to pan his camera across the pretty mountains. He thought about light, framing, and color, about power and prestige, and about the rich. Billy had a Southwestern art-boy aspect—tight jeans and fitted shirts, but at his core he nurtured the seeds of subversion.

Inez appeared with a silver tray loaded with drinks and elaborate hors d'oeuvres. Henri paced around sipping champagne. Anita sat in one of the teak chairs and downed a diet Dr Pepper.

On one of his passes, Henri picked up the empty can and looked at Anita. "Do you know the secret ingredient in Dr Pepper?"

"Dr Pepper has a secret?" asked Billy. "Tell us."

"Here she comes," said Anita, getting to her feet.

They watched an elegant, white-haired woman stride down the corridor, through the scattered light, coming toward them, extending her hand. She smiled and said in a clear, full voice, "I am Sylvia. You must be Anita. Welcome to my home. Please, be seated."

Sylvia liked power and was drawn to it, but she would say "influence" rather than power. Power was too direct, obvious, and blunt. It lacked grace.

Anita was anxious to get a camera in Billy's hands before Sylvia started talking to Henri and before the other guests arrived, but she became transfixed. Sylvia was what Anita wanted to be. Sylvia was everything that Anita's red-clay Texas Baptist mother, who had raised seven kids and cleaned motel rooms in East Lubbock, was not. Anita took the woman's hand and looked into her eyes.

Sylvia understood the effect she could have on younger women. The long pause and the searching, hungry look in the girl's eyes were taken in stride. Sylvia turned, observing in a glance Henri's dress, posture, cigarette, and quizzical smile. "And you would be Monsieur Henri Bashé?"

"Would be? Yes, and intend to be into the future. How do you do, Madame Siskin? Thank you for inviting us to view your famous collection."

"Please call me Sylvia, Henri."

Anita pointed to Billy. "This is my cameraman, Billy Myrdal, Mrs. Siskin . . . Sylvia. He's my partner for the project."

For the project jumped out at Billy. The time frame startled him. He gave Sylvia a faint smile and an unintended, reflexive shrug.

Inez stood apart, her dark eyes fixed on Billy, who pined for his camera and the lost video ops.

"As I explained on the phone," said Anita, "our project is about defining cultures, so we are very interested in your collection and the story behind it. We would also like to film all of your discussions with Henri, who is our primary humanist and narrator."

"Humanist is a profession? What does a humanist do?"

"It's an NEH funding requirement," said Anita. "You need qualified . . ."

"Well, dear," Sylvia turned and smiled at Billy, "you and Mr. Myrdal are welcome to film whatever you like. If you need to film any of the collection out of their cases, I would prefer we do that another day. I've taken the liberty to reserve a handler from the Maxwell Museum for tomorrow morning to remove any pieces you may want to film."

"That would be wonderful."

"I assumed that would be your preference, since my guests will begin arriving anytime now."

"Yes, of course. Thank you so much. If it's all right with you, I would like Billy to film you meeting Mr. Bashé under these beautiful vines."

Sylvia turned to Inez and instructed her to help Billy retrieve his equipment. Inez smiled and nodded gently at Billy as though she were accepting an award. Anita caught the gesture and glanced at Billy. He was oblivious, already sprinting toward the corridor, not wanting to miss the moment. Inez turned as he went by, surprised that someone would run through her mistress's house. She looked back at Sylvia, who nodded, freeing Inez to pursue Billy. Inez could barely restrain herself as she glided across the tiles through the ethereal light.

Anita watched Inez hasten down the corridor after Billy. The maid's innocence annoyed her.

"Anita, have you met Dr. Lucy Perelli yet?" Sylvia asked, diverting Anita's attention. "I believe she spoke this afternoon."

Anita turned and stared into the eyes of her hostess. Sylvia's even manner and mild amusement were disarming and warm. Anita wanted to be that full woman—complete and competent.

"Yes," Anita managed, "we taped her and Henri after the talk. We'll interview her tonight at the party. She's kind of famous, isn't she?"

"Well, she controls a lot of money, I mean a lot in terms of archaeology. These days, that alone is cause for fame. Of course, her relationship with Philip Sachs adds a certain allure . . . one of the great romances of archaeology—a field rife with romance, as you have no doubt gathered."

"Henri has told me stories, mostly about the French in Egypt."

Henri smirked. "Yes, nothing quite so romantic as sex in Ramses's cool chamber. However," he said, working the air with his hands, "I understand the Southwest is equally rife—men and women in common struggle against all that weather. The shared seeking of . . . ah, sherds—as you say."

"You are so French, Monsieur Bashé," said Sylvia, arranging herself in a chair.

"*Naturellement*, madame."

Anita did not want them talking off camera. She squatted down in front of the thick chairs and began to negotiate with Sylvia. "After I introduce you to Henri, could you give us a short tour, so we could be moving past the collections while you talk? Then we would like to film you greeting certain guests and introducing them to Henri. That way we can cut to the interviews later."

"But I won't know everyone, dear."

"Oh, it won't matter. We can always stage the introductions. If there's anything awkward, we can cut it out or reshoot."

"Of course," said Sylvia, touching her chest lightly. "Let us avoid awkward."

Anita paused briefly at Sylvia's comment, not knowing how she should react. Then she laughed.

A little loud, thought Henri. Awkward, even. He was silent. He realized he was waiting for the camera—why squander words? He sipped his champagne and smiled up at the Sandias.

"We have a unique little chapel," Sylvia offered. "Perhaps you would like to begin there."

Henri's antenna shot up. "In the house—you have your own chapel?"

"Well, it's a bit odd, part of the collection, actually. I collect Catholic accoutrements—crosses, virgins, saints, a few relics."

"Relics? Really?" asked Henri. "The body parts of saints?"

With the purity of a nun she said, "Nothing authenticated."

Anita was squirming her way into a knot waiting for Billy's return. Finally she sat on the arm of Henri's chair.

"Relics," he continued, "are an interesting bit of business."

"An interesting and rather considerable business at one time," his hostess replied. "The trade in fakes was enormous—centuries of bone chips, gallbladders, toes, finger joints, slivers of the cross, and pieces of fingernails wrapped in moleskin and preserved in exquisite little silver boxes—offered to every count, duke, cardinal, and even village priest in need of a drawing card."

"Ah, yes. The small step from awe and respect to gifts and recognition."

"And impossible to determine the authenticity of any of it." Only the gentle gleam in her eye and the wistful smile hinted that Sylvia herself may have, from time to time, ignored the ethical impediments of the antiquities trade.

Anita finally interrupted, pleading, "Could we wait until the camera gets here? I really want to video all your discussions."

Sylvia paused, smiled at Henri, then looked at Anita. "Actually," she said, "I need to check a few things. I won't be long."

Anita watched Sylvia cross the tiles under the leaves. She imagined herself walking through the corridor, past the alcoved saints.

Henri observed Anita leaning wistfully toward their graceful hostess or, he suspected, leaning desperately away from herself. He was beginning to understand that, for Anita, actually making films got in the way of being a filmmaker.

She had picked him up at the Albuquerque airport only a day ago. It was their first face to face, and little time was spent on the specifics of the conference or Sylvia's shoot. During the previous year, they traded e-mails. Miscommunication, false starts, and waiting for funding had things between them on edge.

Henri's jet lag, enhanced by drinking nonstop from Charles de Gaulle to JFK and from JFK to Albuquerque International, had him bleached out. His voice was a little drifty, but his mind was spinning its usual brand of loosely connected cultural associations and word games—symptoms of neurological stress that signified creativity in certain intellectual circles.

The year before, Billy had taped an interview with Henri off Britain's Channel 4, cut it down to a series of seven, fifteen-second clips, and showed it to Anita. It was enough to tell them that if they kept the camera on Monsieur Bashé long enough, they would have a film. Henri only lacked editing, which Billy was happy to supply.

Anita hopped off Henri's chair, crossed her arms, and rocked back and forth. Billy was taking too long. That little bitch had cornered him. Usually he was a hyper-responsible gearhead, always prepared and quick. Annoyingly quick. Sylvia's silhouette appeared down the corridor. She was already coming back, and there was no sign of Billy. Anita turned and looked at Henri as if to mute him.

"No words," he said. "Understood."

Anita tried deep breathing and stared up at the blur of canyons and colors, which at first registered as a smear of nightmarish mauve. Either she had not seen the mountain, or she had forgotten it was there. She sat down and waited. The white silk sliding against Sylvia's legs announced her return.

"Are we ready?" asked Sylvia. She glanced back toward the corridor as though she were conjuring Billy forth. The soft running squish-squish of his tennis shoes preceded him. He flashed down the corridor, man and gear flying, came to a sudden stop at Anita, handed her the radio mike, and stood back, ready to roll.

"Speed," he said, just as Inez appeared amid the scattering light and touched a finger to her ear.

"So soon?" asked Sylvia. "I thought we had more time." She looked sweetly, almost apologetically, at the video producer woman and her spikey red hair. "Well, tomorrow morning, perhaps. Our guests are here, and I must greet them. You wanted me to introduce Henri?"

"Please," said Anita. The knot in her neck made her head ache.

Sylvia began, as they walked through the corridor, by introducing the faded saints, snug in their alcoves. Billy slid past for a diagonal tracking shot. "This is Bobby," she said with slightly exaggerated care and charm, looking alternately at Henri, the saints, and the camera. "That's Joey, and here's Jack," she paused, ". . . my fave, Teddy."

Kills The Deer came first and alone. The boys had departed for Saturday night in the LTD on Anita's endowment. It was a mistake to come alone. He knew that. There was never a way to prepare himself for the wealthy white. The experience always overwhelmed.

He had been at this house once before, at night by the back fence, in the late fall. He and his two younger brothers had walked down the arroyo behind the house carrying a deer they had poached earlier in the evening. His memory of the event was very clear in his mind. They stood in the glare of light near the wrought iron fence and scrutinized the huge house with its great timbers. Their truck was a quarter mile away. He was tired, plus he had to pee. He put the deer down, and all three pissed on the cold wrought iron and watched the steamy glow rising up through the blaze of security lights.

As he approached the front door of Sylvia's mansion, Kills The

Deer noticed the video cameras mounted around the house. No doubt there was a video of him and his brothers staring at their steamy apparitions. He wondered if she'd seen it, and if the resolution was good. It was probably transferred to digital by now—the whole thing, the illegal deer, setting the still-warm animal gently on the ground, unbuttoning their pants, pissing on cold iron—all time-lapsed and backed up on DVD or bound in bubble memory. It was a performance, actually. Kills The Deer wanted to get his hands on the tape. He knew someone who had one of the kachinas, who was a friend of the security guy. But which kachina? Maybe it was the truck driver. No, that went to Saltos Transport out of El Paso. Well, he'd figure it out. Kills The Deer brightened a little. He had a project. He had business with the house.

As he came through the door, images of the security video buzzing in his head, he saw Billy's camera, that redheaded woman in a half-crouch, Henri's quizzical smile, and Sylvia, hand extended.

"Good evening Mr. Burnum."

Is this a joke? he wondered. Is this my dream?

"I would like you to meet Henri Bashé. Henri, Kills The Deer Burnum is one of New Mexico's more imaginative artists, famous for his series of surreal kachinas." He shook Henri's hand as though they had never met. "I've heard," said Henri, smile intact, "that you are a man who, how do you say, ah . . . tastes good."

"That would be," Sylvia corrected, "a man of good taste, I believe."

"Mr. Ornery Bashé," said Kills The Deer. "There was a Bashé who ate his mother. Would you be that Bashé, by chance?"

Henri eyed him for a moment, then in a flat voice said, "You would have been my mother's amusement, Mr. Kills The Deer." He looked past the Indian and gestured toward a large room on the left. "Perhaps later we speak? We might seek an, ah . . . exploration of the house."

Kills The Deer turned and looked into Billy's lens. He nodded. There was the redheaded woman, crouched near the camera, attached to Billy's elbow. Where was the other one? The one with the great voice—Lucy? How was it, he wondered, that Sylvia knew him and his kachinas? Had his reputation climbed into the upper reaches of the valley, or had she seen him on the security tape and checked him out? He looked back, but she had already developed greeter's gaze. If she had seen him on the tape, she was not letting on, not in this company. Then he saw Inez, holding something to her ear, lean toward Sylvia and whisper, "Dr. Perry Clark." Of course—the security guy had phoned and announced the Indian artist to the maid. Sylvia probably had no idea who he was.

He should have gone back to the reservation, but he wanted to sell some paintings. Tonight he needed connections more than he needed to escape being an Indian. But the reservation called to him. There he could be invisible. He did not have to be an Indian. What made you an Indian was white people. Without the whites, you get rid of Indians. On the rez, it was possible just to be there.

But that was a lie. The rez pressed him down. As with many things that really mattered, no words described the feeling—only images floated by—whiskey faces, sullen gang kids, dying babies, tired women, and the wandering men.

And hidden away in isolated blocks of air-conditioned buildings were bureaucrats, the pious, born-again Indians at work on special projects, and bloated council men, busy with themselves. Kills The Deer believed the problems of the reservation were caused by these lost ones, desperate to know who they were. In their attempt to concoct an identity, the desperate ones did a lot of pushing and shoving. They created havoc, toxic waste, and excessive noise, importing the white world to Indian country.

To escape, Kills The Deer painted his pictures, made love to his wife, and took long, solitary journeys into the desert.

He wandered through the large double doors into the main room, waiting for other guests, sizing things up. A thin, intense gentleman, very commanding but proper, in black to his neck, was suddenly standing next to him, asking if he might like a glass of champagne.

"Yes. Thank you." Kills The Deer felt self-conscious. He stared up at the ceiling and the great beams. A Chicano muscle-builder in a black turtleneck appeared with a delicate champagne flute on a small silver tray. For a moment, Kills The Deer was absorbed by the fragile beauty of the glass. Was he supposed to take the tray with the glass? The server, catching the Indian's confusion, lifted the glass with one hand while palming the tiny tray in the other. He nodded gently as if to say he understood. Kills The Deer had a glimpse of himself trying to wrest the tray from the massive hand. He smiled, took the ethereal glass, and gulped down the champagne. The waiter had not moved. "Not bad," said Kills The Deer. "What kind is it?"

"A 1975 Joseph Montebello. May I get you another?"

"I would like that. Thank you."

The server gracefully extended the tray, and Kills The Deer deposited his flute.

The room was large and tall—a sanctuary of high, white purity. Long horizontal windows, set beneath the ancient timbers, were meant for light and not the view. Along the right wall several tables displayed artifacts from Sylvia's collection, including painted pottery, figures carved in wood and stone, a variety of Paleo-Indian stone spear heads called Clovis points, ten to eleven thousand years old— and mysterious objects of worship or death. Well-dressed security people kept an eye out for the touchy-feelies. The greater concern than theft was that guests keep their toxic fingers and burning cigarettes to themselves, that the art not be toppled by drunks, and no photographs, please.

At the far end of the room, opposite the large double doors, were three tables draped in pristine Irish linen, covered by trays of food. Several servers stood, ready with mild-mannered smiles.

Lucy arrived with a group of academics who had come in the hotel van. She went through the little greeting ritual, received air kisses from Henri, a smile from Billy behind his camera, and a nod from Anita—crouched as if to pounce. Sylvia extended her hand and said sincerely, "I've heard so much about you, Dr. Perelli. I'm so pleased you've come."

"Thank you," said Lucy. "I appreciate the opportunity to meet you and to see your collection." Lucy was always interested in the artifacts of the wealthy. Collected objects were markers of what the independently wealthy—at least those not overwhelmed by popular culture—found interesting and defining. Their takes on what mattered usually differed significantly from those of the museums, which had to cajole the art crowd, particularly in the Southwest. Although Sylvia's adornments, the house, and careful manner implied propriety, Lucy suspected a deviant strain thrived beneath Sylvia's sheen of social graces—not unusual among the extremely rich.

"Have you met Kills The Deer Burnum?" Sylvia asked. "He's one of our Native American artists. You should find him in the main room." She gestured toward the high double door leading to the east wing.

"In fact, I did, just this afternoon."

"After I'm through here, I'll be giving Mr. Bashé and his videographers a short tour of the chapel. I hope you will join us."

Lucy thanked her and went to look for Kills The Deer, who was standing in the enormous room, sipping his champagne. He watched her enter, then craned his head looking for the man with the large muscles. But he was nowhere. Instead, the intense commander appeared.

"May I get you something to drink?" he asked.

"Thank you. Actually, I am in need of a glass of water, if you don't mind."

"Evian, Spirit Springs, or Perrier?

"How's the tap water?"

"High in arsenic."

"I'll try it, thanks," she said, thinking he was making a joke.

"It's good to see you, again," said Kills The Deer. "I hope I wasn't too rude earlier. I'm not always such a wiseass."

"You were quite entertaining, actually."

"That's it? Entertaining?"

"You expected fear?"

"We try for reverence."

Lucy laughed. "Sorry."

"Well, I *am* an artist. We can't afford to be self-righteous on a sustained basis. It erodes our market position."

Mr. Muscles crossed the floor with Lucy's water on the tiny tray. Kills The Deer watched carefully as she reached for the glass. Not even a pause. She took a sip and smiled.

"How's the water?" asked Kills the Deer.

"Peculiar." She gave a passing server the glass and asked for champagne.

"The champagne here is very good," said Kills The Deer. "It cuts through peculiar quite nicely. The big shots at the rez import Canadian 'natural spring water' for the Agency coolers. It's their favorite, after Bub Beer and Big Rez Cola."

A few guests drifted in, sized up the situation, and headed for the food at the other end of the room. "Henri said you direct a fund for archaeology."

"Yes. There are quite a few sites that are culturally and environmentally important, though they don't make interesting newspaper copy. We try to identify the more important ones and find the money to protect them for future study. What kind of art do you do?"

"I paint."

"What do you paint?"

"I'm big on kachinas at the moment. In some pueblos they're considered ancestors who became cloud people. The kachina cults used to run things. A place for everyone and everyone in his place. It's a little suffocating as far as I'm concerned. But kachinas are crammed full of symbolism according to the New Agers who buy most of the 'Native American' art these days. So I paint kachinas."

"What sort?"

"I've done a trucker kachina, a spinning-top kachina, a hairy biker kachina, a Virgin Mary kachina, a hooker kachina, and a Pope John Paul II kachina."

"Sounds sacrilegious."

"Yes, I get that from neo-traditional Indians. Some guys think pavement is sacrilegious."

"It is."

"Not if you drink enough of this champagne. You can go anywhere and still be with God."

"Do you have a particular style?"

"Abstract expressionistic, fauvistic, surrealism, but with a story. You know?"

"Not really."

"Well, it's like if John Steinbeck had smoked too much Bill Burroughs."

"I'm getting a picture. What did you do before you painted?"

"I thought about being an archaeologist, actually. When I was in high school, I spent a summer working on a Mimbres dig for the university."

"All did not end well, I take it."

"I didn't like keepin' records, and I was a little too advanced for my own good."

"How so?"

"I was a greedy little smart-ass. Some of those pots we were digging were worth ten to fifteen thousand dollars to the Japanese and the Aussies, back when ten grand was a lot of money. There was a fellow, not much older than me, who helped on the dig. He wanted to get into the antiquities business—sort of a dealer in training. Everything on our site went to the university, but this guy bought other stuff for himself from local family collections and from the old pot hunters who made a hobby of working the ruins along the Mimbres River. So when I went back to the rez at the end of the summer, I asked Grandmother Louise if she could make a pot with Mimbres designs and make it look old. She was a good potter. I wanted her to make a pot that would fool this dealer."

"And she did?"

"Yeah. It was really good. I found a picture from a 1930s archaeology journal of a pot I liked. She copied the style, but she changed the design some. The original had two turtles. She made it three and added a lightning-bolt snake around the edge. She called it Racing Turtles Bowl. I wish I'd kept it. Anyway, the fellow bought it. He paid forty-five hundred dollars. I gave Grandmother half and had enough left for my first year of college."

"It must have been pretty convincing."

"It was, at first. But later, the dealer got a lot smarter about Mimbres pots. He tracked me down at school to find out who'd made it. He didn't want his money back, and he wasn't mad. He said the pot was worth what he paid for it. He just wanted to meet the person who made it."

"Did you tell him?"

"Not at first. But Grandmother said it would be all right, he could never prove anything anyway, and maybe she could sell him another pot. Nobody had ever paid that much for one of her pots before. So I took him up to her place. They became buddies. He sold a lot of her pieces over the years."

"Is she still alive?"

"Yeah. She can't see, and she hasn't made a pot in ten years, but she's pretty lively."

"Did she do any more fakes?"

"I shouldn't have told you that story, huh?"

"I like a good fake. You could make the argument that fakes help serious archaeology. There're so many good ones around with fake papers that they depress prices for the real stuff. So the motivation to raid ruins probably isn't what it would be without fakes. I take it you did your share of diluting the market."

He shrugged.

"So you must have heard of Jack Miller?"

Kills The Deer's heart made a nasty jump. He stared at her, looking for a hint that she was playing with him. He drained the last of his champagne and tried to sound indifferent. "How do you know Jack?"

"You know him?"

"I knew him . . . back when." Kills The Deer hesitated. "Everyone in the business knew Jack." He wondered why she wanted to know about a guy who had been out of the business for fifteen years. "I've had too much bubbly," he said, looking for a retreat. "I came here to make contacts for my paintings, not talk about an old friend. I'm a little fucked up. I should disappear for a while."

Lucy knew she had struck gold. "Have you eaten anything today?" she asked.

"That would help, wouldn't it?" He appreciated the shift. "Maybe I'll try some of that cute food they've laid out over there. Well," he extended his hand, "nice meetin' you. Maybe we'll run into each other again."

"Actually," she said with the ease of someone used to having her way, "I could use something to eat. We can get plates, some big-shot water, and find a place to sit and talk. Talking is a quick way to metabolize alcohol. It'll clear your head, and I'd like to hear about Jack Miller."

He had been badly outmaneuvered. It was the champagne. That's what he told himself. He smiled at the idea that talking could clear anything. Talk muddled his mind. He was hungry. This woman, whom he was liking all right, didn't have a troublemaker's gaze. Maybe she wanted an ex–pot hunter to help find some likely prospects for her foundation. Prospects could be land or patrons in her case. Jack would be a good bet for either one. Kills The Deer scanned the growing rabble of attendees for prospects of his own. Not many looked like they were in the money. His best hope, of course, was Sylvia, and he was not going to connect with Sylvia without Lucy's help.

"Jack's got himself a little place outside Silverado. It's kind of a ramblin' shack—rooms added to rooms added to rooms. It's a little like a pueblo in a way. I think a bunch of Mexicans started building it about a hundred years ago. Jack added running water and electricity."

She took his arm and guided him through the crowd toward the food-laden tables. She liked to take a man's arm. It once signified the helplessness of women, but this artifact of manners had been put to a new use—now it was a socially acceptable way for a woman to make contact, to be intimate, yet it allowed for the control and distance that formality provided. Kills The Deer had strong arms. What had these arms done to make them so strong and what kinds of women had they held?

Several guests interrupted to say hello to Lucy, to introduce a friend, or to congratulate her on her speech. One said he had heard the famous writer Ben Wang was coming to interview her. The comments made Kills The Deer think her speech had been brilliant. He became aware of the fact that people were wondering who he was to be escorted by this smart, accomplished, and beautiful woman. Certainly they would have ignored him had they understood he was merely a way for her to learn about another man, and that he was enduring the situation so Lucy would introduce him to Sylvia. The setup made him a little queasy. In spite of her familiar introduction at the door, Sylvia would know him only as that-Indian-who-peed-on-my-fence, if she knew of him at all.

He pulled a pair of sunglasses out of his shirt pocket and slipped them on. As they maneuvered through the crowd, he had an image in mind of a needy child held in the proprietary grasp of a mother negotiating the human sea.

Kills The Deer filled a plate with direct, unambiguous forms of protein and several slices from a small loaf of black bread. The exotics—tucked, wrapped, and rolled in countless colors, layers, and flavors—were intimidating. Delicate food, manipulated into shape by nimble fingers, implied obscure rules and unnatural behavior.

Lucy pointed to some strange, blackish things. "You might like a few of those."

"I don't think so."

"Why not? You have to try things to know."

"Fussy foods piss me off."

He followed her through a narrow doorway that led to the leafy veranda and the slanting sun. She found a bench somewhat hidden from the other guests, and they sat with their plates on their laps and ate. She let the food alter his mood before she brought up the subject of Jack Miller. When she did, she was very direct.

"Was Jack Miller the dealer who bought your grandmother's fake pot?"

Kills The Deer was surprised she was so blunt, but he laughed. "Yeah. He called me up and said there was something wrong with the turtle bowl. At first I thought maybe it had cracked. I said, 'What do you mean?' and he said, 'Who made this bowl?'"

"How did he know it was a fake?"

"By the time he got interested in Mimbres pots, there were so many fakes around there was no way to know what was real unless you knew which dig it came from. He spent a lot of time studying designs that came out of documented digs until he had a good take on what the Mimbres had been up to. He developed a sixth sense about them. Other than Grandmother's turtle bowl, the only time I faked him out was with one a little boy made at Acoma. The boy painted a man and a dog. They were small or far away. Then closer up he painted a man in a tree. The tree bent around with the shape of the bowl so it looked like the man would fall or the tree would break."

"Did he ever find out it was a fake?"

"I told him when he and Grandmother became friends. He laughed and said he should meet the boy, and he would put him to work making fake Mimbres children's pots."

"Was he serious?"

"No, but one night in Grandmother's kitchen, Jack was joking about the loopy stuff the feds funded. He bet Indians could get a government grant to make fake pots. My brothers and some other guys decided we'd try it. We had nothing to lose. We applied for a grant to make Real Replicas—that was the name of the company. We had stationery and business cards. We even started makin' pots, but the big problem was distribution. We gave the guy who processed the loan a bunch of our best fakes. They forgot the whole thing. It would've worked if we had known about marketing and distribution."

"Was Miller in on this scheme?"

"No. Some of our people felt angry about him, because he wouldn't help us."

"He sold your grandmother's pots."

"Yes. But not fakes. Jack sold Grandmother's own designs. They had her name on them. He helped make her a famous artist. Some potters quit making fakes, because they could do better selling art. Plus you don't have to go to jail if they catch you being an artist, usually. When I met my wife, she told me to take some classes so I could be an artist. It was pretty good advice. I haven't had to go to jail for quite a while."

Lucy did not ask if he had really been in jail or why. Kills The Deer started to get up.

"I would like to hear more of your story. I hope you aren't leaving already."

"Just getting some more to eat. Can I get you anything?"

"I'm fine, thanks."

His broad smile flattened his thick lips against the white of his teeth. She could see a dark silhouette of herself in his sunglasses. The sunglasses made him seem faraway, which was what he was. Faraway man. She liked him that way. Maybe he was just different from the other people in her life, though she knew the type—a little crooked, but not really crooked enough to count, because his sense of irony got in the way of being a good liar, and a little too intolerant to make it in the normal world. She decided the best thing she could do for him would be to get Sylvia interested.

Kills The Deer came back with a large sampling of hors d'oeuvres. He put the plate between them. "Thought I'd try some busy-fingers food." He plucked off a bacon-wrapped scallop and popped it in his mouth. "I have a request."

"Yes?"

"Would you speak to Sylvia for me? I could use her help."

"Sure. It might be good if I saw some of your work, though. Did you bring anything?"

He stretched himself out so he could reach into his jeans pocket and pulled out a folded strip of slides. "Just these."

She held them up to the sky—ten bright, hard-edged, surreal images of kachinas dancing, riding a bicycle, looking at themselves in a mirror, kissing in a thorn bush, having sex on a bed of cracked clay, and floating like astronauts in space. Several were wearing mylar-coated sunglasses that reflected other images too small to see in the slides. "How many are there in the series?" she asked.

"Twelve. I think I'll do three more. Then I've been thinking of doing a series of coatimundi as business types and appliance salesmen—coatimundi selling units, but I don't have a theme. I need a theme."

"Coatimundi? Are they like kachinas?"

"They're animals. I've never seen one. I think they don't come this far north. Some people even claim they don't exist—that they're a mythic animal. I've been told they're related to racoons, but much bigger with long snouts and little ears." Kills The Deer was sitting up, leaning forward, and using his hands to describe the animal. "Their claws are like a small black bear's, and they have tails like mountain lions', almost as long as their bodies, that they carry curled over their backs. They're nocturnal and very shy."

"They sound pretty mythological."

"The Mimbres painted them a lot, usually smiling with lots of sharp teeth. They're supposed to live in the ground. Things that lived in the ground would naturally be connected to the underworld where the first people came from. The early archaeologists didn't know about coatimundi. They thought the Mimbres invented them with parts of bears and coyotes and lions."

"Could the Mimbres have thought the coatimundi was in fact a creature made of many animals?"

He took his sunglasses off, glanced over at her, then squinted at the purple mountains. He had never thought about that. If the coatimundi was an everything kind of creature to the Mimbres, it would explain why it was often shown smiling with its sharp teeth bared—life was a joke that bites. A coatimundi made of many creatures would have been a trickster, powerful and magical. Certainly the images on the pots spoke to that possibility. Kills The Deer put his sunglasses on and looked back at Lucy. It annoyed him a little that she had thought of this, and he had not. Then he smiled. She was just the woman to have these thoughts. She was coatimundi. Many things in one. It was a womanly thing to think.

Lucy hoped the smile meant he was not upset. "So what happened to Jack Miller? Is he still dealing antiquities?"

"He put together a huge Mimbres collection over the years. He also represented several potters from the pueblos. A lot of his stuff went to museums and rich foreigners. Jack became one of the more successful dealers in the Southwest. About fifteen years ago, he sold everything and got out."

"Not many people walk away from success." She sipped her champagne and thought about Jack Miller. Did he get religion? Were the feds getting too close? She was suspicious but fascinated. "Why was he so successful?"

"He was there at the right time, and he had a knack—he could look at a ruin and know where to dig. The Mimbres got into his mind somehow."

"But what made him a good dealer?"

"He told great stories. He sang for his supper. It got him invited to all those rich people's dinner parties. He was like an adventurer—a little exotic and strange, you know?"

"He traveled a lot?"

"Yeah. All over the world."

"Does he still, or has he become a homebody since he got out of the business?"

"He has a little place in Alaska. He goes up there for a while in the spring to watch the bears and again in the fall to fish. For the most part he stays around. Are you lookin' for him?"

"I'd like to meet him. Does he see people, or is he a hermit now?"

He figured Jack could handle her. He might even like her. "He has a phone. He's even in the book."

"What's he do now?"

"I saw him in May, and he was building mudmen down by the creek. It's something he's been doing for the last five or six years. He can be a strange man."

"How unique."

Kills The Deer grinned. "You'll see."

She fished the phone out of her bag and flipped it open. "Jack or John?"

"Jack, no initial."

She called information, asked for Silverado, New Mexico, Jack Miller. She wondered if a woman would answer. "Does he live alone?"

"He does now. He was married—they went their separate ways when he got out of the business. She's got a gallery in Seattle." As an afterthought he said, "He still likes women, though."

Lucy pressed more buttons. Kills The Deer held his hand out for the phone and said, "Let me introduce you." She handed it over and nodded a thank-you. He let it ring several times.

FOUR

Jack began to feel safe even though he was in need of self-medication, something to sweat the poison out of his body, but first he had to look at the bowl. He carefully slid the parrot trainer out of the knapsack, unwrapped her from his sweater, and set her on the thick plank table in the dining room. He braced the bowl against a stack of books so she stood upright. Her face was hidden behind the deerskin, and he found himself staring at the slit in the mask to catch a glimpse of her eye. The expectation was ridiculous. He shook it off and considered his immediate dilemma—neutralizing the advancing effect of the sting.

His right arm was pulsating, and the skin on the side of his face felt ready to explode. Getting some protein into his body and sweating the poison out seemed the thing to do. In the kitchen, he downed several glasses of water and swallowed five ibuprofen. He broke seven eggs, separated the yolks, stirred cayenne and hot sauce into the whites, and drank the mix. Then he cut a lemon and sucked on it. He ate several jalapeños out of the jar. Still sucking the lemon, he went into the bedroom, took a down comforter from the closet, and wrapped himself up. He shuffled back to the kitchen, ate more jalapeños, cut up another lemon, doused it with Tabasco, got down a bottle of whiskey from the cupboard, and shuffled into the dining room. This was Jack's version of homeopathic medicine—lots of tincture.

He studied the bowl, running his fingers over the design, tapping the image, pinging the edge to see how hot it was fired, trying to feel his way into the hands that coiled, and scraped, and painted the bowl a thousand years ago. The potter used the Mimbres trick of warping space by painting part of the image on the inside curve of the bowl, which had the subtle effect of making the parrot trainer appear to move, even dance—particularly if the observer had absorbed a poisonous, mind-altering sting. Hadn't she danced before? He couldn't remember.

In the distance, the far, other-world distance, he could hear the phone ringing. Perhaps Becker was calling to explain that she had danced for him, too. Jack was beginning to sweat. He sat—wrapped, and moist—staring at the dancer, sucking on lemon, shifting his head slightly, following her movements back and forth, to and fro. She was dancing. She was dancing for him. He could barely hear the ringing phone, which seemed even farther away. The rings merged into a distant buzz.

He leaned forward, bracing himself against the table with his good hand. He wanted a look at her eyes, but there was nothing but darkness, a thousand-year-old void. He thought he detected a soft flash from the eye slits in the mask, as though the eyes had blinked. Dark eyes. Was he seeing eyes? Then she must be seeing him.

He felt his lips burning from the jalapeños and whiskey. They were swollen. His whole face was swollen, his eyelids so puffy he could hardly see. No doubt the whites of his eyes were bloodshot. Sweat oozed from his pores.

What was she seeing? Was he as hideous to her as he felt? Her intense dark eyes brought the distant buzzing closer, as though it came from behind the sharp black beak of her mask. He listened.

The buzz began to break up, first as the static noise of leaves in the wind, then to surge and release, as small waves roll and break over fine sand—muffled, distinct sounds. Word sounds, strung together. A necklace of words. She was speaking, speaking to him. She whispered.

"I know you. You are the White-Larva. The newborn."

"How do you know English?" he asked.

He could see her eyes narrow behind the slits in her mask. He had disappointed her. "You are not the White-Larva. I have never seen one like you—a man being eaten by a big, ugly bug."

He realized the comforter gave him a distended, embryonic aspect—a creature every bit as bizarre as some he had seen on Mimbres bowls.

"What is wrong?" she asked. "Are you dying? What is this condition you're in?"

He was beginning to drift. He was dying, yes. She would know. The ghost of the Mimbreños was telling his fate. All he could think to say was what he had already asked: "How do you know English?"

"Better to ask, how it is that you can understand the meaning of my words."

"All right. How come I understand you?"

"It doesn't bother you that I am a ghost-spirit talking, yet you are surprised I speak in your words? You should be looking inside your own skull for answers."

"You're telling me that I'm speaking to my own hallucination?"

"You think I am your hallucination? It is not that I speak your words, but that you hear your own words when I speak. I am no one's hallucination. Especially not yours."

He took a sip of whiskey. It burned. Sweat was beginning to trickle down his forehead into his eyes. He felt his pulse in his lip. She was so sure of herself. "Well," he mumbled, "hallucination or not, you've been dead for a thousand years." As soon as the words passed his burning lips, he felt he should make amends, but she was too quick.

"A dying man trapped inside an ugly bug is telling me I've been dead for a thousand years? Why do I find that hard to believe?"

"I've seen your skeleton. You were buried in the wall of a cave high above a river. The bowl you came in was found resting on your skull. Whoever buried you did not punch a hole in your bowl."

"I know. That's why my spirit was never allowed to escape into the clouds. I'm trapped in this bowl instead, but I didn't realize it had been so long."

"Your spirit is trapped in the bowl?"

"Exactly. Trapped in a bowl. And now you have brought me here. Where, exactly, is here?"

"If you were walking it would be . . ."

"If I were walking—as opposed to . . . flying maybe?" She seemed impatient. "Or in your case crawling?"

She was sounding less and less like a hallucination. His breathing was shallow, and things were blurry. He saw her slide her foot over the rim of the bowl and test the table with her toe. Her spirit may have been trapped in the bowl, but some part of her was able to move.

By the time she emerged, she had taken on a soft hue of reddish gold. She was moving around, testing the air and wood. The black of her eyes turned dark brown and the deerskin mask took on a soft, creamy texture. As she set the parrot down and stroked his head, his plumage turned to scarlet reds and neon blues. He was near her feet, flapping and hopping.

She's agitated, Jack thought; and she's been cooped up in a bowl for a thousand years—cramped and cold.

But then, this was all coming out of his own head, wasn't it? He stared out at her tiny, blurry body. She seemed to be prancing around. Loosening up, no doubt. Getting the kinks out.

She could be more than a reaction to the mysterious sting. He could simply be losing his mind.

She moved as he had imagined she would. Even her superior attitude matched his expectations. A thousand years ago she was like this, only much larger. She danced and performed. Even though she was a woman and young, she had power in her clan. He searched for the flash of an eye. Nothing.

What did I expect? After the poison oozes its way through my pores, she'll go back into her bowl, and I'll never see her again. "We are about a three-day walk south of where you were buried," he told her.

She had been attentive to her surroundings. "You have a fine house, filled with many wonderful and mysterious objects I have never seen. What is that and what is its purpose?" she asked, pointing to the low bookcase with a globe on top.

He got up, struggled to the bookcase, selected an appropriate title, and returned with the globe and the book and sat down. "This is a book." He lay it before her, opened it, and began turning the pages. "The small things are letters, which bunched up in the right way make words, which bunched up in the right way make a sentence. String enough sentences together and you can do all kinds of damage. It is possible to look at these words and understand their meanings. It's called reading. About a quarter of the population can actually read."

"Amazing."

"But most of them don't." Talking seemed to clear his head, but his vision was still blurred.

She put her hand up to stop him from turning the page. "What's that picture?" she asked, pointing to a drawing of a tall, fancy man on a large horse staring down at a man the size of a chipmunk.

"This book is a made-up story about a man named Gulliver who traveled all over the world." He pointed to the globe and gave it a quick spin. She jumped back. "One place Gulliver visited was Brobdingnag, a country of giants, who considered him a kind of amusing toy."

All seven and a half inches of her stared up at him. "Well, let me amuse you." She began growing until she was about five foot two or three standing on the table, staring down at him. She was about the size she had been when the bowl was painted, which, in her time, was quite tall. She bent down and studied the globe. "This is Gulliver's world?"

"Actually it's a tiny model of the real world. We refer to it as a planet and it revolves around the sun with several other planets." He peered at the blurry globe. Finally he found the United States and pointed to the Southwest, trying for New Mexico, but hit Scottsdale, Arizona. "We're about here."

She looked at all the lines and squiggles. Nothing related to her experience. "You're joking?"

"No. This is what the world looks like."

"Well, let me tell you something, Larva man, your world is a whole lot different from mine." She surveyed the rest of the room for a moment, then looked at him. "It is unusual that a man with a large house and many things should die without his people around him. What terrible event brought you to this sorry end?"

He was delighted by her energy and grace. He thought, What a unique and talented girl lives in my brain.

"What terrible thing brings you to this sorry end?" she repeated.

"It's not the end," he said. Why should he bother defending himself? She was only an illusion, but he knew that often what he liked about women was illusory, and he learned things from them he would never learn on his own. He explained his condition. "I've only been stung by something, maybe a scorpion. But I'm fine—other than the fact my head hurts, my arm and face are swollen, I'm having difficulty seeing—that, and I'm talking to a masked woman who lives in a secret room in my brain." Even in his hyperstung state, he knew he had stumbled into strange terrain.

She looked down, directly into his good eye, and softly whispered, "I don't think so."

Her even tone, her size, her beautiful copper skin, and her bare breasts threw him. She was so lovely, he forgot he was talking to himself. He tried humor. "You'd never believe you're an illusion living in some guy's head." Pain twisted his smile into a grimace.

She saw through him. "I get it," she said. "Either the sting let me loose to play in your brain, or I'm a ghost—with my own destiny and will—over which you have no control. You'll have to devise a test. If I turn out to be a ghost, you'll have to believe in ghosts. But, if you're right and I'm a manifestation floating around in your skull, you've got serious problems to deal with."

At least she had a sense of humor, dark as it was. For a full-blown hallucination, he thought, this isn't bad. He began to feel thick, like a cube of warm butter. The poison was working its way in through his body. It took a great effort to keep his good eye open. There were stains in the ceiling plaster from the last rain, months ago. He'd better fix the roof soon.

It occurred to him that she could not read his thoughts. Certainly he was unable to read hers. A thought–brain barrier separated them, but could he depend on the barrier to hold? Would she manage to seep through to his side and take over? He decided the more she established herself as a separate entity, the less she would need to penetrate into that illusion he called himself.

"I assumed," he ventured in a thoughtful and respectful tone, as though he were making conversation in a hotel bar, "from the painting on the bowl that you were a parrot trainer."

She looked at the parrot at her feet. He could flap but not fly. She reached down and he hopped to her wrist. "Yes, I trained parrots, but that is not my story." She held the bird near her face and let him gently bite the soft mask. "This is Elu," she said. The parrot turned to Jack and fluffed his feathers. "I was important in the parrot clan. It was my job to draw rain clouds to the valley. When I died, my spirit should have gone into the sky, but my spirit has been absorbed into the bowl. Now it couldn't even escape through a hole poked in the bottom."

"You're going to ask me to shatter the bowl, aren't you?"

"You must, so my spirit will be released into the sky, and I will dance and sing down the rain. I will become like rain and seep through the ground, where the ancient river will take me to my people, then I will come back into this world as a full person. That's what's supposed to happen, but not in my case." She looked at him through her eye slits. "Not yet, anyway."

"Why didn't the people who buried you punch a hole in your bowl?"

"In the last years, the snake and parrot clans lived in the cave to hide from cannibal gangs sent from the north by the chief of the round houses. We were hungry and cold. Most of us got sick. All the others had moved away. We were the last. One day, most of those who lived in our cave went out to tend the field and never came back. A gang wiped them out. There were two of us left, me and my mother's oldest sister, Ellee-bae. I was very sick and ready to die, so she helped me up into the burial place the people made for me. Then she gave me and Elu, my parrot, bitter tea. Everything stopped hurting. I was happy and warm, and I drifted off to sleep."

"And why didn't she put a hole in the bowl?"

"She loved me, and she was lonely. She wanted my spirit to stay around until she was ready to die. When the time came for her to die, she must have been away or too weak. Did you find her bones?"

"Only yours. Your mother's oldest sister . . . Ellee-bae, she made your bowl?"

"Yes. I was her favorite, she loved me best. Maybe too much. So I'm here. From then 'til now. Long time. That's my story."

"Only the very end of your story. I bet there's a lot more."

"You're sneaky. You want to keep me around, because you are dying alone like my aunt. You'll die, and I'll still be trapped in my bowl."

"Actually I do like having you around, but I am not dying . . . losing my mind, maybe, but I don't think I'm dying."

She leaned over the far edge of the table where she could peer down the hallway. "You have a big, elegant house. Lots of rooms for all your women. But they've run away, and now you're alone, except for me and that tiny cat, who incidentally has been keeping an eye on me since I got here. If I'm only a part of your craziness, your cat has a similar affliction."

Jack turned around to check out the cat on the living-room couch. The cat was certainly not tiny, and he appeared to be asleep or indifferent to the event on the dining-room table. "At one time," said Jack, "many people lived here. It's been a while though."

"You lost all of your people to the cannibal gangs, didn't you?"

"We don't have those kind of gangs, but I haven't been paying a lot of attention lately."

"You lost your wife, didn't you?"

"Lost, no, we went in different directions is all. She went north and I went south. About fifteen years ago, I moved down here from Albuquerque."

"Where is Albuquerque?"

"Several days' walk north and east of here."

"Do the round-house people still have cannibal gangs?"

"No. And they don't live in the round houses anymore, though their descendants are still around. They fell apart and spread out all over the place about the same time the Mimbres came undone."

"Who were the Mimbres?"

"You—your tribe. Three hundred years ago, the people who lived near here called the river that ran through their valley the Mimbres River. When the ruins of your houses were found near the river, you were called the Mimbreños, which means 'willow people.'"

"Very odd."

"Why, odd?"

"My name is Willow."

"Mine is Jack."

"Jack? What does it mean?"

"Just Jack."

She was not pleased with his answer. She looked down at her parrot, her face turned toward her shoulder in a self-protective gesture, as though he had insulted her. The gesture disturbed him. She behaved as though he was holding out on her—being disrespectful. She asserted herself in a subtle and powerful way.

Though she was only a figment of his imagination, she was a high-maintenance figment in need of humoring. He felt nebulous. She had become solid and statuesque by comparison. He would have preferred a ghost—a discrete entity who asked only that he smash her pot. Let her be a goddamn cloud person if that's what she wanted. He could only get wet.

He opened his eye. Willow leaned close and whispered in his ear. She was staring at him through the deerskin mask, its sharp beak almost touching his cheek.

"Come back, Jack. I need you. You can't die. I need you to break the bowl and release my spirit."

For a moment, he thought he could hear her breathing. Why would I want to break the bowl? he wondered. There is nothing like it in existence. He closed his eye, keeping his head on the table. She might leave once the poison's out of my system. What if she stayed? Suppose I didn't break the bowl? She'd be mad as hell. Would she stay around if I broke it? Having a womanly apparition around might be easier than the real thing.

FIVE

Kills The Deer gave up and handed the phone back to Lucy. "He's out."

"Do you think he's around? I'd hate to drive down there and find he's not in the area."

"He should be around. I'll try him tonight and call you—the Posada Duran?"

"Yes. Thanks.

"He's not in the business anymore."

"That's what you said."

"But you think he can tell you where to find something you're looking for, right?"

"Yes." She was reserved, hoping Kills The Deer would not ask questions.

"He doesn't need your money, so you won't be able to pay him."

"I didn't intend to pay him."

"You can't expect someone like Jack to tell you much. The feds caused him a lot of grief."

"Was he ever charged?"

"Nope. His idea of right and wrong wasn't always what the government had in mind, but he was careful."

"Did he sell to Sylvia?"

"Probably. You'll have to ask her. She may know another side of him." There was a history of regret in his voice. He had been impressed by Jack's ability to be at ease with anyone—from an effervescent British consul to the old women at the pueblo. "He had buyers in England, Australia, and Japan, but he didn't say much about them." Kills The Deer's voice trailed off. He felt disheartened. He was trading on a friendship for an introduction to a rich white woman, in the hope of making a buck. And there was the added embarrassment that all his talk made him aware of how little he knew his friend.

Kills The Deer was beginning to drift. "Let's find Sylvia," said Lucy. "She would probably appreciate a break from the crackpots and academics."

"How do you tell them apart?"

"The crackpots talk fast and spray you with spittle. Usually, they have terrible breath. The academics, as a rule, only have bad breath."

Kills The Deer remembered he had not bathed for several days. His breath was probably foul as well, given that his stomach was soured by the food, the champagne, and the talk. At this point, he just wanted to go home. "I think I should be gettin' back. Thanks anyway. If you don't hear from me, try Jack early, say I said to call. Okay?"

"Okay . . ." Lucy was a little wistful. She really did want to introduce him to Sylvia, to be of use. "Thanks very much. I appreciate it. I'll speak to Sylvia about your paintings." He was already backing away. He nodded, turned, and disappeared into the doorway to the big room.

Lucy thought about Kills The Deer negotiating his way through the crowd. It didn't feel right to leave him at loose ends. She caught up with him just inside the door. He seemed a little stunned by the noise and the people. She touched his shoulder to get his attention. "Let me ask Sylvia to give us a private tour of her collection. It'll be a painless way to get acquainted."

Kills The Deer smiled. Painless, yes. She understood. She was okay. He nodded. Remembering her fondness for arms, he offered his. They moved through the crowd, toward the far end of the room where a small cluster had gathered around Sylvia, Henri, and Anita. Billy was off getting tape or batteries or lights.

Sylvia had stopped whatever it was she and Henri had been discussing until Billy returned. Instead, she was explaining to Henri the intricacies of the American cocktail party and the various types who attended.

Henri scanned the crowd, pointed out various individuals and asked who they were and what they did. He spotted a youngish couple, fairly sexy, who had engaged a dowdy young woman in what appeared to be earnest conversation. He made a long gesture, aiming his cigarette at them. "What are they?"

"The two in black who are not waiters?" She glanced at Henri's outfit.

"Yes, those."

"They are the latest of many species of environmental fund-raisers."

"Species? Are they endangered?"

Sylvia laughed. "Not these. They reinvent themselves on a regular basis."

Anita was furious at Billy's prolonged absence. She patted Henri on the shoulder, whispered something indistinct from room tone, and marched off toward the huge doors.

A woman who had waited patiently for a turn at Sylvia stepped forward into the space left by Anita. She bowed her closely shaved head. Long, white arms with sharp elbows protruded from her blood-red robe. "Please allow me to introduce myself, Ms. Siskin. My name is Alamanda Frangipani. I am with a progressive environmental group, and we would like your advice on . . ."

"I'd love to contribute." Sylvia stared at the woman's slender white arms. "Do you have a card?"

"Oh, thank you, Ms. Siskin." A long arm darted out, holding a card in its bony fingers. It read:

SUNNY DAY BUDDHIST AVIAN RECOVERY
AND EXOTIC PLUMAGE
We recycle the ones that don't recover.

ALAMANDA FRANGIPANI, executive director.

4400 Nine Gate Road, Sausalito, CA.

www.sunnydayavian.org

Sylvia glanced from the card to Alamanda's long white arms against the blood robe and followed them all the way up to her shaved skull. "And what are you doing in New Mexico, Ms. Frangipani?"

"We've come to buy land. It is our dream to build clusters of environmentally sensitive condominiums near Santa Domingo Pueblo." She glowed, waiting expectantly, as though Sylvia might slip her a deed on the spot.

In the center of the Scholder Room, Inez had carefully drawn her skirt around her knees and knelt down. Billy lay on his back staring through his camera lens. She smiled at him, then turned her face upward, toward the timbered ceiling. The calm, assured tone of her voice reflected the many months she had contemplated the story hidden in the angles of the timbers and in the swirls and undulations in their grain.

"There is no cross in the first station. In the grain, right there," she pointed to a dark pattern in the long beam that came through the thick, outside wall, "you can see the high priest condemning Jesus. The priest asks him if he is Christ, Son of the Blessed One, and Jesus says, 'I am.' Then all the priests condemn him to death for blasphemy against God."

Billy studied the dark pattern, searching for the high priest and the visage of Jesus. Inez was quiet, waiting for him to discover the image on his own. Eventually, she pointed slightly to the left, to the profile of a man with a helmet. "And that is Pilate. He is saying to the priests, 'Shall I crucify your king?' and they reply, 'We have no king but Caesar.'"

"Yes," Billy whispered. "I see Pilate. He is sharp and dark in the wood. And Jesus is vague, below and to the right, and now I see the priests in a row. It's quite obvious. It's amazing . . ." He had meant to say Inez, but caught himself. She seemed too devout to be called by name.

"And there . . . ," she said in a hushed voice, her delicate hand pointing.

Billy focused on her guiding hand, then panned up the massive beams to a ghostly face in the grain. He held his breath and zoomed in for a tight shot. After he had recorded several seconds of the face, he set the camera aside and stared up at the image as Inez told its story.

"Along the way to Golgotha, Jesus passed near a woman named Veronica who used her veil to wipe the sweat from His face. What you see in the wood is almost identical to the image that exists to this day on Veronica's veil."

For Inez, Billy's interest in her vision of the images hidden amid the timbers brought him into the circle of her desire. She quelled the urge to touch his upturned face and perfect lips. Instead, she looked down upon him and smiled.

A mothlike yearning drew Billy toward the girl's radiant passion for her Savior. His soul fell upward. For a moment, Billy was held in bliss, lifted from cool stone toward the loving gaze.

And darkness descended, edged in red. "What the fuck are you doing?" Anita demanded. She leaned over Billy. "We're making a film, Billy. We don't have time for your Merry Maid's vortices."

Inez leaped up and flew from the room. Billy stared into Anita's angry face. "What's wrong, Peaches?" he asked. "She was only showing me the Stations of the Cross."

"You were falling in love, asshole. You're supposed to be working."

"Yes, you're right, of course."

"Right, you're supposed to be working, or right, you were falling in love?"

"Actually, both. I think."

"You think? What the hell does that mean?"

"Well, it was spiritual in a surreal kind of way. Jesus was definitely part of the scene. It was very powerful and . . . peaceful."

"What about us? What about the film?"

"It's okay. No change. Like one of your spiritual hot flashes."

"She's only a child, you bastard." Anita paused and peered down into his eyes. "You're happy about it, aren't you?"

"Yes."

He scarcely heard her whisper, "Oh, Billy." Anita's love for him would rival whatever Inez could offer, but Anita's cravings coiled around her heart in such complex ways, even she could not understand them—the thought of Billy and the impassioned maid entwined beneath the anguished eyes of the crucified Christ gave her a little rush. She reached down, took Billy's hand, and pulled him to his feet. "Let's get to work, cowboy."

Anita had the mike on Henri. The environment was out, and decadence was in. Billy stayed close on the Frenchman with the extra-wide lens to encompass the background of eaters, drinkers, seducers, enviro-hustlers, and habitual schmoozers. Henri, distorted in the curvature of the wide-angle lens, expounded on the end of meaning.

"Futility and absurdity are an expression of decadence. When we no longer find purpose and meaning in what we do, we fall into the decay of petty indulgences, reenforcing the absurdity of our lives with grand houses, grand cars, grand displays." With each "grand," his gesticulations grew wilder and wider. "We can only achieve our cathartic dreams when our great stadiums of savage blood sport become cathedrals for public execution."

A tall, African-American woman in chic, aubergine crepe moved toward Henri. Her voluptuous belly pressed against the yielding crepe, stretching it flat and smooth. She smiled and grasped his arm, pulling him toward her until her mouth was near his ear. The sensuality of her grasp, the stretched crepe, and the warm breath on his ear momentarily stunned him. She whispered. Henri nodded. Dutifully he moved away from the priceless Mayan effigy he had been leaning against while waving flamboyantly.

Sylvia smiled at the woman who strode off through the crowd.

"Who was that woman?" Henri asked.

"I don't know that one," said Sylvia. "She's with security. The insurance company, you know."

"*Excusez-moi.*"

"So what's your game, Henri?" Lucy asked, returning to Henri's rant.

"My game?"

"Yes. Which savage blood sport do you watch?"

"Tennis. There, because you are all alone, your defeat is absolute. With tennis, both blood and brain are smeared in hard clay. And what, as you say, is your game?"

"Being an all-American girl, I have to go with football."

"But what of the baseball—*the* American game?"

"Henri, they give season passes to shrubbery to hide the empty seats."

"Is it true," asked Sylvia, "that professional athletes use bovine hormones to increase their strength?"

"Fake players for a fake audience?" asked Henri. "Good symmetry. Both the observed and the observer are counterfeit."

"Henri and I share a . . . fascination," said Sylvia. "Earlier, we were discussing the enormous market in fake relics, a subject of great interest to me." She gracefully detoured into one of her dinner-party tales, meant to torment the self-righteous. "In the 1780s, Jukulu the Water, a mulatto-Caribbean trader, came from the south, selling relics. He had a small cart pulled by an ebony-black African woman, who told fortunes to the Indians in a harsh language, which Jukulu translated. To the gullible village priests, he sold precious splinters of bone from the feet and hands of saints. These were encased in silver boxes engraved with images of the saints. Some suspected Jukulu and the ebony woman found the small, dark-gray bones in shallow graves at the edge of villages. And if this was so, the priests unwittingly venerated the bones of the very pagan sinners they had, months or years before, saved from Satan's grasp."

"Ah, superstition clings to moldy faith."

"Perhaps, Monsieur Bashé. But truth, whether modern or primitive, may also cling to the illusions cloistered in the implements of faith."

Such reverence made Henri smile. "You have reliquaries?"

"Three, actually. Would you care to see?"

"Care? I would be enchanted."

Sylvia smiled benevolently toward the camera. "Let us begin our tour with the chapel. I think you will like it."

Henri fell in step, and they headed toward the large doors to the central chamber. Lucy, Anita, Billy, and Kills The Deer followed. One of the servers came behind, making offers of wine, crab cakes, fresh salmon, crème fraiche, bread, and crackers.

Sylvia turned left off the chamber and walked beneath a vine-covered glass roof, down a white adobe hallway to the chapel. Billy had trotted ahead so he could film them entering, then stepped aside, away from the door, panning as the others passed by, until his lens beheld a figure about twenty inches high, draped in a red satin cloak, on a black marble pedestal. The arched ceiling enhanced the sound. Every word spoken had a reverberation that augmented the pompous, intensified the shrill, and embellished the neurotic. Anita held her microphone on a telescoping pole, trying to stay above Billy's lens, but close to whoever was talking. The pole swished back and forth in sync with the camera's movement.

The resplendent statue faced away, toward the altar, and every few seconds gave a little snap, then shuddered. The odd movement provoked a familiar sensation in Henri—the snap of fear at the thought of God's wrath, followed by an erotic shiver. The sudden jerk, the tremble, and the odor of damp marble floated up into his mind and through the church of his childhood. For an instant, a wrathful light shot down from the high, ornate window of his memory and dissolved into the shadows of cool stone.

Henri was staring at a wooden replica of the Virgin painted with a thin whitewash. She wore a sumptuous red robe embroidered with little roses made of green glass beads. He moved as though she were drawing him toward her.

She was attached to a small, motorized platter, meant to revolve slowly, allowing the holy gaze to be cast throughout the chapel, but the mechanism was faulty. Instead of graceful rotation, the machine gave its Virgin the jerk and quiver.

"She's broken."

"Evidently, Henri." Sylvia circled the statuette, eyeing Henri to gauge the Virgin's effect. "Don't you love it? The quiver divine?"

"Yes . . . divine," he agreed, turning away from the camera.

But Sylvia would not let go. "It's more of a spasm, really—a found spasm at that."

"I don't understand," he said. "How is it found, as you say?"

"As found art is found. We merely come upon it, Monsieur Bashé. It was not conceived beforehand by the conscious intervention of the artist."

Henri began to suspect Sylvia's response had a tingle of its own. "And what is it you see in her spasm that appeals?" he asked.

"Perhaps you will find this abstract, but as we have found her spasm, so she has found ecstasy in God's touch. That to me has a sweet appeal."

The Virgin snapped and quivered. Sylvia seemed somber and reflective for a moment. "And when you saw her spasm—you thought . . . what?"

He paused, then shrugged. "That she was having an orgasm. You know, the coming."

"Orgasm? Just out of the blue?"

"Please, Sylvia, it is never, as you say, out of the blue." He waved his smoking hand above the snapping Virgin. "Orgasm is always anticipated—consider its text—fear, anxiety, dirty pictures, statistics, lurid tales, analysis, measurement, trajectory, pornographic accoutrement—a crusade of great expectations. The mind is rife with orgasm, cooked to a constant state of preparedness. As with all forms of ecstasy, culture is its context. Ecstasy is not written on a blank slate."

Sylvia's gaze took in Henri for a moment. She saw an amusing but unbalanced verbal gymnast. She turned to Anita and asked, "Do you understand him?"

"Only momentarily. It never lasts," said Anita.

Sylvia directed her little party to the back of the chapel. There, enshrined in a bulletproof glass case inset in the thick chapel wall, were the three silver boxes—four inches square, sealed by a line of silver. The contents, the relics themselves, could be vaguely discerned through a thick, protective square of purple-tinted, faceted glass in the top of each box. The Virgin continued to snap and quiver behind them as they clustered before the relics.

Henri cackled, blew smoke at the Virgin, and turned to scrutinize the silver boxes behind the bulletproof glass. "You seem to take it all rather lightly, Sylvia."

"Playing hookey from the Catholic fold inhibits neither faith nor humor, Monsieur Bashé. Now, I would like to amuse you. Let me show you the control room for the collection, courtesy of the Hanford Insurance Company."

Sylvia led them down the hall to a narrow metal door. She touched in the security code, the door slid back, they all filed in, and the door closed behind them. The small room housed twenty-four video monitors and a large control panel with its own monitor. An operator could switch any camera to the control panel and pan, tilt, and zoom at will. Every piece in the collection was viewed at random throughout the day, and the exterior of the house was constantly under surveillance.

Sylvia was burdened not by paranoia but by her conspicuously valuable hoard of pre-Columbian artifacts. The security precautions minimized insurance premiums. She had not lost a single piece to theft. The long fingers of Indian tribes and foreign governments were the real menace. Her insurance company said sorry, but repatriation was not covered. Much of Sylvia's collection had been ill-gotten by her uncle and grandfather who looted Mexican and Central American temples in the forties and fifties. They also raided grave sites in the Four Corners area until their spotter plane unexpectedly merged with an Anasazi cliff house in the late sixties.

For several years, inspectors from U.S. Customs came to Sylvia's adobe palace armed with warrants, looking for a piece of an ancient temple or a sacred effigy from the grave of some fellow's ancestor. She lost a lawsuit trying to save a beautifully carved jadeite bird to which she felt the petitioners had no rightful claim. She won another suit over a gold mask with emerald eyes. The legal skirmishes had made both sides a little cautious. The government stopped pressing claims that had zero merit, and she often forked over what they asked for without excessive argument. All in all, she was out a market value of $7.3 million, but the issue was never money. It was the loss of her beautiful objects that angered her. Photographs of the reclaimed objects were scattered throughout her displays with cards that said, repatriated by so-and-so, and the date. To Sylvia's thinking, even the local tribes were becoming more reasonable. At least they had stopped trying to repatriate bowls from her special collection of fakes.

She pointed on the monitor to a gully behind the house. "That's where Kirk Douglas, as a very stupid cowboy, took his horse to escape Walter Matthau, the philosophical sheriff, in *Lonely Are the Brave*. The cowboy escapes, only to be run over by a truckload of toilets driven by Carroll O'Connor."

When Sylvia began describing the movie, Kills The Deer was absorbed in the image of the gully and foreground fence—the same gully he and his brothers had walked through with their deer the fall before. He was sure Sylvia had not bothered to look at the tapes. She would never know he had pissed on her fence. Life was a dense web of missed connections. Kills The Deer smiled. He had his theme—the coatimundi of the missed coincidence—the many things, warped by space and time, that in real life, unlike the movies, never quite come together.

Sylvia was giving her guests a succinct summary of the *Lonely Are the Brave*. "It was a story about a terribly stupid, bullheaded man who, against all odds, escapes, only to be struck down by a seemingly random stroke. Meaning, I suppose, that we cannot beat God at his own game."

"Of course we beat God at his game, because . . ." Henri took a quick drag off his cigarette and glanced at the screen with the quivering Virgin, "because, we create gods less devious than ourselves."

"Meaning?"

"We place them on the pedestal, but rig the pedestal to control the spin . . . in this case, the quiver."

"You are not making sense."

"I am making a point." Henri giggled. "Was I supposed to make sense?"

"I was hoping for rationality."

"The French have no rationality. We have a reasoner, a sort of analytic converter."

"I believe yours is temporarily out of order," she teased.

Kills The Deer interrupted the conversation. "Can the camera focus in close on the fence?" he asked.

"Yes, just click on zoom and point to the spot on the screen you want enlarged."

"Do you keep tapes from all the monitors?"

"We use solid state, not tape. It records when the sensors pick up movement."

"So you've stored every movement in this gully since . . . ?"

"The company keeps the images for a year. Unless there's something unusual, of course."

"Like what?"

"Prowlers, I suppose."

"How about critters peeing on the back fence? It must happen a lot."

"That, I think, would depend on whether the species were rare and endangered."

Henri gestured to himself. "I would qualify."

"As a rare and endangered species?"

"*Certainement.* That I am rare is conspicuous. Also, my . . . excursions to understand the logic of culture appear to endanger my health."

Sylvia accepted a flute of champagne from the little tray, took a small sip, smiled. "Culture is not understandable, Henri. It is something other people tell you to do and think and be, without your comprehension."

Henri yawned. He was seeping into jet-lagged exhaustion, but he had one last salvo to fire at humans in large groups. "Culture is the mad cow disease of the soul, constantly eating away, leaving a dry, porous sponge to soak up the latest predigested drivel." He rubbed his eyes and blinked at his hostess.

"Henri, you are exhausted." Sylvia was indulgent, having understood the need to separate a man from his words. "We should continue our discussion in the morning when Anita and Billy come to video."

He nodded. "Of course, I would be, ah . . . be delighted. And thank you for being such a wonderful and entertaining hostess." With half-closed eyes he dug in his pants pocket for the red notebook and the tiny antique pen, then carefully printed, "Found Spasm, Found Ecstasy." He looked up and saw Lucy smiling at him. He had no idea what her smile meant, but a smile's a smile. "What will you be doing tomorrow, Lucy? Doing us the honor of joining us, I hope?"

"I've planned to rent a car and drive down to Silverado if I can get in touch with a gentleman about a new find. But we could have coffee before I go."

She had left him an opening. "You must let us drive you to Silverado," Henri insisted, knowing she would be good for his film.

Anita and Billy looked at each other. They both knew they had to keep Lucy with them. She seemed to be able to handle their delicate, disagreeable, and possibly dangerous celebrity. Their verbal fireworks could be recorded all the way to Silverado. It could prove the anchor piece for the video.

"We'll have Mrs. Siskin's collection filmed before noon," Anita insisted.

"I really . . ."

"Please say yes," Henri pleaded. He was so tired, sweet, and charming.

"Well . . . yes," Lucy acquiesced. It would have been rude to refuse.

SIX

It was getting light out. Jack had fallen asleep, the left side of his face on the table. His right eye was swollen shut and his stung hand lay on his lap, stiff and gross. He opened his good eye to see if he had been dreaming. Apparently not. She sat squatting on the end of the table, the strings of her skirt hanging over the edge. She was watching him.

"I thought you were dead." She sounded more than just concerned, as though it had been a long time since she had cared about someone. "Can you move?"

His tongue had died during the night, and he detected the taste of roofing tar in his mouth.

She tilted her head parallel to his. "Can you speak?" He shook his head, no. "Then I will. I have been thinking. It's the dry season, right?" He nodded. "I might be the last cloud dancer. If you break my bowl beneath a cloudless sky, I might vanish in the air. In the time of my people, the dancers came together in the sky, waiting for the heavy clouds to appear. Then the dancers danced, shaking the clouds and shouting down the rain. The cloud dancers fell to earth in rain and mist, soaking the earth, down deep into the first world, then they returned to life as full people. I want to be sure there are big clouds before you release me. I don't want to be the last cloud dancer in an empty sky."

He raised his head slightly, then slowly sat up. A grayish pink light penetrated the swollen skin of his throbbing eye. He was struck by the fact that even though she lived in his head, she sounded logical, yet he was in a fog. He sat very still, waiting for the pain to subside.

She was determined to make her case. "Who would want her spirit to evaporate into the cloudless sky—never to return with the rain to seep into the earth, never to return to be born again into the world of living and dying? I would be adrift, high in the vast dome of sky, lost and forlorn forever. It would be the end of death."

Poetic as it was, he had never used the word *forlorn* in his life. It was one thing to have a provocative, masked, female parrot trainer living in his brain, and quite another to have her throwing out phrases like *forlorn forever.* The ghost idea was having greater appeal— as long as she was an external agent, she could be as forlorn as she wanted. It would be easy enough to test her claim. He could break the bowl and see if she went away. But what would that prove? He might end up with a handful of shards, and she could simply go off and lounge around in his brain until the next time she was ready to pop out. Surprise.

He was concerned enough about his reaction to the sting that he decided to see a doctor. Standing up was the first thing. It took a while, aided by groaning and swearing. He wobbled his way around the table, bracing with his good hand, until he regained enough coordination to get to the door. He turned and looked back at the parrot trainer. "I'm going to see the doctor," he said. "I'll be a couple of hours."

"Take me with you, Jack. I don't want to be alone in your big house."

"I can't leave you like this, can I?" He hobbled over to a fruit bowl on the sideboard, selected five dried, shrunken oranges, and went back to the big table. Willow jumped into her bowl as he reached for it. "At least I don't have to talk you back in." He set the bowl in the middle of the table and placed the oranges inside. "No one would think to look for a priceless Mimbres bowl under a bunch of dried-up oranges."

Usually there was no reason to be cautious, but a lot of people in the area recognized Mimbres bowls, and the doors lacked locks.

Anybody could walk in. Once in a while someone caught sight of the mudmen from the road and would drive down to investigate.

"Don't let the cannibals get you," she called from beneath the oranges.

"I'm too tough to be cannibal meat. They'd spit me out." The warmth of her laughter made him smile in spite of the pain.

The truck was a hundred feet from the house. Odd, but good, because he could turn it around without putting it in reverse. He was stuck in first gear—his body was too stiff to shift left-handed. Once he got to the end of his lane, he turned north and drove the half mile up the hill to The Sisters' trailer. It was parked near a power pole forty feet off the road.

An old rancher from Wyoming had come down several winters ago with a Mexican woman he referred to as his housekeeper. He set up his trailer and drilled a well. Every winter they came back. One day, he said something best left unsaid. She committed serious disrespect to his body and walked out. When Jack gave her a ride into Silverado to the bus, he heard the story, but it was told in a fast Spanish-Indian dialect. "Stinking old pig" was repeated several times, along with "kicked to shit." After she was on the bus to El Paso, he went back to check on the old guy, but the rancher and his trailer were gone, never to return.

Several months ago, The Sisters and their mother, Marguerite, discovered the well by the power pole and set up their trailer. It was a fairly nice, older Air Stream. One of the larger ones made in the seventies.

Jack had not met their mother, but he knew a few things about her from the stories her daughters told. She was from Texas and had a mother and grandmother in Brownsville. Jack gathered the woman did not care much for men. She was either careless in sex or loved having babies. SuAnn had seen a picture of her father, which came in the mail when her mother was at work. After that, Marguerite got a P.O. box in Silverado. She never, never talked about their daddies.

Snake was quick to fasten on the idea she had been immaculately conceived. "Like baby Jesus," she said with cool conviction. The girls accepted life as it was. Of course, there would be hell to pay later. How she had managed to support all those babies was a wonder to Jack. From what The Sisters said, she had left Texas the way a lot of people leave Texas—angry and fast.

Marguerite's '78 Cadillac El Dorado, which sucked up a lot of tip money at eleven miles a gallon, was parked alongside the Air Stream. It was the cheapest car she could find with enough engine to pull their shining home over the mountains. The El Dorado had expired Texas plates.

The Sisters came banging out the door. Instead of running up to the truck, they stood in a line by the car and watched. Snake waved.

Marguerite stood in the doorway and studied the situation for a moment. She was slightly heavy, but strong legs gave her some spring and a well-balanced stride, which made her sexy in a Brownsville, Texas–girl way.

Something was not right with the man in the truck. She recognized the truck as her neighbor's. She walked over and looked at his swollen face. He hadn't bathed, and he smelled of whiskey. "You must be Mr. Miller. I'm Marguerite. What happened to you?"

"I got stung by something. I can't drive too well. Would you mind takin' me into town?"

Marguerite turned and looked at her brood. All four raced into the house. She looked back at Jack. "What's that about?"

Obviously, they had not told their mother about him. For five days a week, they had been coming over to help build mudmen and never said a word to their mother.

Jack tried to smile. What she got was a twitch and a grimace. "They've been helpin' with some work along the creek bank below my place."

"Work? What kinda work can you get out of those girls?"

"Well, I've been makin' mudmen. They're good help."

"Mudmen? What do you do with mudmen? You sell 'em?"

"I guess you'll have to come see for yourself."

"They never told me." She looked over her shoulder. All four were crowded in the doorway, waiting for Mom to erupt. "They're not s'pose to leave here. They know that." They had been going down the creek and hanging around this man she'd never met. She had no idea what he had in mind—knew nothing about him. She wanted to scream at the man in the truck, scream at her kids, but mostly she felt guilty and angry. It was also quite likely that this fellow had been doing her a favor. The girls were less trouble than they had been in years, so something was going right. That thought only deepened her guilt.

She got a little teary-eyed, but Marguerite was not the kind to let much but anger show through. She cleared her throat and snorted. "Well, that explains why they're always covered in mud."

She was so rattled for a moment she forgot why he was there. "I can take you in, but you'll have to get back on your own, or wait 'til late when I get off shift."

"I can get back, thanks. Do you want to take my rig or yours?"

She liked the idea of his paying for gas. She would have to take his truck back in the morning, not that he was going to need it anytime soon from the looks of him.

"Your rig'll do. I've got to get my outfit—be right back."

The girls scrambled out the door and stood by the Cadillac, ready to make a run for it. "What'd he say?" Snake, the brave, asked.

"Said he intends to make axle grease outta the lot of ya. Something real bad's goin' to happen if you girls don't start listening to me. You've been lucky so far."

"How far's that?" sniped Sadie.

"You're lucky you're not on a white slave ship on the way to Morocco."

Snake liked the sound of Morocco and started singing, "Morocco, Morocco, we are going to Morocco, Morocco. Because we are bad, very bad, bad girls." In her mind, Snake saw a dry, barren island covered with rocks and more rocks.

"What the hell do you think you're doing?"

"I'm singin' a song, Mom."

Marguerite pressed her lips tight and shook her head. She disappeared into the Air Stream. A moment later she came out with her stuff in a paper sack. The brood had circled up for their ritual—Marguerite knelt down, and they all put their arms around one another and hugged. Each of them kissed her on the lips and said, "You're the best, Mommy." Snake added, "And come right home after work."

Jack limped his way around to the other side of the truck, thinking they'd watched too much college football. He was a little apprehensive about the girls. He'd assumed they told their mother what they did during the day, but he should have checked.

Marguerite got in, turned the truck around, and was a mile down the road before she spoke. "I've been meaning to call on you, Mr. Miller. I've been renting that lot from a Robert T. Larson in Laramie. About a month ago, a man came by to check the meter and told me that Larson didn't own the property, that you did. So I called Larson. He gave me some song about he leased from you and sublet to me. Is that true?"

Jack was staring out the window, contemplating Marguerite's hardscrabble life, and taking in scenery. He liked being driven. You missed a lot when you had to stare at the road all the time. He did not want to think about Larson, or property, or Marguerite and her problems. She had to ask, "Is that true?" a second time.

"No. It's not true. Larson was a squatter. He conned you. He's probably trying to get his money back for drilling that well. He could've rented you the well instead, but that would have been too complicated, and you might not have paid. So he rents you the place. You'll have to work it out with him."

"You'll let me stay rent-free?"

"You can stay. I don't care. Your kids are great. It's all right if they come down. I like their company."

"Thank you. It hasn't been easy." Then she became irritated. It sounded like she was trading her kids for rent. "What exactly is it you do together?"

"I told you. We build mudmen."

"You sound like some kind of nut case. Don't you have anything better to do?"

"It would depend on your point of view, I s'pose. I don't do much for the gross national product—in some quarters that alone makes me a nut case."

Her eyes narrowed. "You live alone, don't you?"

"Yes. Is that a problem?"

"What the hell do you think? I don't know a damn thing about you. You could be some kinda pervert for all I know. Some real strange sonsabitches live out here."

Even in his woolly state, it was evident she was emotionally marginal. He had to go easy with her, but he could not let her run over him, either. "First," he said, "I apologize for not coming over and asking you if it was all right for the girls to be down at my place, but I assumed they told you and that you thought it was okay. SuAnn's very savvy. She does a good job of watching out for the others. And supposing I am a nut case, as you put it—why would you want to provoke a disturbed pervert in his own truck out in the middle of nowhere?"

"Like you're a threat—the shape you're in."

Without turning, he said, "You could come tomorrow and see what we've been doing, if you like."

"Thanks, but I have to work for a living."

Her tone indicated it was best to let it ride. He stared out at the landscape. It must have been close to eleven o'clock already. He could not understand how it had gotten so late. It was starting to heat up. By three, it would be in the high nineties. Except for a few crows, everything had burrowed in for the day. At night, the land was alive with every sort of critter. During the day, you only saw cows and cowboys and few enough of them. He was relieved when they got to town. He was in great need of painkillers.

At the clinic, he took his time getting out of the truck. He stood on the sidewalk for a moment, unshaved, his eye swollen shut, and holding one arm with the other. "I'll come by for the truck in a day or two. Thanks for driving me." As he walked up the clinic ramp, he wished he could avoid Marguerite in the future, but that would probably mean never seeing the girls. He had gotten used to them being there nearly every day, calling his name as soon as they saw him, and gleefully splashing across the creek. He liked having them around—flashing between the mudmen, playing tag, the quick wit, the put-downs, remarks about what was "shit-bad" or "honeysweet-good," questions about grown-ups, mean people, why some people, like Marguerite who worked all the time, had no money, and why other people who didn't work at all, had lots of money. And if Marguerite just decided to up and leave—evidently her big threat—could they come stay with him? Kid questions.

They all had their gestures. When they watched him or listened to him tell stories, SuAnn and Sissy had the habit of standing on one leg with the free foot wrapped behind the knee, Sadie was always bopping around, or twisting a hole in the dirt with her toe, or swinging a foot, and Snake stood with her arms crossed and her eyebrows squinched together, deep in thought.

He told them about people who had settled the valley—about the Portuguese Jews who pretended to be Catholics to elude the Spanish Inquisition. They escaped to New Spain only to discover the Inquisition had also crossed the Atlantic. They lived Catholic, died Catholic, were buried Catholic. Their grave stones, however, often had a hidden Star of David carved in a lily, or hovering above the head of an angel. He told them about the Irish immigrants who brought their Catholic–Protestant wars to America and the Southwest, that the most famous gunman of the Irish wars was a boy, about SuAnn's age, named Billy the Kid.

He pushed the clinic door open and was treated to a blast of cool air and one of the strange sonsabitches Marguerite had in mind, waiting to check in. When Jack's turn came, he was amusing himself thinking about some of the more eccentric folks who live in the area when he caught his reflection in the glass divider. "Cash, Jack Miller, none, insect sting," were his first four answers to the sympathetic Latino woman on the other side of the glass.

After lying on the metal table for an hour, maybe two, after having his blood pressure checked and the temperature of his ear taken, and after an indeterminate period of listening to muffled sounds and indistinct phrases drift through the corridors, the door opened and a tall, roundish, pink man with a white beard in his late fifties, wearing a white coat, identified himself as the nurse practitioner. He greeted Jack with a nod and asked what the problem was.

Jack stared at the nurse practitioner—at the pink face with its short white beard, at the white jacket against the white walls. He could not speak for a moment. He glanced around for the parrot trainer—not in sight, to his relief. He sat up. Oh, yes—pain. The pain was real. He looked the nurse practitioner in the eye and said simply, "I need drugs."

"And which drugs might those be?"

"Some serious painkillers and something to reduce this swelling. It could have been from a scorpion. It was dark. I didn't see it."

"All this from a scorpion? I don't think so. This doesn't look normal at all."

"Not a whole lot about this has been normal. Can you give me something?"

"You look like the type of man who would have a much higher pain threshold."

"Well, I obviously look a lot more manly than I am. Can you get me something, please? Maybe cover my entire body with morphine patches?"

The nurse practitioner raised an eyebrow, smirked, wrote legible prescriptions for an anti-inflammatory and Percocet 3, and threw in some starter samples.

Jack left the clinic with more mobility and lifted spirits. Morphine and its derivatives, he was reminded, were powerful spiritual tools.

He turned the corner at the Lizard Diner, walked along the broken sidewalk, past the plywood panels that camouflaged a large hole that had been a five-and-dime before it burned down twelve years ago. It was boarded over so kids, drunks, and old people would not fall in and sue the city. The plywood was covered with graffiti, but in his present state, he was only mildly puzzled by the arty, neon-pink acclaim for Cannibal Soup—oblivious to the fact it was the moniker of a local biker gang.

SEVEN

Henri lay in a pile of magazines on his bed in the Posada Duran. He had finally managed to sleep with the aid of an antihistamine, three prescription sleeping pills, and half a pint of vodka. Although he had lost his ability to ask the hotel operator to hold his calls, he had the presence of mind to unplug the phone. He also managed to get the Do Not Disturb plastic thing turned the right way. All intrusions into his consciousness were put on hold until 11:45, when Anita knocked at the door.

"Henri, are you there? It's almost checkout time. Henri . . . ? Are you okay?"

Henri rolled over and sat up. "Coming, coming. Right away, dear Anita, I am almost to the door. I am opening the door. Good morning." Having managed to get his shirt and pants off before he had passed out, he was standing in the doorway in boxer shorts, arms outstretched, well rested and euphoric. "Anita, you are beautiful. What a gorgeous morning. How are you? Come in. I will call room service. Do you want latte? Sticky buns? I need multiple espresso. Do you think I can get banana and pineapple?"

She scanned the room. "Where did all these magazines come from?"

"I've been collecting them . . . my research. I got them at Shop&Go, down two blocks on the right. There are Shop&Gos

everywhere in America. I have their map. They have one even in Sil-verado . . . are you ready for Silverado?"

"Henri, what the hell happened to you?"

"We're on the way to Silverado . . . remember Bing Crosby? All that singing while driving?"

"Shave and get dressed. We've already been to Sylvia Siskin's and filmed the collection. We tried to call, but you didn't answer. She asked about you. I think she was offended. You should have been there. Anyway, we have to check out now, or we'll be charged for another day."

"Anita, it will be okay. I will call down the desk and extend us an hour." He waved her into the room and went for the phone. "Something is screwed up now . . . no tone for dialing. But no problem. I will get dressed and journey through the hallways to the stairs and extend time." He sat down near the window, lit a cigarette, and took a deep drag. "In France it is difficult to extend the time, but in America, where no one has time . . . one can extend it. There would be a tremendous market for extending time—think of the possibilities." Now he was standing, looking around for his clothes. "People could buy time in different directions." He found his shoes and held them up, triumphant. "Everyone would be going and coming at different rates . . . all at the same time."

"Take a shower. I'll extend your time and find you an espresso." She was out the door.

He recorded his bons mots in his little red book, then stood in the shower stream until Anita returned with his espresso.

Lucy, Anita, and Billy had breakfast early. Lucy had gone back to her room to make calls and check e-mail while Anita and Billy went to video Sylvia's collection. They had agreed to leave by eleven, and Lucy was ready when Billy came for her.

"How'd the shoot go?"

"Tedious. The guy Sylvia hired from the museum didn't break

anything, and Inez was in hiding. Without you and Henri around, this job is seriously slow."

While they waited in the van for Anita and Henri, Billy pulled up images he had transferred from the night before to demonstrate his editing system. "I call it Buddha. He has a huge memory and responds to voice commands. Sometimes I forget he's not human."

"I suppose that would be a problem if you spend all day and night with him."

"Well, I've got Anita. That's some kind of reality check," he said with a wry smile.

Lucy raised an eyebrow. "You must not be a postmodernist. They don't need reality checks."

"At Sylvia's last night, there were some museum people complaining about the po-mos. Did they mean postmodernists?"

"Yes."

"They mentioned Professor Tweed's Sinatra collection. What's that about?"

"A couple of things. Part of it's law. Anything fifty years or older can qualify for restoration and preservation. So Tweed started the Sinatra memorabilia collection. I think it's supposed to be ironic, but you never know these days."

"We have to go there. We could interview Tweed and Henri, shoot Sinatra dolls, then intercut it with Sylvia, Henri, and the twitchy Virgin."

"You won't get much out of Tweed. He had a stroke."

"He can't talk?"

"He can, but he gets scrambled. Which caused an academic dilemma. The postmodernist idea that there is no truth, only multiple points of view, and the value of everything is in question, makes Tweed as legitimate scrambled as he was unscrambled."

"You're kidding?"

Lucy grinned. "It doesn't matter, does it?"

"Right—no reality check. Where is Henri in all of this? I don't know where he's coming from half the time."

"Henri's full of contradictions. He gets loose and gets lost. That's what I like most about him. He's more of a po-mo renegade. Sometimes he's a hyper-relativist—they're not even sure they exist. His thinking is often a neurological response to an excess of coffee, too many cigarettes, lack of sleep, and too much vodka. It's the physiological component of a lot of French theory, actually."

By the time Anita arrived with Henri, it was 12:45. Billy and Lucy were editing Inez's Stations of the Cross. Anita got in the driver's seat, twisted around, and saw Billy immersed in Inez's beams. She rolled her lower lip between her teeth. First a hyperkinetic Henri, now this. She turned around and started the van. "Did you reach your fellow in Silverado?" she asked Lucy.

"Oh . . . yes," said Lucy. She was distracted by a closeup of Inez's pointing hand—the tones, the fullness, the simplicity and sensuality reminded her of a Caravaggio painting. "This is beautiful. . . . Kills The Deer got him this morning and set it up. I'll call him when we get there."

"Excellent," said Anita, and lurched the van into traffic. She drove four blocks, dodging between cars, made a hard turn into a one-way street that wasn't going her way, and pulled into a service station. "We'll fill up here," she snapped. Henri and Lucy were mystified, but Billy was out the door, pumping gas, checking fluids, and kicking the tires. Anita stared at the map while Billy squeegeed windows. "Where the hell are we?" she shouted.

He came over and leaned in to look at the map. "We're here." He said, drawing a path with his finger. "We want to take this street over to here, then to the freeway south."

"It'd be quicker to take this street."

He kissed her under the earlobe and whispered, "It's another one-way. I've been warned about going against traffic, and I promise not to look at the Stations of the Cross until we're through with Bashé and the NEH. Okay, Peaches?"

She drew a long breath. "Okay. You navigate—ride up front with me. I want Lucy and Henri to talk, okay?"

"Sure. I'll operate the camera from my laptop." He planned the trip via the most arduous route he could find. First they would go west, check out the Indian casino and Acoma Pueblo, then south, through the high plains desert, taking an obscure shortcut to Pie Town, connect up with a narrow strip of pavement that shot across the state from Texas to Arizona, then just short of the border, cut south, dropping two thousand feet through several changes in color, climate, and vegetation into the valley of Silverado.

"We should expose Henri to real Indians," Billy said, "then we'll take a dirt road south 'til we hit pavement again." He handed Lucy the map. "Would you mind introducing this leg of our journey to Buddha and our viewers, Dr. Perelli? Please have fun."

Lucy got the map and studied their proposed route. It was going to be a long day. She folded the map to show the half of the state they would traverse and held it up to the wide-angle lens mounted behind the driver's seat. She'd had a good night's rest, was in moderately high humor, and ready for project Henri. She smiled to all and the camera.

"This is the map of our present journey." With a finger she traced the route marked by Billy. "Due to complications beyond our control, we are leaving Albuquerque in the early afternoon—with the current temperature near ninety degrees. We are heading west into a landscape that—according to certain scholars—witnessed some of the most brutal treatment of human beings ever recorded." On the map, she pointed out Chaco Canyon and its suburbs or "outliers," as well as several pueblos and cliff dwellings in the Four Corners area.

"There are others who have painted a more romantic picture—one of gentle, native maize farmers, living in peace and harmony for more than a thousand years. This theory implies that maize contains a spiritual elixir the drug companies have yet to market—a secret X factor that neuters the war zones in the human brain stem."

She put the map aside, looked back at the camera, and continued. "Later in the program, we will address the question of how and why modern humans choose to pursue one narrative over another. Do these preferences have to do with technological advances in archaeological investigation or are they mere psychological manifestations of the prevailing social fashions of the moment?" She paused. "Okay? Good enough for humanism?"

Everyone laughed and applauded. "Well done, Perelli." Anita had found another star who demonstrated a facility for on-camera jabber. The NEH crowd would not find Lucy's patter palatable. Satire was not tolerated by the scholastic aristocracy. Fortunately for Anita, Billy was a wizard of the edit, an expunger *extraordinaire*.

On the long upward stretch out of the Rio Grande Valley and the Albuquerque smog, Henri noticed a sign: DRIVE THRU LIQUOR. "Wait, stop, stop." He waved gleefully. "Drive Thru Liquor. We must all drive thru liquor. America is beautiful. I must have a photograph," Henri shouted. "Return, Anita. Please re-turn."

She acquiesced, pulled onto the gravel shoulder, backed up two hundred feet, and came to a sliding halt just short of the front door.

A Mediterranean-looking man in his fifties, wearing a white short-sleeved shirt and black suspenders, eased his way through the heavy door to investigate the commotion. A good nap had been interrupted by the sound of a vehicle sliding across the gravel. He looked a little disgruntled, peering through the back window of the van at Henri.

Henri waved, then stepped out the side door. "Sorry for our dust. We hurry too much. Tell me, where does one do drive thru?"

With an Italian-flavored accent, the man said, "Sorry, there is no more drive thru. They passed a law. I haven't gotten around to changing the sign. You'll have to come inside."

Henri was undaunted. "For posterity, for our children and our children's children, to save the past for the future, I would like to take pictures of this fleeting phase of Americana. Please let us do the drive thru."

The man could not resist a smile. He had seen a lot, but never a Bashé. He waved them around behind the building and retreated inside. Anita made a U-turn and pulled the van up to the drive-thru window on Henri's side where he could slide the door back and place his order. He craned his neck, waiting for the proprietor to appear, taking in what little there was to take in, obviously disappointed. "It is just a goddamned window with bars."

The window slid back, revealing a smiling face and dark wavy hair. "What'll it be, Frenchie?"

Henri looked up, to the sides, and at the man. In a wounded voice, he said, "There is no drive thru—just a window."

"I lied. So? They wanted the booze, not a car wash. What do you have in mind?"

"I would like to take a picture of your window."

"Open or closed?"

"One each, please. I will buy vodka."

Anita backed the van up and Henri got out with his pocket camera. Billy followed with the digicam, stepping back for a wide shot of the white building, the blank noonday sky, and small, thin Henri all in black looking up at the dark man behind the barred window, beneath the faded DRIVE THRU LIQUOR sign. It was a scene for a short video Billy called *American Moments*. The Italian closed the window. Henri snapped another shot then turned and walked up to Billy. "It should be Drive By Liquor." He went back to the window, which slid open, and Henri placed his order. After exchanging cash for two half-gallon bottles of vodka, Henri asked, "Why didn't you call it Drive By Liquor?"

With a flat, expressionless gaze, the proprietor muttered, "Because . . . I'd have to sell shots."

"Ha, yes, very funny fellow. Goodbye, then. And thank you, too."

"Sure. Goodbye, Frenchie."

In the van, Henri took out his red book and wrote, "Drive Thru Liquor, Drive By Shots—Albuquerque New Mexico."

They turned off the main road into the Sky City Casino parking lot. All got out to stretch and stare at the specter of a giant fun house in the middle of nowhere, flashing lights and neon faded by the blazing sun. The casino was an oasis. It spelled relief. It promised escape from the swelter of the hundred-degree oven that was the reservation world, platters of food, and the possibility of winning ridiculous amounts of money. Henri changed sixty dollars in bills for silver and proceeded to lose fifty-eight as fast as he could stuff them into the slot. He gave up, keeping two silvers for souvenirs, and joined Anita at hamburgers and french fries. Lucy, down twelve, stayed behind. "Would you order me a burger and fries, please? I won't be long."

Anita picked up a pamphlet from the table and read it while she waited for her order. "This is nuts," she announced. "These people claim they have the right, as separate nations, to request military assistance from foreign governments. Who would believe this crap?"

"They took me for fifty-eight dollars. Now they want to conquer America?"

Anita handed him the flyer. "Look at this."

Henri scanned the flyer and nodded. "Acoma can strafe the Hopi Pueblos and blow up the Navajo air bases."

Lucy returned with fifteen dollars in hand. "Broke even," she announced. "It's cold in here, isn't it? Where's Billy?"

"He's at the slots, warming himself with adrenaline," said Anita.

Henri handed Lucy the flyer. "They stole fifty-eight dollars from me. Now this."

She read it while dribbling catsup on her burger. "So sell them those nice Mirage jets and get your fifty-eight bucks back."

"Mirage," said Henri, "describes the . . . how you say . . . whole kit and caboodle."

Lucy nodded. She was eating her burger and observing the casino: mirrored balls floating from the ceiling, sleazy music, clang-ing slots, pale white girls in mules and tight plastic skirts, smacking their gum, large men mesmerized by whirling fruit.

The cold and the country-western whine were getting to Henri. "Anita, I think I would like to see the real thing, the Acoma."

"Don't I get to make back your fifty-eight dollars?"

"I'll wait in the sunshine."

"I won't be long." She went to a cashier, exchanged a twenty for silver, and attacked the nearest machine. It paid out eighty-nine dollars. Whooping sirens and flashing lights broke loose in celebration of Anita's newly gained riches. Henri escaped as the Mellow Fellow crooned "High Hopes," drowning out Willie Nelson's haggard moan about cowboykind's pitiful plight. Again Henri was faced with the great American question—was it irony or bad programming?

He burst out into the bright Acoma sun, a fugitive from fun. Lucy found him lying on a concrete retaining wall, soaking in the heat like a lizard.

They crossed under the highway and followed the signs that pointed to Acoma. Once they passed the art gallery and the long grayness of one-story government buildings, they headed south. The land took over, and everything began to change.

Dust devils of reddish dirt sprang up, danced through the sage, and died. The blue-green of the sage was interspersed with black rock and red clay. Henri's eyes darted back and forth looking for dust devils. He had not seen them since he was a little boy in the country. On the way home from church, always his most impressionable time, a spinning spook came down the road after him. It too was red and transparent. The devil had come for him. He screamed and grabbed his mother's hand. She laughed. "Henri, it's only wind and dust." He turned away from her and stared at his shoes. "What's the matter, sweet Henri?"

"I am foolish for thinking the devil had come to take me."

"Do not bother yourself with the devil. He can only play tricks on small boys."

Anita pulled into a parking lot marked SCENIC VIEW on the north cliff overlooking a broad plain stretching four miles south toward the Acoma mesa. The pull-off allowed tourists to leave their cars, walk to the edge, and stare down at the plain, where for two hundred years the people of Acoma had raised sheep and cattle.

Anita pulled in between identical mobile homes, one from Louisiana, one from Minnesota. Indians in pickups, parked next to card tables covered with pottery and bead work, surrounded the lot on three sides. Rocks held the lighter merchandise in place against the wind. Tourists, unusually pale, of various sizes, shapes, and ages, walked from table to table staring at the wares. The Indians stayed in their trucks out of the wind. The ones with air conditioning had the windows rolled up.

Lucy and crew climbed out of their van and wandered off to various tables. Henri stopped by one to examine tiny pieces of pottery—miniature animals and pots with little designs scratched in them. A pretty woman, soft and round, opened the door of her blue pickup and stepped out into the wind. The truck was parked very near the edge of the rim. Close enough to make Henri nervous. "Those were made by my son," she said in a soft, honeyed voice, "He's only four, but he wants to help."

"Where is he?" said Henri, craning to see in the truck.

"He is with his grandmother, making more pots for me to sell."

"Why are you up here, instead of over there?" He pointed south to the Acoma mesa.

"We are not Acoma. They don't let us set up over there. They don't let us set up in the parking lot down below either." She turned and looked across at Acoma. Her tone was flat, without remorse or anger. "We have a big view." Her words were direct and simple.

He thought she was the most beautiful woman he had ever seen. Her voice was sweet and wise. Her smile enthralled him. He stood there looking into her eyes. "Can I buy everything?"

"You are not American."

"I am French. These people," he waved toward his scattered associates, "are my film crew." He hoped she would be impressed.

"It is okay if you buy everything. I can go home when there's nothin' to sell anymore." She began wrapping each little piece of pottery in paper towels she took from a large box marked Super Absorbent in the back of the pickup. She noticed Henri watching her man in the truck, who ignored Henri's existence. The man sat behind the steering wheel, smoking and staring out across to Acoma.

Was she unhappy? Henri couldn't tell. What did she think of her distant man? Her circumstances seemed sad, but she appeared to accept things as they were. Henri wanted to ask her to go away with him. Instead he asked, "How much?" The wind blew his words toward Acoma.

"What?"

He raised his voice. "How much?"

She nodded and carefully added the items on a hand calculator, smiled her sweet smile, and said, "Fifty-eight dollars."

Had he heard right? He repeated the amount. She gave him a barely perceptible nod and turned the calculator for him to see. He was not interested in what the calculator said. The sun's glare washed out the numbers, anyway. He counted out sixty dollars and handed them to her.

She gave him back two dollars. "Thank you." She folded the card table and set it in the pickup. "I can go home now and watch my programs."

"Which ones—what programs do you watch?"

"I like the soaps and author interviews. We get them off the satellite." She waved and climbed into the truck. Her man continued to stare at the distant mesa. She folded her hands and waited for him to come back to her.

Henri walked to the van, leaning into the wind, thinking about why the woman appealed to him. The wind made him impatient and irritable. He was happy to see the others heading back.

When they were on the road down to the plain, they revealed their treasures, passing them back and forth. Anita had bought a thick turquoise bracelet, Billy had a beaded necklace for Anita. Lucy's prize was an eight-inch black plate with the image of Kokopelli, the hump-backed flute player, carved into its surface. Henri's many small figures drew the most appreciative remarks.

Lucy held the little bear figure in her hand. "If I found this in a store in Albuquerque, it would be a piece of kitsch. But when it has a story, that changes everything. I like it, Henri. Why did you buy it?"

"I fell in love with the woman."

They thought he was joking and laughed. He had nothing to say for once and just looked at the little bear in Lucy's hand.

"It's difficult to know what you've bought until you've had it around for a while," she said. "Sometimes I buy a thing because I feel sorry for the person selling it, then I get home and look at it and see it carries some weight. At least, it reminds me that I was somewhere different, and the people made me remember them."

Henri looked annoyed. "But do you do that with people who sell on the street in Washington, D.C.?"

"No. They only sell cheap tourist junk and knockoffs in D.C."

Henri wondered if the Indians thought of their pottery as cheap tourist junk and knockoffs. He would always remember the sweet round woman. How would she fare in Paris? She would have a stall in the *Marché aux Puces*. People would think she was Tibetan. She would feel lost. Henri stared at the small clay bear.

Billy had him in the lens. "Your little bear has you captivated, Henri."

"No. I was, ah . . . hmm, wondering is there a way of seeing the Indian that is not racist?"

"What are you saying, Henri?" Anita asked. She had an agenda, at least a project, and its lack of focus was making her anxious.

"The whites want either to ah. . . . annihilate or consume the Indian. One is, how you say, hard core racism, the other soft core, but both are racist."

"Consume him?"

"Yes. Make him live in the past and he becomes our Indian . . . the commodity. Or we annihilate him—accept the individual and ignore that he is different. But this also is racist, because his difference defines him as Indian."

Lucy, from long habit, challenged his pessimism: "Can't you accept both the person and the difference?"

"Then you say his difference makes no difference."

"What if the Indian says his difference is only superficial—can't we be united in our humanity and accept him without being racist?"

"Ah, the liberal-humanist ideal. But if he stops the racism by saying his Indianness is superficial, he is the, um . . . co-conspirator in his absorption."

"And he disappears?"

"Exactly. The ultimate definition of the Indian. The disappearing one, the deleted, discontinued, the . . . the canceled man. Our inability to define Indian is, how you say, one coin of liberal-humanist racism—the elimination of the difference. The other coin, of course, is multiculturalism."

Lucy smiled at his seamless logic. "Your argument is like the ouroboros, Henri, the circular serpent who consumes himself tail first. One cannot define what does not exist. Tidy."

He laughed. "Is good, the ouroboros was the alchemists' symbol for unity."

Anita wondered if she could use the piece. Later she would try to sort it out. She couldn't tell if Henri's argument would hold up or if Lucy had undercut him.

They were headed south toward the large parking lot below Acoma—also known as Sky City in the tourist brochures—where they would catch a bus to the top of the mesa. Henri looked back toward SCENIC VIEW. The blue truck was still parked dangerously close to the rim's edge. He imagined the woman, sitting quietly with her hands folded, waiting for her disappearing man. Henri could still hear her soft voice. If only he could be absorbed by her.

As they pulled into the parking lot, they noticed another group of Indians with tables and pickups. The silver tour bus, farting plumes of diesel and carbon on its way up to Sky City, was the last bus of the day. Tourists' cars were not allowed up the hill to the small, ancient Pueblo.

Lucy and the crew stood around and watched the parking-lot Indians tussling with the wind as they packed up to go home. Henri wondered if ancient political intrigues or the simple lack of space had banished these people from the Pueblo above.

An air-conditioned building in the middle of the lot peddled hot dogs, polish sausages, several forms of sugar water, ice cream, tickets to Acoma, permits to take pictures on the reservation, and film. They all bought ice-cream on a stick and went back out into the wind and heat.

"I love the heat," said Henri. "I'm going to move here and become an Indian."

"You'll disappear, you know," said Lucy.

"That, dear Lucy, is the idea. They absorb me. I disappear."

"I think the Indians stopped taking applications several years ago."

Henri brightened. "That's it."

"What's it?"

"The solution. The Indians reopen for applications. White people with the 'crisis of identity,' which is most of us, become Indians—get lots of identity—and the Indians get . . ."

"Money and a few laughs," Lucy answered.

It got too hot for everybody, except Henri. He stood by the van's sliding door, licking his ice-cream on a stick and searching the distance for the blue pickup. Once they were on the road, he discovered he had dripped ice-cream on his black turtleneck and spent several miles concentrating on removing the blight from his person. Instead of going back the way they came, Anita took the northwest road, leaving Henri unable to save the sweet, round woman from the disappearing man, take her back to Paris, and set her up in a stall in the *Marché aux Puces*. Just as well, he thought. His wife would have objected. Having a Native American mistress would not have been the problem—Nina was a Frenchwoman. She would, however, object to uprooting the woman from her people and throwing her into a strange and unforgiving environment. Nina was a wonderful woman. Nina. Of course. The woman on the mesa was his own wife. It was Nina's wisdom, her patience, and soft curves he saw in the beautiful Indian woman.

To continue south, toward Silverado, they had to take a circuitous route north then west through an oppressive landscape of gray lava clots in overgrazed fields. In a draw between two channels of lava they came upon several inert, starving horses, so weak they appeared to have died standing. Billy wondered if they could actually be dead. He could not resist the photo op. Anita stopped at his request, but only to gain bargaining points for later. He got out slowly, staying his distance. If the horses had enough life left to move, he did not want to startle them. At any moment he expected them to fall over—dead and dry as mummies. The skin was so tight around the knee of the nearest horse that it had split.

Billy approached cautiously. Perhaps these were sculptures, a form of Southwestern shock art. The nearest horse tried to back away, but stumbled and sat abruptly on its hindquarters. The horse looked at him through its milk-white eyes. Billy felt a twinge of compassion—to pat the horse, ease it to the ground, and hold its head while it died. But Billy was on the other side of the camera, which kept the world and death at bay. It was a good place to be. He lived in a world of photo ops. He finished with a closeup of the milky cataracts that stared in his direction.

Anita and Lucy watched from the van, horrified by the sight of a dozen horses so near death they were beyond saving.

Lucy was sickened and frustrated that she could do nothing. She was accustomed to making things work.

Henri's observations were almost always more distant than those of normal people, as though his life's work were to witness mass murder on other planets through an orbiting telescope. Henri tried to keep in mind that he lived on a sphere with human heat, but easily lost his focus. He was a radical form of Billy.

Billy got into the van, grim and silent, plugged the camera into Buddha, downloaded, then watched the images on his laptop.

Anita started the van. "Can we get out of here now?"

Billy nodded, but kept his eyes on the screen.

"Your horses are suffering an extreme case of self-absorption," Henri joked.

Lucy rolled her eyes. "Henri, why are you so merciless? Do you see dying horses? Do you see dying people? You are worse than the pot thieves. Eventually you will deconstruct all of life."

Henri cracked the window so his smoke was drawn away from his compatriots—a singular act of conscious compassion. "Culture has already deconstructed the individual to nothing. What is left to deconstruct? Tiny fragments . . . the sherds." He lit another cigarette off the ember of the last, which he let the draft suck through the window crack. "Ultimately, it's culture's job to kill the individual."

Anita glanced up at him. "Henri, you're giving me a headache."

The shortcut to Pie Town took them on a long, rolling, rutted road that jerked the van in several directions at once. Billy, anxious for Buddha, pleaded, "Soothe your circuits, Peaches."

The road straightened for several of miles of deep, multiple ruts where trucks and cars kept making new roads alongside the old ruts during the rainy season. From time to time, rock replaced clay and the road was smooth as a highway. The land became flat, endless, and lifeless.

"We are the last people on earth," Henri said, looking through the slit in the window. "Even the buzzards have given it up."

An hour later Anita saw a sign—at least a post with a board nailed to it. As they got close she slowed down. The sign said PIE TOWN— FIVE MILES. It was a lie. Pie Town was nine miles.

They came in on the north side of the town, which appeared to be deserted. The windows were gray, signs askew, storefronts empty, their paint peeled to dry rotted wood.

"What happened?" asked Henri. "The people have gone away like an American ghost town . . . incredible."

Anita turned down a side street looking for signs of life. Perhaps the heat and wind kept people inside. There were cars, apparently in working order. This gave them hope.

"Dog," exclaimed Billy, pointing to a black Lab asleep or dead next to an eroded adobe. "Crow." Then a little later, with the excitement of a lost explorer, "Cat! Cat in a window."

The west side of town was populated by small trailer houses and old RVs—northern elders, come to escape winter and too destitute to return. Lucy's archaeological mind, yearning to see beneath the surface of things, imagined desiccated inhabitants surrounded by 1950s artifacts.

"Try the east side," said Billy. "It wouldn't be right not to have pie in Pie Town."

Anita dutifully drove east for a block and a half and discovered

Pete's Cafe. It was the one establishment that had stayed open after disaster had befallen the town. Anita pulled up in front, and they all wandered in looking like road-damaged tourists.

Pete's Cafe was where those not yet mummified came to reassert the town's existence and their own. The cafe was partially subsidized by the U.S. Postal Service. The main outlet for the only evident industry in town—placemats with flowers and local grasses sandwiched in clear plastic—was located on a wire rack as you walked in the door.

Lucy and Anita took seats across from Billy and Henri at a table next to the window. Optimistic about the possibility of life, they were automatically drawn to the viewing port. Lucy ordered soup—green pea and lamb—from a young, upbeat waitress with pointy breasts. The others ordered coffee and pie. Henri asked for his coffee in a paper cup.

"Ya want it ta-go?"

"Ta-go, is paper cup?"

"Okay, coffee ta-go. Want that with cow?"

"Cow? I don't think I need cow."

"Okay, coffee ta-go, hold the cow."

A grizzled but cheerful woman in her seventies came in with an older, slightly disfigured man with a hitch in his hip, followed by a thin, ghostly-looking young man. They got something at the counter and left after a few minutes. They did not seem in a hurry. They had time, they just had better places to spend it than in the company of outsiders. The inhabitants of Pie Town were pensioners, renegades, misfits, the old and cold escaping Fargo, San Francisco, and Seattle, and the lonely seeking an excuse for their loneliness. Pie Town was peopled by escapees. No doubt a few escapees from the nation's prisons also managed to find a hot tin house to call home.

When his coffee came, Henri added a packet of the freeze-dried coffee he always carried to boost the caffeine hit and punch up the taste in lieu of espresso. He examined his paper cup, careful to check the details of design and manufacture. He held it caringly, put his lips against the paper to feel the texture—a connoisseur of the paper cup.

He noticed the others staring at him. "The cup made of paper is the only container worthy of coffee. We do not have these cups in France. Their texture is perfect against the lip. They embrace the flavor of the coffee. They are objects of perfection and beauty, and you don't have to wash them."

Lucy peered at him over a white porcelain mug. "Interesting. I think they spoil the flavor."

"I get hiccups drinking coffee from paper cups," said Anita.

"True? You tease?" asked Henri.

"I never tease you, Henri."

The waitress brought the check, dropped it in front of Henri, and stood quietly for a moment staring at Billy.

Anita cleared her throat and said, "Could you tear yourself away and get us some refills?" The girl blushed and trotted off.

"You didn't need to hurt her feelings," said Billy.

Anita grabbed up the check. "This town's so small, they don't bother to break up, they just lose their turn."

"What's that suppose to mean?"

"Never mind."

"What's your problem, babe?"

Henri leaned over and whispered, "The waitress has excessive awe for you." He shrugged and went outside to smoke.

As he stood on the short porch, a faded red Ford 150 pickup turned off the highway and came to a stop at his feet. He noticed a spotlight on the driver's side. Two men got out. One was slightly bent, a wiry tough with a limp. The other, perhaps a younger brother in his early fifties, was short, scrawny, and out of whack. Henri could see something was off in the older man's piercing eyes and in the way his oversized jaw jutted forward, as though his head and the jaw were from different skulls. The scrawny one kept watching the tough one for clues. When the older man marched past Henri without noticing his existence, the younger one nodded slightly without looking.

Henri turned and watched them go into the cafe. The tough looked back and saw Henri watching. The tough did not like being caught out. It made him feel foolish. He hated that. They walked to the counter, taking in Lucy, Anita, and Billy. The women looked like rich bitches. Billy was a pretty boy. His tight jeans made him look like a hired hand who'd never been hired.

They sat down at the counter, and the busty waitress passed them menus. "Afternoon, Lars. Hello, Jacob. Haven't seen you fellas for a few weeks."

Lars, the tough, nodded. "We don't get over this way often."

"I can't blame you. Myself, I'm hopin' to leave—I need a town with a teensy bit more on its plate, ya know?

"El Paso?"

"Way too big. I was thinkin' of lightin' out for Truth or Consequences."

"Town's fillin' up with a bunch of goddamn retirees. Wouldn't go near it. 'Sides, they already got a Sunday's supply of mean old murderin' sonsabitches down there." Lars made a queer gurgling sound that scared the waitress, but when Jacob laughed, she did, too.

His brother's gurgling laugh set Jacob free. He started talking to the waitress—told her they were going to put in the bridge that washed out last fall, but maybe they'd wait until later this fall in case there was another flood that'd wash out the new bridge, were they to put one in, but they'd gotten along all year so far without a bridge, so maybe they didn't really need one.

Lars stared at the waitress's breasts. "Shut your trap, Jacob."

The waitress gave a little jump, then rushed into the kitchen.

"Lars, you should not vex yourself on me."

"Fer the name a God, Jacob, just shut it for a change."

"You are not the boss of me, Lars."

"I am sorely aware of that fact."

Billy pushed back his chair and walked to the counter. "Hi there. Ah, I was wonderin' if there's a shortcut south, or do we have to take the highway west?"

Lars turned and looked Billy in the eye. Years of hate had fixed a clench in his jaw and made his eyes go cold and black. The eyes showed something deep down in the gut, like the desire to kill.

Unfortunately, there was a stubborn core in Billy and a half pint of vanity. He looked into Lars's dead-black eyes and said, with as much cool as he could muster, "The old skunks are mean and ugly this year. Look for an early frost."

It was the kind of put-down you could get away with in the yuppi- fied territories of Idaho and Montana, but not down there. The mean old buzzard and the pretty boy glowered at each other.

Anita knew never to talk to a Texas redneck like that. She sus- pected the ones from this side of hell were just as deadly. In a small Southwestern town, if your victim was a wiseass and an outsider, you had reason to expect an acquittal.

"Billeee!" She was moving toward the door. "We're leaving." She marched out, hoping her force field of motion would draw him with her. Lucy could feel the pull, but hung back to see what developed.

Lars's jaw muscles twitched—he was about to make a move. Jacob came in on Billy's blind side, catching him in the kidneys with three hard blows that put him on the floor. Already Billy was sorry meat.

The brothers stood back just enough to get a good swing and started kicking—ribs, head, stomach, whatever opened up got a taste of boot. Billy, scarcely conscious, had the troublesome sensation he was about to die.

"Stop, now!" Anita screamed from the doorway. She was holding a .38 special on Lars, who glanced over just as Lucy caught him with a fast bottle of catsup against the forehead.

Exploding catsup and glass covered men, floor, and the waitress peering from the kitchen, causing her to emit several abrupt, piercing screams. Jacob clasped his hands to his ears, either from the screams or in anticipation of being shot.

Lars had gone down on top of Billy. Neither moved. Anita walked toward them, both hands on the gun, the gun on Jacob, quietly repeating, "Don't move, don't move, don't move."

Lucy froze, the broken neck of the catsup bottle still in her hand. Jacob wanted to help his brother, but he stayed in a half-crouch, wait- ing for Anita to pull the trigger.

"Get back, Lucy. I'm a bad shot."

The kitchen was quiet. The waitress, unable to breathe and scream at the same time, had passed out. Anita looked Jacob in the eye over the barrel of the .38 as she closed in on him.

He suspected she would shoot. He managed a shy grin and shrugged his bony shoulders. In other circumstances, it would have been an endearing gesture.

Anita was scared—there was something downright untrustworthy about a man who smiles into the barrel of a gun. She was afraid to take her eyes off him. There were several reasons to shoot, but one good one not to. She began barking commands: "On the floor. Do it now. On your back. Arms in front. Stretch out. Roll over." She paused. Her voice dropped. Some red-dirt Texas demon was talking. "Don't fucking move," said the demon. For a moment no one moved.

"Billy?" Anita whispered. She thought she saw his hand quiver. He started to wiggle from under Lars, who had regained consciousness enough to recognize pain and began to groan—a joyous sound to Anita, all things considered.

Billy crawled out of the way and hoisted himself onto the counter. He held his side while blood streamed from his nose.

"Are you all right, Billy?"

He nodded meekly. Lucy had Billy lie on the counter and laid a wet towel over his nose to stop the bleeding. Satisfied he would be all right, she looked down at Lars. "Cover me, Anita. I need to see if I crushed his skull." She took another towel and wiped the catsup off Lars's face to assess the damage. She had nailed him just above his nose. Blood oozed through his skin, and he had a gash across his right cheek, but his skull seemed intact. Any damage would have been to his already dysfunctional frontal lobes. "A little tape and aspirin, and he'll be his old nasty self all too soon."

She went back into the kitchen and checked on the waitress. The girl was leaning over a sink, crying, and rubbing at the catsup stains on her blouse. "Are you all right, dear?"

"This is my only best blouse. It's all cotton. How do you get catsup out of cotton?" She was vexed. "Oh, I knew I shouldn't awore this one to work."

"Boiling water'll take that stain right out. Hydrogen peroxide's really good on blood, but you want to get it within an hour or so." Lucy put her hand on the girl's back and gave her a pat. "Well, we'll be leaving now. Here's a hundred dollars. Buy another blouse."

"Gee thanks. You're super. You know, those guys always scared the piss outta me."

"Smart girl. Take the rest of the day off. If I were you, I'd leave town."

"Soon as I get some water boiled, I'm outta here."

"The blouse can wait. Do yourself a favor and get out now."

Henri waited until the disturbance had settled down, then quietly ventured into the restaurant. Lars was curled up, holding his head, Jacob was on the floor as ordered—face down, stretched out—fingers as far from his toes as possible. Billy lay on the counter, holding his side. Henri smiled at Anita. "You seem to have them, how you say, by the short bunnies."

"It's short hairs, Henri."

"Short hares are bunnies—yes?"

"No. Help me here. Find something to tie these guys with."

The waitress found a roll of duct tape, and Henri and Anita taped Lars's and Jacob's hands and feet. Anita looked at Billy, who was in extreme pain. "You are a fucking idiot, Billy," she yelled. "You know how much trouble we could be in?"

"We're in trouble? These bastards tried to kill me."

Lars looked Anita in the eye and whispered, "We'll be lookin' fer ya."

Anita's eyes narrowed at Lars, then she turned on Billy. "We'd be in a lot less trouble if they'd killed you."

"You know, Anita, a dead Billy would be a problem. Who would video? Who would edit? What would happen to 'Bashé in America'? You would have big problems with NEH. You have to think of yourself, my dear. Talent like Billy is once in a million."

Anita sat down, lay the gun on the table for fear of accidentally shooting someone, and looked at Henri. At that moment, he seemed hilarious. She began laughing until tears streamed down her face. "You are a very funny guy, Henri."

Billy did not see the humor of the situation. "What are we going to do with these two?"

"Leave them here for now," said Anita. "Let's go outside and think about it." She picked up the .38 and was out the door. Lucy and Henri helped Billy outside. Anita was pacing back and forth by the van when the waitress came out, locked the door, and ran to her trusty-rusty Toyota. She waved to her last customers in Pie Town. "Bye, y'all. Thanks for the tip."

Anita stopped pacing and looked at her companions. "This is how I see it. These boys probably have a very bad rep. They're crazy mean and get in lots of trouble. They may not want to report us. If we report them, we have a .38 special to explain. By the time they get loose, they won't be able to catch up with us. That's reasonable, isn't it? . . . Anybody? Reasonable, not reasonable?"

By this time, Lucy was on autopilot.

"I've not acclimated to the Wild West," said Henri.

Billy winced, inhaled slowly, and told Anita to let the air out of the pickup's tires and to put a piece of tape on the end of a spark plug, and put the wire back. "It'll take them a while to get on the road, then the engine'll run rough 'til they check it out in a month or two."

"Good," said Anita. "One thing, though—I don't wanna drive. I wanna get acquainted with Henri's big-bottle booze."

They got in the van with Lucy behind the wheel, Henri in the front passenger seat, and Anita in the console chair. Billy took several gulps from one of Henri's bottles and curled up on the floor. The others took a hit or two.

Henri hummed, "We're on our way to Mandalay," as he hunched down, keeping an eye on the side mirror. He read the legend "Objects in mirror may be closer than they appear" over and over, but there was no sign of Lars and Jacob. Things were quiet in Pie Town. "Why did their truck have a light by the windshield?" Henri asked.

"It's a spotlight," said Anita. "In Texas we use them for poaching deer at night."

"Must be very hot."

"Hot? Why?"

"Poaching is cooking? Yes?"

Anita laughed. When she caught her breath, she explained, "It also means killing game illegally."

He cracked the window and blew smoke into the invisible stream. "Does any animal species recant its dominance over another species and walk away?"

Lucy's heart was still pounding, locked in fight-or-flight mode. "You're saying we should've killed Lars and Jacob in the name of some lunatic Darwinian justification for wickedness and greed? We are not animals, for Christ's sake."

"Dear Lucy, all emotions are grounded in biology. If not, then where are we—floating about, freed from our natural mooring? We can't make up everything as we go along. Our problem is not our wickedness and greed, but that we are wicked and greedy in a world created by our wickedness and greed."

"Then, it makes sense to learn what we are made of so we can figure out how to survive in a world that feeds our instincts."

From the floor of the van, Billy whispered, "She's definitely . . . on to something, Henri. The catsup . . . bottle . . . across Lars's skull . . . was a lot less brutish than Anita's .38 . . . goin' off in his face."

EIGHT

Billy asked Anita to get him some medical attention in Silverado. That required a trip to the hospital emergency room. The doctor, a Pakistani woman with perfect teeth who spoke precise English, checked him over.

The pain in his ribs and stomach consumed his attention, even though Lars's big boot had caught him on the bridge of the nose, causing a slight fracture and blackening both eyes.

Anita wanted to hold him, but she was afraid wherever she touched would hurt. "We have to get his ribs x-rayed, Doctor."

"Forget it, Peaches. I'll be fine."

Anita ignored him. "Are there signs of a concussion?"

"I just need some pills, and we can get out of here, okay? Just relax, babe."

But Billy warmed to the doctor, who was small of body, big of heart, and bountiful of pain killers. She warned him not to take the Percocet until the Demerol shot wore off and that alcohol would enhance the effect of the drugs. The subtlety of language made Billy smile. Sure, X rays. Why not?

Other than the nose fracture, nothing was broken. The doctor taped his nose and ribs and told him to restrict his motion for a few days.

After the hospital, they cruised the main drag for food.

"Up ahead," said Henri. "Chez Jose's. French-Mexican cuisine. We have, as you Americans say, all the luck."

After dinner they found an ancient hotel, the Priscilla on P. Street, which went the length of the town from gully to gully. The P. stood for Priscilla, the daughter of an early miner who had staked out a long strip across the bottom of the gullies on the theory that a fortune in silver lay in the sandy bottom of each gully—a clever theory that never panned out. The Priscilla Hotel was considered a miracle because it had not burned down. Most of the town had—more than once. That made the Priscilla the oldest wooden structure in Silverado.

Henri found this bit of chamber-of-commerce history particularly disturbing. "The structure is, how do you say, way over dues? Any moment it will spontaneously combust." The fact that he drank, took sleeping pills, and smoked in bed considerably enhanced the odds.

As they walked into the Priscilla, a sense of foreboding clouded his mind. "This mustiness is the odor of the ancient dead, Lucy."

"I know, but so is every breath you take."

"Every breath you take? It has an ominous sound." He got out the red book and wrote down, "Every breath you take." He stared at the phrase and smiled. It said so much. He was delighted.

Lucy watched him. Then, warmed by his delight, she reached over and put her arm around his shoulders and gave him a gentle squeeze. Henri looked up, surprised, but she had already turned to the desk clerk.

"Do you have a facility where I could boil some water?" she asked. "I splattered catsup on my dress."

They were given the last three rooms, two next to each other and one down at the end of the hall. Lucy chose the room at the end. All their rooms looked out from the second floor onto P. Street.

Lucy contemplated the street from her window, wondering how many tons of sand Priscilla's father had sluiced before he realized he was wrong, and how many more tons he sluiced before he gave up.

Anita got a bottle of whiskey from the hotel bar and took it up to the room to share with Billy, who fell into a deep, happy sleep, naked except for his bandaged ribs and the exotic mask of soft blue-black that spread from the bridge of his nose to his eyes, a haunting effect intensified by the band of white tape across his nose to his cheekbones. She watched him breathe and let the whiskey slide down her throat. The windows were open, and warm desert air pushed the curtains back—rolling and fluttering in the rays of the setting sun—flicking the lacy light across Billy's naked body.

Someday Billy was going to get them killed. That was Anita's fear. Either that or he would fuck things up so badly she would never get a grant again. Anita still wanted him. Wanted to make love to him. And she liked to watch him glide around with his camera, totally unaware of himself, absorbed in the world in his lens.

The bluish black eyes, bandaged nose, taped ribs, and his drugged state made him unusually vulnerable. She caressed his cock, but the Demerol and whiskey had disconnected it from the part of the brain that operated the essential pumps and valves. His mechanism was out of order.

She gave it up and decided to see if Henri wanted a drinking partner. Besides, they had things to discuss. She took her glass and the whiskey and tiptoed to Henri's door. She tapped lightly. Nothing. She put her ear to the door and listened, then tapped again.

Henri's cautious voice said, "Hello?"

"It's Anita. We need to talk."

"Later, please, I need a nap."

"Henri, open the damn door, please?"

There was a soft snap and a click and Henri, silhouetted against the window light, revealed himself. He hesitated in the doorway for a moment, then resigned, opened up to let her in.

The same curtains were blown back into the room. There were old photos in glass that reflected the light and the fluttering lace. There was a nubby chenille spread, exactly like the one on which her lover lay in semiconscious bliss. She turned to look at Henri. In the fading light, it appeared as though he might have been crying. He wore only boxer shorts and a T-shirt. This was a very different

Henri from any of the Henris she had seen in the last few days. "Are you all right?"

"All right? For God's sake, who is all right? What does it mean?"

"Forget I asked. Should I leave?"

"No, no. Please, stay. My apologies. Have a seat." He waved toward the chairs. "How is Billy? Did the drugs work?"

"The drugs and some whiskey. He's feelin' no pain. At the moment he's semicomatose."

"Semi-comma-toes?" He got his notebook from his pants, which lay on the bed, and wrote it down. He put the notebook back, but it never occurred to him to put his pants on.

"He's smiling," said Anita, "but has no feeling below the waist."

"Ha—his toes . . . are like commas. They cannot stand up. Yes?"

"It's not just his toes."

"Aha."

"A rare problem for Billy," she said, trying to end the conversation.

"Penile dysfunction is a billion-dollar industry—ads, public exposures, drugs, doctors, therapists, and television talk programs dedicated to . . . how you say, limp dick problems."

"I don't want to hear it." She poured herself a shot and set the bottle on the coffee table.

"Yes. I will join you." He filled his glass from his diminishing supply of vodka. "Drink up."

She sat in the white wicker chair and tucked a leg up. "I don't know what to do about Billy. He's going to get us in a bad situation. He's fearless, and he can be a smart-mouth. Being around you makes him more manic than ever. There used to be some downtime, anyway."

"Yes. He caused a brawl. It was a bad scene. He's intense, but he is also . . . magical. He sees what others do not see. He goes too far . . . maybe. For Billy, everything has meaning and relation. He could make a film from random images—everything relates to everything. He has only to find the threads and weave them. Eventually the story comes."

"Except, no one can understand the story."

"For you, it is the opposite. You have a story already in mind, then you find images to make the story. But he finds the story in the images, in the bits and pieces of the world. It's all intertwined."

"And that's the problem. In this intertwined world of his, where do I fit?"

"Oh, dear. I am without a clue. I thought it was the other way around. I saw not much room in your world for him. This is true?"

"I have to make a living. I write the grants, do the paperwork, go to the suck-up parties for the media bureaucrats, do publicity, meetings, and conferences. He's just a goddamn gearhead. He's lost in that stuff and his zillions of images and plays on images. Nobody gets what he's doing."

"You are the perfect matchup. You want to be the filmmaker, but making films does not interest you. He wants to make films, but is not interested in being a filmmaker."

"That was mean, Henri. And it's not true. I want to make a different kind of film."

"You want the money film. I want you to make the money film— then I could find an American publisher for my books. But Billy does not care about that. He loves you, so he's helping make your film. You should let him do his art as well."

"I'm beginning to hate art."

"He hates NEH."

"He'll leave. Then where'll I be?" Henri picked up her bottle and reached over to give her a touch-up. "I'm fucked without him, and I'm fucked with him," said Anita.

"At least you're getting fucked." They got the giggles, missed the glass, and splattered whiskey on the floor. "We should get Dr. Perelli to come in. She's had a bad catsup day."

Henri, in boxers and barefooted, followed by Anita, tiptoed to Lucy's door and knocked.

"Just a minute." They waited, then the door opened a crack and Lucy peered out. "I'm nekkid and on the phone. What's up?"

"An analysis of the effect of cheap booze on the human psyche at ninety-two degrees Fahrenheit in room 227," Henri whispered. "Come as you are."

"I'll be down in a bit." Lucy closed the door, stretched across the white sheets, and picked the phone off the pillow. "I'm back. My confederates in crime came to lead me astray."

"Get rid of those goddamn people. They'll get you killed."

"Philip, please calm down. Thanks for your concern, but you don't have to worry. Other than having to hit that man with a catsup bottle, I've had a great time. You'd love them. Anita's a sexy, Texas redhead with spandex tights. Billy's . . . well, Billy's a cowboy anarchist. And Henri's a dweebie French guy who chain smokes, and survives on caffeine, alcohol, and sleeping pills, and he has a new theory every thirty miles. Him you probably wouldn't like. He's a hyperrelativist, but a gentle soul."

"I have no particular love of gentle souls. Most are brain-dead." He exhaled just short of a snort. "It sounds tiresome—I'm surprised you're so easily entertained."

"Well, maybe I'm feeling tolerant since I'm out of my clothes, lying here on clean white sheets, and talking to you while the wind plays with the curtains. Just your sort of thing, except it's too hot to make love."

"It's never too hot to make love."

There was a long pause, which meant he was fantasizing about her or had gone off on something else.

"Philip? Come back . . . from wherever you are."

"Have you found Jack what's-his-name?"

"Oh, him. He's living down here, and he was home this morning, but I haven't spoken with him. I met a friend of his last night, an Indian named Kills The Deer, who managed to reach him this morning. Kills The Deer says Miller wasn't too coherent. He might be sick."

"Or hung over."

"In any event, I'm going to call him tonight and ask if we can meet tomorrow."

"Why not see him tonight? You could drive back to Albuquerque in the morning and get into Reagan by ten o'clock tomorrow night."

"First of all, the car rental place down the street isn't open until tomorrow morning. And second, it's been a big day for me. I've never tried to crush a man's skull with a catsup bottle before.

Besides, there may be some prospects for the foundation down here. Sylvia said that this spring there was a fire in the foothills north of Silverado. Several thousand acres burned—some of it was private land. I want to fly the burn near the lower areas for ruins and talk to the landowners."

"When do you plan to do that?"

"If there's a plane available, I'll do it tomorrow afternoon. I'll try to see Miller in the morning, though."

Philip was quietly processing. "Well . . . I'll be in meetings most of the day, so I guess you better call in the evening."

"Are you disappointed because I haven't talked to Miller, or because I'm not coming home tomorrow?"

"Both . . . I guess."

"Come on, be happy for me. I saved a guy's life, I didn't get killed, and I have a chance to find some really interesting sites in the next few days. Plus, I'm going to find where your damn toe came from. Let's hear it for me, Philip. Hooray for Lucy. Go Lucy, go."

"I love you." He was laughing.

"I love you, too, Philip. Everything will be fine, don't worry. I'll try to call before eleven, your time."

She rolled over onto her back, spread her arms out, and stared at the long blades of the ceiling fan. They turned slowly, ineffectual against the wind blown in from the desert. She closed her eyes and let her mind skim along the ridge lines where fires had burned the ground clear of grass and juniper, revealing faint traces of early Mimbres pit houses. The desert wind lifted her high into the mountains above the canyons. Wild burros, startled by her shadow, looked up, searching for her in the sun.

Her wings were clipped by Anita at the door. "You okay? I didn't hear you on the phone. It's been nearly an hour."

"Sorry, Anita. I fell asleep. I'll be down after I make another call. Give me ten minutes."

Lucy heard a girl's disappointment in Anita's "Okay." It struck her that Anita was worried she would lose Billy. Did she love him or just need him? Lucy assumed she would not be around long enough to see their melodrama run its course.

She dialed Jack's number and waited for several rings. She was about to hang up when a ragged male voice answered.

"Hello, is this Jack Miller?"

"Yep."

"I'm Lucy Perelli, an archaeologist. I believe Kills The Deer Burnum called you earlier to let you know I wanted to speak with you."

"Oh, yeah. What kind of trouble's he in?"

"None that I know of. Would it be too much of an imposition for me to come out to your place sometime tomorrow?"

"I . . . ah, company is something I really don't need at the moment. I'm having an extreme reaction to . . . to an insect sting. What's this about, anyway?"

"Several things. For one, I'm interested in a frozen toe."

"Sorry to disappoint you, but I'm not much of an expert on frozen toes. Have you tried farther north?"

"I understand that a Jack Miller of 7736 Zuma Canyon Road, Silverado, New Mexico, sent a toe packed in dry ice to a lab tech at O'Connell Biotechnics in Berkeley, California, on June thirtieth of this year. An off-record dating test was requested. Would you like to know how old your toe is, Mr. Miller?"

"Are you with the feds, Miss Perelli?"

"No. I work for a foundation that protects archaeological sites around the U.S. I have neither the desire nor inclination to involve the feds in this. I have other information you may be interested in about the toe, and I would like to know where it was found—that's it."

"Your interest is purely scientific?"

Lucy laughed. "I have no interest in its market value or any illegal activity, if that's what you mean."

"How do I know you're on the level?"

"You don't, but that doesn't mean we can't talk."

"Stunning logic. No doubt you know how to find me."

"Kills The Deer gave me directions."

"Here's a little tip: Never trust a man who gives you directions to my house. Tomorrow, ten-thirty?"

"Ten-thirty it is. Thank you."

"Call before you come, please. I've been a little out of it."

"So you say. I'll be ready for anything. Goodbye."

That damn toe. Berndt Bernowski, Jack's fishing partner, had sent the toe from Juneau. His wife had, actually.

Years ago, Berndt showed Jack an ice cave he had discovered in one of the hanging glaciers in a high mountain valley south of Juneau. The cave had a second opening that drew air, hastening the melt during the summer. Berndt became obsessed by a dark shape they could see deep in the outer wall of the ice cave when the sun was behind it. He wanted to start chopping. Jack wanted to wait.

"So you chop it out," Jack had said. "It's probably a rock. What else could it possibly be?"

"It could be a man. He'd have to be thousands of years old."

"All right. Say that's what's moving toward us at what—six to ten inches a year? Suppose we chop it out now. Find out in five days what we'll find out in twenty years. Then what? The government comes, archaeologists come, reporters come, cameras come. It's a zoo. They'll even run us off. Then the helicopter comes, lifts it out—they take your iceman to a freezer at the University of Washington. You'll get to read about it in *The Juneau Tribune*. Then it'll be gone. There won't be that mysterious thing moving toward you through the ice to wonder about for the next twenty years. You found it, Berndt. You can do what you want. But chopping it out will not bring you any joy, or happiness, or whatever the hell you're looking for."

"Yeah?"

"Yeah. I want us to come here every year for the next twenty years and stare into the ice and wonder what it is. If it's what you say it is, we can let it break away and fall into the sea. No cameras, no archaeologists."

Berndt relented, grudgingly—he knew it would take forever to melt. They made a trip each year to peer into the ice, speculating on the mystery held in its grip. The object slowly moved toward them—year after year for twelve years, until they were certain it was a man, lying on his side. That the form trapped in the ice was human gripped their imaginations. It kept them up nights speculating about his origins, studying maps and reading articles about ancient migrations. Still there were several years of ice between them and their iceman.

In the middle of June, Jack got a letter from Berndt saying he'd had a heart attack. He was afraid he was only good for another couple of trips up the glacier to the cave. He intended to bore through the ice and take a sample of their frozen man so they could find out how old he was, if that was okay.

Jack phoned Berndt. "How's your ticker?"

"Hey, Miller. Don't get old. It's a killer."

"Is it bad?"

"Naw. I have to slow down a little, go on a diet, and take all these damn pills. But I'll be okay. I like my doctor. She's pretty good, and she's pretty."

"Did she say it's okay to climb that glacier?"

"Haven't discussed it."

"And I can guess why. If she says it's okay, then it's okay with me. It's your iceman. Remember to take some dry ice up with you. When you get back, call me and I'll give you a name and an address in Berkeley. Send it overnight. I'll have to set things up. This has to be off the record. Nobody can know about it but you, me, and the lab tech. I don't want to get him in trouble. Same goes for you. What you're doing isn't exactly legal. Okay?"

"Okay, Jack."

"Say hello to Yolanda."

Two weeks later Jack got the toe, packed in dry ice, and a letter from Berndt's wife. She said Berndt had had a series of small strokes.

"I'll keep you informed about his progress. The box (enclosed) was in the freezer with your name on it. I asked Berndt about it. He said I should send it to you. He told me not to look. I didn't—Promise. Best, Yolanda."

Jack called Yolanda. "What's this about small strokes?"

"Don't worry, Jack. Berndt is fine. Right now he is forgetting things, but the lady doctor says he will get better. Between you and me, I think he had those strokes so he could see her more. I'll keep you posted. Okay, Jack? I have to see what Berndt wants. Bye."

Jack made his connection with the lab tech, the son of a Mexican family who worked for him years ago, and arranged to have him date the toe.

"No problem," said Carlos. "I do this sort of thing all the time. My boss doesn't mind as long as I get my work done. I can always come in on a weekend. It may be a while before I get to it, but send it along."

"Just be careful, Carlos."

"No problem, Jack. No problem."

Lucy lay on the bed thinking about her conversation with Jack. Maybe she had been too aggressive. She had to admit she liked Kills The Deer's image of him. It went with the voice. She wondered what he'd have thought if he knew she was naked.

NINE

Jack was asleep in a chair by the heavy, Spanish table where the parrot trainer stood poised in her bowl, which was propped against some books. For an hour, he had tried to conjure her out of the bowl, watching for the slightest motion, moving his head from side to side until his eyelids slid closed and he laid his head on the table.

He yawned and stretched his neck and shoulders. A jab of pain from the sting brought him back to full consciousness. When he looked at the bowl again, she was patting her parrot. He was delighted. Then she stopped. Then started. Then stopped. She was playing with him.

"Wake up, Jack. I watched you sleep all night. You're a mess. No girl's going to want you."

"That bad?"

"Well, not as bad as yesterday."

Gingerly, he touched the side of his face—not as bad as yesterday.

"Coffee," he announced, as though he had been searching for something and suddenly found it. "Will you wait while I make some coffee?"

"Waiting is what I do. Don't hurry, I've got 'til the rainy season."

"I'll be right back." He limped into the kitchen.

He could hear her soft, lyrical voice in the kitchen, even over the sound of the coffee grinder. "I am happy to see you're getting better, Jack. I'll dance for you when you're ready for a little excitement."

She didn't need to shout. Her voice, of course, was inside his head. He could be deaf and hear her. When he turned off the coffee grinder, there was a gentle knocking at the door.

It rattled him. Should he hide the parrot trainer? No. As near as he could tell, she was well hidden in his head. Then there was swollen and ugly, but that wouldn't matter. All the better. Swollen and ugly was just right. Might scare that archaeologist a little.

He opened the door only a crack. There was Lucy with short black hair, looking very field ready in a man's white cotton shirt with sleeves rolled back, khaki shorts, and hiking boots. She had a leather satchel on a strap that crossed down from her shoulder between her breasts. It made her look in charge and sexy at the same time. He regarded the strap, the breasts, and thought women send the damnedest signals—then again, we receive when they're not sending. "I thought you were going to call."

"I didn't want to take a chance you would turn me down."

Miller looked like hazardous waste. Lucy stared at the swollen eye and the grim, dirty, unshaved face. What, she wondered, had Philip gotten her into?

Behind her Jack could see a swoopy, red rental car that resembled a giant tennis shoe. There was a long pause before he said, "I'm hallucinating. Have you had yours?"

"Had my what?"

"Coffee. Sorry. I meant, I mean, I'm having coffee. Would you like some coffee? Christ. You really should have called."

"Well, was I right?"

He opened the door. "I would have—come in—turned you down, but now you are here, and I must treat you accordingly."

"Meaning you won't ignore me."

"Coffee? Or did you want to jump right in with the toe. How much jail time are we talking about?"

"You're taking this in the wrong direction. Do you worry about jail often?"

"Not so much anymore. I've moved on."

"You look terrible. Are you all right?"

"I'll live. Thanks for asking. It's only an overreaction to a sting of some kind."

He ushered her into the living room and watched as she took it in. She was attentive, but it was her job to observe.

She restrained herself or tried. There were many odd, unfamiliar objects, and such things could offer a window into a person, but what window was this—a purple and rose Madonna, a black Christ, a green and yellow St. Augustine, a white hand of Fatima, the skeleton of a carp?

She stopped at a small medicine bag that was meant to hold a talisman. Jack picked up the bag, stiff with age, and turned it so a beautifully made Clovis spear point dropped into her waiting hand. The point was a little under three inches long, half an inch wide, and three-sixteenths of an inch thick. The Clovis had used them to hunt mammoths and giant bison in North America, ten to twelve thousand years ago. She looked at him for an answer.

"I found it in a Mimbres cache in a cave. An elderly Navajo man said it was made by the gods. I wonder what the Mimbres thought?"

She studied the perfection of the point and wondered what form of power it bestowed upon its Mimbres finder. The next object that stopped her was a small horse or half horse, six to seven inches long, missing its back legs and its ears. With Jack's approval, she examined it closely. The horse had been made by a child who had crudely rolled the clay for the legs, body, neck, and head and stuck them together. The little fingerprints were still visible. The child's mother had probably made the two perfect, tiny clay bowls pressed into the sides of the little horse. The bowls, which represented woven baskets, had broken off. All that was left of them were smooth, quarter-round indents on either side of the horse. The child had scratched in a mane and forelock and made a mouth that barely turned at the edges in a sublime smile, which made Lucy smile. "Where did it come from?"

"I dug it out of a clay bank along the Colorado about twenty years ago. Its head and front feet were sticking out waiting to plunge into the river."

She scanned the rest of the room until her eyes caught the parrot trainer's bowl. "Is that from a local dig?"

"Yes, it's Mimbres, but unusual. Very unusual."

She walked to the table, leaned over, and studied the bowl for several minutes. "They were the ones who buried their relatives in a fetal position under the floor of the house."

"That was them."

"It seemed bizarre. Many tribes had a dread of dead souls."

"Which may have had something to do with why a bunch of farmers might have started burying their dead under the house—it would frighten off raiding parties who were terrified of spirits."

"After a few decades it would become the honorable thing to do—showing respect for the ancestors."

She eyed the parrot trainer bowl carefully. "The Mimbres buried their dead with a bowl inverted over the head."

"Uh-huh. Did you want coffee?"

"Oh, yes. Thank you. Black, please."

As he hobbled off to make coffee, she turned her attention to the parrot trainer. She was not an expert on Mimbres imagery, but the drawing had great appeal—it was the body gesture. When Jack returned, carefully balancing a cup on a saucer, Lucy looked up. "The painter must have loved this girl very much."

Hearing Lucy voice his thought about the painter and the girl startled him. The cup slipped from the saucer, shattered, and slithered across the floor from the kitchen doorway into the living room. He just stared at her.

"Are you all right? Can you say something?"

"Ah . . . I dropped your cup?"

"Would you sit down, please?"

"I'm okay. Really. Let me clean this up and make you another."

She got down and started picking up the pieces. To her surprise, it was a fine china cup, or had been, with a delicate weave of pale roses. "Oh, it was beautiful. I'm sorry."

"There're too many cups, never enough shards. Breaking crockery's a serious business. It's our duty to the future of archaeology.

Many shards make for doctoral dissertations and good employment opportunities."

She was on her knees, preoccupied in her search for slivers of porcelain, when she noticed his pants were torn and bloodstained. "You're all bloody. What have you been doing?"

"If I told you, I'd probably have to go to jail."

"Really?"

"I'm a terrible person. The man whose toe you fancy would testify to that."

"And what have you done with your toeless man?"

"Left him in his glacial palace. The toe was the easiest part to get to, and there was no point in digging him all the way out—we'd have had to move him and store him in an industrial freezer somewhere, which would have raised a few eyebrows."

"Do you know if it's a him?"

"I always assumed it was—my chauvinism showing."

She stood up, holding the shards in one hand. "Well, it is, and he's going to change a lot of archaeological theory, produce endless doctoral dissertations and employment opportunities for years to come." She looked at him, waiting for a reaction.

Jack sat down. "You've run the DNA on him?"

"Not personally. The chief lab rat at O'Connell took the toe away from your friend, did the DNA, and verified it twice. He's very good. He has a match. Care to guess where?"

"Tell me."

"Your iceman's not Siberian, he predates Clovis, and he carried DNA markers which relate him to early Europeans. He's around fifteen thousand years old."

"The European thing would cause an entertaining little flap. How did he get himself frozen in a glacier sixteen hundred feet above the sea?"

"I have no idea. Are you going to tell me where you found him?"

Jack avoided her eyes and studied the splatter pattern of dark coffee across the brick floor. "You have the toe?"

"No. I doubt if either of us will be seeing the toe again. Nobody is going to admit he has it or has ever seen it. But what would you want it for anyway?"

"I never wanted it. Can I make you another cup of coffee?"

"Sure." She looked at her handful of shattered cup. "What do I do with these?"

"In here." He got up, limped into the kitchen, and pointed to a wicker basket near the refrigerator.

She found a plastic grocery bag, carefully slid the pieces in, and dropped it into the basket. A water bowl for the cat sat next to the refrigerator. Three turtles graced the bottom and a snake circled the inside rim. "Nice Mimbres bowl," she said.

"It's a fake."

"Louise Burnum's?"

"You've been prying."

She grinned and gave him a shrug, then went back to where he had dropped her coffee, sponged up the spill, and rinsed out the sponge.

He measured coffee into a little espresso maker. "The Louise part's right, but her last name wasn't Burnum. Kills The Deer's grandmother on his mother's side made it." He poured in a quarter cup of water, flipped the switch, and waited.

She was trying to guess his response to her question about the location of the iceman. She had spent years trying to stop his kind. Now she had to deal with him. "So, you have what we want," she said. "And you don't seem to want it since there's nothing you can do with it but get into deeper trouble than you're in already."

"I doubt I'm in any trouble at all. I'm in New Mexico, the toe's in Limbo, California, and the body's in a glacier south of Juneau. You could never find the man in the ice without me leading you to him or locating the cave on a satellite map." The coffee machine began hissing.

"So the iceman's in Alaska?"

"Yeah. Somewhere in six thousand square miles of ice." He handed her the cup and started one for himself.

"Thanks." She stared out the kitchen window toward the creek and the mudmen. She remembered Kills The Deer had mentioned them when he said Jack was a strange man. Seeing the mudmen made her even more curious about Jack. She was going to ask about the figures when he distracted her.

"How many other archaeologists would want in on this?" he asked. "Maybe I should auction it off on the Internet?"

"Put your guy on the Internet, and you'll get Aryan survivalists offering Nazi memorabilia and a three-year supply of beans and rice."

"Princeton would give me a doctorate."

"No doubt."

"These things always come with a curse, you know. It'll cause you a lot of grief. The University of Washington will be all over it before you can get it out of the ice. Five different tribes will claim it's theirs—you'll be up to your fanny in lawsuits. Leave him in the ice. Sooner or later he'll slide into the ocean and we won't have to read about him in *The New York Times* for the next ten years."

"Science, Jack."

"Science is way down in fourth or fifth place. Finds like these are huge. They mean money and status. But you don't strike me as the money and status type. You got down on your knees and picked up a broken cup. You didn't break it, yet you said you were sorry. You're not interested in the iceman. Who wants the big kill?"

"You're very clever. Only he's already had his big kill."

"Your husband? Your boss?"

"Neither."

"Anyway, he's hungry for another big deal, which means he's been dry for a while. Is he losing ground to the young hotshots?"

"Well, I'll let you discuss that with him. His name is Philip Sachs."

"Why should I help Philip Sachs?"

"So what's your plan?"

"No plan." The machine hissed at him. He took his coffee and gestured toward the living room.

She went ahead, talking over her shoulder. "You're just going to let the most important archaeological find in North America slide into the sea?"

"Why not? That's how the Indians would have it."

"It isn't for the Indians to say. The man was not Indian."

"All the more reason they'd want him to disappear into the sea."

He glanced at the parrot trainer, knowing she was taking it all in, then sat down across the table from Lucy. "So why should I give this guy up for the sake of some stranger's career?"

"Dr. Sachs is the Director of First American Studies of the Benning Center for American Archaeology. He's a genius. He has given his life to archaeology. He's a great teacher and has influenced a generation of archaeologists."

"He certainly has a devotee in you."

"He's not some cheap, academic huckster."

"Really? If he were on the level, why would he send you down here to do his dirty work? If it's so important, why didn't he come himself?"

"I was attending a conference in Albuquerque. It seemed logical for me to come down here and talk to you directly."

"Why didn't he contact the feds and the Alaskan Heritage Foundation and tell them about the toe?"

"You're not naive. You know the importance of being the first to announce a major find." Miller seemed not to want anything out of this, or he was driving the price up. "You mailed the toe from New Mexico. There are stiff penalties for failing to report human remains. If the feds get into this, you'll have some other serious problems. At a minimum you've broken three state and two federal laws."

"Stiff penalties? That's appropriate."

"You're not taking this seriously."

Jack rubbed his arm. "Maybe not. In any case, I'm not going to be bullied. I've been watching the man in the ice for twelve years. I liked watching him. I'm not making a dime out of this, I don't care about publicity, and I'm not even the one who took the toe. I sent it to the lab as a favor for a friend. If I'd known it was coming, I would have had him send it to the lab himself. Whatever I've done that's illegal will pale next to the stories I'll give *The New York Times* and the *National Enquirer* if your professor sics the feds on me. The media will make him look like the fool he is—he can kiss off what's left of his career."

She was grinding her teeth by the time he finished. "I'm sorry. I didn't mean to sound like I was threatening you."

"I don't believe that for a moment, but I can empathize. You're trying to make a living like everyone else."

"It's more than just a living, it's our lives. A lot of us would do this without pay."

"Lucky you. Most people don't get to do what they care about. You should take a pay cut as a matter of principle."

"There's no way I can get your cooperation on this, is there?"

"My relations with archaeologists have been nasty and brutal. So you can understand my lack of enthusiasm." The parrot trainer turned slightly and stared at him. He glanced over at the coffee stain on the bricks, recalled the cup slipping from the saucer and Lucy telling him how much the painter had loved the girl.

He looked at the woman who wanted the iceman. "On the other hand," he paused for moment, staring into his coffee, "recent events have changed things. For the last twelve years, a friend and I have been checking out a dark shape frozen deep in the wall of an ice cave, in a melting glacier. As the ice melted, it became obvious that the shape was a person. My friend bored through several feet of ice to the man's toe which was sent to me to have dated. I would have been happy had it remained a mystery for the rest of my life. But now I have to think about it being exposed and probed, about investigations, the inevitable hearings, lawyers, and ham-handed politicians. Who, in their right mind," he paused to consider his current state of mind, "would want that?"

"We can protect you."

"A written guarantee from your Dr. Sachs wouldn't protect a lab rat, much less a pot thief."

"Can we think about this for a day or so before you make up your mind?"

He appreciated the fact that she could back off and give them both a chance to reconsider the consequences. In spite of everything that had been said, she seemed calm and composed. She was a striking mix of Italian and something, maybe Irish. He had been so occupied with himself and the situation that he had not bothered to see her as anything other than a threat or an annoyance. Under almost any other circumstance, he would think she was attractive and someone he would want to know. Her take on the parrot trainer made her more than intriguing. The shape and fullness of her mouth caught his attention. The sensation woke him up. He smiled. "I'll call when the poison's out of my blood. Maybe I'll be a little less hostile."

"I caught you at a bad time, and I was pushy. It's just that the find would be very significant for Philip—in several ways." She wondered if she should have invoked Philip again, but it was meant to put things in perspective—at least for herself. It was a way of saying, This is for someone who's important to me—so I may be as interested in you as you seem to be in me, but it's not going anywhere.

Pleasantries and graceful gestures got her out of the house without botching their truce. He watched her drive off before he went back to the table and his untouched coffee.

As he sipped, the parrot trainer emerged from her bowl and grew to her normal size. She sat on the table, pulling her legs up to her chin. He could see her dark brown eyes beneath the mask.

"What are you drinking, Jack?"

"Coffee. I don't think you've had coffee."

"I watched you with that woman. You like her, and she likes you even though you're ugly." She stretched her arms out, then stood up and pushed her bare foot toward him. "You will fall in love with her."

She was brazen and a little intimidating. He tried being dismissive. "What do you know about love?" He should have known better.

"I was in love with all the men, but that was a secret. I pretended not to see them," she turned her back to him, gently swished her strings, and looked over her shoulder, "but I missed nothing." She jumped down and sat next to him. "Because I could not have a lover, I loved every one of them."

"You were a virgin?"

He saw a flash beneath the mask as she rolled her eyes. "Yes, I was a virgin. It meant more corn for the village. When I was old enough to have a man, the corn maidens came to my dreams. They told me it was a parrot clan woman's desire for men that makes the corn grow." She rose as she spoke, standing tall and straight and looked down at him. "A parrot woman full of yearning will enchant the clouds to gather in the mountains. In the late summer, the corn maidens sent the flute player into my dreams." The memory of the flute player excited her. She began turning slowly, around and around. "His playing filled me with a desire. I woke up craving every man in the village. I burned for several days. My passion enticed the clouds until the sky was dense and thick with rain for the yearning earth." She was speaking quickly, caught up in her memories.

"Our ancestors' spirits were released through the holes in their burial bowls when they died. They sat in the sky above the mountains and waited. When the clouds came, the ancestors danced on them, making lightning, and shouted back and forth, making thunder." She had begun to spin, discharging a stream of words. "Then the rains came. First as small drops that sprinkled across the plaza, waking the air, drawing the people out of their houses. We breathed the new air into our dried, summer brains and we shouted, danced, and whirled around." She was turning so fast she became a blur, emitting an eerie wail. Her parrot began flapping its wings, hopping in the air, and trying to mimic his mistress's wailing.

She collapsed, rather dramatically, Jack thought, on the table. The parrot hopped over and rubbed its head against her mask. She sat up and slid over next to Jack, her legs hanging over the edge of the table, and patted the parrot.

"Some families did not make the hole in the burial bowls. These families would only release their ancestors when there was a dire need. If the clouds were stubborn and withheld their rain, a priest went to those families. He would say it was time to set the spirits of their ancestors free. The unbroken bowls were uncovered. Those without bowls to break gathered in the plaza in silence and listened for the ancestors. Then by a signal from the priest to the boys on the roof top to the women below, the bowls would be struck, letting loose the ancestors to shoot up all at once, to dance lightning and shout thunder."

Jack's eyes followed her body down from mask to her breasts and belly to her swinging legs. "So the ancestor became more powerful the longer the bowl was unbroken?"

"Some said that."

"And you've been waiting a thousand years?"

Her deep, throaty laugh was as playful as it was menacing.

He laughed. "God help us. Why was a parrot clan woman chosen to seduce the clouds?"

"The parrots got their feathers from the rainbow, and parrots can talk. Because we honored and respected the parrots, said sweet things to them, and fed them treats, the parrots spoke to the clouds for us. They would say, These are the best people, very kind and generous. You should rain down so their corn will grow."

"Pardon me for being slow, but why did you need the parrot if you could seduce the clouds?"

"It's not easy getting rain. Sometimes you needed a little oomph— like parrots and letting loose the ancestors."

"And for you, when it rained—what was it like? Did you dance and shout?"

"For me it was different. When I got my first breath of the coming rain, the tingling in my womb began slowly turning. When the raindrops began, the sensation spread through me like a glimmering snake whirling its way through my body, throwing me one way, then another, until the tingling came through my skin and seeped into the ground with the rain. My fire fizzled out. I became light as a rainbow feather. Then I waited for another year, until the corn maidens brought the flute man to make my dreams juicy."

"You were an orgasmic virgin."

"I was still a virgin."

"Well twirled, though," he teased.

She knew her fireworks had his attention. After all, he was a man. "I helped bring rain. The corn grew. My people ate and had more babies. And, yes, I loved getting 'well twirled.' It filled me up and reminded me of my purpose until it was time to do it again."

Then she stopped swinging her legs and looked at him through her mask. Her voice lost its exuberance. "But in the end, everything we did to make rain failed. Everything failed."

"You were more successful than you could ever imagine."

"That's a surprise. I thought we were all done for. We thought we lived at the end of life. There was a long time with little rain. Way to the north, the poorest farmers there were dying. They did not have streams to irrigate their farms and depended on rain even more than we did." Willow's words seemed to transform her entire body. She stood up and began telling her story with many gestures and extraordinary dexterity. Jack watched as she became emaciated.

"After many deaths, they began to look for ways to make it rain again. Their tall headman wore a hideous mask." To show the height of the tall chief she stretched her body to six feet and her mask transformed into a dark, shapeless face, matted in hair and dried blood. "He told them they needed to build more shrines and roads for promenade and rituals, of which they already had more than they needed. Most of his people believed him, or didn't know what else to do, and they began building and digging and clearing and making grand things to honor this man, who claimed he was their god."

She reverted to her normal self and tilted her head to the side. "There was even less food than before. Some people wondered if he was a god at all. There were rumors he ate and shit like everyone else, but he was different from other people. He had lighter skin, he was very tall, and he knew how to build big buildings, but he didn't know how to make rain.

"A few of the northern people, who lived in little pueblos farther to the west of this tall god, came down to our valley to learn about our five clans and how they brought rain, made rules, kept peace among ourselves, and stopped men who wanted lots of power.

"These rebellious northerns were sworn to secrecy. Each clan took some of these people in and taught them what that clan's responsibilities were, who its animals were, and in what ways the clans could work together. Then the northerners went home and started clans in their own pueblos. A few even buried their dead in their houses.

"What we told them caused a lot of trouble. Some pueblos turned away from the tall chief and his people. His hatred was aimed at those who abandoned him as a god. He sent cannibal gangs to kill whole villages, and he sent a gang to terrify us. We were warned they were coming, and we moved out of our village into the entrance to the middle world. But the northmen found us." Willow sat on the table, drew her legs up, and looked at Jack. "They ate one of our young men in the field below the cliff. We were not warriors and seeing that made us sick with fear." She was quiet for a while. When she resumed, there was a vengeful edge in her voice. "But we tricked them into death.

"Even after we were rid of them, we had another year of drought. Everything was coming to an end. We wanted to know if there was a way to change what was happening, so we thought we would go down into the first world and ask our ancestors. The great-grandmothers and grandfathers, who had told the stories about the formless beings, said there are three worlds—the first world is the world of beginning and death, from which all people emerged and where they go after they die and become cloud spirits, and rain down into the earth again. The second world is a long, dark passage where the formless beings became animal-people. In the second world, Coatimundi, the animal of many parts, divided people from animals and led them up into the third world of light and rain and growing things and showed them how to live. At first it was too bright, and everyone was blinded by the light. Coatimundi made all the people hold hands, and the animals gripped the tails of other animals in their mouths, then he led them from thing to thing and explained the third world and how it worked. Of course, some animals lost their grip."

"What happened to them?"

"They bumped into things. That's why they have stubby noses." Her laughter echoed down the corridor into the many rooms and made the house feel alive.

"When their eyes began to work, the people could see the dome of the sky that rests on the earth like an overturned bowl.

"Everyone makes this journey between the first world and the third world many times." She paused for a moment, then with a rueful smile added, "Except for myself."

Jack recognized Willow's view of the world as a primitive version of those familiar to many modern Pueblo Indians. It lacked only the benefits of manipulation through time and Catholicism. What intrigued him about Willow's cosmology was that there was no celestial world beyond. The sky was a bowl that matched the underworld sky. The two bowls were separated by a thick layer of earth and rock. Willow's worlds were symmetrical, and the patterns of life and death were as cyclical as nature itself.

"At the time when things were bad," she said, "we went down into the second world and searched for days, thinking we might see our ancestors to learn how to change the way things were going."

"Does the passage that leads into the second world begin as a steep slope just past where you were buried?"

"Yes. But the second world was mostly tunnels and big cave rooms. One room was alive. We could hear it breathing, and it watched us with a thousand eyes. In another place we saw Coatimundi painted on a wall by the ancient people. Farther on we found the entrance to the first world. It was beneath a pond that glowed from the underworld sky. But we decided not to go down into the first world."

"Why?"

"We were afraid. When the ancestors died and returned to the first world, did they lose their form again? Would they have eyes to know us by? They might think we were an enemy and kill us. And even if they didn't, would going into first world upset the balance between life and death? Of course we didn't think of these things until we found the entrance. We could not know the answers, so we turned back."

"How did you get into the second world?"

"For several days we wove a rope from willow bark until it reached far into the darkness. A young man from the snake clan went down first. A few others, including myself, decided to go down.

"I saw the rotted bodies of the northmen in the torchlight. I was full of joy and pride, because I was the one who made the plan that tricked them."

"How did this trick of yours work?"

"We had carved little holes in the cave wall to display our magic parrot feathers, which the northmen discovered when they came to look for food. They also found an olla of soup we made from cactus buds. The soup made your head a little foggy and agreeable. We drank a little at night to get rid of our hunger. But the northmen drank lots." She laughed and imitated the men staggering around.

"Parrot feathers glow after you drink this cactus. The more you drink, the more they glow, until you see a powerful magic shining from their tips. The northmen were half crazed. 'Where did you find these wonderful feathers?' they asked. Their eyes were shining. They grinned and showed their teeth. We knew they would eat us.

"I showed them the passage that slanted down into the second world. 'Our feathers come from a blind woman who raises her parrots down there.' They edged along with their torches and stared into the darkness below. 'How do you go down?' they asked. I told them that each man had to grab hold of another's wrist, making a long line, so the ones in back could keep the ones in front from falling. Then my aunt sang a wailing chant. She told them it would protect their descent into the second world if they chanted as loud as they could. I waved a handful of glowing feathers in their faces as they practiced the chant."

Willow let go with an ungodly, wailing moan that sounded like a choir of drunken coyotes. Willow's arms flailed the air, conducting her chain gang wailers.

"The cactus and the chanting made them ecstatic. We formed them into a long line and led them into the passage—each man secured by the grip he had on the man behind him. Then it became very steep, and the rock was slick and smelled of fish oil."

Willow reached up, grasping an imaginary hand as her feet slid forward, spilling over the table until she teetered on the edge. "The leader slipped, swinging around with his torch," with her free hand she waved an imaginary firebrand above her head, "burning the second man, whose shrieks of pain were lost in the wailing chants of the others. The second man tried to let go, but the first clung with a death grip, pulling the second along, and that man held tight to the next who clung to the next and so on, until they were all pulled wailing and screaming into the second world."

Willow collapsed in a heap of tangled limbs. She seemed to have generated several extra sets by the time she landed. Her masked head emerged from the tangle.

Jack was dismayed and a bit unnerved, but he gave her performance a positive critique. "You have an extravagant and distinctive style. Transforming, even."

She ignored him and went on. "A few on the end managed to break away, but we came at them with long poles and pushed them over, and they fell into the darkness. Their screams were loud and long and echoed through the many passages of the second world." She assumed her former proportions and limb count and sat on the edge of the table, swinging her legs. "It was a perfect day."

"Gruesome, but ingenious. How many died?"

"I think twenty, maybe more. We saved one for a lesson."

"I hate to ask."

She leaned toward him. "The three brothers of the young man the cannibals ate, took the man we saved to his home in the north. The four of them walked through the mountains for seven days, traveling until they saw a great round house many stories high. The house was white and shining in the early dawn. Their captive was home. He realized they meant to let him go. He was very happy.

"They pointed toward the great house on the other side of the valley, and he nodded his head and smiled. A broad road led to the great house. They pointed to the road, nodded and smiled and demonstrated that he should walk backward down the middle of the fine wide road toward the great house. After they were sure he understood, they gave him several big drinks of the cactus juice to keep him from passing out, stuffed grass in his mouth to stifle his screams, carefully cut and peeled the skin from his head, turned it around, and sewed it on backward, leaving little eye holes to see through and another hole to breathe through.

"After he had rested they gave him sticks for canes and helped him practice walking backward. They walked along with him until they were near the great house of white stone. It was quiet. No one was in sight. They kept walking toward the house. The only sound was from the birds and the moaning of the backward man. No one was cooking yet, and the only odors came from morning dew on the sage. When they came to a shallow gully, the brothers ran down the gully and out of sight. Even though the backward man was getting weaker, he kept going. Maybe he believed his people could save him. But no one came, so the brothers began screeching like owls. Still no one appeared at the door of the round house.

"Then a short, thin northman emerged from behind the house. He stared at the backward man for a while, not believing what he was seeing—then he began to shout. People came running and stood in the road watching the backward man coming toward them. They were so quiet they could hear his moaning and the skritch, skritch of his canes. They looked at his quivering legs and naked butt, at the streaks of blood down his back from the tight necklace around his neck. The man, whose face had been young and beautiful, now had a flap of skin for a nose. The eyes were vacant bone-white holes. The mouth was drawn back by stitches into a thin, twisted leer. The people did not recognize him. Since he had no clothes, they did not understand he was one of them. I am sure they thought he was a demon.

"The brothers only knew that the northmen were frightened because they recoiled as the backward man moved toward them, feeling his way with canes. The tall chief appeared in the doorway and walked into the bright sun. He wore a huge mask matted with layers of dried blood, mud, and hair. There were only holes for his eyes, nose, and mouth. For several moments he stood with his head tilted toward the sky, holding his palms open to the sun. After a long time, he lowered his massive head. From the top of the white stairs he watched the backward man come toward him. It was quiet except for the moaning and the scritching canes. Then the tall man understood—the man was one of his own. Through the hole in the tall man's mask, the brothers could see him smile. He admired this hideous trick.

"His smile was terrifying, because his teeth were not those of a human being but the sharp pointed teeth of a cat—teeth made to tear raw flesh. This man-cat was a true demon, who ruled his people with terror.

"The brothers hid until dark, then started home. We were even more afraid of the northmen after that."

Jack was no longer thinking, What a charming girl lives in my brain. "They say you should choose your demons carefully."

She ignored the possibility that he was talking about his own demons. "Fortunately, the northmen had bigger problems than us."

"You've given me a lot to think about. I'll be back in a while."

He got up and walked outside into the early heat. Where, in the deep pool of his unconscious, had Willow's story materialized? Years ago, he suspected the Mimbres had developed an early form of kachina, and for a hundred years archaeologists had written about the Chaco cannibals. But there were many details in her story that were unfamiliar.

After wandering through the mudmen for a while, he began to relax. His arm was not as stiff, and his face was feeling like his face. He went back to the house and looked at himself in the bathroom mirror. He shaved, showered, and changed clothes. He fixed some eggs and toast, which he ate in the kitchen.

He cleaned up the dishes and went back to the living room and put the dried oranges back in Willow's bowl. "I'm going to be gone for the rest of the day. I have to get my truck and go into town." Simple good manners had made him tell her his plans.

She called after him, "Have a nice day," with a soft taunting laugh.

SNYDER COUNTY LIBRARY
1 N HIGH ST
SELINSGROVE PA 17870-1599

TEN

He walked up the lane to the dirt road without limping. The stiffness in his arm and the swelling in his eye were gone. He could wink. Winking was an important form of communication with children. He had not winked at an adult for years. Something was amiss with adults.

This time The Sisters all waved at Jack, evidence that Marguerite had a change of heart. Her head hovered beneath the open hood of her Caddy. Except for Snake, the Sisters were sitting in the car. Snake stood on the trunk, holding her cat with one arm while she pointed to the sky with the other. Except for the lack of stars, it looked as though she was giving the cat an astronomy lesson.

Cadillacs, Lincolns, and LTDs, between fifteen and twenty-five years old, had been the cars of choice for Southwest marginals, but that phase was about over. You could get three hundred thousand miles out of a Toyota. Junker 'yotas speckled the back lots and roads of the high plains desert, suppressing property values—and thereby saving the land by destroying the landscape.

In the West, the perversity of aging automobiles was the main reason women of a certain age and income bracket even bothered with men or marriage.

"Havin' kids," Marguerite informed Jack, "all starts 'cause the car won't." She was considering the mysteries of the wires beneath the hood as she imparted her insight into the mysteries of creation. She looked up at him, actually smiled, and shouted to the girls, "Get me some baking soda and a hammer. Now . . . please." They scrambled out and fled toward the trailer. Snake, having given up on the cat, stood on the trunk and gazed at the sky.

"You wouldn't want to trade that truck for this Caddy, would you? It's a classic."

"So's the truck." He hesitated for a moment, second-guessing what he was about to propose. "You can use the truck whenever you need."

"Careful what you offer." Marguerite giggled. "Old cars and desperate women are erratic."

Jack wondered if desperate women attracted old cars. "Well, the truck's available, no strings attached." That was a lie.

She saw right through his scam. "All right, I asked around. You've got quite a reputation, but it doesn't include child molestation. I realized you've been doin' me a big favor."

"I'm glad it works out for you. Anytime you want to stop by and see the mudmen . . ."

"I've seen my share of mud kids already. But maybe." Her confessional had her talked out, so she stared at the engine until the girls returned with the hammer and baking soda. Marguerite spit on the battery terminals, poured the baking soda over them, and watched the bubble and fizz with great satisfaction. She gave the terminals a couple of light whacks with the hammer.

"We'll see. Try it, SuAnn." SuAnn dove into the car and turned the key. The Cadillac's eight huge cylinders cranked over, popped, and roared to life. Marguerite smiled. Born free—until next time. "Men 'n cars are more goddamn trouble than a toad in a toilet."

Jack smiled. "I've heard that bitter women and cantankerous machinery can cause a good man to come unhinged."

"Guess I never met a man who hadn't previously experienced one or the other."

"Well, it's good we got that out of the way. I just came for my truck and to thank you for driving me in yesterday. I've got to go back in for some pills I forgot to pick up."

Pleas came from the car. "Can we go, Mom? Please?"

"Yeah. We won't be no trouble," said Sadie.

"Jack won't mind, will you, Jack?" Sissy asked.

Snake was still absorbed in the sky.

Marguerite looked at Jack for approval.

"You can come, but you can't ride in back. You'll all have to squeeze into the cab. Are you staying or coming, Snake?"

She leaped off, with a somber "I'm comin'."

As soon as they were settled in and on the main road, Sissy wanted to know, "Who was that pretty lady in your house this morning?"

"She your girlfriend?" asked SuAnn.

"You never told us you had a girlfriend," said Sadie.

"She's t-r-o-u-b-l-e," said Jack.

"That spells trouble," said Snake.

"How'd you know what that spells?"

" 'Cause us girls ain't nothin' but t-r-o-u-b-l-e."

"Why's the lady trouble?" asked Sissy.

"She asks too many questions."

"She's sure pretty. What kinds of questions does she ask?"

"You don't get the idea, do you?"

"You mean the idea that we ought not to be askin' so many questions?"

"That's the one."

"If we don't ask questions, we'll grow up stupid. You don't want that, do you?"

"How did you know about that lady, anyway? Were you spyin' on me?"

"No. We came down to tell you that Mom said it was all right for us to help with the mudmen. We saw through the back door."

"We was spyin'," said Snake.

"Were not. Just shut it, Snake."

"What'd she say to make you drop your coffee?" asked Sadie. "She said she was in love with you, didn't she?" The girls started giggling.

"She said I was too ugly to love."

"You're not that ugly," said SuAnn.

Sadie squinched up her eyes. "She didn't say that. He's just pullin' your toe."

"Yeah, Jack, you're pullin' our toes. She thinks you're yummy."

"Where do you get that?"

Sissy, the analytical one, weighed in, "She picked up all those sharp little pieces from the cup you dropped, and put them in a bag so you couldn't cut yourself, and put them in the trash for you."

"You girls are trouble."

Snake, who was sitting on SuAnn's lap next to Jack, staring at the road, said, "Already told you that."

"Could we change the subject?" It was a demand more than a request, partly because he thought The Sisters might be right about Lucy, and partly because he had heard it before from Willow. And what about Willow? Had they seen him talking to himself? When were they going to start nosing in on that one?

Nobody said a word for half a mile. They stared out at the cacti, at spiky stuff, and the occasional cow. Finally, Sissy broke the silence. "Snake stares at the sky all the time. It's real strange."

"What's up there, Snake?" asked Jack.

"Birds."

"Aren't neither." Sadie shot back. "You lie."

"I see birds. Lots."

"Bullshit."

Jack interupted the flow. "I'd appreciate it if you weren't so crude, Miss Sadie."

"Okay, but she doesn't see birds."

"How do you know?"

" 'Cause if they was there, I'd seen 'em too."

"Tell me about the birds, Snake."

"I can only see 'em when they're straight up and the sky's real blue. I don't know what they do up there. Sometimes they fly around in big circles. Sometimes they make swoops. They're tiny, 'cause they're so high."

Snake rarely said anything. It was one or two words when she did. He looked at her. On SuAnn's lap she was almost at eye level, but she was still staring down the road.

"Snake's full of it," said Sadie. "She gets away with everything 'cause she's littlest."

"Maybe she can see better than the rest of us. The Indians and ancient sailors could see things we can't. Don't be so sure of yourself. Okay?"

"Prove it."

Jack slowed down and pulled off the road. "All right, everybody out."

Their eyes got big. "Are you mad at us?" asked Sissy.

"No. No. It's okay. We're just going to take a look at Snake's birds." He reached into the glove box and took out his binoculars.

"Jesus. I thought you were gonna make us walk."

"Yeah, you shouldn't scare us like that," said Sadie. "We're just little kids."

"I didn't think you scared that easy." He kept the binoculars at his side, but looked up at the sky. "Okay, Snake, can you see birds?"

She stood against the truck, leaned her head back, and cupped her eyes with her hands. Jack and the others waited. Snake studied the sky for several minutes.

"Well, eagle eyes," said Sadie, "where's your damn birds?"

"They're gone. Sometimes, when you look at 'em they go away."

Jack studied the sky with his binoculars for a while, then put the caps back on. "Birds all gone. Sorry."

"Weren't never no damn birds," SuAnn muttered.

They were silent most of the way into town. The older girls were quiet because they felt Jack had sided with Snake, and they were sick of her. She was always seeing things, and she ratted on them, though Snake saw it as reporting the facts. Mostly, they were irked because she seemed so independent and bullheaded. She acted as though she could take it or leave it. At the same time, they wanted to be like her—to take it or leave it—but that was hard to manage.

Jack pulled into a diagonal parking slot in front of the drugstore down the street from the Priscilla Hotel. After they got out of the truck, Sadie grabbed his arm and pointed. "There's your girlfriend, Jack. She's comin' out of the hotel with a bunch of people."

"She's not my girlfriend. I just met her, and it wasn't a particularly amiable meeting."

"What's that mean, amiable?"

"Friendly. Which it wasn't."

"You never told her name."

"Lucy Perelli. Dr. Perelli, probably."

"Who's those queers with her?"

Jack shook his head. "People not from here." He disappeared into the drugstore. The Sisters stayed outside and kept an eye on Lucy and the people who were not from there. The girls started edging toward the hotel, pretending to look in the window of a used-book store, then an antique store that was going out of business.

Sadie squinted evil eyes at them. "Wonder what they're up to."

"The redheaded lady and Mr. Lean Jeans robbed that bank in Winslow," Sissy whispered. "The skinny guy in black's the boss."

"What would Dr. Perelli be doin' with people like that?"

"She's a doctor, so she's rich. They coulda kidnapped her little baby for ransom. They're in negotiations."

"You said they were into bank robbing."

"It's called diversicatin'."

"Whatever," said Sadie. "But that redheaded lady ain't no lady."

"Shut your friggin' flap tops," SuAnn said a little too loud, which drew the attention of the bankrobbin' kidnappers.

"Now we're in for it," whispered Snake, and they made a run for the drugstore as Jack was coming out.

"What's happenin', ladies?"

"Nothin'."

He looked up the street and saw Lucy and the other three staring at them. Lucy waved. Jack waved back. Lucy said something to the others, and they all started walking toward Jack and the girls. Jack groaned quietly. The girls took a deep breath and waited.

"Hello, Jack. I'd like you to meet Henri Bashé, Anita Parker, and Billy Myrdal, who are doing a video documentary on Monsieur Bashé, an infamous French social theorist. And this is Jack Miller, the man Kills The Deer told me about, and one of the reasons for my coming to Silverado." Lucy looked at The Sisters and smiled. "Are these yours?"

He nodded to Lucy's collection. "Good to meet you. This is my crew: SuAnn, Sissy, Sadie, and Snake. They work for sandwiches."

The girls hung back. SuAnn looked everyone in the eye and nodded, Sissy and Sadie looked at their feet and uttered a feeble " 'Lo." Snake looked straight up at the sky without a word.

Anita went right to work. "What is it you do, Mr. Miller?"

"Little enough you wouldn't notice."

Anita was not giving up. She looked at The Sisters. "So you're Mr. Miller's crew. What do you do?"

There was a long pause, then Sissy said, "We're makin' a bunch of mudmen. They're gonna blow up when it rains."

This made no sense to Henri, but he was fascinated. The man looked rough. He'd either taken a bad fall or been in a fight. The children were impoverished. Their clothes were torn or badly worn. Various of them had scars, sores, scabs, and flakes of dried mud. Henri had never seen Americans like these, close-up.

Jack had two things going for him as far as Anita was concerned. On one hand, Lucy had business with him. That made him special. And on the other hand, he wasn't afraid of a fight. Anita, obviously, had a small crack in her personality. She walked over to him and stood so close she had to look up at him. Her head was tilted at nearly the same angle as Snake's. "Our video has a lot to do with deconstruction. It's one of Henri's main interests. Could we interview you?"

"No, thanks."

"We're sponsored by the National Endowment for the Humanities. Anyone who knows Henri's work would feel honored to be in a film with him. You should let us explain our project. I'm sure you'd change your mind. It's really important work."

"You could interview Snake, here. She's an expert on the flight patterns of high-flyin' migratories."

Anita looked at Snake, who was still looking straight up. The girls were trailer-trash kids, something she understood all too well, but she did not grasp Jack. He seemed impervious to the importance of the NEH, or being videographed with a famous person. Indifference made him a challenge.

Billy wanted them all in his lens. He had never seen anything like The Sisters. They were all akimbo, askance, and sly. The man was well muscled and tanned. His large hands were cracked from work.

Jack smiled, nodded, and headed for the truck. The girls broke and ran. They were all piled in and away before Anita could dig out a card or get his e-mail address.

"So much for diversicatin', bankrobbin' kidnappers," said SuAnn.

Jack did not bother to ask what that was about. His mind was turning around Lucy and her video geeks. The young fellow's eyes were black-and-blue, and he held himself like he'd cracked a rib. The redhead had busted out of a holding pen somewhere in Texas, and the skinny French guy in the black turtleneck with the alcoholic pallor was falling apart in slow motion. Interesting. Then there was Lucy. He wanted to know more of her story.

"When we get back, are we gonna make mudmen, Jack?" asked Sadie.

"We need to eat first. What do you want for lunch?"

"Peanut butter and strawberry jam sammiches."

"Yeah, peanut butter and strawberry jam sammiches. And milk," Sissy demanded.

"Jus' jam," said Snake.

"From jam we am and in jam we be," said Sissy.

"That's stupid," snapped Sadie.

"Says you, Sadie. Stupid is as stupid does."

"I'm really, really sick of that."

"So stop callin' me stupid, bat girl. I ain't, an' you know it. Jack, is it true that witches are caused by fallen angels doin' it with human women?"

"Doin' what with human women?"

"You know."

"I'm drawing a blank on the angel–human connection. It was there, but now it's gone."

Sissy's fascination in the procreative possibilities between fallen angels and human women went out the window when they were passed by nine primer-gray Harleys ridden by an irritable-looking pack of Indian-Chicanos with Anasazi designs tattooed on their arms and faces.

"Soup, Soup," hollered Sadie. "Cannibal Soup."

"How do you know about them?" asked Jack. He had an uneasy memory of seeing their name in neon. "Are they in a band?"

"They're bikers. Mom has a friend who rides with 'em. They eat at her cafe, too."

"They look like a nice bunch of boys."

"Yeah. They give Mom stuff."

Philip began glancing at the phone, expecting Lucy's ring. She should have been back. It was 11:45 in D.C., 9:45 in Silverado. Philip liked things to go according to plan. He had spent his life creating situations and environments he could control. He had avoided the universities as much as possible and academic politics altogether. He taught, but he got in and got out. Having so much clout spoiled him. He was accustomed to being important, but his celebrity was beginning to wane. *The New York Times* did not call for his opinion. Not lately. They called those bastards at the Smithsonian and the Peabody.

He had spent the day around Washington and on the phone preparing the groundwork for a major event, selectively creating a buzz that would blossom into media and money. He was professionally discreet, never overcommitting. He hinted at paradigm shifts, but hedged his pledges, smoothing his exit with shy smiles and small, guarded gestures. Philip never set off false alarms, so people were attentive to his tease. He knew how to play when he held a good hand, or in this case, a cold toe. Unfortunately, the key to the toe was held by Jack Miller, whom Philip pictured as an incoherent drunk. He worried about Lucy. What he had asked her to do was probably a little risky, but he had to move. A young Beloit archaeologist had heard about a new find in a glacier and for some reason thought Philip was involved. The man had tried the office, then the house, to no avail—Philip screened his calls. And next, what—postdocs from Bakersfield? It was time to take risks.

Lucy's involvement with the crazies was making him anxious for several reasons. They could hurt her, which would be terrible, and also interfere with her finding out where the toe came from. She had actually broken a catsup bottle on that thug's head. Philip felt his forehead. How could she break a bottle against a guy's head? He was not so sure he could do it, but does anyone know what he'll do until he has to? He knew he was ready to take some major risks to find Miller's iceman. Otherwise, he would end like the other near-dead, wearing pastels and clutching a golf club. He wouldn't have to crawl into a hole, he was being pushed.

He flinched when the phone rang, then waited with the receiver near his ear and his thumb on the button until the message played out and he heard her voice. "Hi, Philip, it's me."

"I thought you were going to call earlier."

"I'm sorry. I just got back from flying the burn Sylvia told me about. I went up after the sun was low enough for good ground relief. I lucked out. Found a great local pilot whose plane was rigged to take pictures. He flies a lot for the Forest Service, so he knows the canyons and the currents. It was pretty rough, because it's so damned hot. But I didn't eat, so at least I didn't lose my cookies. He said the Forest Service guys had been looting these burns for decades. It must have been a common practice—remember the guy we met from Colorado who had the huge Anasazi collection?"

"Wasn't he some kind of official who had access to everything—helicoptered stuff out of the hills?"

"Right. Jeff flew for him. Anyway, we found four pit-house sites on private land that haven't been raided. I picked up maps before, and located each site. We took six rolls of film. I can do some calling in the morning and arrange a meeting tomorrow or the next day with the landowners. Pretty good for an evening's work, wouldn't you say?"

He was quiet for a moment; then, unable to restrain himself, he blurted, "What about Miller?" There was a long pause while Lucy came down from her adventure high, got over the insult of his indifference, and refocused on the fact that Philip was desperate. "I'm sorry," he said, "it's just . . ."

"It's okay, Philip. I understand."

"Some jerk got wind of a find in a glacier and somehow tied me to it. There's a leak in Berkeley. I've got to move on this as quickly as possible. Has anybody else contacted Miller?"

"No. From the way he talked, I'm pretty sure I'd know. He's more or less on the sidelines." She told him Jack's story in as much detail as she could recall. "I'll see him tomorrow. I doubt I can get a map from him right away, but I think he'll do the right thing. He's pretty smart, doesn't need money, and he likes his life the way it is. Giving us a map and getting rid of us is the best way to maintain his version of sanity. He's not the kind who needs or wants to be in the public eye."

"I could always sic Ben Wang and the media on him."

"That's mean, Philip. I know you're joking, but we don't want Miller angry. He could do us a lot of damage."

"Of course. I'm not interested in overexciting Mr. Miller. You never said anything about running into Ben at the Siskin party."

"He was the buzz, but never showed. Saved again."

"Well, I'm sorry I was self-centered. Sounds like you had an extraordinary day. It's just that I haven't been able to get excited about the outline of a pit house for about thirty years."

"Well, I am, sweetheart, so fuck you and good night," she said sweetly.

Philip laughed. "Wish you were here."

ELEVEN

Nothing qualified the Joaquin-Jimenez as a river other than wishful thinking. It was a creek that disappeared into the streambed from place to place and from time to time.

Early in the morning Lucy parked near the lower side of the house and walked down to the creek. What she saw was so unexpected it delighted her—the sheer number of figures, the work and dedication involved, the variety of styles and shapes, the beauty and ghastliness of the characters revealed in the angled light, their shadows stretching toward the creek as though they had come en masse from a morning swim. She had seen a few of the figures from the kitchen the day before, but had no idea they were a small part of a sizable colony.

Jack interrupted her intrigue from the kitchen door. "Good morning, Dr. Perelli. Would you like coffee?"

She waved, "Yes, thank you," and returned to the figures under construction. Thin willows were used as an armature for the mud. The still visible joints were wrapped with strips of willow bark to keep the boughs fixed at a required angle. The secret, she saw, was the willow bark wrappings, which pulled and turned the figures in subtle ways, creating their stance, gesture, and illusion of motion. She was bending over, peering at the bark wrappings on the calf and knee of a running figure, when she heard his voice directly behind her. She guessed by his halting tone that he had been as absorbed in her form as she was in the mudman's.

"Here's your, ah, coffee." It sounded almost like a question. She straightened up, turned around, and accepted the pale blue porcelain cup. It was clear that he'd been captivated by her ass. She sipped her coffee, amused by his lack of subtlety. Maybe he was recovering from a long drought.

"What happens when it rains?" she asked, then nodded toward the mudmen.

He was relieved to be let off so easily. "They wash away."

"You've done this before? And you let the rain wash it all away?"

"Yes. They were inspired by an Indian who told me about the first people being unformed mud. I give each of them a story to remember them by."

"But they're beautiful. You have to save them this time."

"Then I won't get to see them erode. Disintegration is the best part. At first it's slow, they change color, then little rivulets form and begin to erode the mud away. Gradually the willow armatures are exposed. Then there's the finale."

"What's the finale? They all fall down?"

"Try harder. You're the archaeologist."

She tried to imagine what could possibly make for a finale in a field of melting mudmen. Her eyes came to rest on the willow bark bindings of the figure she had looked at earlier. She grinned. "The bark slips when it's wet and releases the boughs. They explode?"

He laughed. "If I do it right, it's kind of a slow dance. Then they come undone, and it's mudmen everywhere."

"You're serious."

"Entropy's highly underrated. I never understand anything until it starts falling apart."

"You could photograph them. You could do a book of your work. I've never seen anything like this, Jack. People should see it. This is extraordinary."

"Yes. Pictures of mudmen melting in the rain. Big market there. I could get grants. I've always dreamed that one day I would write the great American grant proposal explaining the importance of mud to art bureaucrats and fashionistas. I'll start tomorrow. No, tomorrow is shopping day."

She laughed. "You sure live in another world, but then, you were a looter."

"So, I'm a sociopath in your layer cake of hell?" he said, burrowing into the clay with his bare toe.

"No, no. I didn't mean that at all."

He turned and stared at the mudmen.

She wondered if she had upset him. "I'm sorry. I didn't mean to insult you. Anthropologists and sociologists are outsiders, too."

"Their job is to understand culture. My job was to steal artifacts from it. I was a criminal." He remembered Willow and shrugged. "I am a criminal—another vocation that keeps changing its definition. What I did for a few years wasn't considered illegal for most of history. Archaeologists and museum directors have been raiding ruins for centuries." He looked at her. "And just because you operate within the law doesn't mean you're not a criminal. The Indians still think archaeologists are a bunch of thieves and grave robbers."

"A lot of that's changed. Other than a few nut cases, we have pretty good relationships with most tribes."

"Only because unemployed archaeologists discovered they could make a living by hiring themselves out to the tribes to justify native claims to water, coal, and gas. Which requires turning a blind eye to any evidence of prehistoric violence or anything else Indians don't want to hear about, like a frozen toe."

"Some contract archaeologists do more important work than a lot of academics. Most of those native claims are justified. As for the blind-eye business—what do you expect? A lot of them work for the tribes because they know the Indians have been screwed on a systematic basis for several hundred years. Some archaeologists believe there are issues more important than the precious, elusive, and ever-changing truth."

He turned and looked at her in the slanting light. He grinned. "Some of my best friends are archaeologists."

"We blame the bad stuff on the looters, dealers, and private collectors."

"You met Sylvia Siskin, didn't you?"

"I have. Nice collection. I assume you've done business with Miss Sylvia."

"Comin' and goin.' I sold off most of her daddy's Mesoamerican collection before the repats kicked in the door. I also sold her several exquisite Mimbres bowls. We have a long history."

"Did you, by chance, assist Sylvia Siskin in the acquisition of her reliquaries?"

"Chancy world, isn't it? Estaño Obrero made up several of those for me. He suggested they be soldered shut. It would save time, and we wouldn't have to rob graves. I made up the story about Jukulu the Water. It was a winning combo."

"Did she know they were fake?"

"In my world, fake is just another word for reliquary. But I always sold with a money-back guarantee."

"Are you avoiding my question?"

"She had me take them back to Estaño to install the little crystal windows. After that he put those little windows in all his reliquaries. Sylvia has a great touch. She also added the black fortune-teller who pulled Jukulu's cart."

"Did Estaño make many reliquaries?"

"You would like one?"

"Of course. I collect all kinds of fakes. My Clovis fakes are as beautiful as your real one."

"And I thought you were a saint. When I got out of the business, I lost contact with Estaño. Sylvia has the only ones in the States."

"What happened to the others?"

"One went to a little museum at Cambridge. Thirty-one went to Italy for resale in Europe and Russia, and ten went to a very secretive buyer from Japan. We usually fooled the museums. At least they pretended to be. But galleries and dealers challenged authenticity to get the price down. Once you'd overcome that hurdle and gotten your price, they'd ask if you could reproduce similar items at a reduced price if they bought in quantity. So they got you in the end. It saved time hunting up buyers, but glutted the market. Working fakes takes a lot of time. Very few people make real money at it. A lot of them just do it for the fun of screwing snobs."

"Did you like screwing snobs?"

"At first, yes, a lot. After a while, it was just making fools out of fools. You have to hate them to keep it up."

"So why did you keep doing it?"

"Because I figured out a few tricks, got to know several remarkably rich folks, and by chance met some useful scoundrels, all of which allowed me to make truckloads of money. But the majority of what I dealt were real goods. Only about fifteen percent of what you deal in can be fake. Building trust, you know. You broker authentic items for resale, but you refund a fake."

"But you stopped everything, even the legit part."

"The life took on a strange, sucky sensation. Putting a value to everything poisoned me. Others do it and fine—nothing. But not me. The blood got sucked out and cold air drifted in."

Lucy was a little dubious. "And you just quit?"

"Yep."

"Sylvia Siskin must have missed you."

He gave Lucy a wry grin. "Well, I did make her a fortune."

"At great sacrifice to yourself, no doubt."

"I was in business. Not unlike yourself."

"Archaeology is more than a business to me. I keep sifting through the ashes just to figure out what glue held cultures together and why it lost its stickum."

"I've always thought of it as a hypnotic trance."

Lucy nodded. "With various moral and spiritual mood elevators to reinforce the illusion of cohesiveness."

"What's the glue du jour?"

"Shopping. 'Living the good life.' It keeps us entranced."

"Whatever holds it together, as long as it doesn't kill too many people at once, I have to go with, like everyone else."

"There's an interesting equation—one good life equals X number of deaths. *The Times* should run a daily tally."

She sipped her coffee and studied one of the more grotesque mudmen. "I meant to ask about a couple of borderliners we ran into in Pie Town named Lars and Jacob. Are they from around here?"

"They're the famous Raw Bone and Rat brothers, respectively. They come with the territory. Lately, they seem to be particularly out of control. Federal regs on mine-waste discharge cost them a mining operation that'd been in the family for seventy years. Then the EPA sued them to clean up, which put them in Chapter Seven. They haven't handled extreme poverty all that well. There's a rumor that they've been robbing banks in Arizona and Colorado. They're also suspected of murdering a hitchhiker. They're not the kind to tango with."

"Unfortunately, we tangoed. Raw Bone has an ugly lump between his eyes and a nasty gash due to my zeal with a catsup bottle. If Anita hadn't had her .38, they would have beaten Billy to death."

Her choice of enemies alarmed him. It wouldn't be a bad idea if she left New Mexico immediately. He eyed the leather satchel. "Are you carryin' a gun?" He bet she'd never fired a gun.

"Of course not. I've never fired a gun."

"Would you like to learn, or would you rather I just drove you to the airport right now?"

"They don't even know we're down here."

"Oh, they do. They're using the last of their gas money cruising every motel in the county looking for you. Your crew look like escapees from an infomercial, and you don't exactly look like local material. Be careful, okay?"

"I do live in D.C., you know. But thanks for the warning. I'm leaving soon, anyway. I came down here to find your iceman's whereabouts and to locate some sites for the Preservation Fund. Yesterday, I flew the area burned over by the fire. We spotted four early pit-house ruins. I need to talk to the owners and look at the sites, then I'll discuss them with the state archaeologist in Santa Fe. I realize I'm asking the wrong person, but do you know any virgin sites?"

He laughed. "I do, in fact. Sometimes it's hard to tell from the maps if they're on government or private land, which means surveys. I never spotted any of them from the air, even when I knew where they were—most have to be walked. It takes a lot of time.

You're better off dealing with what you've got for now. You could come back later and check out the others."

"What about Raw Bone and Rat?"

"They'll be in the lockup sooner or later."

"I hope sooner." She shuddered. "I'd like to see your maps, if that's okay?"

"Sure." He nodded toward the house. "It may take a while, fifteen years of maps."

Halfway to the house, Lucy turned for a last look at the mudmen—intense and alive—a colony of dancers, poised, anticipating the next movement. Waiting for rain—for the last dance. She had no reference points in her life for a Jack Miller—no sense of what it was that connected him to anything familiar.

In his living room he had a long cabinet with thin, wooden drawers made for maps. Several maps had notes in red ink and pages clipped to edges, diagrammed with trails, small details, and sketches of pots and other artifacts, numbered, dated, and annotated.

"You've left quite a record of your handiwork. Isn't that dangerous?"

"It would take an army of government accountants to figure it out. They'd never find anything illegal anyway." He pulled a map from one of the top drawers and spread it out on the dining room table. He glanced at the parrot trainer for a moment. She made a coy move, turning and raising her shoulder. Jack smiled.

"What?" Lucy asked.

"Nothing."

She knew she'd missed something, but her attention was quickly captured in the detail of the map. The pit-house areas were well marked, as were trails that were not on the original Forest Service map. She was impressed by the amount of detail he'd added. "You covered a lot of ground here."

He watched her study the map for a moment, then, not knowing why, he was compelled to turn back to the drawers and pull out several more maps. He rolled them up and handed them to her. "There're about twenty-five sites on these maps. They've never been touched. One is a Classic Mimbres site. I don't need these anymore. They might as well be yours. Most of the guys who own the sites could use some of your money."

"This is a little overwhelming."

"It should keep you out of trouble for a few years."

For Lucy's purposes, she had been handed the directions to a gold mine. The effort that had gone into finding the sites was mind-numbing. He was being incredibly generous. It occurred to her that she might have to ask for his help in deciphering his notes, which would bring her back, time and again. She smiled at the thought and wondered if it had occurred to him as well.

"No one has ever given me anything like this, Jack. Thank you. It means a great deal to me."

"I have another site I'd like to show you that's not on those maps. Have you ever done any caving?"

"Sure. Some of our sites are in West Virginia and Pennsylvania caves," Lucy said.

"What are you doing tomorrow?"

"I intended to see some of the ranchers who own the sites in the burn. Why?"

"I recently found a cave the Mimbres believed was the entrance to the underworld. It's full of interesting stuff. The upper chambers were occupied around 1130. We could get into it and out in a day."

Lucy realized he was staring at the parrot trainer bowl again.

"I'd need to pick up some gear and supplies this afternoon, if you want to see it tomorrow," Jack continued.

"Yes, very much. Is it something the Fund should try to protect?"

"No. It's on government land. I just thought you, more than any-one I know, would want to see it."

"I'll get my ranchers out of the way this afternoon."

"You don't mind going with a novice, do you?"

"I have to guide you?" Lucy asked.

"It's just that I'm not great with heights. I'll want to take my time."

"I don't mind that, but we need to tell someone you can trust where we're going and when we expect to be back. Any candidates?"

"How about Kills The Deer?"

"Has he done any caving?"

"Oh, yeah."

"He's not exactly next door."

"We can set it up so if we don't call in by ten A.M. the day after tomorrow, he'll come down. I can give him directions on the phone and fax a map from the copy shop. We'll take enough food for three days. Does that sound reasonable?"

"Sure."

"Shall we tell your crew?"

"I'd pass. Henri is already undergoing disaster, Billy's damaged, and Anita's only on call for her .38. Kills The Deer will be fine. Would you suggest he have some gear ready, just in case?"

"I'll do that, and I'll pick you up at ten-thirty. Okay?"

"Okay."

"You haven't mentioned the man in the ice."

"I figure you'll tell me when you're ready. If you're ever ready."

"You've been figurin', have you?"

He watched her walk to her car and wave goodbye. Was he trying to pull her into his life? That would be completely pointless, everything considered. Then why had he given her his maps and offered to show her the cave? He felt a little out of control, a little confused.

After she left, Jack sat down and looked at Willow. "How come you never talk to me when someone else is in the room?"

"You're a simple man. It's disturbing to have too many things in your head at once."

"I've noticed. You did let me know what you were thinking, though."

"Yes, but I waited until there were no demands on your attention."

"Was it your idea to give Lucy the maps?"

"What were you going to do with them? Someday this place will get washed away. If she has the maps, they will bring her back to you. She'll need to ask about the squiggles on the corners."

"It crossed my mind."

"And you think it didn't cross hers? You're certainly brave to go down into the middle world," she teased. "You must be falling in love."

"What?"

She had moved out of the bowl, grown to normal height, and was sitting on the table with her legs crossed and her arms wrapped around them. The parrot sat at her feet and glared at Jack. "Your voice changed." She sighed. "There was desire in it. You used to hold back, this time you were tilting toward her. And you were very quick to take my suggestion to give her the maps. You didn't fight it for a minute. Something happened when you were outside with her. Didn't it?"

"So—you who knows everything I know, only better—what happened?"

"She was enchanted. She wants you to love her."

"But does she love me?"

"She's in the habit of loving Philip, and you're a dangerous man, remember?"

"I can't be that dangerous. She agreed to spend a day alone in a cave with me."

"Maybe she needs dangerous."

"You just said she was in love with Philip. What would she need me for?"

"You're a sweet man, Jack, with a dash of idiot. She wants to change her life, but she hasn't admitted it. Philip has to show her how lame he's become before she'll cross the creek. That's part of what you're doing for her. She'll see him better because of you."

"You don't understand this world. I'm the lame one here, not the hero. I can't stand this culture, and I'm completely subsidized by my past transgressions. I build mudmen with little girls. I'm not embarrassed by that, but it doesn't make me an example of modern manhood."

"You're a rogue, Jack. You don't need to worry about your manhood."

"You know, I had a nice thing here, until you two materialized."

"Are you going to make love to her in the cave?" There was a catch in her voice.

"I'd make love to her on the roof," he said, oblivious to Willow's longing, "but there's the Philip question, remember? How does that get resolved?

"Leave the Philip question to Philip. He can't stop himself from resolving things in your favor."

"You're so sure."

"There've always been Philips in the world. Most of them are destined to self-destruct."

"Why do you think I'm in love with her?"

"You've got it bad." The parrot, seeking pats, gave her finger a gentle squeeze with its beak. She let him step on her hand, then raised him to eye level and stroked his head. "I don't like you going down into the second world. Suppose you don't get back?"

"Oh, you're not concerned about me. All you care about is escaping the bowl."

"Would you want your spirit trapped in a piece of clay for the rest of eternity?"

Jack stared at her. "Why am I doing this to myself?"

"Trust me, you're not. It's all happening to you because you had to go poking around in Hans Becker's notes."

"What do you know about Becker?" Jack asked suspiciously.

"A raw man killed him."

"A what?"

"A raw man. One who never became a full person. This one was a Scorpion person's spirit."

"Does this raw man have a particularly nasty sting?"

"Particularly nasty. He drove Becker a little mad. The raw man wanted the second world to himself, and he's welcome to it. He wanted you to find me."

"If I go back tomorrow, will I get stung again?"

"He stung you to make you fall and break the bowl so he would be rid of me for sure. How was he to know you wouldn't bring me back to the cave? You yourself considered returning the bowl, remember?"

"I might have thought that for a moment."

"Your 'for a moment' got you a nasty sting."

"So, as long as I intend to break the bowl when it clouds up, I'm safe from the raw man?"

"Yes. And if I were you, I wouldn't change my mind. He followed you home. He's here in the house, listening to everything you say."

"How do you know this?"

"Before you were stung, remember the strange light across the canyon, jumping around like a moth?"

"It's all a little fuzzy."

"That's how raw men are. They usually go home in the evening, curl up in old baskets or jars left in caves, and dream bad dreams. But that evening, after he stung you, he followed you home."

Jack glanced around at the pots, cupboards, and other possible hiding places. He thought he smelled the stench of rancid butter drift through the room. For a moment, he found himself believing a raw man was in the house. "What kind of spirit is a raw man?"

"They are hungry ghosts who wander around, causing trouble. In the beginning, Scorpion person asked Coatimundi to make him the headman. So Coatimundi took his soul away, and he became a shaman with great power. But when he died, being soulless, he could not become a cloud person, and he could never return to the first world. He was left to wander without shape. Raw men have been know to slip into the mind of an idiot and make him an important person."

"Coatimundi had a sense of humor."

"Coatimundi is many things. He is full of tricks. He taught parrot to talk and to tell wicked jokes to embarrass people. Sometimes he hid an arrogant person's fetish so the person's magic would disappear."

"Were Coatimundi stories secret to the parrot clan?"

"Everyone had Coatimundi stories, though every clan had stories that were secret. But you know how that is. The deer clan said that first-deer had sharp teeth which frightened rabbit, so every night rabbit would gently rub deer's teeth with a stone until they were flat and only good for grass. Deer was always painted with sharp, laughing teeth to remind us who we were.

"The clans argued about who did what, but they agreed these things happened before time began. There were old ways of doing things, particularly with the dead. The traditional people would not talk about their dead. They took them into the mountains at night, and some clans did this 'til the end. Those who practiced the old ways said the others had strayed and would come to a bad end. They were angry that we buried our ancestors under our houses and painted images of animals and people because, they said, it caused trouble in the spirit world."

"Why *did* you bury your relatives under your houses?"

"Those who had no family were buried in the plaza between the houses. We buried people we loved in our homes. There is a comfort knowing Great-grandmother is sitting under the floor."

Jack laughed. "It also meant that it was her house and forever the house of her children and her children's children."

"That, too. Some people who came to our village had heard where we buried our people and thought it was terrible. Some refused to come inside, because our houses were haunted by the dead. A man who came to trade shell beads said entering our house would be like going down into the underworld. My mother had to bring him his supper on the roof. He was afraid spirits of the dead would get him."

"You were afraid to go into the first world."

"Yes, it's true." She thought about that for a while. "It was entering the unknown. I even wonder if I'll become a cloud person and rain down into the first world and come back as a full person in this world. Maybe it's different now."

He never imagined she would question her destiny. "When you were a child, did you know about the first world?"

"In each house there was a hole, the belly root—what you call a *sipapu*—near the fire pit. We were told the belly root went down into the first world. When a baby was born it was held over the belly root so a spirit from the first world could enter its body.

"Sometimes Grandfather would put a flat rock over the belly root when he left. One day, when the grown-ups were gone, I took the rock off. I cupped my hands around my eyes and looked down, but it was too black to see. Then I heard something and put my ear over the hole. At first I only heard a sound like people laughing far away. After a while, I thought I was hearing words mixed in with the laughing, but I couldn't understand them. It was gibberish. Every day, when the grown-ups were gone, I'd listen.

"One day I remembered the grandmothers had said everything was backward in the first world. So I thought I was hearing backward talking. I learned the sounds and taught the other children. The grown-ups couldn't understand us."

"Nothing's changed," said Jack. "The kids still listen to the underworld, they still talk backward, and we don't understand them."

"You have a belly root?"

"More like an underbelly." He pointed to a screen in the wall. "It's called TV, but it serves the same purpose. It sounds like gibberish."

She stared at the blank screen for a while. "There's nothing there."

"Even when it's on, there's nothing there."

"The belly root always reminded us of where we came from and that we would always come back. It was important for us to know we would return. The clowns at the festivals painted black and white stripes around their bodies and did everything backward to remind us of where we come from."

"Nice to have a sense of direction."

"This time, if I come back, I'll be in your world. I'll be like you and your people."

"Then you can watch the TV to find out who you are and to discover the meaning of life and what will become of you. Which is something I've always wondered about the Mimbres. Why did your people come apart?"

"My father said that several times over the years, we had very little rain, but we became better farmers. We built more and more places to catch water and made ditches for water. We planted wherever plants would grow. Since there was more food, people had more babies. Then there were several seasons of very little winter snow or summer rain. People had to start moving away to look for places where there was moisture. Many of them did badly. When the corn tassels dried up for many seasons, people began to listen to the old stories.

"The traditional people pressured my family and others to stop making images, but our paintings had become popular with the people who came from the place where the sun rises in winter. We celebrated with these people. They gave us food and we gave them painted bowls. Many of our people began making paintings for food, but finally they gave up and began moving to the other side of the mountain.

"When you moved to a new place, it took a great effort to start over. Houses, dams, and irrigation ditches had to be built and new fields cleared. Sometimes people settled unlucky land and had to start again. If there wasn't enough food stored to get them through the next season and the game had gone away, the people died." She became agitated, paced back and forth, and became thinner and thinner.

"The people who crossed the mountains found the light was different there. So were the wild plants and the taste of the water and the time when the corn tasseled. Unfamiliar spirits lived in the hills and caves. Those things go deep into people and change how they dream and think. Perhaps some were taken in by other tribes and made to learn new songs, dance new dances, and think new thoughts. Even if they survived, they were no longer the same people."

He noticed she was losing her color. Even the parrot's bright plumage turned gray. Willow was on the verge of fading away completely.

"My family and others who stayed behind all died. So my people disappeared, forever."

Jack knew the Mimbres had never disappeared. Their cloud dancers still lived in the minds of people at Zuni, Hopi, and Acoma pueblos, and of many who walked the streets of Albuquerque, Santa Fe, and Taos. They lived in Kills The Deer's bold kachina paintings.

Jack believed that the stories the Mimbres painted of their world were the origin of the kachina cults. Certainly, kachina images were painted on their bowls. Now their world was reflected in the political and ceremonial complexity of many pueblo societies and in their wary attitude toward individuals who strive too much for power. The power hungry were the butt of mockery to the modern Pueblo Indians, just as they had been to the Mimbres painters.

"Your people had powerful thoughts," he told her. "It was your people who changed the ways of other tribes. Perhaps some tribes absorbed you, but your thoughts absorbed them. Your people outlived the Anasazi hierarchies. The importance of the cloud people is still alive in the pueblos in the north. You left your thoughts with many tribes."

What he said pleased her very much. Her color began to return, and the parrot became bright and animated. It amused her to think the Anasazi had become Mimbres.

Jack wondered if he should tell her what had happened to the pots, that Mimbres imagery covered the Southwest like pavement, and that he'd bought his house with a single Mimbres bowl, possibly one painted by her aunt. But he thought better of it. She would hound him mercilessly if she thought her bowl was too valuable for him to break.

TWELVE

It was evening by the time Lucy finished talking to the ranchers about the newly found ruins on their property. She caught up with Henri, Anita, and Billy in the hotel lounge, discussing the day's events. They had gone to the museum, and Henri had gotten the curator to take them into an inner sanctum of mysterious Mimbres objects, shards, large fertility stones, and boxes of bones that belonged to the U.S. government.

Anita was looking for a conspiracy, at least a story of egregious bureaucratic neglect. "I'll bet the feds have bones stashed in basements all over the country."

"Excuse me," said Lucy. "I hate to interrupt, but I told Jack Miller about our Pie Town escapade. He said Lars and Jacob are locals known as Raw Bone and Rat, which probably tells us everything we need to know about them. Oh, yes, there's a rumor they rob banks and maybe murdered somebody."

Anita flinched. Henri seemed stricken. Billy just shook his head.

"Sorry to up the paranoia level before bedtime, but you needed to know. Well, I have a call to make. See you tomorrow."

"Lucy, don't abandon us. It is, how you say, our hour of need." As they watched her go, Henri whispered, "Maybe we should leave town now."

Billy moaned, "I think I'll get my own .38."

"It'll take two weeks to get a permit," said Anita. She smiled and gave his arm a gentle squeeze. "Best you stick close to me, sweetheart."

Henri lit up. "I know—we get the Robo-Cop, pepper canisters they use on the, ah . . . disorderlies, and the kids."

Anita stopped him. "I don't think I want to be in the area when you're wavin' a can of pepper spray around, Henri."

The room was saturated with the day's heat. Lucy undressed and lay across the chenille spread, her mind full of Jack Miller, mudmen, maps, and the ranchers, who had initially regarded her interest in their land with suspicion, but who had come around for various reasons that did not necessarily involve money. Some took to the idea that another civilization had farmed the same land a thousand years ago. It was quite a day. She sat up and began dialing Philip's number, then hesitated.

She put the phone down and lay back on the bed. Jack would give her the iceman's location if she didn't rush him. The thought of Philip's impatience made her jaw clench. She drew a deep breath and watched the ceiling fan whirl ancient dust through the hot room.

The phone rang. She let it ring, staring up at the fan, and waited for the ringing to stop. Six rings. The front desk must have checked the bar for her. Philip knew she was in her room. On the seventh ring she rolled over and picked it up. "Hello."

"You must have a very large room."

"I had to run all the way from the other end of town. How are you?"

"Are you irritated with me?"

"I'm not sure."

"Did Miller tell you where the iceman is?"

"I had a great day, Philip. Truly wonderful. And I am making progress on the iceman. I'm sure Jack will tell me tomorrow or the next day. If I try to rush him, he could clam up. So I don't need to feel any pressure from you." Her heart was racing.

"You're overreacting. Why?"

"You started in on Miller and the iceman right away and I . . ."

"You know how important this is."

"I'm sorry. I guess . . . I was just frustrated, because it was a great day for me, and I didn't have anything to tell you, and I don't know what else I could have done to move things along with Miller. We've discussed it, and he's thinking about what he wants to do."

"How much time does this guy need?"

"There's no way to rush him. The only way to get anything out of Jack is to play it straight. I've never met anyone quite like him. I don't know how to read him."

The silence that followed meant Philip was considering several scenarios. She'd probably made Jack out to be a little too interesting.

"I'm glad to hear you had a great day. I can't say the same for myself. I received an e-mail from an Indian named Sillcot, in Cleveland, no less. He's heard about the toe, and he's threatening a lawsuit already."

"Where's he coming from?"

"He's with the Native Peoples Defense Fund. These are the young guys with law degrees. They're not like the old radicals, but it's going to be a nasty fight."

"Well, you need them as much as they need you."

"They're a goddamned distraction."

"In my world that would be true, but it's not in yours, and you know it."

He laughed. "Well, publicity is necessary in what you and your sexist friends refer to as Big Penis Archeology."

"How did Sillcot find out about the toe?"

"I don't know, and that's what has me on edge right now. So far, no one has enough information to break the story, but that could change quickly, particularly if someone else gets to Miller."

"I don't think Jack will talk to anyone else right now."

There was another pause. "What did you say that made him so amenable?"

The hotel was at its hottest. The bricks had absorbed the afternoon sun, turning the room into an oven. "Let me call you back in a minute. This room is too hot." She walked into the shower, stood under the cool spray soaping the day's sweat off her body, watched the suds swirl into the drain, and thought about the rain-washed mudmen consumed by the Joaquin-Jimenez River. She reached out, picked her phone off the sink, and pressed the speed dial for Philip's apartment number. "Hi, I'm in the shower. What were we talking about?"

"I asked what you and Jack talked about."

"Well, let's see, we talked about his mudmen, art, entropy, and a cave he's taking me to see tomorrow. He also gave me detailed maps to several untouched sites, mostly ridge-top pit houses, and a Classic Mimbres ruin. It was very generous, which makes me think he intends to give us the iceman's location."

"He just gave you the location of the sites?"

"He said he has no use for them. He's been out of the business for quite a while."

"You said something about a cave?"

"Yes. He wants to show me a Mimbres cave. Evidently, there are some interesting things in it."

"You're going into a cave alone with him? That sounds ridiculous." His voice was beginning to annoy her. "Who's backing you up?"

"Jack's friend, Kills The Deer, the one I met in Albuquerque. Jack's faxing him a map to the cave. We intend to come back before it gets dark. If we don't call in by the next morning, he'll come look-ing for us. Plus, I'll have my phone with me."

"That little static toy barely works in the open. You expect to call from a cave? I don't like this, Lucy. You just said you didn't know how to read Miller. That's a real confidence builder. Why's he doing all of this for you anyway?"

"I'm not sure. It may be his way of feeling us out—to find out if we're setting him up—before he decides to give us the iceman. Maybe it's simply that he likes me."

"That's what concerns me."

"That's sweet of you, Philip. Don't worry. It's a quick trip, and we'll be out before dark. I'll call you as soon as I get back to the hotel. Okay?"

"Not that anything I said would make any difference. What about your Pie Town thugs? Any sign of them?"

She hesitated just long enough for him to know something was off. "What happened?"

"Nothing. Nothing's happened. They live around Silverado, though."

"They'll be looking for you."

"I assume so."

"Damn it, Lucy. This has become a fiasco—you've hooked up with three losers who are wasting your time, using you in their stupid video, over which you have no say or control. You hit a guy with a catsup bottle, he's after you, and now you're going down in a cave with an unpredictable looter."

"And all for you, remember? I don't need this. I'm doing the best I can. The only dangerous part of this is Raw Bone and Rat, and I'll be out of here in two days anyway."

"Excuse me. 'Raw Bone and Rat'?"

"They're what the locals call the thugs from Pie Town."

"I am so reassured by that. I'm going to get the next flight to Albuquerque. I'll be in Silverado by tomorrow afternoon."

"And do what? Defend me from bad guys?" She heard glass breaking in the bedroom and turned off the shower to listen. She must have forgotten to lock the door.

"Ah, Lucy, dear. It's just me, Henri. Sorry, I dropped a glass." There was a slight waver in his voice.

She covered the phone. "I'll be out in a minute." Perfect timing, Henri. She returned to the phone. "It's Henri, I think he's drunk. If you come down, he could interview you for the video."

"Are you joking?"

"I want you to stay in D.C. There's absolutely no reason for you to come down. You'd complicate things with Jack. So, please, stay home and organize the project. You asked me to find out where that toe came from, and that's exactly what I'm doing. So let me do it, all right?"

"When will you be back at the hotel?"

"Probably ten o'clock, my time."

"I'll be here."

"Thanks for your confidence in me and your appreciation of my efforts. Good night, Philip."

A day in a cave with Jack Miller was beginning to sound better all the time.

She dried her hair, slipped into her robe, and went out to deal with Henri. A vodka bottle sat on the table. He was on his hands and knees feeling the carpet.

"The glass just slipped out of my hand. Please be careful . . . little slivers . . . everywhere. I've made a big mess. Wear boots until the vacuumer comes in the morning. I'm very sorry."

"It's all right. Don't cut yourself."

"Too late." He held up a bloody finger, smiling, pleased with himself.

"Very good, Henri. Why don't you wash your hands, wrap your finger in tissue, and I'll pour you another glass of your favorite beverage." Her irritation with Philip made Henri's intrusion a relief.

"I heard the shower and waited outside for a while, then I thought to come in if the door was unlocked, which it was. It was rude, I know. I'm sorry."

"Please stop being sorry and get cleaned up. I'll deal with the glass."

"Yes, yes." He headed for the bathroom and returned a few moments later, his finger wrapped in tissues. He accepted a glass of vodka from her. "I overheard you say to your Philip that he should come down to interview with me, but then it was of course a joke. Why, of course a joke?"

"I can't believe you were eavesdropping, Henri."

"I know. I can't help myself. Why a joke?" He sipped his vodka, watching her out of the corner of his eye, and waited.

"Philip hates postmodernists."

"Particularly inebriated French postmodern-deconstructionists?"

"Particularly them."

"Well, certainly I am inebriated and French. With the postmodernists I am, how do you say, fed up." He toasted the air with his vodka. "To hell with the po-mos." He was well buzzed. Another toast: "To hell with the decons." He grinned at Lucy. She shook her head and laughed. "You're down here on a mission?" He almost sounded sober for a moment. "Looking for a toe . . . like a spy? And Jack is the key that unlocks the mystery?"

"You're out of line, you know?"

"So I am." He poured himself another and raised his glass to Lucy before taking a gulp.

She was not sure what kind of trouble Henri was going to cause, if any. He could only embarrass her. He clearly thought she was deceiving Jack. She needed to disabuse him of that notion. "Yes, I'm on a mission, sent by my friend, Philip, to find the origin of a very old toe. The origin of which is known only by Jack. And this you should keep in your head—Jack knows why I am here. I'm not pulling a fast one on our friend Jack. Okay?"

"*Oui,* madame."

"I think it's time for you to go back to your room and fall into a deep sleep."

He began a dutiful struggle to a standing position. "I should say . . . though, that the deconstruction of America is an impossible task. The va, va . . . vastness of the American midriff is too . . . squishy and impenetrable to deconstruct. Wonderful word . . . squishy—onomatopoetic. Decades of social theorists have probed . . ."

"Don't forget your bottle."

"Yes, yes. Going, going." He managed to open the door, then turned and said, "Culture is merely a prison in which to dehumanize the individual. Remember that." He gave her a slight head bob and backed into the hallway.

As Henri passed Anita and Billy's room, he heard one of Anita's rants learned at a young age from a demented red-clay Texas relation whose hatred of men was the all-consuming fire of her life. "Snake bastard, goat fuckin' mother whorin' sonabitch." Henri had no idea what set her off. She needed and loved Billy, yet hated everything about him. Anita was a conflicted woman.

By the time he made it to his room, the ranting had transformed to sighs, then whimpers. Elongated, the whimpers became moans. The moans drew Henri to the air vent above the baseboard in the wall between their rooms. As the moans became more distinct, he stretched himself out on the floor and tried to peer through the vent. He was allowed only a view of the shaking white iron legs of the bed. He was too drunk to get horny, but he wanted to watch. It had been a long time. He listened and thought about Nina. She moaned as loudly as Anita. Funny, Nina-Anita. Was Anita as good as she sounded? He missed his Nina. Why was he in this strange country when he could be home, curled around his beautiful wife? He was a dumb ass of a man who could barely make a living. He lay on the floor feeling sorry for himself until he noticed the moaning through the wall had become a deep roar, growing louder and louder. Jesus, he thought, what's she doing to him? Henri pressed his face hard against the floor to get a better angle of the bed, but to no avail. The roar became deafening, intimidating Henri. He crawled backward, pushing himself into a sitting position, then realized the sound—roaring, popping, revving, rumbling—was coming from the open window. Henri scooted over to the window and looked down on the street full of motorcycles. Many motorcycles. He loved motorcycles more than anything, except possibly Nina.

After watching awhile, he went downstairs to stand on the curb and smoke. He sucked the odor of the hot, revving engines, gas, exhaust, and the cigarette deep into his lungs. Reverberations of engines rattled around in his skull down to his toes until his bladder signaled his brain—the first time he'd seen motorcycles he was so young, so excited, he'd lost control. Ever after, when caught in a rapture of motorcycles, he had the urge. He wobbled back into the hotel and went to the men's room in the bar, smiling all the while—one never forgets peeing one's pants out of delight—and returned to the street, relieved. Henri watched the parade, even stepping off the curb to feel the blast and bluster of exhaust and machines.

For no good reason that he could see, the parade began to notice him. He realized the sidewalks were empty. It was just Henri, bikers, and rolling rumble under the dark blue sky. He was abuzz in vodka heaven.

Several bikes began circling him in their vultures-inspect-roadkill fashion. His eyes jumped from one face to the next. There was one particular face. The face stopped. It was a tough, lean, Indian-Chicano face with hair on its lip and chin.

The man grinned. "Enjoying yourself, little man in black?"

"Since I was a boy," Henri gestured at knee height, "in Villon, I have loved motorcycles and the motorcycle guys. They would come after dark, blasting down the cobblestone street, roar around the fountain in front of the police station, and disappear into the black night.

"When I first saw this, I was six years old. I bravely opened the door of our shop and stood in the blinding lights as the bikers flashed by. I was so thrilled I pissed my pants," Henri laughed, "but they were short pants."

"Leon Marquez," said the man, extending his hand.

"Henri Bashé." Henri shook Leon's hand. It was warm and sticky. He pointed. "Your hand. It's all a bloody mess."

Leon examined the bloody hand and smiled. "Sí. I tried to kill some guy, but he got away. Too bad."

"I'm sure he had it coming." Henri sounded serious, having no idea what one was expected to say, then his humanitarian instincts kicked in. "I have bandage and antiseptic in my room. Come, I will—how you say—fix you up?"

"I see you are a true gentleman, Frenchie Bashé. It is a rarity, in these days. Thank you."

Three other gentlemen, Leon's bodyguards, parked their bikes and followed their wounded leader and Henri. As they entered the hotel lobby, the night clerk became unusually rigid and mute. Henri, on the other hand, had regained partial sobriety. All that reverb temporarily restored his motor skills, allowing him to bounce up the steps, gracefully retrieve four glasses from the little lounge on the second floor, and open the door to his room, without a misstep. "Handsome tattoos," he said of the designs on their shoulders and forearms as the four bikers marched by.

"Thank you, Frenchie," said Leon. "Very old. Anasazi."

"Have a seat," said Henri. He poured the four triple shots of vodka and retrieved his kit from the bathroom with his various medicinals. He sat on the floor and began to wash and dress Leon's hand. Leon and his friends smelled of woodsmoke. The last time Henri smelled woodsmoke was when he had visited his grandmother in the country. "Are you from Silverado?"

Leon laughed. "No. We live in the hills with the night dogs and the pumas. There were biker gangs in France when you were a boy?"

"Several years after the war there was still the black market, so there were many gangs. They rode bikes from the war. Some were German, some British, French, Italian, and American. The police could never catch them, because they went down steps and narrow streets. They were my heroes. They let me help them work on their bikes even though I was a kid."

"Did you ever have a bike?"

"I was eleven when I got my first bike—a Harley Davidson 45. I put it together with parts from three other 45s. It was my greatest achievement. But I was too light to do the kick start. I had to ask big guys I could trust to do the start. Bad guys would, how you say, take it for a spin. If the spin was too long, they would run out of gas.

"The gas was expensive. I usually siphoned it from the police car at night in front of the station—just a little each time." He put his ointment and bandages back in the kit. "And there you are, Señor Marquez, all fixed up. New again, yes?"

"Much better, thank you." Marquez went to the window and looked up and down the street. They had been in town long enough for the local police to call the highway patrol for assistance. "We're leaving now. You are a gentleman and friend, Frenchie Bashé."

Henri followed them down the stairs and watched them ride off, flashing under the street lights, then leaning into the corner at P. Street and Grant. The engines echoed back through the town. They were bigger and louder than those he had heard as a child, but his first night of the motorcycles would always be larger in his memory.

On his way back, he remembered the night clerk's trauma and looked for him. "Mr. Night Man, where are you?" But there was no sign. Henri stood at the counter and waited, thinking about rebuilding his 45. He had known everything there was to know about the 45 Harley Davidson—a victory unparalleled in his life, for reasons he could not explain. He was still living his youth when he heard someone stir behind the counter. The surprised face of the night clerk emerged from below. "Good evening," said Henri. "Napping?"

"No, sir. I was waiting to be sure all the gang had left. I am terrified of them. I can't help it. These are very bad people you took to your room, do you know?"

Henri gestured with one hand, then the other. "Good, bad, good bad, it depends on many things. They seem like nice guys."

"These men are some kind of Mexican Indians who know how to go through the desert at night without roads so the agents can't follow them. They live in caves, where they can hide from planes and helicopters. They bring drugs from the Mexican mafia in Nuevo Casas Grandes over the border. These people kill people. They are bad, bad people."

"Sometimes even good people are not so good. You can never tell."

He smiled and went up to his room.

Henri sat up. It was four o'clock and quiet. He must have been awakened by a noise. He listened, hoping for Anita's moans. Instead, he heard growling. He got up and looked out the window. The street below was filled with black dog creatures running up the gulch. One of them stopped in the street, raised its head at Henri, and began to moan.

He woke with an erection. Anita and Billy were going hard at it. He listened, horny and dreamy, then the moaning stopped.

"Billeee."

"Peaches, I can't row with a rope."

It was getting light out. Anita's voraciousness would not let Henri sleep anyway. Everything between them would now be tinged with his knowledge of her consuming passion. It would color everything. The thought inspired him to go to work on another project.

He got up, showered, got some coffee in the hall machine, added his freeze-dried, lit a cigarette, and began transferring his list of words from the little red book onto a legal pad. He had gathered hundreds of words since the beginning of the trip. Anything that rang in his brain went in the book—words from billboards, magazines, men's rooms, conversations, words misunderstood, and words mispronounced. He began scanning his list, making marks, underlining, drawing arrows, combining, dissecting, yes, even deconstructing words. Matching and mating words—words that could be translated into cash money.

Luck followed Henri. His latest piece of luck, other than the questionable association with Anita, now at least made interesting by her sexual voracity—was a chance seat companion on a train from Brussels to Amsterdam the year before. An American, a gnomish woman with a pixilated brain, offered him a job finding names and slogans for new companies. Henri was paid on commission. His names went into a database with a date. If the name was purchased and he was in with it first, he received 20 percent. Plus it was fun, plus it tore the world into the little bits he cherished, and best of all, it commercialized absurdity. At the moment he was supporting himself and Nina with word play for pay.

So far he had sold many names, including Anna-Retzia, an L.A.-based clothing line; Juvenalia Teen Fashions; Bondo Zee, a Dutch manufacturer of sex toys; Vortex Vixen, a distributor of sexy, New Age accoutrements—and several slogans, including "The last best place" to the Morioka Prefecture travel bureau in northern Japan. For his names and slogans he had already received eighty thousand American dollars, before taxes. Henri knew this could not last, and he had to make euros while the sun shined. He had a long list worked out an hour later when Billy knocked gently at his door.

"Come in, come in. I am ready."

Billy entered, tentatively. The room was blue with smoke. He had never seen Henri so early. "What's up?"

Henri leered. "Have a bad night?"

"You've been listening?"

"There's a vent in the wall under the sign that says, 'no peek, no listen.' I covered my ears and sang nursery rhymes."

"What are you working on?"

"Making money," he said, halfway through his first pack of cigarettes and flipping yellow pages. "I send lists of words to Rae Tesme, a small woman from Hollywood, and she sends me a lot of money. Words for money. I have excellent, how you say, brand-eye coordination. What are we doing today, young Billy?"

"It's too smoky in here. That's the secret, isn't it? Your brain can't get any air. You don't think, you hallucinate."

"At the moment I'm working on a name for a New Age drink with carbonated essence of awe and respect. So far I have Awesome Indian Fiz, Sacred Zip, and Rez Wiz."

"I'd lose the Rez Wiz."

"But I like Rez Wiz."

Billy clapped his hands in a show of enthusiasm. "Want to do some editing? Buddha's warm and waiting. Also, I want to show you something I'm working on."

"What's that?"

"It's a short piece about how people use archaeology to say what they've already made up their minds to say."

"You Americans dig to create a text for yourselves. Ancient relics help to . . . obscure your loneliness. You need to hear the whisperings of prehistoric people in the rooms of your house. In Europe we want to revisit our lost empires. And never forget, our cavemen were better artists than your cavemen."

They stopped for a jolt at the coffee nook and walked down to the van, hidden in the hotel's back lot—in case Raw Bone and Rat were on the prowl.

Billy had a scene ready to go. "This is all done with pieces from discarded footage and outtakes. I call it Reel Anthropology. You find the best stuff in outtakes. This was shot somewhere in the South Pacific, I got it out of the discard bin at *Geo*." The clip showed a man in the foreground in Western clothes, squatting on the jungle floor, watching a naked native man trying to start a fire by striking flint sparks into a cone of dried moss. The man's little daughter sat on his leg as he struck the flint, waiting for the fire to start. All this flint striking was going nowhere. The white guy got bored, took a cigarette from his shirt pocket, and lit it with a Zippo lighter. The little girl's eyes flashed from her father's striker to the Zippo. Billy zoomed in on her face and froze the scene. "The edited film is always an illusion—the outtake is the reality."

"*Oui, certainement.* So it is. As the conscious life is merely a dream—and our dreams are the reality, but don't tell Lucy I said that."

THIRTEEN

"You're going away?" asked the voice behind the deerskin mask. She had her legs stretched out over the edge of the table, toes pointed, arms and fingers reaching toward the ceiling.

"I'm going on a picnic with the archaeologist, remember?"

She put her arms down, hands flat on the table. She was thinking. She looked at her breasts and gave them a jiggle.

"You're very sexy for an appar—"

"To my cave?"

Jack heard the jealousy in her voice. "I'm just showing her the cave. It's not like we're having sex in your parlor."

"Really? She wants to have sex with you, and you want to have sex with her. What have I failed to grasp?"

"Philip, her man for all reasons."

"All the wrong reasons, you mean." She arched her back, her nipples hard and rosy. "Thinking about you with her fills my body with passion. I think it's time for rain."

"Are you coming on to me?"

"What would you do if I were flesh and blood?"

"This is very weird. I'm being seduced by my own apparition."

"You don't have to go to the cave. You could bring her back here."

He was lacing his boots, giving her a sidelong look, trying to imagine her watching while he made love to Lucy. He decided, if she didn't talk, it would be like having his cat watch. "I'm supposed to put on a peep show for a phantom voyeur in a bird mask? I'm not sure I need that."

"It's time for the clouds to come. You can smell it in the air."

"I was supposed to meet Lucy ten minutes ago." He was all laced up, the bags with the climbing gear were ready by the door, and he was looking for a watch he thought he'd left in a drawer a couple of years ago.

"You have a surprise coming, Jack. I only wish I could be around to see the look on your face when you figure it out."

"See you tonight. Try not to spook the cat." Talking to Willow was making him feel as though he were in two places at once. Disorienting. He was glad to be headed to town.

He had a feeling she wasn't staying around much longer. Perhaps he had created Willow in the hope she would explain that single, obscure gesture, but he had absorbed her and her thoughts as he had The Sisters'. They had worked their way into that place that reminded him of who he was. It had been the summer of Willow and The Sisters. What a lucky man he'd been—the magic of Willow, the dancer and storyteller, and the giddy joy of the endlessly playful, teasing Sisters. He had been overly blessed. Soon they would all be gone. In losing them, he would lose a part of himself.

Then there was Lucy. He was taking her into the middle world of the Mimbres. Where, he wondered, would that lead?

In the secluded parking lot behind the hotel, Anita slid the van's door open, jumped in, and slammed it shut. She was pale and breathing hard. "I think they found us."

"Who?"

"Raw Bone and Rat is who. I was in the lobby, drinking my coffee and reading the paper. I looked up and saw Raw Bone drive by in that red pickup we deflated. He stared right at me."

All three had a flicker of panic—eyes darting from window to window.

"Did he drive by again?" asked Billy.

"I didn't stay around long enough to find out."

"It's real bright out. I doubt if he could see through the reflection in the window."

"He was wearin' sunglasses."

"They'd be the cheap ones."

"Yeah. Probably."

"Probably," said Henri.

"They're gonna find us." She glared at Billy. "When they do, they'll kill us, because you had to be such a macho jackass. I want to leave town right now."

"In daylight? We'd be too easy to spot, they could follow us out of town."

"Oh, Christ almighty, baby. What're we gonna do?"

"Be cool, honey bunny."

"Don't quote *Pulp*-Fucking-*Fiction* at me, goddamn it. Those assholes want to kill us."

"Do you have your .38 on you?"

"I hardly have clothes on, for Christ sake."

"All right. All right. Look. If we stay together and stay in town, we'll be okay. Go get the .38 and bring Lucy back with you. Maybe we can hide out at her friend's place."

"Jack Miller?"

"Yeah, him. He'll have guns."

"Okay, Billy, but I think we'd be better off makin' a run for it." She also liked the idea of hiding out at Jack's. It was a conundrum. She slid the door open, looked both ways, sprinted to the back door of the hotel, bounded up the back stairs, and nearly ran into Lucy, who was just leaving. Anita was startled, "Lucy? Where you goin'?"

"Jack's taking me into a Mimbres cave. We'll be back tonight." She was wearing her many-pockets jacket, a pack, and loose ripstop pants over sweats, the height of bulky-butt caver fashion.

"Billy sent me up to get you. I saw Raw Bone drive by the hotel. I couldn't tell if he saw me or not, but they are definitely looking for us. I'm scared. I want to get out of town."

"Jack's waiting for me in the lobby. He can tell you what to do."

Jack was sitting on a long Naugahyde couch, reading *The Albuquerque Journal.*

"Jack, you remember Anita? She's afraid Raw Bone and Rat know we're here."

"Hi, Anita. I remember. Very Texas. In the best way, of course."

Her concerns were not with her lowlife roots. "I'm really scared of these guys. I've seen them real close. They would've killed my partner if it weren't for Lucy and my .38. Do you have any suggestions?"

"You're safe in the hotel. They won't come after you here. They'll wait 'til you leave and follow. Just keep your .38 handy. When you're ready to leave town, I'll see they're distracted."

"You will? Gee, thanks."

"Lucy and I are going to take a look at a cave. We'll be back by dark."

"People get lost in caves all the time." Anita felt safe with Jack. She would have liked him around on a more permanent basis. For a brief moment, she indulged the idea of being looked after instead of looking after.

"We're well prepared. Don't worry about us and don't worry about Raw Bone and Rat. You'll be okay. One thing to keep in mind—Lucy whacked Raw Bone pretty good. He might not recognize any of you. And when Rat wasn't lookin' at that .38, mostly all he'll remember is your eyes and some spiky, red hair. Dark glasses and a scarf wouldn't hurt if you have to go out."

Lucy leaned over and put her hand on Anita's knee. "I know you've got a lot of footage to go over. The van's well out of sight. You can edit all day. The desk or the bar will get you anything you need. Just keep Henri off the street and you'll be fine."

"You know," said Anita, "I'd love to see this cave. Maybe I could come along. I've got good legs."

"I'm sorry," said Jack, "but we only have two harnesses. I wouldn't want to take you in without proper gear. These things take some planning. Some other time, maybe?"

"Sure. Sorry I was so pushy."

Anita watched Jack and Lucy leave, warmed by Jack's attention and reassured by his advice. She wanted to throttle Lucy. "Cave, my ass," she mumbled as she headed back to her room to get the .38.

She returned to the van wearing large oval sunglasses, her red hair hidden under a black silk scarf decorated with blood roses, carrying an extra box of cartridges, and an eighteen-inch piece of heavy rebar. She handed the rebar to Billy. "Just in case I miss the bastards."

"It's got good heft," he said, slapping the bar into his hand. "Where'd you find it?"

"In the basement. It's on loan from the janitor."

Billy was editing a piece on Henri. Both men seemed unconcerned about Raw Bone and Rat—Anita would take care of everything. She absorbed the situation quickly, accepted responsibility, and climbed into the front seat, where she had the best view of the outside world. She ate energy bars and drank two Big Bounces of Super Joose, while she kept watch in a heightened state of anxiety, depleting her serotonin, ravaging her synapses, jiggling from cheek to cheek in an incremental creep toward panic. Henri and Billy edited, oblivious to her impending fragmentation. She unconsciously caressed the .38, and fantasized Raw Bone's repeated demise by various techniques, executed by her in an assortment of flashy outfits, while Jack waited for her back at the ranch in a state of throbbing arousal.

Bits and pieces of what was being said in back, mixed with sound effects, intruded on her fantasies. Billy was showing Henri a series of car crashes. "That one," said Henri. Billy froze the final frame and began compressing sounds of wreckage into extended bass explosions with deep reverb and an eighties' video-game slam. "Okay," said Henri, "now about twelve frames of car crunching . . . That's great, Billy. Now for the denouement."

"*Day-new-ma?* What is?"

"Something like . . . the final release—the purge. Or perhaps, in these times, only the gesture before the pause announcing the next thing."

"Gush of blood?"

"Gushing's good."

Billy fingered Buddha and popped up a Renaissance painting of a wincing woman slicing through a man's carotid artery in the act of beheading him. "Give me a second—I can spurt the blood and give him a flick of eye flutter . . . There we go."

"Good gush. Spurting blood—the release from consciousness—absolute catharsis and classic resolution to the human comedy."

"Missed it," said Billy.

"Missed what?"

"The funny part."

Jack and Lucy left the highway at Becker's yellow metal house. The chicken was still pecking away in the shade of the rusty tractor. As Jack negotiated the hairpin turns up the mountainside, Lucy asked, "How did you find this cave, and how long have you known about it?"

"A German, named Becker, flew off the rim of a canyon in a red Taurus and died at my feet, leaving a map with directions."

"You're joking, I hope."

"The flying Taurus is too mythological?"

"Too preposterous."

"Truth is preposterous. Check the sheriff's report. Just don't say anything about the map or the cave."

She was quiet for a while. Her thoughts were with Anita, the .38, and Billy's bruises. She studied the hairpin turns below—nothing following them. And nothing down on the highway. There was a truck parked off the highway in the distance, which she thought had been there when they went by.

"You said Raw Bone and Rat had a mine the EPA shut down. What kind of mine?"

"Mostly gold. It was an old underground vein they'd been working for years. Gold miners have to put the ore through a hammer mill, then wash it with cyanide to leach out the heavy metal. There was enough gold in the vein to keep the brothers going even when the price dropped, but the feds made them stop the cyanide from seeping into the river."

"So they've been making a living by poisoning everything down-stream for years?"

"Along with the rest of the gold miners."

"Now these guys are crazed, because the government put a stop to it. Can't they get a job?"

Jack shrugged. "Would you hire them?"

Lucy shook her head in disgust.

He glanced at the flash of gold on her ears. "Nice earrings. Philip give you those?"

"Thanks." She forgot which she was wearing and reached up to touch them—small, 24-karat gold seashells. "Yes. A birthday . . . present." Great, she thought, I can't wear gold anymore.

She was quiet too long.

"Sorry," he said.

"Don't be."

"Being self-righteous is complicated."

She laughed. "Yeah, Mr. Grave Robber. You'll get yours."

"You have no idea."

She was intrigued. "You could tell me."

"Yes, and it would be as unbelievable for you as it is for me." He pulled off the road. "This is it. We'll cross over those rocks and work our way to the bottom. There's a deer trail about halfway down. The cave is across the canyon, under an overhang. It's so well hidden, you can't even see it on the other side of this ridge."

"Tell me what's so unbelievable."

"Later maybe. Let's get our stuff. I want to concentrate on the cave."

They crossed the ridge and started down the trail. This time the trip was different for Jack. He was no longer thinking about the parrot trainer, or Hans Becker, or where the cave would be. He was thinking about Lucy. They hit the deer trail and were soon across the floor of the canyon. He pointed out handholds and the zigzag path that led from ledge to ledge.

They worked their way up the cliff face. He had a backpack and a larger nylon bag containing two climbing harnesses, two hundred feet of rope, helmets, head lamps, batteries, water, protein bars, and enough food for three days. Since he was an amateur at climbing and acrophobic, he used the rope to pull the bag from ledge to ledge.

The trip was faster and surer than the first. She watched him moving above her, aware of his agility and strength. He reached the wall under the mesa in half the time it had taken the first. They sat on the ledge overlooking the small valley, its detail made pale and shadowless by the high sun. Both the road and the pickup were hidden by the ridge of black rock on the other side of the canyon.

"We've crossed into another world." She looked down at the base of the cliff, toward the half-hidden pool. "Listen. There are children swimming and splashing below." For a moment, she was a teenager testing out the new boy.

He looked down at the secret pool. His face was expressionless—too sober to play, she thought. Then he closed his eyes. "They're shouting. One's a joyful shrieker with gills and wings. She can breathe air or water and can fly or swim. She's just escaped from a cavern beneath the cliff that leads to the sea."

"What else goes on in your mind?"

He glanced at her. "Well . . . I converse on a daily basis with the masked woman in the pot I found in the cave behind us."

Lucy remembered him looking at the parrot trainer. She was cautious. "Is that what you meant by unbelievable?"

"But harmless."

"Does your apparition have a name?"

"Willow."

"That makes sense. Mimbres is Spanish for 'willow.' Does she follow you around or stay at home?"

"Strictly housebound."

He began pulling the bag with their supplies the rest of the way up the cliff. "The Mimbres thought of this world—the world of trees, rivers, sun, and sky—as the third world. We are about to enter their second world—the cave, which was the underground passage connecting the surface to the first world, where they originated. Their first world was much like the third world. It even had an underworld sky that hovered overhead like an inverted bowl. The Mimbres believed that in the time before time, they were led from the first world up into the second world by a spirit creature who made them half animal and half human. They lived in the dark as animal-humans before Coatimundi took them to the third world. He also separated animals from humans and gave the humans souls.

"To the Mimbres, the universe was very self-contained. When people died, their spirits became cloud people, similar to today's kachinas, and made rain. Then they came down in the rain, soaked through the earth, and emerged in the first world. After a while, their souls were reborn in human beings in this world."

"A very circular world—no heaven or hell. The Spanish priests who came to convert the northern pueblos four hundred years later must have had their patience tested trying to unravel that tidy little knot. Why do you think the Mimbres believed in kachinas and their cyclical world?"

He hesitated for a moment and looked off toward the rock ridge. It reminded him of the spine of a dinosaur. He wanted to sound halfway reasonable. "Well, the Mimbres left a lot of hints on their pots that relate to contemporary kachinas." He looked at Lucy and grinned. "Willow filled in here and there."

Lucy rolled her eyes. "We have a cave to explore," she said and swung her legs over the ledge. "Let's get on with it."

He pulled two hundred feet of nylon rope out of the big bag, a set of rock drills, bolts, a hammer, swivel clips, the harnesses, sweaters, and gloves. He carried the rope, and they divided the rest of the stuff into their backpacks.

Lucy examined the harnesses. "Where'd you get these? They look brand new."

"They're nylon halter strapping. I put them together at Jerry's Saddle Shop yesterday. They come with a lifetime guarantee."

"Mine or yours?"

"We'll know more after the test." He pointed to the opening of the cave. "That had been a crevice in the wall. It must have taken a while to chip a doorway large enough for an adult."

The shape of the tapered opening was not lost on Lucy. There was no doubt this was the entrance to the earth's womb. Sliding her body through the opening into the interior of the cave was strange, oddly sexual, and amusing. She assumed Jack had his own thoughts about it, but kept hers to herself.

They slowly panned their flashlights around, searching for details and getting a physical sense of the cave and its treasures. She examined the plain ceramic ollas, the stone ax, scrapers, knives, awls, and bone daggers with her flashlight, and peered into the baskets. She shook her head at the tightness of the weave. Jack shined his light on the pile of rose-colored shells, then scooped them up and handed them to her. It was something she would never have done without first measuring, numbering, and photographing, but the beauty of the shells sent a thrill through her. "Thank you," she said, taking them to the doorway, into the daylight.

"In the winter," he said, "the children would hold them in the shaft of sun to let the light reflect on their faces."

She smiled. "Did your parrot trainer tell you this?"

"No. It's a kid thing, though, isn't it?"

"Yeah . . ." She looked at him. "It is a kid thing."

He dug out the helmets and head lamps and took her farther into the cave, through the tunnel into the next room where the parrot trainer's skeleton sat behind the reconstructed stone wall. Jack stood quietly and stared at the wall, which was illuminated by the lamp on his helmet. "There's where she's buried. The German, Becker, found her."

"The man in the flying red Taurus, whose last act was to give you a map?"

His laughter bounced around the room. "He didn't exactly give it to me. I took it."

"Old habits . . ."

"Aren't you glad I did?" he asked.

Lucy ignored his question. "Was she exposed when you found her?"

"Yes. Originally the crevice had been filled with a sandy clay as the stones were set in place. Becker did a good job of removing enough clay to get at the bowls without disturbing her. He set the bowls on the floor to sketch them. That's where I found them. I don't know why he left them. He may have had to leave in a hurry and intended to come back."

"How many bowls?"

"Two small ones and the parrot trainer."

"Where're the others?"

"I put them back when I rebuilt the wall."

She was pleased he had reburied his parrot trainer.

He pointed his light at the olla against the opposite wall and watched as she gently lifted the stone lid.

The fanged snake stared up at her. "Ooh, that's wonderful." She shined her flashlight into the olla, studying the fragile balance of bones. "It may have been a kind of talisman. Something for protection." Her voice reverberated from the jar. "Slivers of mica were inserted in the eye sockets to make them glow. The skeleton had to have been carefully reconstructed with hide glue. He looks ready to leap out at transgressing spirits."

Their voices echoed deep into the cave, drawing them toward the slanted passageway into the Mimbres underworld. Jack unzipped his pack while Lucy held a light on the operation. He removed the hammer and steel drills and began the arduous process of pounding a drill into the rock for the bolts that would hold the rope. After a while, Lucy took over. They traded back and forth for an hour until they got two pins anchored in the rock, tied off the rope, and let it play out into the darkness below.

Lucy offered to go first.

"You're sure?"

"Quite. I told you, I've done this before. I'm fearless."

"Well, be fearless, then. Going down is the worst part for me, and I'm not that great at going up."

"You did pretty well on the cliff."

"Kids and women carrying babies went up and down that cliff every day."

"Let's go." She snapped the rope through her harness swivels and, with one hand on the rope in front and one hand behind, began walking backward, testing the surface. The slant became steeper and steeper until it reached about forty-five degrees. Getting out was going to take time and lots of upper-body muscle. She had descended about 150 feet when her voice echoed through the cavern, "God almighty."

As soon as the line went slack, he snapped on. The anchor pins gave him the confidence to descend the chute at a run. In less than fifteen seconds he could see what had inspired Lucy's "God almighty"—a pile of bones and human skulls lay on the first plateau of the cave. These were the northmen, the cannibal gang. This was Willow's surprise—something he could not have guessed. No amount of intuition on his part could have contrived her story and then discovered the proof for it.

Lucy looked back at him, catching the edge of his face in her head lamp. "What do you think—a sacrifice?"

He sounded vague. "How about mass murder?"

They had to step among the skeletons to continue into the cave. Willow was taking a new shape in his mind. An old phrase of grade-school propaganda, "new dimensions and important breakthroughs," jumped into his thoughts. He had always hated the phrase. But he was certainly faced with a new dimension.

Lucy studied the jumble of skeletons, trying to determine what had happened. Some were scattered, others were in a pile. Apparently, six had survived the fall and managed to crawl away from their dead brethren. She made a disturbing discovery in the pile—finger bones clutching the wrist bones of another skeleton. "This almost looks like a communal suicide—as though they all held on to each other's wrists and plunged to their death. These all appear to be adult males. Do you think they're Mimbres?"

"If this was a Mimbres suicide, there would be women and children. Perhaps the Mimbres tricked an enemy."

She stared at the bones, wondering why Jack would jump to such a conclusion. "A trick? I can't imagine how."

Jack was staring at the bones, imagining Willow's glee when he told her about finding the bones of her dead northmen. "Let's get going."

They unsnapped the rope and continued their explorations at a gradual descent for another hour without finding anything as astounding or unsettling as the skeletons. They came upon formations of quartz that reflected their lights into separate rays of color dancing over the walls. Once past the quartz, they entered a low tunnel that forced them to crawl on a downward slant for eighty feet before emerging in a large room where their lights glittered off slivers of mica in the rock.

Lucy turned, letting her head lamp treat them to the explosion of light. "Zowie. Mimbres disco or a secret Bee Gees' hideaway."

Jack was equally impressed, but for other reasons. This was Willow's room of a thousand eyes.

They turned their lights overhead and discovered the ceiling was covered with fur. They were looking up at hundreds of sleeping bats. For several minutes they stood, staring at the furry creatures, until the light began to ruffle the ceiling sleepers. They turned their lamps off and waited in the dark, beneath the soft ruffle of leather wings. The scene at the bottom of the chute had stayed with them—the mesh of human skeletons and the image of fingers bones clutching wrist bones.

"Would you like to start back?" he asked.

"Yes, I would." She turned her lamp on and they began retracing their path toward the chute and the jumble of bones.

If Willow had started out as a projection of Jack's mind, some repressed part of himself, she was certainly doing a good job of establishing an identity apart from his. How could he have known about the skeletons? Perhaps Becker had made the discovery and Jack had unconsciously translated a phrase as he skimmed the notes. He would have to go through the notes again and search for a reference. There was the room with a thousand eyes, but she had not mentioned the quartz formations. He could not help scanning the walls for the image of Coatimundi.

"Oh, God, no," Lucy's sickened shout echoed around him. He looked up to see her silhouette amid the skeletons. What alarmed her was not evident to him, until he saw a snake slithering around her ankles. Then with greater speed it began spilling over skeletons, and over the rocks toward Jack. It took a moment for the horrible sensation of a snake to become 150 feet of nylon rope freed from its pins at the top of the chute. They stared up into darkness that consumed their light. His first thought was that the rope had been abraded against a sharp edge, but when he found the end, he could see the rope had been untied from the pins.

They looked at each other for a moment, then in one voice said, "Raw Bone and Rat." They switched their head lamps off and waited, scarcely breathing.

Jack put his mouth to her ear and whispered, "Back away around the bend and stay to the inside."

They held hands and quietly retraced their steps through the skeletons in the dark. After they made it around the bend, safe from falling objects, they stopped and leaned against the wall.

"I didn't see anyone follow us," said Lucy. "How did they know?"

Jack went over the landscape in his mind until he had a plausible answer. "About a quarter mile this side of the bar, there's a farmer's lane that crosses the valley and takes off up the hill to an abandoned mine shaft. It's a high point over the valley. If they saw us take the logging road, they had plenty of time to find the pickup and spot us before we even reached the cave."

"We have at least twenty hours before Kills The Deer shows up." Their predicament excited her. Circumstances beyond her control gave way to a liberating sensation—as though they were strangers on a train. "You can tell me your life story."

"I think I'll spend my time devising ways to kill Raw Bone when we get out of here."

"Well, I pretty much tried that, which is what got us into this situation, so I'd advise against halfway measures." She was quiet for a moment, then asked, "Do you think they might wait around to see if anyone comes to check on us?"

"I seriously doubt it. They're not the waitin'-around kind, and if they did they wouldn't stand a chance against Kills The Deer."

"I wish I'd finished the job."

"It wasn't very professional of you."

"What will you really do, when we get out of here?"

"Get you on a plane."

"I mean, to them?"

"Send them on a wild goose chase. Juarez would be good. A week of that town would finish them off. The Mexican mafia would wrap them in razor wire and roll them back across the border."

She laughed at the thought of Raw Bone and Rat stomping through Juarez, checking the motels for her.

"Let's see if my phone works." She took the cell phone out of her pack and pressed the number for the hotel and got static. "Do these things work anywhere?"

"Could I interest you in some champagne, Dr. Perelli? Personally I would like to fog my sensory system a little."

"You have champagne? I have a cardinal rule—never refuse champagne when trapped in a cave. We should eat something, too."

They turned their lamps on and descended deeper into the cave, searching for a suitable spot to dine and sleep. They found a relatively flat surface where the two of them could stretch out and call home for the night.

He pulled two candles from his pack and gave them to her. She was melting wax on the rock for stickum when she heard a champagne cork pop.

"I brought it along to celebrate a successful caving adventure," said Jack.

"It's supposed to be bad luck to celebrate before there's something to celebrate."

"There're a lot of rules about the celebration business I don't know about."

"Celebrations are immersed in rules."

"Around these parts, they generally get drunk. That's if it's just a bunch of guys."

"And now you understand something else about culture."

"It's one of the few things men do understand about culture. Actually, I've noticed males don't think about culture so much as we go along with the program. We think of ourselves as the result of a two-million-year-old experiment run by females. We're the human variant of lab rats. Have some champagne." He handed her a plastic cup and poured.

She toasted him. "It's been symbiotic."

"The fact that you've bred us to be brutes confuses the guilt issues, don't you think?"

"It would, if we thought about it, but we don't."

"I often wonder why certain women are attracted to certain men."

"I usually run contrary to type, but then, I already have a mate, so my unconscious brain automatically filters out other prospects."

"Really?" He had fallen into the trap of believing she was interested in him.

"But then, I'd be the last to know, wouldn't I?"

He smiled and began sorting through the pack. "For cave cuisine, we have provolone and cheddar, vacuum packed, sliced roast turkey, honey mustard, rye and sourdough, canned peaches, little yogurt cups—lots of those—and energy bars in nine flavors that protect the rain forest."

In candlelight, among cave shapes, consumed by thoughts of murder, mating, and escape, they drank champagne, and devoured turkey-provolone-mustard sandwiches.

"I'm surprised we haven't found paintings or petroglyphs," said Lucy. "You would think that during the last thirteen thousand years, someone would have managed to get down here with ropes or ladders and leave us a few animals on the wall?"

"I'd bet on Coatimundi."

"You seem to know a lot about this place for someone who's never been down here before."

He was quiet for a long time, trying to find a way to make his story halfway reasonable.

"Jack?"

"It's just an . . ."

"Just tell it." She laughed. He looked so serious in the flickering candlelight. "Trust me."

"Okay." He sipped champagne from the plastic cup. "When I found Becker, his notebook had blown out of the car. I retrieved the pages, took them home, and tried to translate them. It's been a long time since I read German, and it was slow going. I started scanning for words that could be tied to his map. What I'm going to tell you could have come out of Becker's notes, even though I wasn't conscious of it at the time. I really don't know. I'm just looking for a rational explanation of how I could have known about the skeletons."

"So some of what you know has come from simple, rational deduction, based on what you've read and heard, and some of it has come from Willow, a manifestation of your overly stimulated imagination?"

"I think so. Willow's stories seem to be a mix of accepted ideas and fantasy. She told fascinating as well as gruesome stories. What she described as the Mimbres belief system was an early kachina cult. Then she took it further, claiming some of the Chaco outlier groups to the north adopted many Mimbres ideas, which threatened the Chacoan lords who sent cannibal gangs down to terrify the Mimbres. Most of the Mimbres had already moved to the Rio Grande side of the mountains, but the Chacoans found a few of them in the valley below this cliff and made an example of a young man by hacking him to death and eating him in plain sight. When the Chacoans came for Willow she told them there was a treasure of parrot feathers, which they could get to by linking themselves together, hands to wrists, in a human chain and descending into the second world. Her aunt taught them a chant to protect them from evil spirits—a high wailing chant that masked the screams of those who clutched their comrades' wrists as they fell to their death."

Lucy sipped champagne, going over the details in her head, trying to make sense of his story. "How good was your German?"

"I studied it for a year in college. I could read the easy stuff."

"Did you ever think in German?"

"Sometimes, when I dreamed."

"What else did Willow tell you about the cave?"

"She said there was a room with a thousand eyes that was alive and breathing, which could have been the room with the mica and the bats. She mentioned a wall with a drawing of Coatimundi. Finally, there was a glowing pool in a large room with spears sticking up from the floor. The Mimbres believed the pool glowed from the light of the underworld sky. They didn't go into the pool, because they were afraid if they went through to the other side they might upset the balance of life and death—they were unsure of what would happen."

"She didn't mention the chamber with the quartz?"

"No."

Lucy's laughter was warmed by the champagne. "A thousand years is a long time. Maybe it slipped her mind."

"Maybe I never learned the German for 'quartz'?"

"So this has been going on since you took the bowl from the cave and got your sting?"

"The hallucinations began on the way home. The conversations started later."

"But they don't seem to have abated along with your other reactions?"

"No. In fact they are more lucid, even contentious."

"Contentious? How?"

"She claims she's a ghost whose spirit was trapped in her burial bowl a thousand years ago, that she is not a part of me, that she is not my hallucination."

"She talks. Does she move around or come out of the bowl?"

"She steps out of the bowl and grows to normal height."

Lucy gave him an inquisitive look. "She has a physical body? Have you touched her?"

Where, he wondered, was she going with this? He shook his head. "No. I don't think there's anything to touch."

"Does she always wear the mask?"

"Always. Sometimes I can see her eyes."

"Have you been under a lot of stress recently?"

"Besides the sting, a disembodied toe, and you? No."

"I cause you stress?"

"Not enough to cause hallucinations."

"So tell me, why would I be a source of stress for you?" She was smiling, teasing.

"I live a very quiet, protected life. I'm not used to being affected by strange women. Not for a while, anyway. You're causing . . . complications."

She was conscious of the fact that she had been flirting. She wondered if it had been obvious to Jack. She was used to flirting with men in a very harmless way, checking out her attractiveness or power or whatever it was she had no name for, but she was careful professionally. Whatever was going on between them was different. She could not tell where the boundaries were. It made her a little anxious. "You've managed to isolate yourself from everything that irritates you, haven't you?"

"I have several lifetimes of projects in mind. I stay immersed. It keeps me sane. What's your secret?"

"I went in the other direction. I may be sane, but I'm not all that happy with the current state of things. You immerse yourself in experiences. I created a bureaucracy that needs constant feeding. It's rare that I even get out to look at sites anymore, much less for them. That's why your maps mean so much to me. Mostly, I raise money. That's my life, asking people for money. I want out for the same reasons you stopped dealing. Everybody becomes a mark."

"What do you want to do?"

"Play in the dirt."

"Like me?"

She laughed. "I have all your sites to dig, remember."

"Playing in the dirt is about the only thing that makes sense anymore."

"It lets me pretend I still live in the natural world."

"There's an extraordinary Mimbres bowl of two bears connected by an umbilical cord to an embryonic man in the middle. To the front and back of the man are little corn fields. The man throws his hands up against the bears, against his creators. He cannot deny them, yet he wants to escape this insufferable bondage to nature. We want the easy life of crops, machines, wheels, gasoline, and electricity—we want the subsidy."

"The man was connected to the bears by an umbilical cord? Why bears?"

"They're smart animals with human traits. At one time there was an unusually strong connection between Indians and bears. When I was a kid, I went to Alaska to work on a fishing boat. Eventually I ended up living on an island that was home to several bear clan elders. The Native Cultural Council was controlled by Fundamentalist Christian Indians, who thought the traditionalists were a troublesome bunch of pagans because they objected to the council's cutting down the forests, building dams, and putting the bears out of business.

"When I came to the island, the old men told me stories about bears, how bears used to be people, and how to think about bears, but they never said the name of the bear in their own language."

"Why not?"

"I think they believed the name was part of the bear. When you say his name, it reverberates in the bear's spirit and calls forth a powerful and dangerous bear."

"How did they talk about the bear, if they couldn't say its name?"

"By calling it other names. 'A dark place,' 'sticky mouth,' 'four-legged human,' and 'fierce mouse beast' are a few I remember. A place called Badger Creek is really Bear Creek, but you have to live there awhile before you figure that out."

"So the metaphor takes your mind away from the real bear?"

"The bear clan guys would say it keeps the bear's mind away from you."

"They must've had some pretty stupid bears."

"You're lucky there're no bears around, 'cause they'd eat ya."

"If you were with me, I wouldn't have to worry about bears."

"You think I could save you from a bear?"

"I'm betting I'd outrun you."

"It doesn't always work. They like to chase down the lively ones."

"Did you meet the bears the old men talked about?"

"I've become well acquainted with several bears, but I don't know if they were the same ones. I ended up living on the other side of the island where Jessup Conklin loaned me one of his shacks."

"So you just went over the mountain to see what you could see, and there was Jessup?"

"I met him in a bar on the mainland. He was getting old, and it got too hard on him to winter out there alone, so he started staying in town from November through the first of May. He said if I'd help him out with a few things, I could meet the bears. Well a 'few things' turned into about fourteen hours a day, and I didn't see a single bear. He'd point up at the mountains from time to time, at little black holes in the snow. 'The bears live up there in those caves. They'll be comin' down any day for the sedge grass. That's what they eat in the spring.'

"After a couple of weeks of that, I realized I'd been snookered. One afternoon, I walked out into a field above the tide line to look at the first flowers to bloom. Because they were a dark chocolate color, Jessup called them chocolate lilies. There was a little field of them, and in the middle of the field was a nice soft patch of grass. I lay down and fell asleep.

"Maybe an hour later, I became aware of the fact that I was not alone. My eyes were closed, and I didn't know if I was dreaming or not, but I could hear the sound of big things chewing. It was a slow kind of chewing. Then I opened my eyes. All around me were bears. They obviously knew I was there, but they didn't seem to care.

"I lay still for a long time, just to be sure. When I sat up—slowly—they were digging up the chocolate lily bulbs and eating them. The bulbs were a bear delicacy. Tastier than me, at least. Some of them looked over, but went on digging and eating and digging and eating.

"After a while I went back to Jessup's and told him I woke up in a patch of bears.

"He looked out the window and said, 'Mokie, Honey, Tansy, Adam, Geraldine, and Christabol. They wintered pretty well, 'cept Adam. He's awful skinny, but he's old, like me. He's all hunkered-lookin', like me. That's not necessarily a bad sign.'

"He'd go out and talk to them. He loved his bears. All his stories were about bears."

She poured them another cup of champagne. "So, tell me one."

Jack took two rolled rubber sleeping mats out of the bag, gave Lucy one, unrolled the other for himself, then stretched out on his side. He propped his head on his arm and sipped champagne. "My favorite Jessup story was about a thin ghost of a man from California, named Joaquin, who came for a stay and brought a violin. One evening after supper, they built a campfire to help keep the mosquitoes down, and Joachin played his violin for Jessup. In the twilight, the shapes of several bears came over the sand dune from the sea where they'd been diggin' clams. This made Joaquin nervous, and he stopped playing. Jessup motioned him to keep on, and he did.

"The bears sat a few feet behind them and listened to the violin. Jessup was curious about what the bears were up to and kept watch out of the corner of his eye. After a while, the bears began to sway, rolling their heads back with their mouths open and their long tongues licking the air."

Lucy's head filled with images of huge, dark beasts rolling their heads and their long, red tongues licking the air. "Jack, why did they lick the air?"

"Jessup said they wanted to taste the music."

"To taste the music? Incredible." She was quiet for a moment, playing the images in her head, then she unrolled her mat next to Jack's and lay down, pressing her back into his chest. "I'm getting cold. Is this okay?"

"I think I can get used to it."

She reached around and pulled his arm over her shoulder. They lay next to each other for a long time before she said, "Good night, Jack."

"Pleasant dreams."

As she drifted off, she became a giant brown beast, with chocolate lily breath, licking the air for the taste of music.

FOURTEEN

By three o'clock, Anita had become blasé about Raw Bone and Rat. She hated editing, which was hard on her eyes and her bottom. A well-metered consumption of alcohol lessened the pain. Around six-thirty she suggested they all go in for dinner. Billy and Henri stumbled out of the van and squinted at the sky.

"I can't take any more of the NEH today, sweetcakes. Me brain's burnt. Maybe we can go for a walk after dinner."

"We, and I emphasize the we, cannot go out of this damned hotel until Jack gets back from his little 'caving' expedition with Lucy, so he can cover our asses while we leave town, which can't be soon enough. Let's go eat before they close the kitchen."

They passed through the bar on the way to the dining room. Tiny, carefully placed lights made the glass shelves lined with whiskey and scotch glitter in the antique back-bar mirror. A tall, flamboyant woman with broad shoulders and largish breasts, in her mid forties, sat at the end of the bar holding a drink with one hand. With her other hand she rubbed an arm and shoulder made sore from hours of driving. She stared at herself through the glittering gold of whiskey and scotch.

Henri stopped, seeing she was distressed, introduced everyone, and asked, "Would you care to join us, madame?"

He was small, harmless-looking, sort of stylish in his retro black outfit, and had a soothing French accent, all of which disabled her sanity detector. In addition to which, she was somewhat inebriated. Still, she knew better.

Henri saw her hesitate. "You are weary from the road and should have a little something to eat. Yes?" he asked brightly. Henri could never consciously seduce. He was merely doing his duty to the human race, which made him quite attractive at first.

"Delores McKenzie," she said in a faded Oklahoma accent, which was asserting itself the more she drank and the closer she got to home. "I'd be happy to join y'all." She picked up her drink and followed them into the dining room. "I'm on my way to Oklahoma City to see my mama after three years of workin' for a bunch of evil cocksuckin' snakes in San Francisco. I got canned, 'cause I bruised their feelings. Hated their guts, too."

"For which evil cocksuckin' snakes did you work?" Henri asked.

"A save the endangered species, environmental group who figured out how to save themselves foremostly."

Anita was trying to ignore Delores. "We should order, if that's all right with everybody?"

"Honey, you be from Texas. You shoulda said. Where 'bouts you from? I'd put money on the lovely Lubbock Valley."

"Could we just not talk about Texas?" Anita murmured without looking up from the menu.

"Whatever you like, dearie."

"We still want to hear about your evil cocksuckin' snakes," said Henri.

The waitress took their orders for dinner and a round of drinks. Delores asked for a triple scotch before opening fire on the snakes in question. "The outfit I worked for was started back in the fifties by some serious, committed folks. In the eighties, the lawyers more or less took over when they realized they could get shit-rich suing greedy, deep-pocket corporations and settling out of court for massive amounts of cash that went straight through the foundation and into the lawyers' pockets."

This was a revelation to Anita. "They got away with that?"

"Sorry, sweetheart. This is the land of milk and honey we're talkin' about."

"I want, how you say, my cut," said Henri.

"But that was the old days," said Delores. "Next the re-lay-tors got in the truth." She giggled. "I meant trough, sorry—this Glen Livid's smooth, but it causes tongue slippage." She took another sip. "The re-lay-tors persuade wildlife agencies and environmental-studies departments to do game counts of the glitzy endangered species on private lands." She stopped to finish off her scotch. Anita and Billy looked at each other with the same thought: Delores would make one hell of a video. She fulfilled the requirements of their one shared credo—well-informed rage was the meat of a good documentary. Anita had a guilt flash for having dissed the woman at first glance.

"The re-lay-tors find a good match between impoverished rancher and chic endangered spee-cees. Then the bankers threaten foreclosure on the hard-pressed rancher who sells his land to the foundation . . . they put it back on the market. The new buyer signs a no development agreement with the feds—which, of course is a gift to the superrich."

"Why's it a gift?" asked Anita.

"They get huge tax breaks for conceding to the no-development stipulation, allowin' them to accumulate tens of thousands of acres of the great open West for their personal playground." She paused to get acquainted with her newly arrived triple. Henri had his book out, taking notes, attentive as a jackrabbit in hostile environs.

"Naturally the re-lay-tors take their grab from both sales. Repulsive amounts of money—locked for decades inside cows eating grass—are set free—*sploosh*! Everyone is swimming in liquidity of one sort or another."

Henri smiled. "America is beautiful."

Delores sipped. "But this new breed . . . the accountant commandos, are takin' over, pullin' in fast cash usin' commissioned hit-n'-run freelancers to charm money from the enfeebled rich. The freelancers're stylish n' sincere—like TV news anchors or Hollywood escorts—very effective with trust fund dowdies and liberal lambs burdened by inherited wealth."

Anita felt a lot better about sucking up to the NEH. In the world of grift, Anita didn't even qualify as pond scum.

Henri's admiration for things American spiked to new heights. He savored the twisted rationality along with his vodka. "I believe we saw the charming freelancers at a party recently. Very clever people, madame."

The front-desk lady came up to their table. She bent down and whispered to Anita, who excused herself to take a phone call and followed the lady into the lobby.

Anita held the house phone away from her ear. The man on the other end was shouting, maybe drunk. It took her a few seconds to realize it was Philip. "You were supposed to call an hour ago," he shouted. "What the hell's going on? I was about to . . ."

"Hello. Hello. This is Anita. Stop your goddamn shouting. Lucy and Jack are still out. We expected them back by now."

Philip was not used to back talk, now he was screaming. "Why the hell hasn't one of you gone to look in the cave?"

"Unless you want some dial tone, just jack back, professor. We don't have a clue where their so-called cave is. Besides, we can't leave the hotel because of the Grimm Brothers, Raw Bone and Rat. So we're screwed down for a while."

"Do you think you're making any sense at all? Are you drunk?"

"Screw you, boner. If you want her, come down here and find her yourself." Anita realized she was drunk. She was about to apologize when Philip threw the phone across the room. She could still hear him screaming in the distance.

By the time he picked up the phone, his scattered wits were back in their box. "If Lucy comes in, please tell her that I'll get there as soon as I can. Maybe I can get a plane out of Reagan late tonight. I'm very sorry I yelled. Things are a little stressed here."

"Yeah. Know the feeling. I'll warn her." Anita handed the phone back and nodded thanks. The manager looked embarrassed. Anita smirked. "You should've heard what he said to me," was her over-the-shoulder shot as she headed back to the dining room.

They all looked at her, waiting for a report. "It was Dr. Big Bone, looking for bad-girl Lucy who failed to call in on time. He's got a mean side to him—had the audacity to suggest I was drunk."

"You are drunk," said Billy.

"I know that. My point is, I don't need anyone telling me I'm drunk. It's fuckin' rude to tell people they're drunk . . . Billy."

Henri's anxiety was fighting the calming effect of the alcohol. "Perhaps . . . maybe . . . should we drive out to Jack's house and look for clues?"

"Clues?" asked Anita.

"Yes. One always looks for clues—the map with, how you say . . . X is the spot."

"That's pointless," said Billy. "If they were in a cave, I doubt they'd be there now. They'll show up when they're good n' ready."

"I think we should go out to Jack's," Henri insisted. He was getting very worried for Lucy and felt they should do something, anything.

"I have . . . four words for you," said Anita. "Raw Bone and Rat. Remember them? They sure as hell remember you, and me, and Billy Nose over here, and the van. I don't want to get caught on a back road at night."

"What if we had a different car and wore disguises?" asked Billy.

"Where's this 'different car' coming from?" asked Anita. "Lucy didn't happen to leave us the keys to her rent-a-car."

Billy smiled at Delores. "You got a little time on your hands, don't you?"

"For you, honey, if God hadna already beat me to it, I'da created time. But do you mind tellin' me what part your good buddies, Raw Bone and Rat, are playin' in all this?"

"We encroached on each other's territory, so to speak." He pointed to his nose. "A lady named Lucy catsuped Raw Bone in the head, and my precious here put her .38 in Rat's face. The ladies let them live, for reasons I'm a little vague on. Now they're out hunting us down. So how about you join the party, see the world?"

"You still have your .38, sweetheart?" Delores asked.

"On my very person, as we speak," said Anita.

"We'll need to unload my car. You end up with lots of useless stuff after three years in San Francisco."

Anita was eating her lamb chops and thinking. The protein

seemed to have a positive effect on her reasoning abilities. "Jack and Lucy might make it back tonight, and we can't do much in the dark, and we're drunk to boot. Let's unload Delores's rig tonight and be ready to go in the morning. I'd rather go out there in the daylight. Besides, we might find those kids that hang out with him. They might know something." Anita thought it would be a chance to appear heroic and brave to Jack, and, failing that, catching Jack and Lucy in a compromising situation would vindicate her suspicions.

In their intoxicated state, everyone seemed to think it was a reasonable plan and indicated as much via various grunts and murmurs as each devoured his meal, except Henri, who had substituted vodka martinis for overcooked lamb chops. He pulled out his little book and made a few notes. He had written, "Delores's rig, .38 sweetheart, catsuped Raw Bone, shit-rich," and "hard-pressed ranchers," when Delores looked over and scanned his list.

"Whatcha writin,' daddy?"

Henri looked around the table. He smiled and put the notebook away. "I love to dream up, how you say, scams. I have a company—Arte Marte, good name, don't you think?"

"What's it do?" asked Delores.

"On the Web we will sell Picasso's Pouch in a Purse, Einstein's Brain on a Chain, Pope Soap on a Rope, Glands of Guilt in crystal jars, and several other items—Ear of Vincent, of course, and Ernest Tincture of Testosterone. How you say . . . gifts for loved ones."

"Need a partner?" asked Delores, only half joking. "I usetabe 'n advertising. Wrote slogans."

He was trying to light a cigarette, but the coincidence caused a loss of coordination. He peered at Delores, flicking his lighter. She was making him dizzy.

Anita held up the bill and a credit card for the waitress.

The restaurant employees were awed by Henri, whom they had mistaken for Ben Wang, Big Writer, whose reported arrival in town was big news. The manager, waitresses, and two of the kitchen crew gathered around Henri.

"The staff and I have a request," said the manager. "We only now realized you were in town and a guest at the hotel. We would be honored if you would write a few words for us to frame for the restaurant entrance. In addition the management would like to cover your bill for the evening. We are so honored to have you as our guest."

"Really? Any words at all?" He knew something was wrong but was too drunk to realize he was the beneficiary of mistaken identity. "Well," he looked around the table, "what should I write? Anyone?"

They were as dumbfounded as he, except of course for Delores, who had no way of knowing that no one in America, outside of a few fringe professors, would have a clue as to who this man was. Henri was fairly clueless himself, but he enjoyed the prospect of gifts and recognition.

The waitress provided him with several sheets of hotel stationery and a ballpoint pen. He wrote, "To all the fairies and elves who grace this wondrous palace in Silverado, the entropic heart of America." Then he tore another sheet into scraps and copied random words from his red notebook, signed them, and gave them out as tips. The staff stared at their scraps, smiled at Henri, said their thank yous, and wandered away puzzled. One said, "Ben Wang fortune cookie."

"Let's deal with the car tomorrow," said Delores. "I think we all need our pillows about now. It was great meetin' y'all. I'll see you in the morning." She gave Henri a peck on the cheek and wobbled off.

Billy and Anita helped him out of his chair and guided him up the stairs to his room and bed. His last words were, "Words for money, that's my motto—*Palabras para dinero. Les mots pour les Euros. Verba pro pecunia. Worten für geld.*"

Anita debated if it would be too personal to remove his shoes. She compromised by slipping them partway off.

Back in their room, they heard one shoe hit the floor, then the other. They began undressing each other, slowly caressing and kissing. Billy was a three-way marvel, cameraman, editor, and body parts, but he could be as impractical and stubborn as a hood ornament. She had to work hard to get what she wanted, and she wondered if it was worth it, until she saw the footage, or the series of edits, or felt that big thang sliding into her velvet lining.

Henri, startled out of a drunken stupor, opened his eyes and listened. Ah, they're at it again. He slid off the bed, crawled to the vent, and lay stretched full out on the floor. He peered through the horizontal louvers of the air vent at the legs of the bed and Billy's bare feet and ankles. Ha, he was doing her from behind. Henri's imagination bloomed. Billy's feet were anchored solidly on the floor, but the bed was slamming into the wall in unison with Anita's muffled moans.

Then it stopped. Henri saw Anita's feet hit the floor and spring out of sight. She's jumped him, thought Henri. She's on his stick. Billy's feet were making little hops across the room. Then the feet staggered back to the bed and disappeared. Henri heard the springs sprong and Anita whisper, "Nice ride, cowboy. Don't forget the lights."

Henri fell asleep on the floor dreaming of Nina—her round peach bottom, her creamy thighs, the light of the moon streaming through the open window on a summer night.

Henri sat up, fully clothed except for shoes, and realized there was knocking at his door. He scuttled over to the bed and crawled under the covers.

"Henri, it's Anita. It's time to go. Are you decent? Can I come in?"

He started to take his clothes off, thought better of it, and sat on the edge of the bed. His head hurt. "Of course I'm decent. I am a Frenchman. Do come in." He had forgotten how he had arrived in his room.

Anita poked her head in. "Hi. Thought you should sleep. We've got Delores's car unloaded. I'll get coffee and rolls from the kitchen. Meet you out back in ten minutes, okay? Don't forget your disguise."

"But I don't disguise. I wear black."

"Stay here, I'll get you something in dark brown." She slammed the door. He heard her trotting down the stairs.

When Anita finally returned, she had a stylishly large Hawaiian shirt, borrowed from Delores. He put on his French sunglasses and instantly took on the demeanor of someone fleeing San Francisco in the wrong direction. Anita imagined she'd changed his life. She couldn't see him ever going back to black, or to France, for that matter. From here on, life for Henri would be one gay luau.

The other outfits were simple. Billy wore sunglasses and an Arizona Diamondbacks baseball cap so he could hide his nose under the bill. Anita was wearing her rose scarf and sunglasses. Delores had on black slacks and a yellow silk blouse over lavish, unfettered breasts.

It was after ten o'clock when they headed off to Jack's. Delores drove, Anita rode shotgun, or more specifically .38 revolver, and the boys slouched in the back. They were excessively obvious, just not what Raw Bone and Rat were looking for.

Anita, .38 held with both hands between her legs, safety off, was having an extreme case of trigger itch. Fueled by caffeine, the open road, and Jim Morrison at full volume, the fear was beginning to express itself as rage. If she saw Raw Bone and Rat, she was just going to start shooting.

Billy could see she was upset, just how upset, he had no idea. "Peaches, honey, please put your gun in your purse. We'll see those fellows long before they figure out who we are, and I doubt if they'll—"

"Just mind your own fucking business, Billy Nose. Remember who got us into this, macho boy? I don't want to get killed because you suffer from a bad case of testosterone poisoning."

"Well, you're the one who's set to blow your toes off because you can't control yourself."

"He's right, honey," said Delores. "You best put that thang in its holster. It makes me nervous, too. I've known too many people who shot friends by mistake—so they said."

"Well, honey, when this 'thang' goes off, it won't be no fuckin' mistake." But Anita snapped the safety on and laid the gun on her purse. She had Jack's address from the phone book and was reading numbers off the mailboxes. "I think it'll be comin' up pretty soon. It'll be 7736."

They could see The Sisters down by the creek, hard at work on the mudmen. Delores pulled her 1990 Honda off the two-lane blacktop and bumped her way down the clay ruts toward the house. As soon as The Sisters heard the car, they bunched up and waited while mud caked on their hands and squished up between their toes.

"Truck's not here," said Anita. "We'll want to talk to those girls along the creek."

Delores aimed the Honda toward the right corner of the house, keeping the girls in sight. She stopped the car, and everyone piled out. Anita looked back over her shoulder, checking the highway. She had the .38 ready, just in case. They all waited and listened, but everything was quiet. Evidently, they hadn't been followed. She walked down the slope toward the girls with the others trailing behind.

Henri, still suffering from his hangover, could not take his eyes off the mudmen. He was not watching where he was going and almost fell. The mudmen seemed peculiar, something out of a religious ritual—Indian or Mexican. But this was Jack's work. What kind of man made such creatures? Henri wondered if Jack was an artist or simply unstable. What did he do with these things? Henri stood and stared and the mudmen stared back.

Anita scrutinized The Sisters, trying to remember their names. "SuAnn, Sissy, Sadie, and Snake? Right?"

"Yes, ma'am," said SuAnn.

"We just dropped by lookin' for Mr. Miller and Dr. Perelli. Have they been around?" Anita tried to hide the .38 in the folds of her skirt, but they all got a look.

"Is Jack in trouble?" asked Sissy, eyes fixed on the fold in Anita's skirt.

"Mr. Miller and Dr. Perelli went to look at an old cave yesterday. They were supposed to be back last night, but we haven't heard from them, and we're getting concerned."

Sissy's words came out a little jerky. "We haven't seen Jack for a couple of . . . of days."

Anita thought Sissy was being evasive, which made her think the girl knew something. They stared at each other for a moment.

"Ya gonna shoot him?" asked Snake.

Anita realized they had seen the gun. "No, no. The gun's not for Jack. It's for somebody else." She was flustered. It was too hard to explain.

"You gonna shoot the lady?"

"No, dear. I'm not gonna shoot the lady. If Jack comes back, please tell him to call Anita at the Priscilla Hotel. Will you do that for me? I promise I'm not goin' to shoot Jack or the lady. Okay?"

"Who you gonna shoot?" Snake persisted.

"I'm not shooting anyone." She turned and looked back at the highway for a second. "The gun's just . . . for target practice."

"Who you scared of?"

Anita was too rattled to say. She already had the girls worried about Jack. She glanced around as though she had just noticed the mudmen. "What are these things? You made these?" Then she really looked at The Sisters. She was surrounded by aboriginals. Anita heard a truck on the highway and twisted around as something zoomed down the road. It was just another mufflerless Toyota pickup, but she was jangled.

Billy came up and put his arm around her and gave her a squeeze. She was shaking. He whispered in her ear, "It's okay, babe. It's okay. Let me have the gun, you're scarin' the kids."

She glanced around at the mudmen, thought of using them for target practice just to break the tension, thought better of it, and handed the .38 to Billy. The safety was off. He snapped it on and put the gun in his pocket. It was a tight fit. The Sisters giggled, except Snake, but they were all relieved.

"Do you think it would be all right if we looked in the house?" said Billy. "We thought there might be a map to the cave."

Sadie wasn't letting them near the place. "You'd never find it if he had it. For one thing he has lots of maps. For another, his house is a mess of junk and weird stuff. Anyways, Jack wouldn't like you goin' in there at all. No way."

"Besides," added Sissy, "if he had a map to this cave, he'da taken it with him."

"Well, you girls should know," said Billy. "We'll go back to the hotel and wait. If you hear anything, or you want to get a hold of us just call the Priscilla Hotel and ask for Billy or Anita. Okay?"

"Sure. We can do that. We got a phone at home. 'Bye."

" 'Bye," said Billy. "Henri, we're going now." He turned to Anita. "Well, it seemed like a good idea last night."

Henri disengaged himself from the powerful grasp of the mudmen and followed behind.

The Sisters watched the strangers walk back to the Honda and leave. As soon as the car was out of sight, they looked at one another, all with the same thought, even Snake. "Wash off first," said SuAnn. They went to the creek, got the mud off, and dashed to the house. They had never gone into Jack's house without being invited, but this was different. This was an emergency. They searched the house, but the only maps they found were Forest Service maps on the wall of Jack's office, which made them realize they couldn't make sense of a map anyway.

After an hour, Sadie had a revelation. There was no cave. "I betcha they're off doin' it."

Sissy's eyes got big. "Really? You think they're doin' it?"

"Remember how she looked at him in front of the drugstore? She wants him bad."

The Sisters' sex education consisted of overheard remarks and snippets of this and that between Marguerite and her friends, and listening with their ears pressed against the cold aluminum of the trailer house, back near Mom's bed, whenever they were banished to the outside so Marguerite and some fellow could have some "peace and quiet." What they heard was neither peaceful nor quiet.

The Sisters went back down to the creek and stood storklike among the mudmen and debated sex. SuAnn and Sissy had most of the basics down, but none of them understood the size-passion question. Snake was grossed out, of course. She didn't even want to think about Jack doing those things—she wandered off and smeared more grease on Oliver Oil.

FIFTEEN

When he woke, she was sitting up with her head lamp on, staring into the darkness. He waited, thinking she had heard something. She flinched when he asked, "What's the time?"

"I don't know. Just a minute." She searched her pockets for the watch. "Six-thirty. The sky's light by now."

"How long have you been awake?"

"Not long."

"Let's make some coffee and eat something." Jack turned his lamp on, set the helmet on a rock so he could see Lucy, and rummaged around at the same time. He pulled a tiny camp stove out of Lucy's pack, spaceman coffee, and the granola bars, then got the water started. "We have some time on our hands before Kills The Deer gets here."

"You're pretty confident he'll find us."

"I'm afraid he's all we've got. He better get here."

"If I can get us out before he gets here, I get the iceman, okay?" Lucy asked.

"You think there's another way out?"

"Maybe."

"All right. If we get out, the iceman's yours. What've you got in mind?"

"Willow's glowing pool."

"Sunlight?"

"It's the only thing that makes sense to me. I've never seen one, but I've heard of sunlit cave pools. I'd guess we're still thirty to forty feet above the canyon floor. The pool could be the same one we saw from the ledge."

He wondered if Lucy was betting on unconscious suggestions by Becker or if she thought Willow was more than his projection. Maybe she was simply as scared as he was and willing to try anything. "You believe it exists?"

"Don't know. We might as well look." She grinned. "So far Willow's done pretty well."

"What if she's right, and we come up in the first world?"

"I won't get my iceman."

They stuffed their pockets with granola bars and fresh batteries and started to retrace their route to the ceiling of the bats.

A half hour later they were staring up at the blanket of bats on the ceiling in the room with mica eyes.

"Did you hear these guys last night?" asked Jack.

"I must have been asleep when they left, but I heard them coming back this morning. They flew down to check us out. I could feel the wind from their wings."

After a long time of maneuvering through crevices and narrow passages, they came to a chamber large enough to stand in, with a single flat surface. Their lamps scanned the wall and discovered a three-foot-high drawing of Coatimundi wearing a mask of a smiling man. He was sitting as a man would sit and his thick tail was arched over his back. On the end of his tail perched a young parrot, wings spread for balance, its beak open. Coatimundi's head was turned, as though he were having a conversation with the parrot.

Lucy peered at the bird. "They're definitely in cahoots, deciding the fate of human kind, no doubt."

"Willow didn't say anything about the parrot," said Jack. "You would think . . ."

"Try not to, please. You live in another world, and you don't even know it. You think you're a rational, conservative man, but you're not."

"Things happen."

"Things happen?" She laughed. "Let's see if we can find Willow's underworld pool."

The chamber became a steep decline, then fingered off in separate directions. They consulted Jack's compass and decided to take the cavern to the right as it would take them in the direction of the canyon. After some arduous climbing, crawling, and descending, they entered a chamber the size of a two-story house with a domed ceiling covered with stalactites. The floor resembled a field of stone spears. They made their way through the stalagmites until they came to a dark pool.

"There's something odd about the smell in here," said Jack. "This place doesn't smell like the rest of the cave."

"What's odd?"

"Fresh water or wishful thinking."

As they approached the pool, the light from their head lamps was split by the surface of the water, reflecting high on the chamber wall and at the same time penetrating into the pool and beneath the wall.

"It isn't glowing," Jack said in a matter-of-fact tone, but he was disappointed.

"Damn it," said Lucy.

They turned their lights off and stood in the dark for several minutes, waiting, and hoping. The dimmest light appeared. Gradually, it began to brighten.

"Do you see a glow?" he asked.

"Yes, but is it in our eyes or in the water?"

The glow stayed with them whether they closed their eyes or looked away. "It's a mirage," said Lucy.

"Can a mirage leave an afterimage?"

They concentrated on the pool and waited, closing and opening their eyes. The glow seemed to come from under the wall, deep and far away.

Jack moved his hand in front of his eyes. "I can see my fingers. It's skylight filtered through God knows how many feet of water. How are your lungs?"

"Better than average, but I have no idea how long it'll take to swim to the other side. What about you?"

There was a long pause and she wondered what was going through his head. Finally he said, "Raw Bone and Rat could still be out there."

"Watch your eyes," she said. "I'm turning my lamp on." After her eyes adjusted to the light, she checked her watch. "We'd have enough time to call off Kills The Deer. He won't leave Albuquerque for over an hour."

"Who goes first?"

"You're sure you want to do this?" she asked.

"Don't think about it. We can do it. You can swim a long way in sixty seconds."

The light went out, and he heard her helmet hit the floor. "What are you doing?"

"Stripping. We get to ogle each other if we make it. Breathe deeply for about three minutes before we go in. It'll force more oxygen into your blood."

They stood naked in the dark, inhaling and exhaling like yoga masters. Lucy took his hand and pulled him down so they were sitting at the edge of the pool.

"Ready?"

"As I'll ever be."

She let go of his hand. They slid into the water, testing for depth, then pushed off. They touched hands, inhaled, and dove under the wall toward Willow's underworld sky, swimming side by side. After Jack had counted twenty seconds, the light was only slightly brighter. He could feel the turbulence from Lucy's arms and knew she was still next to him, but the dim glow only made his chest tighten. Was he running out of air already? Her hand thrashed against his arm. One of them was beginning to lose it.

His lungs ached. He tried not to think, just swim toward the light. It was getting brighter, wasn't it? Definitely brighter. He had lost count. His hand scraped the rock above. He tried going lower, but he was losing control of his arms. That's how he'd drown. He wouldn't sink. He thought he would sink, but that would come later. First, he would be pinned against the ceiling, trying to move forward, but his legs and arms wouldn't cooperate. They'd wave back and forth. From below he'd look like a disjointed bug, new to water, swimming desperately, going nowhere, signaling to the trout, Dinner is served.

His head hit the rock and stung, but pain was good. Pain brought him back. He turned to look for Lucy. She was gone. He looked toward the light. They were close. What happened to her? A hand came from below and touched his face. She had become disoriented and dropped beneath him. He looked down and saw the whiteness of her body. He jerked her arm and she regained direction. They flailed toward the light, lungs ripping apart. For a moment, the light became blinding, then dimmed. He reached up, hitting the rock. She brushed past him, disappearing into the blast of light, then her legs thrashed up through the water. She had broken the surface. He came up beside her, inhaling water and air, coughing and gasping, drowning and breathing at once, too panicked to feel elation. Instead he felt he had emerged into Willow's underworld—everything turned on its head. The world was not the one he had left—years ago.

They clung to the ledge, eyes shut against the brightness, gasping like fish drowning in air. When the pain in her lungs subsided, she opened her eyes enough to squint at him. At first, all she could see was the light glowing through his dark hair, his eyebrows, and vertical, wavy lines. The lines were red. The light hurt, and she closed her eyes again. She could not imagine what caused the red lines. She barely opened her eyes and reached out to touch his face. The red ran down her fingers to her arm and spread across the pool. "Jack, you're bleeding. It's your head." She put her hand on his head to find the cut and pressed her fingers against it. The bleeding stopped. "Do you feel all right?"

He was still gasping, but could talk. "I've . . . never felt . . . better." He squinted and smiled while she washed the blood from his face.

"I don't think it's bad, cuts just bleed a lot in the scalp. You'll have to keep it compressed." She put her other arm around him and pulled herself against his body and whispered, "We did it," and kissed him on the cheek.

His eyes opened to slits. He could barely see her, she was so bright. It was a strange sensation, feeling the full press of her body, yet barely seeing her, seeing only a bright ghost where he should see a full person. For a moment he thought of Willow, whom he could see as full and real, but could never touch. More than anything he wanted to feel the pressure of Lucy's lips against his own.

He felt the press of her body ease away. Far, far away, it seemed. She took his hand and raised it to his head to compress the cut.

"You'll have to keep pressure on it until the bleeding stops."

He turned toward the ledge of the pool so he could talk to her without seeing her naked body. "Tell me something."

"What?"

"It didn't bother you to press your body against mine. Which I enjoyed very much, but you couldn't kiss me on the lips?"

"Had I kissed you on the lips, you would have kissed me back, and I would have wanted you to."

"And that would have been . . . ?"

"Dangerous, I think."

"So are we lucky or unlucky?"

She looked at him and smiled. "We're lucky we're alive."

In a soft, amused voice he said, "I suppose that'll have to do."

He looked up at the ledge where they had been the day before, looking down, imagining children splashing, shouting, and shrieking for joy. He began to notice the numbing cold of the water. After a small eternity, he hoisted himself up on the rock. "I'm going to check out the road for our friends. You should probably stay here 'til we know things are clear. If you don't see me in an hour, head downstream toward that yellow trailer house by the highway. You'll probably find something in there to wrap around yourself. It'll be a good place to watch for Kills The Deer and flag him down before he heads up here. I should be back in thirty minutes. I'll bring you something to wear—there's a change of clothes behind the seat in the pickup." Without looking back, he stood up and walked out into the canyon and up the hillside.

Lucy watched him disappear through the trees, stepping from stone to stone, crossing the creek. She liked him naked. She liked his ass and his agility and grace. The hand balanced on his head brought a smile. He didn't flinch at every step—a barefoot boy with cheeks.

Picking his way through the brush, avoiding the stickers as much as possible, he made good time. He returned to the sensation of breaking through the surface of the pool into daylight, to emerge in Willow's first world—a naked explorer in an alien land.

The sun's heat drove the numbing cold from his body. Jack began to feel human. He reached the bristle-back rocks that hid the road and his truck and stood quietly, breathing slowly and deeply from the climb, listening for Raw Bone and Rat.

His truck was farther up the road from where he crossed the dinosaur's back. He guessed the brothers would have parked behind him, but they were not in sight. Their vantage point to the east was hidden by a rise in the road. If they were there, being spotted was not a worry until he started off the mountain. The truck seemed untouched. He opened the hood—nothing out of place. The bag of clothing behind the seat included boxers, khakis, a sweatshirt, socks, and sandals—in case he fell in the water one day.

He dressed to keep his hands free, plus he could get through the stickers faster with pants. The sandals sped his descent and spared his feet. He already had his quota of stickers. He had stopped bleeding and no longer needed to hold his hand on his head. He could descend in dignity.

Lucy had been lying on the rock, letting the sun warm her body. When she heard him coming, she sat up, her back to him, proper and modest. Neither knew how to behave, and so surrendered to custom. They understood what they were doing, and still they did it, even though their bare flesh had been pressed together half an hour before. He undressed to his boxers and dropped the clothes and sandals beside her.

"I brought you some clothes," was all he could say. He turned, walked across the stream, and waited on the other side of the willows as she dressed.

She came up behind him, her sense of humor restored. "The promise of civilization," she said, "is that we will go to our death with grace."

He touched his head gingerly. "I wasn't doing a very good job on my own."

"We need to get to a phone and call Kills The Deer."

As they came off the mountain, Jack scanned the suspected lookout for Raw Bone and Rat. They were probably asleep, happily dreaming of their devious deed.

Jack stopped at The Little Grande Bar, picked two quarters from his ashtray, and used the well-beaten pay phone welded to a steel post in the parking lot. "Good morning, KD."

"I was nearly out the door."

"Well, I'll tell you all about it later. If anything happens to us, it'll have something to do with a couple of brothers named Raw Bone and Rat. Do you plan to come for the mudmen?"

"I wouldn't miss it. When do you expect rain?"

"My personal weatherwoman says soon. I expect a thousand-year flood."

"Raw Bone and Rat?"

"Yeah. Dangerous boys. Lucy hit one of them in the face with a catsup bottle. Made him mean."

"That'd make me mean."

"She had reason. I'll tell you later. I'm goin' home to sleep. Take care."

She was sitting in the truck in his clothes, listening.

"They're going to remember me down here as the Catsup Kid."

"I'd bet that's not what Raw Bone calls you."

"By the way, you owe me one iceman."

"So I do. We'll take care of that tomorrow."

The drive to town took an hour, but it seemed much longer. Neither of them had ever studied the world with such care. He pulled up in front of the Priscilla, truck running, his mind in neutral. He smiled. "Keep the clothes."

Lucy wished he would turn off the engine and talk to her, but he wasn't moving in that direction. She resigned herself to the situation and started to open the door, then she stopped. "May I have a kiss?"

It was not the kiss he objected to, but the feeling of loss that would follow. She was moving toward him, reaching for his shoulder.

A car horn blared, making them turn to look back. Lucy recognized Anita waving or warding off mosquitoes.

Anita knew what the hand-to-the-shoulder gesture meant. And the shoulder was bare.

Lucy looked at Jack in his boxers. "We're trapped. I'll let you go. I'll call you later, okay?" She jumped out of the truck to face her overwrought companions.

Jack smiled in spite of his irritation with Anita. He drove home thinking about Lucy's lips.

When he opened the door, silhouetted in boxer shorts against the blank brightness of the sunlit world, he heard a soft giggle that quickly became uncontrollable laughter. He closed the door and waited for Willow to subside. She was sitting on the table with her legs spread.

"Welcome home to you, too," he said.

"So how was cave life?"

"Not all it's cracked up to be."

"For two days, I've been lying here, thinking about you and Lucy. It's time for me. I'm ripe. Turn me loose, Jack. I've got a thousand years of pent-up passion ready for rain."

He nodded at her legs. "Would you mind?"

"You're offended?" She drew her legs together. "I'm horny. I have an entire weather system to seduce."

"We found your glowing pool."

"And the skeletons?"

"Yes. And the wall of eyes, Coatimundi, and the spears."

"That must've put your rational mind on spin."

"It did. But we got trapped in the cave and what saved us was Lucy's logic, or lack of logic. Anyway, your glowing pool led back to the third world, not into the first."

"Obviously, you didn't go into the first world, because you've come back to me."

"We went into the pool. That's how we escaped the cave."

"Of course you did. That's why you're here in short pants. You just didn't go into the first world. You would have had to die to do that. Then you would have seen the shapeless ones. They almost got you, didn't they?"

He touched the top of his head. "You could say that."

"I'm glad you made it back. I'd be in a fine fix otherwise, all lusty and nowhere to go. I've been here thinking about you and Lucy making love. . . ."

"Sorry. It didn't happen."

She ignored him. "And I'm getting ready to make it rain. I've waited a thousand years. You're going to see rain like you've never seen rain. And I love you."

"You loved them all."

"True, but you're the only game around, now."

He laughed and went to the kitchen window to check on The Sisters. The girls were conferencing. Sadie had her hands on her hips, staring at the house. They had seen him drive up, but fortunately their angle of view prevented them from seeing him get out of the truck half naked. The sky was pale blue. He came back. "Not a cloud in the sky."

"Tomorrow, or the next day, or the next. The clouds will come. Are you ready to break my bowl?"

"Yes, of course," he said, but the question made him feel abandoned. "Where should I break it?"

"In your fireplace. The chimney will shoot me into the clouds."

"May I glue the bowl back together?"

"And what will you do with my beautiful bowl? Trade it for another house?" He was sure he hadn't told her he'd traded a bowl for his house. She caught his surprise and laughed.

"No," he said. "It should go back where I found it."

"My aunt would like that. It may even bring you good fortune, Jack."

There was a knock on the kitchen door. Jack dashed down the hall to the laundry room for pants and a shirt. When he returned, Sissy, under commission, was waiting at the door. She had probably seen him flash past the living-room door toward the hallway.

"We was worried about you. Those friends of Lucy's came lookin'. They're a nosy bunch. They wanted to see in your house, but we wouldn't let 'em." She waited for praise.

"Thanks. I appreciate that."

"We were beginnin' to wonder if you'd run off for good. What'cha been doin'?"

He thought of all the clever ways he could answer her, but gave up. "Lucy and I went to look at a Mimbres cave. We got trapped and couldn't get out until we found a pool that came out the other side. It was an adventure."

" 'Zat why you come home nekkid?"

"Yep."

"Did Lucy come home nekkid, too?"

"No. I had clothes in my truck. Why all the questions?"

Sissy stared up at him and took a breath. "If you fall in love with Lucy, will she come and stay here, or will you have to go away and be with her?"

"It's okay, Sissy. I'm not going away with Lucy. For one thing, there's another man in her life."

"That doesn't mean a thing. That stuff changes all the time."

He hadn't expected that. He was quiet for a moment. He had become attached to them. It had never occurred to him that it worked the other way. He didn't want them depending on him, and of course, at the same time, he did. Finally he managed to say, "Besides, I wouldn't want to leave you guys without something to do."

Sissy caught her lower lip between her teeth and squeezed hard. She mumbled, "Thanks," and turned and ran as hard as she could toward the others, who awaited the verdict.

Jack closed the door and watched Sissy and her sisters, then heard them shout. The girls seemed so faraway. They waved, innocently reminding him that they would be the ones to leave. Marguerite was too unstable to stay around for long. Willow would be gone. Lucy, too. He drew a deep breath and let it out. He could feel the emptiness in his chest. He was drowning, down into the world of the dead—a mudman without willow bark hidden in his joints to put a dance back into his life.

The desk rang at three o'clock, forty-five minutes before Philip's plane was due in. Lucy was still waking when Anita knocked on the door.

Anita had her outfit on. "I brought your disguise," she said, and handed Lucy a shopping bag. "Billy and Henri wanted to come along. That okay with you?"

"Sure. We should stick together. Are you packin'?"

Anita reached into her bag and pulled out her .38. "Don't leave home without it. Oh, yeah. We don't dare take the van out. We'll need to take your rental car. Delores heard Oklahoma calling. Billy and Henri went down to help her repack."

"Too bad. I liked Delores, what little I saw of her." Lucy pulled out a large black hat, wraparound dark glasses, and a strapless black top from the sack. "My God, they've got a transvestite boutique in Silverado." There was also a tube of ultradark red lipstick.

The pull of Oklahoma had become downright magnetic. Delores gave everybody wet kisses and long hugs. When she left, her memory lingered with the odor of lavender and the fumes of a Honda in need of a ring job.

"She was unusual," Henri said, slightly mystified. "I have never known such a woman. She gives the wet kiss."

Delores fled east. San Francisco and the enviro-scammers had filled her with hate, the rednecks with fear, and the Silverado crew with longing. It was a confusing and explosive mix. She was fifty miles outside Truth or Consequences before she got pulled over for speeding.

Philip's plane was late. Henri suggested they wait in the smoking bar. The others rebelled, so he got a double vodka and joined them in the restaurant that looked out on the lone runway. He was pleased Philip was late. "Lucy, maybe you could give Billy and Anita some background on the First Americans debate and the great Professor Philip Sach's migration theories. At least they should know when to turn the camera on."

Lucy sipped her coffee and studied Henri. She guessed he knew very little about the subject and could use some background before taking on Philip. She knew Philip could hold his own against Henri. In fact, it would probably be good for them to have a go.

"Okay, but this is going to be an extremely compressed version of Who's on First 101. This question of who was here first has become an Abbott and Costello routine. There are eighty-seven theories being researched from Tierra del Fuego to the Bering Strait. The theories make claims that date from forty thousand years ago to twelve thousand five hundred years ago and include various groups who migrated from Iraq, the coast of southwest Pakistan and India, or northern Siberia coming from the west, and people from Europe coming directly across the Atlantic or skirting along the ice from northern Europe across to Iceland, Greenland, and Newfoundland. There are theories that Africans crossed the Atlantic to South America and others that people migrated across the Pacific to Chile. These various theories study rates of change in languages and DNA, carbon date bones and wood associated with certain tools, and compare skull shapes when they have skulls to compare. Technologies for shaping tools from stone, as well as types of tools, are another marker for who, when, and where. It's quite a time to be throwing theories around."

Anita was recording and taking notes. She kept writing for a while after Lucy paused, scanned her notes, and looked up. "Philip? Where's he in all this?"

"He believes early southwest Asian populations migrated toward the Mideast and up into Europe, while a related group migrated along the coast of India toward Micronesia and north along the Pacific rim. They had elongated craniums, much like Europeans, which distinguished them from the rounder skulls of the north Asian Siberians or the American Indians. The present-day Native Ainu who live on Hokido, Japan, are descendants of these people. He estimates the migration of the ancestral Ainu into North America happened around the height of the glacial period, fifteen to eighteen thousand years ago, depending upon whose data you believe."

"Data-based faith," said Henri, as he wrote it down.

"You could say that, Henri." She continued with Who's on First. "The ancestral Ainu, in Philip's view, came to populate much of North and South America. Around twelve thousand years ago, they developed a stone-tool technology, which we call Clovis, either on their own or from outside influences. There is some evidence that Solutrean technology from Europe may have been introduced on the Carolina coast. However it came about, in a relatively short time, Clovis technology covered much of North America. The spear points were effective for bringing down very large animals, like giant bison and mammoths. This state of affairs continued until north Asians migrated from Siberia and absorbed or killed off the American-Ainu population."

Anita could see the plane from Albuquerque taxi toward the gate. She had one last question before Philip arrived. "Does Clovis, New Mexico have anything to do with Clovis points?"

"Only indirectly, but at the time it seemed highly significant. The first Clovis point was found in Blackwater Draw near Portales in 1932. Portales was dry, meaning the archaeologists, after a long day of digging under the hot sun, had to endure several miles of a mud-rutted road in a Model A Ford to the town of Clovis to find a drink. So we have the Clovis point rather than the Portales point—please do not take this to mean that archaeologists are all a bunch of vindictive drunks, though there are those who dispute this disclaimer.

"There are some basic problems with Philip's theories, which I'm sure Henri will, for your amusement and the camera, get into with Philip."

Henri nodded at Lucy. He loved the idea of having Philip for lunch on camera. He was smiling into his vodka when the flight from Albuquerque pulled up to the gate.

Philip was one of the first off. He had come prepared for July in the Southwest—a pale green short-sleeved shirt, cutoff khakis, and sandals. His single light bag proclaimed that twenty-four hours in Silverado was more than enough. He had on sunglasses and looked inscrutable—certainly not academic or professorial. Anita thought he looked like a pale, slightly overweight Robert DeNiro playing a mobster on vacation.

Lucy walked through the clutch of greeters, embraced Philip, and gave him a kiss. "You didn't have to do this, you know. But I'm glad to see you."

"What happened to you?"

"We got trapped in the cave and didn't get out until this morning. It was pretty frightening, actually."

"Nice outfit. Southwestern?"

"I'm in disguise—Raw Bone and Rat, remember?"

An archaeologist is trained to look at the surface of the land and imagine what lies beneath. With Lucy, this talent extended to Homo sapiens. The tension in Philip's neck and back made him walk with a tentative gait, as though the ground were not where it should be. He did not have the stifled stride of a man angry at his girlfriend for spending the night with a stranger. This was about him, not her. He was moving like a man who knew he had miscalculated.

He was gentle with her, but his eyes wandered, even though he seemed attentive to what she said and to her touch. She would have to wait.

Lucy introduced everyone and suggested they get back to town and get something to eat. Philip said he had to make a call to Washington and would meet them in front.

Anita excused herself to use the ladies' room, while the others went to get the car. She inspected her lipstick and pushed a few loose strands of red under her scarf, checked the overall look long enough for Philip to have gotten through to D.C. She sauntered out and stood around the corner from the phones. He was talking to someone named Tom. ". . . Because I don't want Ben Wang . . . Miller or Sillcot until I'm back." She caught something about finding an iceman. The rest was lost amid the intermittent security announcements and the incessant country lament that plagued small airports from Montana to New Mexico. She scooted out into the sun and jumped in the backseat with Billy and Henri, fantasizing about the possibilities of doing something on Ben Wang.

"He's still on the phone," she announced to Lucy. She was particularly curious about what Philip knew on the Jack and Lucy front. She also wanted in on the bigger game, whatever it was—Philip had not come all the way across the country just to rescue his little girl.

Billy sat in the middle with Henri to his left so he could do a wide-angle pan from Henri to Philip in the front passenger seat. He had Lucy adjust the rearview mirror so he could get a three-quarter shot on Philip's head from the back and see his face in the mirror at the same time.

Philip got in and gave Lucy a pat on the knee. He looked at her hand, not at her. He sat back and let the landscape blur past, but Anita's curiosity about migration theories interrupted the flow.

"Lucy mentioned your American-Ainu theory, Professor Sachs," said Anita. "It sounds terribly interesting. We were wondering just exactly what their migration path to the Americas might have been. Would you mind if we filmed as you explained it to us?"

Philip hid his irritation. The last thing he wanted was to perform for Anita, but he pretended it was an honor. "No. Not at all. The ancestral Ainu were a maritime culture. Depending on ocean currents and the amount of water held in the glaciers at any given time, their routes brought them to various islands in Southeast Alaska and down the Inland Passage. Over time they migrated along the coast to South America. There were several migrations before the arrival of the north Asians from Siberia several thousand years later."

"Isn't your theory a bit fragile, Professor?" asked Henri.

"Fragile? Perhaps you could be more specific."

"What evidence do you have to support your ah . . . position?"

"Well, Henri, I wouldn't expect you to be up on an area so outside your field. Little physical evidence of these early migrations remains as the sea level was about three hundred and fifty feet lower than now. However, there is a growing body of evidence that supports the migrations of ancestral Ainu into the Americas during the last ice age. For example, there are DNA markers in archaic Europeans, Southeast Asians, and American Indians that fail to show up in early Siberians in northern Asia."

"Do you believe this Kennewick man who was discovered in a riverbank in the Northwest several years ago was related to your Ainu?"

"Possibly, but he was born about a thousand years after Clovis disappeared. He could have been from yet another wave which came from Southeast Asia, or a survivor from the first. There's also a rumor that Kennewick's carbon dates were contaminated, that he was actually what was first believed—a white pioneer."

"You archaeologists just seem to pull theories, how do you say . . . out of the air."

Lucy looked at Henri in the rearview mirror and laughed. "As a general rule, you operate in a vacuum, Henri. Why the sudden interest in facts? Next, you'll be asking for objectivity."

He was irritated, but ignored her. After all, he had Philip to chew on.

"Your theory," said Henri, "is meant to discredit the Native Americans' claim of being the first Americans. In effect, what you're saying is that the Siberians came later, massacred an entire civilization, and therefore the American Indian has no claim to the lands and water the Europeans have taken from him. You've constructed a nice little rationale for all that Aryan, racist nonsense, haven't you?"

You little frog bastard, thought Philip. He smiled. "The American Ainu may simply have been absorbed by the Siberians. As for racism, our profession has difficulty even describing *race*, Mr. Bashé. Even genetically speaking, the concept is not easily defined."

Henri laughed. Absorbed, indeed. He dug his little red book out and wrote, "genetically speaking."

"Interesting," he said, tucking the book back in his pocket, "that you fail to define race, yet your theories support racism."

Philip was unfazed. Henri was just another intellectually lazy, French academic. It seemed pointless to continue the conversation, and he did not appreciate Billy's incessant camera.

To Henri, Sachs was an American bully. They were silent the rest of the way into Silverado. When Lucy pulled up in back of the hotel, Henri was first out.

Anita was about to quiz Philip about the iceman and Ben Wang when he turned and thanked her and Billy for coming to pick him up.

"Perhaps we shall see each other later. Right now, Lucy and I have some catching up." He had his bag and was already heading for the back door of the hotel. Lucy directed him up the stairs, opened the door to the room, and followed him in. He took a notebook from his bag and started writing. Then he looked around for a phone.

"Ah. They have a phone. I won't have to use my cell." He grabbed the phone and put it to his ear. "Dial tone, too. How convenient." He looked at his watch. "The pilot announced that Silverado is famous for its museum of silver ore samples and Billy the Kid. We certainly have to take that in."

He sat on the edge of the bed, rapidly punching numbers. "Tom, it's me. Did you get through? Yes. No? Okay. Keep trying. You have the number here? That's it. 'Bye."

Philip abandoned large pieces of the world when he was absorbed in a project. Lucy understood being focused, but Philip was still avoiding her gaze. He jumped up, whirled around, and stared out at the street for a moment. "I think I'll take a quick shower. Would you call Miller and tell him I'd like to come out this evening?"

"This evening?"

"Sooner's better. I'd guess he's ready to cooperate." He gave her a quick smile. "Wouldn't you?"

She was stunned. He was implying that something was going on between Jack and her. She wondered if Philip really believed it. If he did, he was accepting infidelity as a trade-off for the iceman. Perhaps he was only fishing for confirmation of his insecurity about her. It would be natural for him to test the water—not wanting to believe she was losing interest, yet afraid she had.

At the same time, he was right. She had betrayed him—she felt guilty about what had gone unsaid with Jack. They hadn't made love, but then in some way they had. She wondered if Philip had seen into her, the way she could read him? Who had betrayed whom, and when?

He had undressed and was heading for the shower. "The faster we get this done, the more calls I can make east tonight."

"Did you want me to go with you?" she shouted over the spray.

"Of course," he shouted back. "I'll need directions."

She sat on the bed and pulled the phone over. "I think it's me that needs directions," she said to the open window, and began dialing Jack's number. The phone rang for a long time. She waited, hoping he was home, wanting his voice in her head. "Hello." He'd been running.

"Hi. It's me."

"I was hoping it was."

"You're all muddy, aren't you?"

"Yep. What's up? Want to take me to dinner?"

"I do, but it'll have to be another time. Philip got panicked when I didn't call last night. He just flew in from D.C. Now he wants to come out and talk to you about the iceman. How are you with that?"

"Right now?"

"Yeah."

"Might as well get it over with. See you soon."

"Thanks, Jack. We'll leave in a few minutes."

Philip came out of the shower as Lucy hung up. "Is everything set?"

"Everything's set." She was not ready for a showdown with Philip, but she needed him to say something about what was happening to him. She watched him get dressed. "Why are you acting like a nut case? It's getting on my nerves."

"I know. I'm sorry." He had several maps rolled and secured with a rubber band. He finally looked her in the eye. "It's just that . . . I'm under some awful pressure right now. Everything's ready—almost ready. Miller's cooperation is essential. My career is in this bastard's hands."

"It's probably not a good idea to think of him as a bastard. He certainly hasn't been, but if you keep this up, you'll turn him into one."

"I know. I know." He was jerking around the room, trying to see if he had forgotten anything.

She sat very still on the edge of the bed and watched. "What's wrong, Philip? I've never seen you quite like this."

He stopped and looked at the ceiling fan as though he had just noticed it. Then he turned and stared out the window into the distance. "I've got myself in a trap. Ben Wang's really into this, and he's pushing the hell out of me. He wants to know everything. It was a mistake. I don't know . . . I don't know where he's taking this. It could all backfire. Even if we find the iceman and it fits into my migration theory, I'm afraid he'll still screw me. I'm pretty sure he sicced Sillcot's Indian radicals on me, which he'll use in his piece for *Atlantic* on the racism of archaeology. Then he got himself locked into the *Geo* film. He's everywhere. The whole thing's very distracting."

She shook her head. Letting people like Wang get the upper hand was not a good sign. "I'm sorry, Philip. I really am."

He turned and stared at her. "Right now, I need to take care of business with Miller. Can we go?"

This was not Philip, who was thoughtful and considerate, even gentle. In his desperation, he'd been making deals with bastards and now they had him trapped. She felt terrible for him. She bit her lip and stood up, flipping her keys. "Let's go."

She drove fast. Her mind raced over what he might have said and to whom. Philip was quiet, watching the flashing fence posts and the barbed wire stream past.

Jack had gone back down to work with The Sisters. They were putting finishing touches on the mudmen and snipping the nylon string that had held the willow armatures in place until the bark wrapping and the clay had dried. He was surprised to hear Lucy's car turn off the highway and bounce onto the dirt road. The girls and Jack watched the dust plume that followed the car toward the front door. He looked at the girls and shrugged. "This won't take long."

"Is that Lucy?" asked Sadie.

"Lucy and Philip." He looked for a reaction, but they had no idea what was happening. They just waited for an explanation. "I'll tell you about it later." He washed his hands in the creek, then walked up to the house to greet his guests and show them in.

Everything was cordial. They pretended they all had the same agenda. Jack looked over at Willow. She played indifferent, though her back was arched slightly in a "look at this, Jack" tableau. His stifled laugh became a wide smile, which made Philip a little paranoid.

Philip reacted by turning away, pretending to study the architecture and the layout of the house. He wondered if Jack was going to pull something. "This is an extraordinary place you have, Miller. Do you mind if I have a look around?"

"Help yourself. Would you like coffee or wine?"

"Oh, I'm afraid wine would put me into a coma right now. I'll have coffee—black, please." He began to wander through the house with Lucy while Jack made coffee. They took in the rambling museum, scanning the walls and shelves of carved saints, arrays of crosses, a collection of early clay figures made by children, a pile of army-issue Navajo saddle blankets blackened with ancient sweat, a box of square, hand-forged nails, old tools, and a variety of objects retrieved from under the desert sun. Philip studied the rooms meticulously. In the office, he found Becker's drawing of the parrot trainer pinned to the wall, a pile of photocopied notes in German, and the German-English dictionary. The edge of a loose page poked out of the dictionary, inviting inspection. Philip opened the book to where Jack had left Becker's map. Lucy had not seen any of this before. Philip's interest in the notes alarmed her, particularly since he could read German fluently.

"We should get back," she insisted. "I'm sure the coffee's ready."

But Philip picked up the map and the drawing. He had noticed the parrot trainer's bowl on the living-room table and had made the connection between the drawing and the bowl and read enough in the notes to get the idea.

Jack announced from the office door that their coffee was waiting in the living room. He was surprised to see Philip turn toward him, holding Becker's map and the drawing.

Philip's arrogance filled the room. "You seem to have solved a mystery. This is the image on the bowl in your living room. I take it the map is . . ."

"Something I came across in the desert."

"Quite a coincidence. And X marks the cave you and Lucy went to investigate?"

"It does."

Philip's gaze fell on the Forest Service map Jack had used to follow Becker's directions.

Lucy took his hand. "It's none of your business, Philip." She took the map and the drawing from him and put them back on the desk. "Let's have our coffee."

He relented and followed her out, but not before realizing most of the private land shown on the Forest Service map was on the alluvials that fanned down to the main river along the highway. Everything else was federal. He had no idea where the German's map fit in the maze of contour lines. He only glanced at the map, noticing the cross near a ridge line, which he assumed put the entrance to the cave away from the river terrain. Obviously, Jack had not retired from anything.

They sat at the heavy Spanish table in the living room, Lucy and Philip on one side facing Jack. To his right, Jack could see through the arched doorway into the kitchen, through the glass door, and down the slope to the river, the mudmen, and The Sisters.

Philip sipped his coffee and stared at the parrot trainer bowl at the end of the table. Lucy was tense, both hands holding her cup. She looked straight at Jack.

Without taking his eyes off the bowl, Philip said, "When Lucy told me she was going caving, I assumed it had something to do with her Fund work, which of course always takes place on private land." He turned and looked directly at Jack. "But if I remember correctly, she said your little expedition was not for the Fund."

Philip was making it clear that he knew Jack had stolen a bowl from a grave site on federal land. He delivered his speech as though Lucy were not in the room. He was threatening without stating anything specific.

"Well, I did not come to talk about your caving experience, although it was undoubtedly an exciting adventure . . . in many respects."

Lucy had not touched her coffee. She was looking sideways at Philip. Whether from embarrassment or anger, her face began to redden. Being humiliated by Philip was something entirely new to her. "Damn it, Philip, that was uncalled for."

Jack's initial response to Lucy's confusion and rage was to throw Philip out, but he glanced at Willow, reminded of her comment about Philip's self-destruction. No doubt she was gleeful under her soft, white mask. Jack took a breath, trusting that Philip would fry in his own fire.

Philip unrolled his maps on the table. He had come with an entire speech, but now that was not necessary. He did not even bother to ask. He had Jack in a corner. "These were the most detailed maps I could find of the Alaskan glacier fields. They're done from satellite photos. You should be able to pinpoint the exact location of the cave." He began arranging the maps so Jack could read their descriptions. "Which area do you need?"

Lucy looked away, shook her head in disbelief. "Excuse me," she said, getting up from the table. "I think I'll go look at mudmen." Ignoring Philip for the moment, Jack watched her go through the kitchen door and step into the evening sun.

"Which area do you need?" Philip demanded. He had gotten up and was standing next to Jack. For a moment they watched Lucy walk down the hill toward the mudmen. One man was watching a woman walk out of his life, while the other hoped she was walking into his.

Jack pointed to one of the maps. "Let's try this one." He pulled the map out and laid it on the table. "I've never seen the area from the air, so this is unfamiliar to me. The man is in an ice cave in a hanging glacier in a valley above the sea."

The high feeder valleys were filled with hanging glaciers that sent melt down in the summer along with occasional chunks of ice the size of a double-wide. Jack's finger traced a path into the bay to a rock incline, and crisscrossed upward toward a glacier in a valley hundreds of feet above the sea. The massive main glacier lay directly to the north. Philip's eyes were fixed on the moving finger. He hunkered over Jack, watching the finger inch up the incline toward the hanging glacier.

The finger followed along the edge of the glacier, then began a zigzag up the middle. Philip watched as if he were waiting for a reluctant uncle to finish signing his will. He held his tongue. Jack stopped at a tiny dark wedge halfway up the glacier, more than a thousand feet above the sea. "This wedge is very much like the shadow cast from the vertical slope of the cave."

Philip felt a surge of joy. He stared at the shadow that held the secret to his revival. It was his. He looked down at Jack, smug that he had gotten what he wanted. Neither man acknowledged the fleeting blackmail. No confrontation necessary. Philip looked back at the wedge of shadow, imagining his ancient man, press conferences, television interviews, helicopters, and book contracts.

Jack could hear Lucy in the distance, as though she were calling for him to come out and play. Her magnetic pull drew him away from the map and Philip. "Would you like more coffee?" asked Jack, finding escape in hospitality.

"No." Philip was a little sharp. He was plotting his new life.

"Well, I think I'll get myself some," said Jack. He glanced at Willow, who had stretched her arm out and gracefully opened her hand as if to say, Pay up, buster. She was too sure of herself, he thought. He went into the kitchen and stood in the doorway. Lucy was watching Snake chasing her sisters through the waiting figures and their long, skinny shadows.

Jack got out the jams, peanut butter, bread, and a gallon of milk and fixed them their favorite variations. He put the sandwiches, milk, and cups in a cardboard box and walked down the hill. They took a break to gobble down their snacks.

Philip's daydream was interrupted when he realized it was too quiet in the kitchen. He folded the map in half, rolled it up, and, clutching it in his hand, went to investigate. From the kitchen doorway, looking down the slope toward the creek, beyond the army of mudmen, he could see Jack standing near Lucy and a cluster of fierce little girls wolfing down sandwiches. For a moment Philip forgot his victory. His instinct was to take Lucy away.

When The Sisters saw Philip marching down the slope, clutching a pipe in one hand, they stopped. As he came closer, they could see it was not a pipe, only a rolled-up paper. This was Lucy's man. The one who was keeping Jack from going away with Lucy. They all lined up, as Marguerite had taught them, to be introduced. They had clay dust in their ratty tangles and smudges of clay on their clothes, legs, and arms. Snake's smudges were a compound of oil, grease, and clay. Then there were the peanutbutterjam sammiches clutched in their dirty little grippers.

Philip walked straight toward Lucy, ignoring Jack, The Sisters, and the mudmen. He wondered if the stories of children being raised by wolves had any basis in fact. He touched Lucy's arm. "We need to get back to the hotel, dear. I'm expecting a call." He shook Jack's hand. "Thank you for your cooperation. You've done the science of archaeology a great service." He could not help grinning.

In spite of Philip's subtle tug, Lucy stood and stared at Jack for a moment. "Thank you, Jack. I'm sorry . . . I'll let you know about your iceman." Then she turned and shook hands with each of The Sisters. "Goodbye. I really liked meeting you. I wish I could stay to see your mudmen do their dance." Suddenly the world was out of kilter for everyone.

Jack and The Sisters watched as Philip and Lucy walked around the far end of the house and disappeared. After a long pause, Sissy broke the tension frozen in the air above the mudmen. "When's it gonna rain, Jack?"

"Soon," he said, "very soon."

Willow had promised. Jack and The Sisters would watch the mudmen do their dance. He looked at the sky. Willow was good at her job. It was beginning to cloud up in the southwest already.

He gestured toward the sun, which was just beginning to settle into the low, thin clouds, "A day, maybe two."

The girls said good night, crossed the creek, and ran home through the trees to wait for Marguerite. Tonight was buffalo wings.

Jack went into the house, poured a glass of whiskey, and sat down. Willow was waiting. She sat on the table with her legs tucked under and stretched her torso and arms.

"You did very well, Jack. I'm impressed. I was right about Lucy's lover, wasn't I?"

"Yes. There was no point in blackmailing me, and he didn't have to humiliate her."

"He's angry. She's been too patient and loyal for too long. She resents him and he knows it, yet his whole future depended on you and her. He's the one who's humiliated. Since he can't win, he's forcing her to leave him."

"But he's very possessive. He came down and basically dragged her away."

"What do you expect? He's insecure. He can't help himself. He's not the kind to let go, even if it's destroying him. She'll have to leave him."

"And then what? Will I see her again? You said she liked me."

"Like you, fuck you, love you. All are different. She has to be around you to fall in love."

"Maybe she'll come back to poke in the dirt."

"Oh, yes. Your generous gift of the maps to my people's houses." Then, reminding him it was her idea, she said, "That was a clever stroke."

"You're always right, aren't you?"

"I'm old, Jack. Very, very old."

Philip watched the colors in the sunset as Lucy drove.

She forced herself to be calm and motherly toward him. "Why did you have behave like a bully? Jack was willing to give you the iceman. You didn't have to blackmail him. I've never seen you act that way to anyone."

In an offhand tone he asked, "How's that, dear?"

"You were an asshole, Philip, and you know it."

"I was only protecting myself. He could have decided to change his mind, or cause trouble later on. I don't have to worry about that now."

"I think you're a damn fool."

Philip was so enchanted by the new life the iceman would give him, he forgot that on occasion the giver forgets to remove the price tag.

SIXTEEN

The next morning was overcast and windy. Philip and Lucy were like the weather, erratic and moody. At breakfast, Anita offered to drive them to the airport for the morning flight to Albuquerque in Lucy's rental car and return it to the agency afterward. Henri, who was still asleep, was not mentioned. Best to let sleeping dogs sleep. Philip looked out at the wind whipping papers and plastic cups down the street. He got up without excusing himself and walked out of the dining room. Five minutes later he was back.

"The airport says it's too windy for the plane to land." He was brooding. "The wind is suppose to break in the afternoon. We'll have to take the seven P.M. flight." He would be forced to waste a day in Silverado.

Lucy suggested that what he needed most was to make calls, which he could do from the room. If he slept on the red-eye back to D.C. that night, he could work most of the next day in his office. Philip nodded, got up, and went upstairs. Lucy finished her breakfast in silence, signed the check, and went up to the room.

Lucy, who'd had little sleep, was irritable and distracted, mulling over the events of the evening before. Philip was on the phone pitching a *New York Times* reporter. She slipped into her shoes and left. Philip watched her go. There was nothing he could do that would have made a difference. He waited for the door to close, then began dialing again.

She nearly ran into Henri, coffee in hand, on his way down to help edit. "Good morning, Henri. I have a favor to ask. Philip's using the room to make calls, I wondered if I could use your room for a while. I didn't get much sleep last night."

"But of course. Weren't you suppose to leave this morning?"

"Too windy. We're going out on the seven P.M flight."

"Oh. That is good. I'll ride out with you."

She would have liked to tell him to stay, but smiled instead. "I'll come down later and see how you're doing." She stayed in his room, looked through his pile of magazines, and tried to nap, without success. Around noon she wandered down the hall past her room, where Philip was hammering at some overworked soul about Sillcot and his band of bastards.

Anita was in the front seat of the van, performing her hypervigilant routine on caffeine and energy bars. Billy and Henri were arguing over every cut.

Eventually, the tension and bickering drove Lucy back upstairs to Henri's room. She stared at the phone for long periods at a time, then finally fell asleep just before Anita came to fetch her for dinner. As the airport manager had promised, the wind was dying down. The plane would land. Everything was A-OK.

Philip was pleased with himself at dinner, but had almost nothing to say—a little small talk about the heavy air and the dark clouds forming to the southwest. He still avoided Lucy, who ignored him, and listened to Henri and Billy talking about the edit. Anita drank three glasses of red to calm down.

To Henri, Lucy seemed out of focus and on autopilot. He knew Philip had to be the cause of her distress, which heightened Henri's desire for revenge. Anita decided it was best to leave the van and take Lucy's rental car to the airport. They all packed in, with Lucy and Philip in front and the others in back. Anita's face was hidden behind her large dark glasses and the rose scarf. Billy pulled a cap down over his nose.

Anita shrugged at Henri in his standard blacks. "You can scrunch down if we see them."

He took a long drag off his cigarette. "Scrunch down is good," he said, and wrote it in his book.

On the way to the airport, they admired the desert in silence. After Lucy parked in the lot, they trooped into the terminal. Lucy and Philip checked in, then joined the others in the restaurant to wait for the plane.

As Lucy sat down, she apologized in a distracted tone. "I'm sorry. I forgot. I have to make a call. I'll be right back."

"Can we order something for you?" asked Henri.

She looked back at him and smiled. "That's so kind, Henri. Thank you. I'd like a glass of red." She walked outside in the sun and tried Jack on her cell phone.

"Hello."

"Hi. It's Lucy. We're at the airport, waiting for the plane. We couldn't get out this morning because of the wind. I just wanted to say goodbye and apologize for Philip's behavior. He was wretched."

"You don't need to worry about his little blackmail. I intended to put the bowl back in Willow's burial chamber. So there won't be any evidence, anyway."

"Is that why you didn't get angry when he was trying to blackmail you?"

"I really don't give a damn about Philip. I already agreed to give you the iceman, remember. That was our deal."

"He hasn't always been like this."

"Well, he is now. Which reminds me, I got a call from a Sloan Sillcot, who represents an Indian legal firm with a long, self-righteous name. They're demanding the location of the iceman, who he claims is an American Indian. Sillcot says his group will sue if Philip takes the iceman. He also said he got a call from Ben Wang, who's doing a story on Philip. Sillcot heard about me from Wang. Do you know about any of this?"

"Philip said Wang has gotten out of hand—that he's dangerous. He'll use anything you say. I've never had to deal with him, but it sounds like that's about to change. You and I have just become part of the story."

"What's Wang look like? Sillcot said he wants to talk to me."

"A very dissipated Eleanor Roosevelt with stubble."

"You're kidding?"

"Not at all." She laughed. "He's a very good journalist."

"Yes, and he kills."

"His target will be Philip, who probably deserves it. If we don't talk to him, he can't say much about us."

"I'm glad you called. I was wondering when you might be back to look at the Mimbres sites I showed you?"

"When's good?"

"Anytime after the end of the rainy season. Some of that country will be pretty slick for the next few weeks."

"I'm looking forward to the end of the rainy season. I should get back."

"I'll keep you posted."

"Goodbye, Jack." She looked up and saw the bright clouds consuming the sun. A warm breeze was rearranging her hair. She walked into the terminal, remembering the sunlit pool, kissing him, and the touch of their bodies.

Anita had Billy stand back and to the side, so he would not be in Philip's face with the camera. She wanted to engage the famous professor in her project but was a little unsure of how to proceed.

"Professor Sachs," she began, without asking if they could video him, "I understand you went out to meet Jack Miller yesterday. I was interested in knowing what the two of you had in common. Mr. Miller's background seems a bit . . . contrary to your own?"

Philip turned to Billy and stared at the camera. "Turn that damn thing off. You didn't even ask for an interview. You will get a hell of a lot further if you develop some manners."

"I'm sorry," said Anita. "You seem to be very involved with the media. I didn't think you would mind."

Philip checked to see that Billy had lowered his camera. "Why would I have anything to do with a notorious antiquities thief, who builds mudmen with children as his principal activity in life, and whose irresponsible actions in a caving incident damned near killed Lucy?"

"Actually we would like to know about your current work on the iceman. I understand Ben Wang's doing an article on you? Is that really true?"

"How in the hell did you find out about that?"

Anita was not a Ben Wang. She stuttered a little, then simply said, "Is it supposed to be secret?"

Philip stared at her. "We're inside. I don't think you need sunglasses." She snatched them off, dropped them, and they clattered across the floor. Philip was annoyed that Lucy had gone outside probably to call Miller. After Anita had collected her glasses and herself, Philip smiled and seemed to relax. He wondered if she was as naive as she seemed. Perhaps these two could be useful, maybe even help balance what Wang might do to him.

"Yes. It's a secret, but less so with each passing day. This is a delicate project, Anita, and I'd appreciate it if you wouldn't go into this in your video just yet. I'll be more than happy to give you a long interview in a week or so, and the opportunity for some spectacular footage. It is possible I could guide some funding your way. It will be worth the wait, I promise. Is that okay with you?"

Before Anita could respond, Henri gave Billy the nod to start the camera. Billy moved back and to the side so Philip was unaware he was being filmed. "Professor," said Henri, "I would appreciate your response to a few questions, please." Without pausing, Henri launched into Philip. "Haven't you archaeologists done everything you accuse the pot hunters of doing—raiding people's burial grounds and stealing sacred relics? You bloated university museums and basements with artifacts and bones of the not-so-long dead, constructed buildings the size of football fields many stories high for squirreling away your loot, until it became obvious that collecting loot was not nearly as profitable as collecting information.

"Now you look back at the information you've collected and say, more, we need more. More doctoral dissertations, more data, more computer programmers. You archaeologists—who name, define, and categorize—represent official culture and suck life from the cultures it dominates. So now, the cultural saviors vilify the pot hunters as criminals. But the role of the criminal is to deconstruct official culture. So, hooray for the criminal."

Anita was breathing hard and chewing her lip. The NEH wasn't going to like this.

Philip leaned toward Henri for the kill. "Bashé, before you and your multiculturalists, postmodernists, and deconstructing relativists are through, you will have caused more suffering and death than all the plagues of history, because you will have eroded the possibility of hope. You are the destroyers of dreams."

Henri shot back, "You and your gang devised a flimsy methodology to support authoritarian structure. You are intellectual monsters who have climbed out of . . ."

Philip smiled. "Bashé, fuck you and your hyperbolic bullshit."

Henri looked over at Billy. "Hyperbolic bullshit is good. How was the focus?"

"Fine," said Billy, holding a straight face.

Henri had gone way over the top as far as Anita was concerned. She couldn't even talk. The little bastard had probably screwed the promised interview with Philip Sachs—forget the funding. And Billy, the idiot, had the audacity to video Henri's attack, despite her attempts to wave him off.

Philip turned and looked at Billy. "That was a very stupid, costly mistake, Mr. Cowboy-cameraman."

Lucy returned as the flight was being called. She tried to look normal, but nothing about her was normal. She saw them turning, one after another, to look. Her face felt flushed. She wondered if they noticed.

"I see your plane is boarding," said Henri. "So this is goodbye. Goodbye, Lucy, I hope we meet again. Goodbye, Professor Aryan-theory."

Lucy kissed Henri on both cheeks, and wandered off toward the gate.

"I'll e-mail you," Anita called as Philip went through the door.

"E-mail is to writing," said Henri, "what New Age is to the soul."

Anita turned on him. "You don't know shit about the soul, Henri. You don't have a spurchall bone in your body."

"Spurchall?" He turned to Billy. "What is this spurchall?"

"She's saying spiritual, Henri." Billy had his camera running.

"Ha, spiritual, of course." He took a long drag deep into his lungs and considered the concept of spiritual. "I had no idea you were spurchall, Anita. You always impressed me as one of those desperate women whose goal in life is to escape their parents' dreary fate, which suggests the spurchall is merely a ticket to abundance." He took another drag off his cigarette. As he exhaled, he realized how harsh he had been, and was about to apologize when she exploded.

"Fuck you, Henri. You little sonofabitch." She turned to Billy. "The two of you have screwed me with Sachs and Wang. You can walk back to town." She headed for the door.

They stood in the terminal and watched her march toward the car. "She missed the denouement," Henri said, a little sad.

"You could have waited until we got back to town."

"They have cabs here?"

"I haven't seen any. There was an airport limo, but it just left. I think we have to hitchhike."

"Oh, you mean with the thumb, like Clark Gable?"

"Unfortunately, Claudette Colbert has left the building."

"Well, it will be a nice walk. I see the clouds have cooled the heat of the sun." Henri simply accepted the state of affairs and headed for the door. It was a long walk, and Billy was still sore, but he followed his buoyant friend down the highway and into the great out-of-doors.

Lucy and Philip buckled in and waited through the squawk of announcements and the pilot's love affair with his voice. They were in the air before Philip said anything. He looked out the window and asked, "Why did you go off and leave me with those idiots? That woman . . . Anita, asked me about the iceman *and* Ben Wang in front of that little French bastard. What the hell business do you have telling her my business?"

"I never said a word about the iceman or Wang. When I called Jack to apologize for your behavior, he told me Sillcot called him demanding the location of the iceman. Evidently, Wang told Sillcot about Jack. What I would like to know is why in the hell you told Wang about Jack."

Philip stared out the window for a while. Finally he looked at Lucy. "I screwed up, dear. Can we just leave it at that?" He was quiet for a while and went back to the window. He queried the world below, "Why the hell did I ever talk to Wang?" Then he turned back to Lucy. He had a slight panic in his voice. "Jack didn't tell them where the iceman is, did he?"

"I didn't think to ask, but you certainly gave him cause to," she said and smiled.

Henri and Billy hadn't gone more than a mile when a faded red Ford pickup shot by going in the other direction. Inside, Raw Bone glanced at the strange little man in black.

Billy caught a glimpse of Raw Bone as his head jerked back. "Have a nice day-new-ma, Henri." They ran across the road and up the hill into a clump of scrub juniper to the sound of screeching brakes. Raw Bone put the truck into a slide, momentarily lost control, and came to a stop at the edge of the road.

Billy figured he could outrun them, but Henri was helpless. Billy crawled over next to him and whispered, "You stay put, no matter what. I'll lead them into the hills as far as I can." He left his camera with Henri and crawled through the trees toward Raw Bone and Rat. He lay behind a rock until they had come within a few feet of him.

"I heard one of 'em," said Rat.

Rat, Raw Bone, and Billy were all holding their breath, listening—waiting for one of them to make a move. Billy jumped straight up, stared Raw Bone in the eye, got a glimpse of the shotgun at his side, and made for the trees. He ran for three seconds, then dropped behind a boulder. He felt a sting in his arm and heard a blast. He was up again, very close to the trees. The gun pumped, ejected the shell, slammed in another. Billy dove sharp to his right. The second blast missed. He was up and into the trees before Raw Bone had a chance for a third shot. He could outrun them, and a shotgun was fairly useless in the trees. Billy only had to let them stay close enough to keep them on his trail. He led them into the hills for a little more than two hours. By the time they gave up and headed back to their truck, it was dusk.

Billy hoped Henri had wits enough to stay hidden until Raw Bone and his brother got in their truck and left.

But no. After the third shot, Henri waited for half an hour, then ran for the road when he heard a truck. Of course, no one was going to pick up a delirious little man in black, waving his hands—one of which held a video camera—in the middle of nowhere. And no one did. Some slowed to stare, then sped away.

Enraged, he began running toward town. Several yards later, he slowed to a jog, then a resigned walk. Far up ahead, he saw several bikers in the twilight, cruising in pairs toward him. They turned off the road into the hills on his left and immediately dropped out of sight—where and how mystified him. He could hear the sharp rap of their bikes, but no bikes appeared in the hills among the cacti and spiky stuff. For a moment, he had hoped they might belong to Marquez and his gang, but these bikes were not throaty, low-riding Harleys. Twenty minutes later, he found the mysterious escape route—a dry arroyo that went up into the hills. During the rainy season water from the arroyo was funneled into a large culvert under the highway and out into the desert.

Henri was nervous, wondering if the next vehicle would be his death. He was exhausted and decided to get off the road and try to nap in the culvert. His wish was denied when he slipped going down into the arroyo and slid into a small, fine-needled cactus.

He lay still for a while, decided nothing was broken, and crawled into the culvert. He'd been sitting in a nest of dried brush for over an hour, picking stickers from his arms and hands, when he noticed several animals watching him from the foothills—possibly the night dogs Leon Marquez had mentioned. He wondered if they were hungry. Perhaps they were wondering if he was good to eat. They began moving through the rocks toward him, their long, thick tails waving over their backs. Their teeth seemed to glow in the dusk. He promised himself, should he escape Raw Bone and Rat and the toothy menace in the hills, that he would go back to his lovely Nina and never leave Paris again.

The animals stopped several feet from the culvert and watched, almost as though they wanted to be sure Henri was all right. He decided they were merely curious and began talking to them. They listened with great interest.

"What kind of animals are you?" he asked. "Certainly not tigers, nor lions, nor bears. I have been told that, being French, I am inedible. Or was it indigestible? The point is, I am bad eating."

He found his cigarettes, crumpled from the fall, and a book of matches. He sat and smoked as it got dark. After he lit his second cigarette, the shy creatures crept to the edge of the culvert, staring in fascination at Henri's glowing ember. When they heard a car approach, they scurried back into the hills. Henri was sorry to see them go.

Raw Bone should have given up on Billy and gone home by now. Henri walked out into the arroyo to look down the road. He had great confidence in Billy's ability to outwit Raw Bone, partially because he could not face the idea of Billy's death. A car zoomed past. He was up high on the bank, which made him visible for an instant as the headlights flashed by. Henri stood in the darkness, wondering what he should do. He was out of cigarettes. He was hungry. No one would stop when there was light, they weren't about to stop in the dark. As this realization registered, a vehicle skidded to a stop just before the culvert.

A spotlight snapped on, pivoted, and fixed on him. In his depleted state he remembered spotlights had to do with cooking deer. He also remembered who had such a contraption, and started running down the bank, out of the blinding light. Fortunately, he tripped as Raw Bone got off a shot. Henri rolled into the arroyo, got up, and ran for the culvert. He lay down in his nest of brush and listened. It was quiet for several minutes, then he heard feet sliding down the banks on either side of the road. They had him trapped.

Henri lay still and flat, facing the desert, trying not to breathe. The two men stood in the dark, waiting for him to make a move. Then, from behind, he heard Raw Bone's hobnails on the metal culvert just as a diesel truck began to downshift. No doubt, Raw Bone's pickup was in the middle of the road. As the truck approached, Henri saw a man silhouetted near the mouth of the culvert and heard Raw Bone shout, "Hey, creep, here's somethin' hot n' tasty. Too bad I'm outta catsup."

There was a blast. The echoing pings of buckshot ricocheted through the culvert. The silhouette man fell backward as the hail of shot penetrated his skin. Overhead, the truck rumbled past, leaving the dark and the sound of Raw Bone's heavy breathing in the steel tunnel and the fallen man's moaning, scraping his boots against the earth, trying to crawl. It crept into Raw Bone's brain that he had shot his brother.

"Jacob? Jacob? Where are you, Jacob? Oh, Jesus Christ." Raw Bone's boot just missed Henri's rigid body as he stomped toward the other end of the culvert shouting for his brother. "I told you to stay clear, you goddamn fool. Talk to me, you goddamn fool."

To his relief, Henri heard the bikers. The first shot had drawn their attention. By now they were moving out of the hills, down the arroyo toward the highway, lights off, engines idling, coasting toward the culvert.

When Raw Bone heard them, he headed up the side of the bank to his truck, leaving his brother. The bikers cut their engines and listened—Raw Bone running toward his truck. Henri lay still, waiting. Then the flashlight found him. A man walked around and pointed the light at Henri's head. Things seemed extremely quiet. Henri wondered if Rat was dead. He sure as hell was quiet. Everyone was waiting for something.

Henri looked up, squinting against the light. "Thank you, for saving my life, very much." This was a guess. Who was holding the light? Would he shoot or just stomp Henri to death?

The man turned and called for Anzapi. Another set of boots. Some whispering. This seemed like a bad thing, but these men smelled of woodsmoke and that was a good thing—Marquez smelled of woodsmoke.

"Frenchie Bashé?" It was Marquez. "What happened, caballero? You okay?"

"I'm very lucky at being unlucky."

"No extra holes in your body?" Marquez laughed.

"Sí. No extra holes. But I don't know about my friend Billy. They chased him into the hills. I don't know if he's alive."

The bikers left Rat groaning in the arroyo and rode up the bank to the highway with Henri, holding Billy's camera, on the back of Marquez's bike. They had gone less than a mile when their headlights picked up Billy. He was panicked, but much too cool to show it. By their sound, they were off-road bikes. At least they weren't Raw Bone and Rat. He stood his ground as they pulled in around him. By the time his eyes adjusted to the headlights, he heard a voice shouting over the rumble of engines.

"Billeee, Billeee! It is me, Henri. Everything is okay. Leon has saved our asses."

The desert night was cool, and the ride back to town put a chill through Henri. Fearing for his life and Billy's for hours, having his armful of cactus stickers, running out of cigarettes, almost being killed by Raw Bone, the cold air, and the noise and vibration of the bikes left Henri shaking. He struggled off the bike in front of the hotel and smiled at his saviors. He was near tears, but upbringing and genuine gratitude forced the words, "Please, allow me to buy you a drink," through his chattering teeth.

"A drink would be good," said Marquez. They parked their bikes in back of the hotel and met Henri in the bar. He asked the bartender for two bottles of Chablis. The man was not going to be rude to Henri considering the backup, but his face showed consternation—he had no Shablee. "On second thought," said Henri. "Could we have two bottles of your best scotch, nine glasses, and a pair of . . . tweezers." The tweezers appeared with the rest—it was a prickly country.

After they had pulled up extra chairs and settled in, Henri started tweezing stickers. "You changed bikes, Leon. I like the Harleys better." The scotch appeared and Henri toasted his friends, "For saving our asses."

"The Harleys bottom out in the rocks," said Leon. "Who was the man shooting? What was that about?"

"He's called Raw Bone. He was trying to kill me, but shot his brother by mistake."

"We know them. They're bad guys. We'll take care of them for you—not to worry about Bone and Rat. Okay?"

"Very thoughtful of you. I am grateful." Henri raised his glass and smiled. The golden scotch and his dangerous friends warmed his heart.

Billy wondered if doing a video of the bikers would be worth the effort. There would be a lot of bullshit involved, plus the possibility of bodily harm, but it would be unlike anything anyone had done. After his second double and a couple of beers, he put the question to Marquez.

Leon was thoughtful. He was used to hearing stupid ideas, but it was not good to discuss such ideas with people you didn't know. "You could make a very interesting film," said Marquez, "because we are interesting people who do interesting things, but you would probably get killed. One of us might kill you. It's possible. So, to save both of us a lot of trouble, I must say no. Thank you for asking."

Billy was relieved. Besides, Anita would have hated it. He watched the bikers with Henri. The Frenchman was describing the strange animals who came out of the hills, who listened to his questions and watched him smoke in the darkness of the corrugated-iron tunnel.

Billy had seen the rental car in the hotel lot and the light on in their room. He wanted to go up and tell Anita about Henri and Raw Bone and Rat, and being saved by Marquez. He had spent all that time in the hills wondering how to make Anita happy and affectionate again. She was right about his little films. He was self-absorbed, but that was his protection. Meanness was hers, he guessed. It was an impasse. They had started out all sweetness, harmony, and sex. It was simple. It worked, and they didn't need to talk about why. When they started to fall apart, neither one could talk about it. He just assumed the solution was to go their separate ways.

Billy thanked the bikers for saving Henri. They shook hands all around. Henri had consumed too much scotch and was slowed to a slur. "Sank you, Señor Marquez, for letting me play Androcles to your lion. In Paris, my beautiful Nina and I will dine out for several months on the tale of your good deeds."

Leon looked at his bandaged hand. "Paris must be a boring place, Monsieur Bashé." He patted his French friend on the shoulder. "Next time you come, I will take you to the mountains and to Juarez. They do things there that will give you years of dining out, as you say." He nodded and his crew followed him out.

"Are you all right, Henri?" Billy asked.

"I am feeling quite fine." He waved the tweezers. "I'm getting more arm hairs than stickers, but everything is proceeding accordingly. You should go up to Anita. She needs you. Do what she wants and she'll come around—even put up with an occasional, how does she say . . . arty, jerk-off flicks. But let her finish "Bashé in America," so we can all make some money, and I can go home, okay?"

"Okay, Henri." As Billy stood up he caught a glimpse of Anita coming through the bar. She saw him and sprinted into the restaurant, wrapped her arms around him and squeezed. She was killing his ribs, but he really wanted her to hold him. "What happened to you, Billy? I went back, but you'd disappeared. Then I saw that red pickup. I was scared bad. I was sure you were dead. Oh, God, Billy, I love you. I love you, baby." Oblivious to Henri, she took Billy's hand and led him away.

He heard Henri call out, "Good night, cowboy."

Willow stood up and was doing a kind of slow dance on the table. She stretched her arms high and swung her bottom back and forth, letting the strings of her skirt slide over her rounds. She thrust her breasts toward him and gave them a slight jiggle, then her hands slid down, barely touching her nipples, over her stomach, to the woven belt that held the skirt. She untied the belt, letting the string skirt fall to the table. She pushed it toward him with her toe.

"What are you doing, Willow?"

She spun around in a full circle. "It's time, Jack. Thinking of you and Lucy helped me entice the clouds. There'll be rain in the morning."

The scent was in the air. "Time to break the bowl?"

"Sooner's better."

Jack picked up the phone and pressed Kills The Deer's number. "Hi, it's Jack."

"Hey, Jack. Everything okay down there?"

"Yeah, it's goin' to rain tomorrow morning. Didn't want you to miss the show. The clouds are heavy, and it's real quiet."

"I'll be down by daylight."

"Drive careful," he said, and hung up. Willow was watching him, fantasizing, doing her slow dance.

"I have a request," he said.

"Tell me."

"I would like to see your face. Will you take the mask off before you go?"

"If you found me undesirable, it would break the spell. There would be no rain and I would vanish in the sky. Would you have me risk that?"

"No, of course not." He felt as though a lover had separated herself and gone away.

The gesture he had seen in Becker's drawing had started all of this, and ultimately drew him to Lucy. He had been smitten by the greeting, the solicitation, the invitation of a gesture. "Come into my house," said the gesture. It was the gesture of love. And Lucy saw this also.

Willow made him think of being held by Lucy in the water, the touch of her naked body against his, invisible in the bright sun.

"What are you doing, Jack? I can feel something happening in me. You are making the tingle all through my body."

It was time to let go of the ghost who lived in his mind. "Goodbye,

Willow." As he reached for the bowl, she leaned toward him and kissed him. He could feel the passion of her kiss, but she was gone, drawn into the bowl. With the sensation of the kiss still pressed against his lips, he threw the bowl into the fireplace, shattering it against the bricks. He thought he heard a gust of wind go up the chimney, but the imagination does things.

SEVENTEEN

Before daybreak the wind whirled through, blowing brush, loose boards, nests, and small birds from their resting places. It was barely light when the wind stopped. It became quiet and still.

Jack woke out of a deep sleep. A fine, warm drizzle started. It was more like steam. He dressed and walked outside to check the sky. He felt the embrace of the mist. He was replaying Willow's last dance in his mind when he remembered her toe pushing the skirt across the table toward him. He went inside to look—the table was bare.

The phone rang. The ringing reminded him of Willow's first words, "You are the White-Larva." He never did ask her who the White-Larva was—damn. The phone was still ringing. He stared at it, letting it ring twice more before he finally answered.

"Ben Wang, here." It was Eleanor Roosevelt with stubble and asthma. "I'm looking for a Jack Miller who used to deal in Indian artifacts?"

"You found him. What do you want?"

"I understand that several weeks ago you came into the possession of a frozen toe. You sent the toe to Carlos Martinez, a lab assistant at the O'Connell lab in Berkeley, for an off-record carbon-fourteen dating. His work indicates the toe is approximately fifteen thousand years old. The chief lab tech, Mickey McGregor, identified DNA markers in the toe that appear in early Europeans. I understand this toe came from an ice cave in an Alaskan glacier. Do I have the facts straight so far?"

"Where did you get your facts?"

"I'm doing a story on the find, and I'd like all the background I can get. I understand that Dr. Lucy Perelli was sent down to see you by her close friend and mentor Dr. Philip Sachs and that the two of you were trapped in a cave together. Could you tell me something about your time in the cave?"

"It's all turned to tabloid, hasn't it?"

"I'm under the impression that she was very persuasive in getting you to divulge the location of the man in the ice. Is that a fair statement?"

"Who put you on to me?"

"Does it matter?"

"Why are you setting up Lucy Perelli like this?"

"Do you feel Sachs has betrayed you and Perelli?"

"You are quite the bastard."

"I often hear variations on that theme. But I am only doing my job. Did you and Dr. Perelli make love in the cave or at any other time?"

"Fuck you very much, Wang. 'Bye."

He sorted through his notes for Lucy's number in D.C., got her answering machine, and waited for the beep. "Lucy, this is Jack, call me."

"Don't hang up, I'm here."

"Screening your calls?"

"Yeah. I tried to call you."

"So has Ben Wang talked to you?"

"Yes, but not for long. His biggest interest seemed to be if we'd had sex in the cave. Philip set this up. I don't know if he thinks I cheated on him or what, but this is totally, fucking out-of-bounds."

"I won't disagree, but he's desperate. I had another reason for calling. Would you like to meet me in Juneau to see the iceman?"

"God yes. Can we get there before Philip?"

"I think so."

"Is it raining yet?"

"Drizzling. I expect the whole thing to go off pretty soon. Kills The Deer's due any moment. You'll have to come next year."

"I will, of course. I should have stayed this time. When can you be in Juneau?"

"I'll meet you at the Juneau airport under the polar bear, the day after tomorrow. You'll get in before I do. You can rent a car at the airport and get a room at the Tlingit Motor Lodge. I see The Sisters just showed up. I should go, but, ah . . . I wanted to say . . ."

"Yes?"

"It's going to start soon."

"Is that what you wanted to say?"

"I . . . feel . . ."

"What? Tell me, Jack."

"Remember Willow's gesture?"

"Yes."

"When you first saw it, do you remember what you said?"

"That the painter loved her very much."

"When I think of that gesture, I think of you."

"Keep the thought. I'll see you soon."

"Not soon enough." He paused for a moment. "Has it occurred to you that we are having this conversation because of a stolen bowl and a frozen toe?"

Jack dialed Finley, a long-time fisherman friend of his and Berndt's in Juneau, got his answering machine, and left a detailed message. As he hung up, he heard Kills The Deer's pickup come off the highway.

Kills The Deer parked at the far end of the house and walked down the hill, watching The Sisters moving slowly among the mudmen, checking for changes. As Jack walked into the kitchen, Willow flashed lightning through the clouds and shouted down a thunderclap. The sky let loose.

A tall mudman with a narrow face slowly released his long right arm. The girls cheered. The cheer brought Jack out the door and down the slope. Another mudman's roundish, popeyed head opened up and shot mud into the air. The girls went wild, dancing and twirling in the rain, chasing one another through the mudmen, around Jack, and into a startled Indian.

"This is my friend, Kills The Deer. These are The Sisters—SuAnn, Sadie, Sissy, and Snake. Say hello, ladies."

They looked at one another for a second, then shouted, "Hello ladies," and laughed, and fell down, and rolled in the mud like exuberant colts.

The thin bands of willow bark that had held back the gestures of arms, legs, ankles, wrists, and heads began to slip. The poised dancers moved—some slow and graceful, others in awkward jerks. Some, unable to contain their enthusiasm for a moment of life, exploded. Then came the disintegrating flurry of flying mud and willow stays. The entire colony let loose across the rising water. The single exception was Oliver Oil, who stood stout and resolute, waiting for the flood's full onslaught. The Joaquin-Jimenez was rapidly becoming a river.

"If this keeps up," said Sissy, wet to the bone and squinting into the rain, "we'll be headin' fer high ground."

They were all stomping, right foot, left foot, right foot, left foot, through the mud of melting men and chanting, "Angels, devils, angels, devils, angels, devils." They all fell down again, laughing and howling. The rain intensified. The Joaquin-Jimenez filled its banks and began encroaching up the hillside.

Jack looked at the sky—at Willow's handiwork—and knew he'd better start clearing some things out of his house, though he expected he had several hours before water reached the door. He left the roiling river to the roiling girls and walked up to his house.

Kills The Deer followed, laughing. "Where'd you find those strays?"

"They found me."

"They'd put a terror in most folks."

"For good reason. Go dry off. You'll find clothes in my bedroom." Jack went to the big closet near the shower to round up sheets and towels for The Sisters. From time to time, he had company, in spite of himself, so he had a closet full of linens and towels he'd found at the Salvation Army in Silverado. He liked the sound of Salvation Army. What a concept.

The Sisters trooped up to the house, leaving a muddy track through the kitchen and into the shower room. First they washed their clothes, then themselves. Wrapped in towels and sheets, they trooped back out to the living room and ate their sammiches.

Jack fetched a plastic ice-cream bucket from the closet and collected the fragments of the parrot trainer bowl from the fireplace. The Sisters watched. They wondered if Philip got mad and smashed the bowl or if Jack did. They all were reluctant to ask. Maybe it was Lucy. This was grown-up stuff. Sometimes it wasn't a good idea to ask questions.

Jack set the pieces out on the big table, six pieces of paper, and a bottle of glue. "Let's put this back together before the river comes for us."

Kills The Deer built a fire and set the girls' clothes on a rack to dry. They all sat around the table and put the bowl together. There were lots of cooks in the pot. No one would claim it was a perfect job, but it stayed together.

SuAnn studied the fractured parrot trainer. "Is she dancing, Jack?"

"Yes, definitely dancing."

"She has a long skirt made of strings."

Jack smiled, thinking of those strings sliding over Willow's bare bottom.

Lightning cracked through the clouds and thunder shook the windows. "That was too close for comfort," said SuAnn.

"I'm goin' away for a few days," said Jack. "When I get home I have to put this bowl back where I got it. So I need you to hide it in a safe place for me until I get home."

"Our trailer is about as safe as it gets, which isn't sayin' a lot," said Sissy.

"We could bury it in a box under the trailer. Nobody goes there but us," said SuAnn.

Snake came over and whispered in Jack's ear, "Will the lady in the bowl talk to me, too?"

Jack looked her in the eye. "What put that idea in your head?"

"I heard."

"The lady's name is Willow. Every time it thunders, she's talkin'."

But Snake knew a secret. "She didn't talk like that to you."

"No, she didn't," he said. Evidently, Snake could hear as well as she could see. He wondered if she'd seen Willow out of the bowl, but Sissy intervened before he could ask.

"Can we help you put the bowl back where you got it?"

"You'll have to swear an oath never to tell."

"We'll swear," said Sissy, looking around. "Right?"

"Right," said the others.

"When you see where the bowl goes, it'll scare the pee out of you."

Their eyes got a little wide. "Okay," said Snake. They all agreed that they would do anything to see where the bowl went. "Are we goin' to see a dead person?"

"Yes, a very old dead person."

"We've seen worse 'en that," said Sadie. " 'Sides, we're tough."

"Suppose this particular dead person could suck your brains out through your ears?"

"Fer one thing, our brains's too big to get sucked through our ears. Fer another, dead people don't suck so good. So there."

"Don't I get to come?" asked Kills The Deer.

"You have to swear," said Sissy.

"I can swear pretty good."

"If Jack says you can, then you can," said Snake.

"Well, he can come if everybody'll help me load up those two trucks out there with as much stuff as we can before the flood comes through the door. But first we need to build a frame for the back of my rig and stretch a tarp over it."

Kills The Deer's truck already had a metal topper so he could haul his paintings around. They used some old two-by-fours and nailed a top together in half an hour. It was a high, awkward-looking structure, but sturdy. Jack backed the truck to the front door, and they were ready to start loading.

"There's too much stuff in your house to get it all in the trucks," said Sissy. "How're we gonna decide what to take?"

Jack walked through the house. The others followed, a little dismayed at the variety and volume of usless things. "Why don't we just take what we want to save," said Jack.

They looked around and each of them found something they liked best and started with that. Snake's first pick was the coatimundi skull. SuAnn, the deep quiet soul, cradled a tin retablo of an olive-eyed Christ Child. Sissy's take was a faded door panel painted with a yellow bicycle. Sadie took a wildcat skull and a root in the shape of a lady with thick hips that reminded Jack of Marguerite. Jack filled a box with roots of every shape and laid dried roses and tulips on top. Kills The Deer, the lover of irony and "symbology," took a box of saints, or *santos*. These were carved, wooden figures, about a foot high, that, at one time, had been painted or dressed in fine fabric. Now they were bare and gray and faceless.

Before the first trip to the truck, Kills The Deer asked, "Do you know how they lost their faces?"

The sisters shook their heads.

"It's because of the jackrabbits." He held up a *santo* for them all to inspect. "Years ago, in certain villages, the little saints were made by several carvers. The masters made the heads. Masters are perfectionists. They wanted the little glass eyes to stay in the faces forever. So they took a chisel and split the face from the head so they could set the eyeballs from the inside. Then they drilled small holes from the front, only big enough for the glass eyes to see through. From the back of the split face they drilled a larger hole, but stopped before going through. Then they glued the eyes to little sticks and pressed them behind the eye sockets. They used jackrabbit glue to put the chiseled face exactly back in place without disturbing the face or the beautifully carved lines of the hair.

"Sometimes the saints were left behind in a falling-down house when an old person died. If the glue got wet, the faces popped off and hopped away."

"Ha," said Sadie. "I don't buy it."

"Well, I buy some of it," said Sissy. "But it sounds a little far-fetched."

Jack gave Kills The Deer a shrug. "They're a hard sell."

"I liked it fine," said Snake—her way of saying Kills The Deer was okay. "But we better keep that bowl dry."

After an hour, they decided all the stuff they could get in the trucks was in.

"What about our place? Will the flood get it, too?" asked SuAnn.

"Your trailer's about fifty feet higher off the river than my house. You'll be fine. We'll take you home before we go. Will you look after my cat while I'm gone?"

"The bowl *and* the cat?" asked Snake.

"I know. It's a lot to ask."

"Better take cat food."

Jack and Kills The Deer took the girls and Jack's cat up to their trailer and left Jack's truck with them. Snake rode up with Kills The Deer. She was quiet. Snake had a lot on her mind. The trailer was on a knoll high above and well away from the river.

The Sisters took the cat and the bowl—bundled in towels and plastic wrap—waved goodbye, and made a dash for the trailer.

Kills The Deer drove Jack through the storm, east into the foothills of the Black Mountains toward the Rio Grande and the freeway to Albuquerque. Water poured from the arroyos, filled the culverts, and flooded the road. They slowed to a crawl to get through the low spots. The steeper slopes were beginning to erode, jettisoning cannonball-sized stones down the hills. Within hours the banks would absorb the water and ooze over the road. It would be weeks before the highway department had the mud, rocks, and trees cleared away.

Once they started up the steep part of the mountain, the real threat was from trees with shallow roots in the thin soil. Lightning cracked across the canyon at the same instant thunder boomed through the cab. Jack looked up at the sky—all those years of stored-up lust. He imagined Willow, grown to the size of a mountain, stomping lightning out of the clouds and making thunder with her hands. She was beginning to scare him.

A heavy branch smashed into the grille, another cracked the windshield and snapped off the wiper blade on Jack's side. "Damn it, Willow."

The truck veered across the road and onto the shoulder. Jack looked up at the storm as though he expected to see her swaying her thighs and breasts, with thunderous moans—the thousand-year orgasm.

Kills The Deer leaned forward and peered through the cracked windshield. "There's no willow up here, Jack."

Jack looked at him, "Did I say willow?"

They kept checking the temperature gauge to see if the radiator was leaking. About a mile up the road they came to another tree. At least this one was already down. They got out the chainsaw and cut their way through.

The storm was confined to the west side of the range. The rain stopped and the wind slowed once they crested the mountain and started down the other side, winding through the canyons that opened into the wide valley toward Truth or Consequences.

Kills The Deer peered at the booming little town on the Rio Grande. "The mayor of that place named it after a 1950s game show. Did you know that?"

"I heard it was supposed to be Truth *and* Consequences, but the city council balked."

As they turned onto the freeway toward Albuquerque, Jack felt they were finally out of range of his overzealous cloud dancer. With luck, her thousand-year lust had run its course, and she was seeping into the first world of her ancestors.

The grass, trees, and shrubs in the mountains usually helped slow the water, letting it absorb into the ground, slowing its run to the gullies and arroyos. But three months before Willow let loose, tens of thousands of acres had burned the ground bare in the watersheds that fed the Joachin-Jimenez. When Jack, The Sisters, and Kills The Deer saw the river rising, they were only seeing the runoff from the low valleys. Kills The Deer and Jack were well on their way when Snake and SuAnn saw the accumulated runoff from the massive burn. A wall of water fifteen feet high shot through the canyon below the trailer, headed toward Jack's house.

SuAnn put her arm around Snake. "I'm afraid Oliver's history," said SuAnn.

"I'll make him lots tougher next time," said Snake.

But they were both thinking of Jack's place.

The wall of water hit Jack's rambling house so hard the windows barely had time to explode before the adobe walls fell in on one side and blew out the other. The water moved so fast it sucked bricks from the floor.

Before the plane crossed the Grand Canyon on its way to the dreary-cool of Seattle, Jack fell asleep, enraptured by Willow's final, irrevocable liquefication of love.

EIGHTEEN

During the flight from Seattle to Juneau, he looked down on the massive Canadian glaciers that fed the fjords and the sea of the Inland Passage. The pressure of the top ice turned the glacial face a translucent green, as if it were lit from inside. He imagined colonies of mammoths frozen in these glaciers. Depending on the depth and movement, they might be spread thin as butter by the pressure of the moving ice. Others—their great ivory tusks, enormous heads, and fist-sized teeth intact—were waiting, ready to walk out into a green meadow and begin grazing or trumpeting for territory, a mate, or the approaching menace of men with spears tipped with beautiful, fluted points.

Somewhere, in all that ice, were men, women, and children, who had huddled together to hold the last of their warmth against the catastrophic summer storm that would not thaw for thousands of years.

A cheerful announcement of glacier facts jolted Jack back into the moment, compressing an expansive daydream to an insipid travel brochure. The crew was ordered to cross check and prepare for landing.

Lucy waited in front of a giant stuffed polar bear standing upright in a Plexiglas case. The traffic to the airport was light, so she had several minutes to absorb the strange beauty of the bear and study the quiet irony in its sublime expression.

When the loudspeakers began squawking, she turned her attention to the deplaning passengers. She caught sight of Jack, still flight dazed, dodging the lungers and greeters crisscrossing his path. He made his way to the periphery of the lost and reunited and found himself looking up at the white bear. Lucy came from his blind side, slipped a hand around his neck, pulling herself into him, and kissed him on the lips. The polar bear had seen a lot of this. For Jack and Lucy, it was the first time their lips had touched.

They pressed together until their awareness was pierced by the tittering of Tlingit girls gathered to view the great, white bear.

Jack became serious and formal. "Excuse me," he said to Lucy, "have we met?"

Lucy had a mischievous grin and a glint in her eye. Except for the bout of giggles, the girls were well mannered. And clean. He wondered how The Sisters were doing.

They waited at the baggage carousel, leaning into each other as though they had been apart for months. "We need to start right away," said Lucy. "We'll be too late if we wait 'til morning. I talked to a friend in Philip's office who said they'd already left D.C. and arranged for a transport helicopter from Anchorage to take them out to the glacier."

"Big helicopter? Hmmm. And to think your tax dollars are paying for it. Well, we'll have to get you outfitted, buy supplies, and see if Finley's boat's ready. Look for a large green duffel bag with an orange tag. I'll try Finley." He went to the pay phones and dialed Finley's cell phone.

"Finley."

"Hi, it's Jack. Where are you?"

"Working on Hilde's transom."

"No need to get personal."

"I can tell by your voice, you need to leave today."

"I do."

"I've got krill in the heat exchangers."

"That only happens to spaceships when the aliens attack."

"Yeah, welcome to Juneau."

"We can be in the bay in three hours, then it'll take an hour to get through the ice to the glacier, right?"

"Somethin' you need to consider—there's been a big snow up high. Most of the way the trail to the top of the main glacier is clear. Beyond that, it's gonna be slow goin'."

"We only have to get down there in time to hike in before dark. Lucy and I can stay in the cave overnight and leave early."

"The sooner you stop talking and get over here the sooner . . ."

"We'll be there in an hour—hour and a half."

"I'll have this fixed by then. Bring us something to eat, we're starving."

"Smoked salmon?"

"Microwave burritos would do us fine."

"Burritos it is. How's our friend Berndt?"

"That lady doctor he had the crush on got engaged, put him in a funk for a couple of days."

"I'm sure I'll hear about it when we get back. See you soon." He hung up and turned to find Lucy crossing the terminal with his duffel bag.

"Philip isn't likely to leave for the glacier until tomorrow, is he?" she asked.

"No," said Jack. "We should be on our way out before he shows. They'll never see us."

"I don't care if he sees us. I just want to see the iceman without him around."

Jack drove into Juneau so Lucy could look at the scenery. Her head pivoted back and forth trying to take in everything. She had never seen anything like Juneau. It was a glacier park with a thousand-foot waterfall on one side, a bay with fishing boats and ocean liners on the other, and hundreds of small, cedar-sided houses hanging on the hills in between. The predictable governmental structures she screened out. She wanted the storybook town.

They drove up the main street of Juneau to Moose Goods Mercantile, where they outfitted Lucy for the climb to the ice cave: crampons, snowshoes, and energy bars. On the way down to the docks, they stopped for supplies at the Juneau Market. Inside, she found an odd combination of New York, rural Midwest, and Indian faces—an interesting mix of colors and types, all without a ripple of expression.

"Finley wants us to get him microwave burritos."

"In the land of salmon, he wants frozen burritos?"

"You've never had a good microwave burrito, have you?"

"Far be it from me to malign the microwave burrito," she said, scanning the frozen-food bins for Finley's favorite.

"Find burritos," said Jack. "I'll get us the best salmon you ever tasted." He started down another aisle.

"Don't go. I'll never find you again."

He turned and came back to the cart. She gave him a great, juicy, supermarket kiss. There was random clapping, even a halfhearted whistle. He turned red and imagined the butcher pronouncing them man and wife in frozen peas—the Jolly Green Giant as best man. What about The Sisters? Would Lucy move to New Mexico? He felt kissing in public had the taint of corny movies, which explained why a supermarket kiss seemed to have such binding force.

At the docks, Jack nodded toward the giant cruise ships farther up the harbor. "Those food-boat captains like to play chicken. A couple of years ago a cruise ship nosed its way into the side of another. Peeled off its one-inch-steel sliding like it was tin and left an entire stateroom exposed. Something like that happens every three or four years, but that was the first time I'd seen interior decor."

"It must get pretty boring," said Lucy, "all that food and shuffleboard. After Philip's big find, they'll be cruising the fjords searching for men in ice. There'll be ads in *American Archaeology*."

They found Finley's boat, the *Hilde H.*, and hauled their gear onto the deck as Hilde came out of the cabin. She was a big woman in her midfifties, with reddish blond hair.

"Hi, Hilde. This is my friend, Lucy Perelli. This is Hildegard Hansen, half owner of the *Hilde H.* and Finley's partner."

"Hello, Lucy, welcome aboard. Good to see you, Jack. Finley's below, futzing with a heat exchanger." She walked over to the hatch, peered down, and said, "How's it coming, Finley?"

Finley's reply was muffled, but sounded positive.

"Jack is here with his friend."

A skinny, coverall-clad man in his early sixties climbed out of the hatch, flashed a toothy grin through a bristle-brush beard, and shook hands with his guests. He had steel-hard hands and steel-gray eyes. "Howdy, Miller. Nice-lookin' lady. Didja bring burritos?"

Jack handed over a bag of groceries, and Finley headed for the cabin. "Come on, fellows, let's get in my tummy."

Jack sat in the pilot's seat and swiveled around, checking out the boat. Things looked tidy and well maintained. "How much longer can you afford to fish up here?"

"Hilde came into some money, otherwise we'd be cleanin' fish for the goddamn Japs."

"Finley, they're not the goddamn Japs," said Hilde, "they're the goddamn Japanese. And when the money runs out, we might consider ourselves lucky to be cleaning their fish." Hard work had given her powerful shoulders, a round, firm bottom, strong legs, and an attitude.

"She's got a nice ass on her for bein' a well brought-up lady like she is. Her daddy was an admiral in the Norway navy. She's a smart one, too."

"Father was an ensign, Finley." She indulged Finley's crudities, jokes, and flights of fancy, because he knew how to fix anything, took chances, liked to explore the nooks and crannies along the coast and islands with her, plus she found him an endearing mate beneath the covers.

The *Hilde H.* was a thirty-two-foot steel-hulled fishing boat, driven by twin diesels. She was well designed and well made, but obsolete, not unlike Finley and Hilde—they had come late to the boom days of the independents and stayed long. The old Juneau had already changed by the time they came. Fishing had become corporate and international. An inheritance from Hilde's grandfather, a Norwegian fish broker, had literally kept them afloat. They were proud of their boat and their life on the water. Hilde and Finley wanted to be honest fishermen. It didn't seem a lot to ask, but for reasons they could never fully grasp, it was. Hauling Jack and his friend to the glacier wasn't fishing, but, as Finley said, "It's cash money, right in the old pocket, see." His primary goal was to avoid being caught in the machinery of civilization. "The job of the big boys is to catch the lunkers and give 'em somethin' to do. Our job to stay outta the net." For Finley, staying out of the net involved a variety of activities, legal and otherwise.

They cast off in the early afternoon, bubbling backward into the harbor. Once they turned and were clear of the dock, Hilde slowly pushed the throttles forward, leaving a deep wake. The envy and longing of landlocked tourists followed them into the distance. They took the channel to open water and headed south. Finley microwaved burritos, and they drank the expensive red wine Lucy had splurged for.

"She's runnin' pretty good," said Jack.

"Helps to get the krill out."

The sea was glass, which helped them spot deadheads, the barely submerged logs that occasionally sank small boats. They had been out about two hours when the giant flukes of a whale broke the surface, rose fifteen feet in the air, and put an end to any doubts about the existence of pure beauty.

The Inland Passage tended to send people, even the experienced and cynical, into a trance. The sea air mixed with wind blown down from glaciers; whales, seals, seabirds; the sky and mountains reflected in the dark water; submerged ice the size of a ship; and the lurking deadheads aroused senses people were unaware they possessed. The extremes of death and beauty made people who worked the water for a living fatalistic and almost mute, except in Finley's case.

An hour later, they turned east toward Koosnuku Bay and negotiated the masses of sea ice that had once been locked in the glacier. Finley had rigged lines from the bow to the throttles and the steering cables, which allowed him to pilot from the bow and watch for ice. Within half an hour, the still, cold air that hung above the water had everyone, except Hilde, in sweaters or jackets.

Finley beckoned Lucy to the bow and pointed to the water directly below. "I think of the ice beneath the surface as a kind of dream." He was quiet for a moment, thinking about the dream, or allowing for emphasis, Lucy wasn't sure. He pointed to the jagged icebergs around them. "These icy structures rest on dreams the size of mountains. Eventually, the dream melts and these small islands of reality submerge into the sleeping sea. The sea is like sleep and the things that live in the sea are its dreams."

She could see the underwater ice disappear into the dark water far below the surface—into the deep, sleeping sea.

Later she found Jack in the cabin. "Your friend's a sweet dreamer. It's such a contrast to his rough exterior."

"This place allows him to think the way he does. It's what's kept him here."

The islands of floating ice made navigation more treacherous the closer Finley came to the glacier. He headed to a spot on the left bank where the mountain met the water. They nosed in near a sandbar a mile from the five-hundred-foot wall of the translucent green, which periodically sheared off giant calves of ice without warning, sending out waves as high as thirty feet.

Jack jumped from the bow to the sand. Lucy swung their gear out to him, then leaped over the water to the shoreline.

Finley yelled, "Three o'clock tomorrow, right?"

"Three o'clock." They waved Finley off, hoisted their packs, and headed toward the trail that would take them to the top of the glacier. Once they left the shore, it was a steep, rocky climb on a trail that saw little use. They skirted the edge of the glacier, staying on hard ground. Near the top they rested, ate climber's junk food, drank water, and attached their crampons. The sun's reflection off the ice made them shed some clothing even though it was nearly seven o'clock. They had four hours of good light.

The hanging glacier of their destination was in a high valley several hundred feet above the main glacier. The climb was difficult, too steep for snowshoes, but not so steep Jack had to fight his fear of height. Some areas were blown clear of snow, leaving patches of bare rock with a glaze of ice.

Other times they sank into pockets of snow. The climb was taking longer than Jack had anticipated. The last half mile to the high valley was a constant fight through two to three feet of snow. Once they reached the level snow on the hanging glacier and put their snowshoes on, life became much easier.

They had climbed fifteen hundred feet up from the sea by dusk. The climb up had taken its toll on both of them. They stopped and looked across the main glacier at another high valley nearly two miles away that held its own hanging glacier. The valley was steep and angled to the south, ending at a cliff a thousand feet above the sea. "Lucky we're not over there," said Lucy. "I don't think I could have made it."

Jack stared at the valley. "No," he said, and fell backward in the snow, where he lay for several minutes, his snowshoes sticking straight up. "I don't think I can move. I can't imagine what tomorrow will feel like."

"Come on, Miller, get a move on. I want to see your iceman before it's too dark."

"It's already too dark. We've always needed the sun coming through the ice to see it. We still have another hour of this before we get to the cave."

It was near dark by the time they found the iceman's cave. If the snow had been a foot deeper they would have missed the entrance. In spite of the snow, there would be enough direct sunlight in the morning to illuminate the iceman suspended in the cave's outer wall.

They crawled in through the opening, managed to get their pads and sleeping bags rolled out, and fell asleep in their clothes. She reached over and touched his hand. "Thank you."

"Just keeping a promise." He smiled and fell asleep.

Lucy sat up, feeling the deep *wump wump* of transport-chopper blades in her gut. The sun illuminated the ice cave. "Jesus. It must be late." She realized they were about to be invaded by Philip, Ben Wang, and a *National Geographic* film crew. She had already rolled her sleeping bag into a ball and was stuffing it into its sack when she noticed Jack had not moved.

"Would you like me to make you some coffee before you rush off?" he asked.

"Jack, please. They'll be here in minutes."

"It's okay. Listen."

The helicopter was already growing fainter and fainter. She

crawled through the snowy entrance and peeked out at the receding chopper. It was crossing the glacier toward the valley high above the bay. Jack crawled out behind her. They stood on the bank of snow that protected the entrance to the cave and watched the huge transport move into the valley two miles away.

Philip was up front next to the pilot, studying the terrain, looking for the wedge of shadow Jack had shown him on the map. He was getting agitated. "This map was photographed in the late afternoon. It doesn't correlate with much of the detail we're seeing down there. All that damn snow isn't helping either."

The pilot, irritated from the start by Philip's pushiness, was not pleased they were chasing around looking for an ice cave with a useless map. Once they reached the top of the ridge, the pilot banked around and started down again. Philip was searching the valley for Jack's wedge when the chopper seemed to rise several feet. "What the hell are you doing?" he yelled into the microphone.

"Avalanche," the pilot yelled back. "I think our blades set it off."

Philip watched the mountain drop out from under them. His heart fell away with the mountain. He pressed his face against the window.

He was not sure what the avalanche would do to the ice cave. Perhaps nothing. It might go over the top or around, leaving the destiny of his status unhindered.

"Search the mountain after the snow settles. It has to be here. The snow would have gone over the cave. We'll find it."

He looked at the *Geo* producer for confirmation, for hope. The woman was shaking her head in dismay.

On the other side of the glacier, Jack and Lucy saw the snow below Philip's chopper begin to fracture as though a large china platter had shattered in slow motion. The chopper's *wumps* were muffled under the thunderclap. They could see the avalanche begin to move down, gaining momentum, until it exploded across the edge of the valley, out over the sea. For several moments, even the chopper disappeared as snow billowed into the air.

The chopper hovered above the valley, then began moving up and down the ridge. Philip, the pilot, Ben Wang, and the media crew stared out the windows, searching for an object that could have made the shadowy wedge on the map.

Long after everyone else on the chopper knew no ice cave would be found in the valley, that the entire trip was a wash, Philip gave in. The avalanche would have taken the iceman down to the sea and buried it beneath tons of snow.

He could not look at the others. The man who had worked so hard for so many years could not comprehend that something so unjust, so out of his control, could have happened. He assumed that eventually—in months or years—his iceman would melt free of the compacted snow and ice and dissolve in the sea, unexamined by science, consumed by fishes.

Lucy turned and looked at Jack. "Did you lead him on a wild goose chase, or did they misread the map?"

"You and I had a deal, remember. If you got us out of the Mimbres cave, I'd give you the iceman. I was never obligated to Philip. And, without the iceman, Wang has no story, except maybe a sidebar in *Golf Digest* on Philip's handicap. If you want to give the iceman to Philip, that's your call."

"No. This one will always be yours, Jack." She was angry at Philip, but she also felt sorry for him. "At least he thinks his iceman has gone to sea. He won't have to waste the next five years searching for him." She knew his insatiable ambition would lead him on to other glories.

Jack took her by the hand. "It's time to see your iceman."

They crawled into the cave and sat on his sleeping bag, peering into the thick wall of ice illuminated by the sun. In the middle of the thick cave wall they could see the iceman through twelve to fifteen feet of ice, lying on his side with his back to them, about four feet above the cave floor. Jack had never seen him this early in the morning, with the sun coming in at a direct angle. The intensity of the light made the entire wall glow, surrounding the captive man.

Neither of them spoke. They sat, studying the man in the ice. After a long time Lucy said, "I think there are two people. The smaller one is a woman. See where her arm comes around his body? She's holding him. Her hand is pressed against his back. The edge of her face is just above his head."

Jack cupped his hands against the brightness of the sun and leaned forward. His eyes did not easily adjust to the light. He tried to imagine the shape of a hand on the man's back. There seemed to be something there, but the sun coming through the ice made it difficult to see a distinct image.

"Now look just above the man's head," she said. "See how strangely it's shaped? What you're seeing is the edge of a woman's head. The eye is closed. If it were open, she would be looking directly at us. Her lips are near his ear, as though she is whispering to him." Lucy waited for a moment. "Can you make her out?"

He was silent for a long time. "Maybe . . . I see what might be the arch of her forehead, but it's blurred."

"Relax for a moment. You're trying too hard. Don't look directly at her, but down slightly. The light bending around her face will illuminate her features if you don't look straight into it."

He looked down toward the middle of the man's head, closed his eyes for a moment, then slowly opened them. He began to make out the line of the woman's jaw, her cheek, and her closed eye. "My God. They've been in an embrace for fifteen thousand years." He looked at Lucy. The glow of light through the ice illuminated her face. She had that glint he'd seen beneath the white bear.

She smiled, sliding her hand over his shoulder, her lips near his ear, and whispered, "Tell me, Jack, what's she saying to him?"

ACKNOWLEDGMENTS

Thanks to Diane Reverand, editor *extraordinaire*.

I would like to thank the following individuals for their kindness, time, and help. They are in no way responsible for my transgressions.

David Alt, Geology, University of Montana
Brad Baker, fisherman
John Peterson Baker, diver and pile driver
Harry Benjamin, artist
Anthony Berlant, artist
Frank Bessac, Professor Emeritus Anthropology, University of
    Montana
Susanne L. Bessac, anthropologist
Cynthia Ann Bettison, director, Western New Mexico University
    Museum
Nan Bovingdon
J.J. Brody, research curator, Maxwell Museum
Ray Dewey, antiquities dealer, Sante Fe
Brenda A. Dorr, curator of archaeology, Maxwell Museum
Dumont Maps and Books, Sante Fe
Kurt Feidler, chief of spinal cord injury, VA Medical, Albuquerque
Loreen Folsom

Thomas A. Foor, Anthropology, University of Montana
Douglas Gavin, builder of Harley 45s
Christopher Hill, Anthropology, Boise State University
Laura Holt, librarian, Museum of New Mexico
Carla Homstad
Ann M. Irwin, deputy director Environmental Affairs Division, Texas DOT
Amy Jameson, assistant manager, Maxwell Museum
Charles A. Johnson II, lecturer
Charles Jonkel, president, Great Bear Foundation
Gertrude Lackschewitz
Steven A. LeBlanc, director of collections, Peabody Museum of Archaeology and Ethnography, Harvard University
Mike McKay, owner of Rainbow, one ornery Scarlet Macaw
Nicholas Potter, bookseller, Sante Fe
Paul Perry, writer, adventurer
Wanda Raschkow, archaeologist
Elaine Rose, teacher
David Rosenthal, Anthropology, Museum of Natural History
Karen Rossmen, museum services manager, Western New Mexico University Museum
Curtis Schaafsma, curator of anthropology, Museum of New Mexico
Harry J. Shafer, Anthropology, Texas A&M
Brian S. Shaffer, Geology and Archaeology, North Texas University
Cordelia Thomas Snow, Historic Preservation Division, ARMS, Santa Fe
D. Gentry Steele, Anthropology, Texas A&M
Barbara Theroux, Fact & Fiction Books
Sally Thompson, research anthropologist, Continuing Education University of Montana
Janis Thompson-Bouma, archaeologist
Clint Traver, rock climber
Laurie Urfer, illustrator
Michelle Valintine, Foreign Languages, University of Montana
Cristina S. VanPool, Archaeology, University of New Mexico
Lynne Wolfe, designer

BIBLIOGRAPHY

Those readers who are interested in ancient migrations, antiquities thieves, Mimbres culture, postmodernism, deconstructionism, and bears who can taste music, may find the following books and articles of interest.

Baker, Tony. *The Clovis First/Pre-Clovis Problem.* 1997 http://www.ele.net/ art_folsom/preclvis.htm.

Bassett, Carol Ann. "The Culture Thieves: They gain a fast buck. We lose the history of an entire civilization." *Science 86* (1986): 22–29.

Baudrillard, Jean. *America.* Translated by Chris Turner. London and New York: Verso, 1988.

Braden, Maria. "Trafficking in Treasures: In attempting to stop the booming artifact trade, laws have been passed to deter looters, but some collectors are complaining as a result." *American Archaeology* (2000): 3 (4): 19–25.

Brody, J.J. *Mimbres Painted Pottery.* Santa Fe: School of American Research, 1977.

Brody, J.J., Catherine J. Scott, Steven A. LeBlanc, and Tony Berlant. *Mimbres Pottery: Ancient Art of the American Southwest.* New York: Hudson Hills Press, 1983.

Brody, J.J., and Rina Swentzell. *To Touch the Past: The Painted Pottery of the Mimbres People.* New York: Hudson Hills Press, 1996.

308

Carr, Pat. *Mimbres Mythology.* El Paso: Texas Western Press, 1979.

Chatters, James C. "The Recovery and First Analysis of an Early Holocene Human Skeleton from Kennewick, Washington." *American Antiquity* (2000): 65(2)291–316.

Cushing, Frank. *The Mythic World of the Zuni.* Albuquerque: University of New Mexico Press, 1988.

Davis, Carolyn O'Bagy. *Treasured Earth: Hattie Cosgrove's Mimbres Archaeology in the American Southwest.* Tucson: Sanpete Publications, 1995.

Fewkes, J. Walter. *The Mimbres: Art and Archaeology.* Introduction by J.J. Brody. A reprint of three papers by Jesse Walter Fewkes published by the Smithsonian Institution between 1914 and 1924. Albuquerque: Avanyu Publishing, 1989.

Goodstein, David, and James Woodward. "Inside Science." *The American Scholar* (Autumn 1999): 83–90.

LeBlanc, Steven A. *The Mimbres People: Ancient Pueblo Painters of the American Southwest.* London and New York: Thames and Hudson, 1983.

———. *Prehistoric Warfare in the American Southwest.* Salt Lake City: University of Utah Press, 1999.

Lekson, Stephen H. *The Chaco Meridian: Centers of Political Power in the Ancient Southwest.* Walnut Creek, California: AltaMira Press, 1999.

Miller, Joaquin. *True Bear Stories.* New York: Rand McNally, 1900. (When I was a boy I read Miller's story about the bears who could taste music. I trust Joaquin's ghost will not take offense at my retelling his incredible and beautiful tale.)

Minnis, Paul E. *Social Adaptation to Food Stress: A Prehistoric Southwestern Example.* Chicago: The University of Chicago Press, 1985.

Moulard, Barbara L. *Within the Underworld Sky: Mimbres Ceramic Art in Context.* Santa Fe: Twelvetrees Press, 1981.

Nelson, Ben A., and Steven A. LeBlanc. *Short-term Sedentism in the American Southwest: The Mimbres Valley Salado.* Albuquerque: Maxwell Museum of Anthropology and the University of New Mexico Press, 1986.

Nelson, Margaret C. *Mimbres During the Twelfth Century.* Tucson: University of Arizona Press, 1999.

Norris, Christopher. *Deconstruction: Theory and Practice*. Revised ed. London and New York: Routledge Press, 1991.

Snodgrass, O. T. *Realistic Art and Times of the Mimbres Indians*. El Paso: O.T. Snodgrass, 1977.

Stanford, Dennis. 2001. *Northern Clans, Northern Traces* (interview). http://www.mnh.si.edu/arctic/html/dennis_stanford.html http://www.mnh.si.edu/arctic/html/dennis_part_2.html

O'Toole, Fintan. "The Many Stories of Billy the Kid: Was the legendary Western outlaw actually an Irish terrorist?" *The New Yorker* (1999): Dec. 28: 86–97.

Patent, Dorothy Hinshaw. *Secrets of the Ice Man*. New York: Benchmark Books, 1999.

Preston, Douglas. "The Lost Man: Is it possible that the first Americans weren't who we think they were? And why is the government withholding Kennewick Man, who might turn out to be the most significant archaeological find of the decade?" *The New Yorker* (1997): June 16: 70–81.

Schaafsma, Polly, ed. *Kachinas in the Pueblo World*. Albuquerque: University of New Mexico Press, 1994.

Shafer, Harry J. "Extended Families to Corporate Groups: Pithouse to Pueblo Transformation of Mimbres Society." Revised version of a paper presented at the XI Mogollon Conference, Las Cruces, New Mexico, 2001.

Silverman, Max. *Facing Postmodernity: Contemporary French Thought on Culture and Society*. London and New York: Routledge Press, 1999.

Steele, D. Gentry. "Facing the Past: A View of the North American Human Fossil Record." Unpublished monograph. n.d.

Steele, D. Gentry, and Joseph F. Powell. "Paleobiology of the First Americans." *Evolutionary Anthropology* (1993): 2 (4): 138–46.

Swift, Jonathan. *Travels into Several Remote Nations of the World by Lemuel Gulliver*. London and New York: MacMillan & Co., 1894.

Thomas, David Hurst. *Skull Wars: Kennewick Man, Archaeology and the Battle for Native American Identity*. New York: Basic Books, 2000.

Thompson, Sally. "The Sacred Bird: The Scarlet Macaw Among Puebloan Peoples." Chapter 25 from *The Large Macaws: Their Care, Breeding and Conservation*. Fort Bragg: Raintree Publications, 1995.

Turner, Christy G. II, and Jacqueline A. Turner. *Man Corn: Cannibalism and Violence in the Prehistoric American Southwest.* Albuquerque: University of New Mexico Press, 1999.

VanPool, Christine S. and Todd L. "The Scientific Nature of Postprocessualism." *American Antiquity* (1999): 64: 33–53.

Whittlesey, Stephanie M., ed. *Sixty Years of Mogollon Archaeology: Papers from the Ninth Mogollon Conference, Silver City, NM.* Tucson: SRI Press, 1999.